Milly Johnson is a joke-writer, greetings card copywriter, newspaper columnist, after-dinner speaker, poet, winner of *Come Dine With Me*, *Sunday Times* Top Ten author and winner of a Romantic Comedy of the Year award in 2014 and 2016.

She is half-Yorkshire, half-Glaswegian so 1) don't mess with her and 2) don't expect her to buy the first round.

She likes cruising on big ships, sparkling afternoon teas and birds of prey, in particular owls. She does not like marzipan or lamb chops.

She is proud patron of Yorkshire Cat Rescue (www.yorkshirecatrescue.org), The Well, a complementary therapy centre for cancer patients and the Barnsley Youth Choir (www.barnsleyyouthchoir.org.uk) who have conquered the world and are now moving onto other planets.

She lives happily in Barnsley with Pete, her long-suffering partner, Tez and George, her teenage lads, Teddy the dog, Hernan Crespo, Vincent and Theo the cats and Alan Rickman the rabbit. Her mam and dad live in t'next street.

Sunshine Over Wildflower Cottage is her twelfth book.

Find out more at www.millyjohnson.co.uk or follow Milly on Twitter @millyjohnson

milly johnson

Sunshine over Wildflower Cottage

SIMON &
SCHUSTER

London · New York · Sydney · Toronto · New Delhi

A CBS COMPANY

First published by Simon & Schuster UK Ltd 2016
A CBS COMPANY

3 5 7 9 10 8 6 4 2

Simon & Schuster UK Ltd
1st Floor
222 Gray's Inn Road
London WC1X 8HB

www.simonandschuster.co.uk

Simon & Schuster Australia, Sydney
Simon & Schuster India, New Delhi

A CIP catalogue record for this book
is available from the British Library

Export TPB ISBN: 978-1-4711-4084-6
PB ISBN: 978-1-4711-4048-8
EBOOK ISBN: 978-1-4711-4049-5

Typeset in Bembo by M Rules
Printed and bound by CPI Group (UK) Ltd, Croydon, CR0 4YY

Simon & Schuster UK Ltd are committed to sourcing paper
that is made from wood grown in sustainable forests and support the Forest
Stewardship Council, the leading international forest certification organisation.
Our books displaying the FSC logo are printed on FSC certified paper.

This book is dedicated to all the wonderful pets I've had over the years. From the many goldfish I rescued from fayres, to the battalion of beautiful cats I've adopted. From the budgie we had that couldn't fly properly and used to divebomb into walls, to the gorgeous dogs who looked at me as if I was Angelina Jolie. From the hamster with the *Guinness Book of Records* stretchy cheeks, to the white rabbit who just wandered up the street and into my heart. They have brought me far more than I ever gave them and I have loved them all so much. I consider myself very lucky that they were part of my life and our family.

Author's Note

In 1985 my path crossed with the actress Shirley Stelfox's. I was on my summer vacation from university working in a hotel in Wales and Shirley was part of a film crew staying there. She was party to all my ambitions to be an actress and then witness to my crisis when I realised that I was totally on the wrong track. Really, all I ever wanted to do was write books but didn't feel I would ever be good enough. So Shirley made me put down my serving tray, sit with her and not move until we had sorted out my life. She told me that it was absolute nonsense not to give my dreams everything I had to make them come true and that if I didn't believe in myself, why would anyone else?

So I did give them my best shot – and they did come true. And I never dared to contact her and tell her what impact her kind words had upon me because I didn't think she'd remember me. Then on 7 December 2015 Shirley died without ever knowing what she'd done for me. Learn from me and always deliver the thank-yous that grow in your heart.

And never underestimate the power of a small kindness. A ripple at one end of the ocean can cause a tsunami at the other.

God bless you, Shirley Stelfox – and thank you.

We can judge the heart of a man by
how he treats his animals

IMMANUEL KANT

Chapter 1

A person could have been forgiven for thinking that by driving to the hamlet of Ironmist, they were crossing the boundaries of time as well as county divisions. Viv Blackbird half expected to see King Arthur and the knights of his Round Table in her rear-view mirror when she had passed the grey stone castle on the crest of the hill. The castle was the seat of the Leighton family, she knew. They owned most of the land around here and had done since before the Big Bang. The area from the hilltop down to the hamlet below had once been called *High-on-the-Mist,* though the name had long since been contracted to Ironmist, or so the internet told her. Viv was headed for the bottom of the dell where the Wildflower Cottage Sanctuary for Animals was situated. As the road turned sharply away from the castle and began to dip, she could see how the old name had suited it perfectly. A low mist had settled in the bowl of the valley. It was as if the ground were made of smoke. It looked both beautiful and weird; but then weird was good sometimes.

A black horse was trotting along the road. Its rider was a

woman who was wearing her long hair loose and it was as black as the horse's mane. Viv dabbed her foot on the brake, even though she was hardly speeding anyway, and swung out to the other side of the road. The woman didn't even acknowledge the consideration. In fact, if anything, she gave Viv a look that said *what is your car doing on the road anyway?* Viv hoped she wasn't representative of the welcome she was going to receive. She'd never lived in a place as small as this but knew they had the reputation of being cliquish. She also hoped there weren't any horses in the sanctuary. She didn't like the unpredictable massive things and couldn't understand how anyone would want to climb up onto their backs and give them free licence to throw you off and then trample all over you.

Viv turned down what she presumed was the main street through Ironmist, passing a pretty row of cottages, a barber on one side of the road, a pub called The Lady of the Lake on the other. A woman was washing her front step with a bucket of water and a scrubbing brush. An A frame stood outside the Ironmist Stores and Post Office holding a handwritten sign which read: *MR WAYNE HAS HAD HIS OP AND HE'S FINE.* Viv smiled. That notice gave her better hope that she was about to join a friendly community.

Jesus. She slammed on her brakes as a dog wandered into the road. A huge beast of a thing. It was larger than the dog that had played the title role in the TV adaptation of *The Hound of the Baskervilles.* A tall, squarely-built young man approached the car, holding up his hands apologetically. Viv lowered her window as he indicated that he wanted to speak to her.

'I am so sorry,' he said. 'My fault. I let go of his lead. Are you all right? You're shaking like a jelly.'

Viv looked at her hands clamped onto the steering wheel and noticed that her little finger was vibrating.

'I'm okay, thank you,' she replied, though she didn't entirely feel it. Thank goodness she hadn't been going any faster.

The man stroked the big dog's head. 'He's called Pilot,' he said. 'He's twelve. I love Pilot.'

The man's size had deceived Viv. Up close, she could see he must only have been about eighteen or nineteen and mentally, he seemed to be much younger.

'Well, you make sure you hold on to his lead properly next time,' Viv said softly.

'I will,' he replied. 'Where are you going, lady?'

'To Wildflower Cottage, the animal sanctuary,' replied Viv. 'Am I heading in the right direction?'

The young man brightened. 'Oh yes. That's where Pilot lives. Don't tell them, will you? They won't let me walk him again.'

'I promise I won't.'

'You need to turn right just after the café. It's on the corner. It's called the Corner Caff.'

'Thank you. That's very kind of you.'

'My name's Armstrong. If they ask, will you tell them that I'm doing a good job? I'm going to take Pilot for a biscuit at the bakery up the road. They make biscuits with liver in them especially for dogs. Pilot loves those.'

'I will,' smiled Viv.

'See you. Come on, Pilot.' And with that, Armstrong tugged on the lead and he and the giant shaggy dog began to lumber up the hill.

Viv set off slowly in case anything else should run into her path. She didn't want to start off her new job in an animal sanctuary by killing something. The café on the corner was painted bright yellow and hard to miss. She swung a right there and was faced with a stunning view of the bottom of the valley. In the centre of it sat a long cottage couched in a bed of fairy-tale swirls of low mist and to its left was a tall tower with a crenellated top. Viv's jaw tightened with nervousness as the car ate the distance towards it.

She parked as directed by a crooked wooden sign saying 'Visitors', at the side of a battered black pick-up truck. As she got out of the car, she noticed sprinkles of flowers in the mist, their violet-blue heads dotted everywhere she looked. The second thing she noticed was the biggest cat she had ever seen in her life walking towards her, muscles rippling under his velvet black fur. She'd thought her family cat Basil was huge but this guy was like a panther. The cat rose onto his back legs in order to brush his face against her thigh. As Viv's hand came out to stroke his head, a voice shrieked from the cottage doorway.

'For goodness sake don't touch him. He'll savage you.'

A tall, slim woman had appeared there. She was wearing a long flowery hippy dress and had a mad frizz of brown hair. 'He's called Beelzebub for a reason. Bub for short.' She walked towards Viv with her hand extended in greeting. 'Viv, I presume,' she said. 'I'm Geraldine Hartley. We spoke on the phone.'

Viv had rung the sanctuary as soon as she spotted the advertisement in the *Pennine Times* and after a surprisingly brief conversation, Geraldine had offered her the job right there and then, subject to a personal reference and an assurance that Viv had no criminal history or accusation of animal cruelty. The wage was basic, cash in hand, although meals were included as was a small grace and favour house.

Her friend Hugo, who now had a scientific research job down south in London had supplied a glowing appraisal of her abilities and character. She'd taken the risk of giving a false address in Sheffield and so far there had been no comeback. It wasn't the most professional organisation she'd come across.

Viv shook her hand. Geraldine had a very strong grip. She also had the most beautiful perfume. Viv instinctively breathed it up into her nose and her brain began to dissect the scent: *rose – definitely. Violet – probably. Orris . . . maybe.* It was floral, but with a hint of something else that she couldn't quite pin down. Complex, but there wasn't a scent yet that she couldn't separate into its basic elements, given time. Her olfactory senses judged it to be delightful and something that her mother would love.

'Welcome to Wildflower Cottage.' Geraldine brought her back into the here and now by lifting her arms and spreading her hands out towards the sky as if she were an evangelist about to address her congregation.

'It's so pretty here,' replied Viv, opening up her boot and taking out her luggage. 'The mist is very unusual.'

'We get a lot of it,' said Geraldine, lifting up one of Viv's suitcases. 'Come on in. I expect you're dying for a cup of tea. Or are you a coffee girl?'

'A tea would be lovely, please,' replied Viv. She didn't say that she was already full of tea having stopped off at a service station halfway through the journey and had two pots of the stuff whilst soul-searching at the table. *What are you doing?* her brain threw at her. *Have you really thought this through?* She had texted her mum and told her that she was stuck in traffic, because she knew she would be worrying why she hadn't been in contact to say she had arrived. She didn't ring because she thought that hearing her mother's voice might have had her abandoning her plans and running back home.

Viv followed Geraldine into a spacious, rustic kitchen-lounge with a heavy beamed ceiling, thick stone walls and a Yorkshire range fireplace. There was a massive furry dog bed at one side of a bright red Aga and a cushioned cat bed between a long oxblood Chesterfield sofa and an old-fashioned Welsh dresser. A bird with round angry eyes was hopping about on the stripped pine table in the centre of the room. Suddenly it took flight and swooped towards Viv, who ducked and screamed.

'Viv, meet Piccolo,' said Geraldine. 'He gets excited, bless him. We've had him from an egg which his sneaky mum hid from us. There's nothing wrong with him but he's imprinted on us. He thinks he's a cat with wings.' She called him and Piccolo flew towards her, landing on her hair. 'It doesn't hurt me,' she said, seeing Viv's look of horror. 'Unless I move too fast and he feels the need to grip on.'

She crossed to the Aga and put a large kettle of water on it to boil, still wearing her living breathing owl hat. 'You'll find that this is not your typical animal sanctuary.'

Bub swaggered in and over to Viv, butting her leg with his large head and making friendly chirrupy noises. She bent down to stroke him, remembering just in time to pull her hand back as his paw came out to strike her, claws extended.

'Told you,' laughed Geraldine. 'He's a duplicitous bugger, that one.'

'I met one of your helpers up the road,' said Viv, attempting to be friendly. 'Armstrong, I think he said he was called.'

'Armstrong Baslow, yes. Did he have a rather large dog with him? Please say yes.'

'Yes.'

'It's the first time I've let him take Pilot out. The old lad needed a walk and with being by myself at the moment, I haven't had time.'

'Pilot – that's Mr Rochester's dog in *Jane Eyre*, isn't it?'

'It most certainly is. You can blame me for that. But as a rule of thumb, if the name is ridiculous, it'll be something Armstrong has thought of. When Pilot first came to us, I thought he looked exactly as I'd imagined the Pilot in the book to be. Poor soul had been wandering around the moors for God knows how long. Someone had obviously dumped him. But he took to the name straightaway, bless him.'

She laughed and Viv warmed to the sound. Geraldine must be a nice person to have such a lovely, tinkly laugh, she decided.

'As for Armstrong's name, in case you're wondering, his father was a space enthusiast,' Geraldine continued. 'He died last year and they sent his ashes up to heaven in a firework, can you believe?'

Viv was hypnotised by the owl's antics. He was on the edge of the table now and seemed to be reprimanding the cat with angry flaps of his wings and squawks. Then he jumped down onto the floor beside him.

'Oh my God . . .' Viv shooed at the predatory Bub by her feet. She was sure she was about to witness the last few seconds of the bird's life.

Geraldine laughed as she watched Viv in full panic mode whilst Bub flashed her the sort of look he reserved for viewing things he'd done in his litter tray.

'Piccolo is safer than the rest of us with Bub. They have what Heath always calls "an affinity".'

'Heath?'

'Heath Merlo, the boss,' explained Geraldine. 'I thought

it was serendipitous that his name means "blackbird" in Italian. It was like a sign that you were the one we should take on. Mind you, we were hardly overrun with applicants.'

It was the first time Viv had heard mention of 'Heath'. She'd presumed that Geraldine was the one in charge.

'Heath is away with Wonk at the moment.' Geraldine went into further explanations. 'Wonk is our three-legged donkey. She's having a new prosthetic limb fitted because she's outgrown the other one.'

'You have a three-legged donkey here?'

'Yes. She had a rich owner who left us Wonk when she died on the proviso that we would look after her. Her legacy goes a long way to supporting us. Come on, I'll give you a very quick tour whilst the kettle is boiling. It takes an age and I don't help matters by always over-filling it.'

Geraldine beckoned her to follow and they left the owl cawing an angry protest at being left by himself with no one to entertain, stomping up and down the table on legs that looked too long for his small body. Viv was sure the low mist had thickened since she had arrived. Walking behind Geraldine, even at a close distance, Viv couldn't see her feet and it was as if she was floating.

'I've never seen mist like this before,' said Viv.

'It is unusual,' replied Geraldine. 'Legend has it that years ago the valley was a sacred lake inhabited by a water nymph called Isme who was trusted to look after all the creatures who lived in it, but she fell in love with the local bad boy – the Lord of the Manor's son. One day he stripped the lake of all of the fish and Isme's furious father forced his daughter to take revenge by dragging the young man into the lake and drowning him. Heartbroken, Isme withered away and the lake dried up with her until all that was left was a lingering mist and the wildflowers which had taken seed in the places where her tears had fallen.'

Viv bent down to a vibrant blue patch of them. 'Love-in-a-Mist. How beautiful.' She had recognised them immediately.

'I see you know your plants,' smiled Geraldine. 'They flower continually.' She picked out a plump purple seed case hidden inside its lacy netting. 'I think they're as pretty when they pod, don't you?'

They carried the faintest scent of strawberries tinged with smoke. Viv could pick it up, just, but it was almost missable, even to her.

'We'll start from furthest away and work our way in,' decided Geraldine. 'Our birds.' She lifted a large stiff leather glove from a hook outside the door and Viv wondered why she'd need that.

'At the back of the house, there, is our food preparation area,' said Geraldine, pointing to an outbuilding with an arched barn door. 'Do you want to see inside?'

'Not really,' said Viv. She guessed it wouldn't be full of packaged ready meals.

'Thought not,' grinned Geraldine. They walked down the dirt-track road. Viv didn't really need to see the birds – she'd hardly be interacting with them. And she didn't like birds even more than she didn't like other animals. The Alfred Hitchcock film *The Birds* encapsulated all her worst nightmares: their capriciousness, their flapping wings, their ability to peck out your eyes. She shivered at the thought and hoped they were all locked away.

They arrived at the aviaries clustered around a central grassy area where perches were studded into the ground.

'This is our flying arena,' explained Geraldine. 'And there are our birds. None of them would survive in the wild. They're all damaged in some way, poor dears.' She sighed. 'Come on, Vivienne, let me introduce you to our family.' Geraldine walked to the first cage.

Staring at Viv was a large tawny owl with the most beautiful feathery face.

'That's Melvin. He was found with terribly broken wings. He can fly after a fashion now but it's not a very good fashion. His partner in crime is Tink there.' Sharing the same shelter was a much smaller owl with eyes that seemed to take up half her head. 'They used to talk to each other through the wire, so Heath decided to test them in the same aviary and they bonded. It's very sweet to watch them when they are perched together. They lean on each other.'

Tink was tongue-clicking at Viv as if she was warning her off looking at her fella. Viv sent a silent psychic message that Tink had nothing to worry about – she would be staying as far away from them as possible.

They moved on. 'In here is Beatrice, our eagle owl. Rescued from a wardrobe – I kid you not – where a stupid prat was keeping her as a pet.' Geraldine shook her head in dismay.

Beatrice's orange-ringed eyes swung over Viv as if she were of no value.

'Come on in,' said Geraldine. 'Beatrice is a love.' She pulled the latch back.

'Are you kidding?' said Viv.

'No, not at all.' Geraldine opened the door.

'I . . . I can't,' said Viv.

Geraldine put her left hand into the glove.

'You'll be doing this in no time if you choose to. Beatrice

is a good one to start off with because she gets on with everyone.'

Viv would rather have eaten her own head than interact with birds. Especially large terrifying things like this one.

Beatrice started making a 'yarp' sound.

'That noise tells you that she's happy I'm around,' said Geraldine. 'She's bonded to me. And I've bonded to her, haven't I, girl?'

The bird lifted up its wings and seemed to rise up as if on a heat thermal, coming to perch on Geraldine's outstretched glove.

'I have arm muscles like you wouldn't believe,' chuckled Geraldine. 'She's quite a weight, I can tell you.' Geraldine gave the owl a scratch on her head as she addressed her. 'And you've just had your twentieth birthday, haven't you, my love? Okay, off you pop.' She jiggled her arm up and down but the owl gripped on.

'She's spoiled,' laughed Geraldine. 'Go on with you. I'm showing a guest around.'

In the next cage was a large white owl that started flapping her pepper-speckled wings as soon as they neared.

'Just as Beatrice loves everyone, Ursula hates everyone, even Heath.' Geraldine clucked at the bird in greeting. 'We keep trying to get her to trust us, but we haven't made a lot of progress, I'm afraid.'

The large white owl stared at Viv with 'I want to kill you' eyes and started bobbing her head up and down.

'Why is she doing that at me?' said Viv, feeling ridiculously intimidated.

'Well I never,' Geraldine said, raising her eyebrows.

'What?' asked Viv.

'That's very interesting. She's interacting with you.'

'Is she?' asked Viv.

'Yes, she most certainly is. She's taken her eyes off you to bend her head. That's a sign of trust.'

'Oh.' That bird was a rotten judge of character, thought Viv.

Geraldine grinned. 'There is no rhyme or reason why birds love you or hate you. They just do.' She pointed across to a cage. 'There's a red-tail hawk over there called Sistine that I found entangled in thorns and I nursed her back to health. But is it me she's grateful to? Oh no. She's Heath's girl.'

There were hawks and eagles and owls and the ugliest bird Viv had ever seen in her life: a white-headed vulture. The inside of his aviary looked like a Toys R Us for birds. He had a tyre on a rope, a ladder, a huge rubber Kong, a climbing frame.

'Frank turned up in a Manchester scrapyard. He can't see very well but he likes to play,' smiled Geraldine. 'He's likely to run off with the hosepipe when you clean him out.'

Viv hoped that Geraldine meant a general 'you' and not a specific one. She wouldn't be cleaning Frank out. Ever.

'Like fresh eggs for breakfast?' asked Geraldine as they made a slow walk back towards the cottage. 'We've taken in some ex-battery hens. They're just getting used to being outside and having room to move. They're learning to scratch for worms and insects and their egg yolks are lovely and golden as a result.'

That nearly put Viv right off eggs for life. She had always been quite squeamish and once hadn't eaten cod from the chippy for over a year after hearing that it ate any old rubbish it could get its jaws on, unlike the more discerning haddock.

The sanctuary was also home to three limping geese, all with deformed feet, who still managed to swagger around like drunken John Waynes; and a blind baby goat called Ray who was glued to the side of his sighted twin Roy. In a run with a wooden shelter in the shape of a giant Toblerone were two hedgehogs – a strange albino one who looked as if she would glow in the dark and another with incredibly short prickles, as if he'd had a tough-guy crew cut: they were introduced to Viv as Angel and Bruce Willis. They wouldn't survive in the wild, Geraldine explained. They'd taken in lots of hedgehogs over the years, and patched them up and sent them out again – but only if they knew they'd be safe. There was a huge black hairy pig called Bertie who had formed an attachment to a beautiful pair of shire horses who looked as if they were wearing shaggy fur boots. As soon as they spotted Geraldine, they started walking across their field towards her.

Even though there was a sturdy barrier between them, Viv instinctively took a few steps back.

'You don't have to be scared of Roger and Keith, duck,' said Geraldine. 'They're as gentle as spring lambs.'

'They're huge.' The hairs on the back of Viv's neck stood up as two tonnes of horse approached the fence. They could cause a lot of damage if they were suddenly spooked: flatten her like a pancake, kick her into Kingdom Come. She'd err on the side of caution, thank you, and not get too close.

'Roger and Keith have been at Wildflower Cottage for ten years,' explained Geraldine. 'Heath's father took in four shires from a disgusting farm near Saddleworth, but Pete didn't make it through the first night and we lost John only a few weeks ago.' She sighed. 'He was such a dear fellow. I'm only glad that he had a few safe, happy years with us.

He's buried in our graveyard with all his sanctuary brothers and sisters behind the house. I can't bear the thought if we have to—' She pulled herself up short and shook her head. 'Anyway,' she said then, as if she was forcing herself to move on. She extracted a tube of Polo mints from her pocket. 'Want to give one to the horses?'

Viv declined hurriedly.

Geraldine tilted her head and looked down into the eyes of the much shorter Viv. 'I must say, you're not at all what I expected.'

'Oh?'

'In a nice way, I mean,' Geraldine said. 'Some people have sounded perfect on the phone and when they arrive ... well, I've known I've made a huge mistake. But I don't get that feeling with you. Though you're not at all confident around animals, are you?'

'I wouldn't do them any harm,' Viv replied quickly, to dispel any fears Geraldine might have on that score. 'But admin is more my thing.'

'Well, that's what we need really. Someone efficient. Heath has let things slide and hasn't got the time to sort out the backlog and I'm not very good at that sort of thing. I can't use computers and I don't like being on the telephone, as you might have been able to tell. I much prefer to roll up my sleeves and pull a pair of wellies on.'

'I passed a lady on a black horse when I drove down the hill. Is that one of your animals too?' asked Viv. Did she see Geraldine bristle slightly?

'No. That'll be Antonia Leighton. She lives up in the castle at the top of the hill. Let's go and get that cuppa,' said Geraldine. 'Are you hungry? That's one good thing about working here; everyone in Ironmist thinks we're starving, so they're always sending us cakes and bread from the bakery and pies, butter, vegetables, you name it. It's a very kind place.'

So that was Antonia Leighton, thought Viv. She hadn't recognised her because she looked very different from the smiling picture she had seen in the glossy magazine. She was the daughter of Nicholas Leighton, the man that her friend Hugo had said would be a very useful person to get to know. And he was the real reason why Viv was here.

Chapter 2

'Bloody hell, Stel, what's up? Your head's the colour of a stick of rhubarb with high blood pressure.'

Linda leaned over the coffee table and handed her friend a plastic fan. There were five women in the room and all of them had small whirring blades cooling their faces, even Iris, Linda's eighty-two-year-old mother. And surprisingly Caro too, who was floating through the menopause as if she was aboard an enchanted craft with an anti-menopause cloaking device, had beads of perspiration pushing out of the pores on her forehead. She dabbed at her temples with her fingertips. *She even makes sweating look elegant*, thought Gaynor.

'Thought you didn't get hot flushes,' she said, tapping her fan on the table, hoping that would somehow rev up the dying battery.

'I don't usually. My thermometer might be getting more and more on the blink, but I haven't had that experience you seem to get where you say you feel it rising up from your feet,' replied Caro.

'I used to sweat so much in bed, Dennis used to have to

sleep in a wetsuit,' sniffed Iris, putting down her fan in order to sip delicately from her special china cup covered in irises which she lifted from a matching saucer.

'Slight exaggeration there, Mother,' said Linda. Her hair was plastered to her face with perspiration. 'Dear God, this can't be normal.'

'I didn't get the sweats until I was over a year into the full-throttle menop— oh bugger, my battery's knackered as well,' said Stel, banging her fan on the side of the sofa in an attempt to revive it.

'Here, Stel.' From a drawer in the dresser behind her, Linda retrieved another fan from the job-lot stored there and tossed it to her. Linda's husband Dino was a market dealer (Aladdino's Cave) trading in allsorts and novelties which he imported from the Far East.

This quintet of friends always jokingly referred to themselves as 'The Old Spice Girls'. They'd known each other for ages; but two years ago they'd decided to make their meetings a regular Sunday event from 5.30 until 7 p.m., to galvanise them for the week ahead with pots of tea and finger food.

If they had been actual Spice Girls, it wouldn't have been too hard to choose their names. The preened and perfect Caro would have been Posh Spice. With her rounded vowels and cultured ways, she made Victoria Beckham look like Pat Butcher. Iris would have been Blunt Spice, since the brake on her mouth had long since failed, much to the frequent embarrassment of her daughter. Linda would have been Bountiful Spice because everything about Linda was big: her hair, her bum, her appetite and her heart. Gaynor would have been Bitter Spice. She was twisted up in knots about her husband running off almost a year ago with a cheap young tramp, and fed off his frustration that she wouldn't give him a divorce. And Stel Blackbird would, at the moment, be Sad Spice. Her much-loved only daughter Viv had left home that day in order to work in a godforsaken place up on the moors. She'd said she only intended to work there through the summer, but Stel had said the same to her parents and then had never moved back to the family nest.

'Linda, you do know the central heating's on, don't you?' said Gaynor, feeling the radiator. 'No wonder we're all wilting.'

'It's what? But it can't be . . .' Linda broke off her sentence as the penny dropped and she turned slowly to Iris, her eyes narrowing to slits. 'It's you again, isn't it, Mum?'

'I must have forgotten to turn it off,' said Iris. 'I thought I'd warm the room up a bit for everyone.'

Linda bobbed next door to turn off the heating, chuntering profanities in her mother's direction.

'It's always cold when you first come in. I was only trying to help.' Iris lifted up her shoulders and dropped them as if hurt.

'It's seventy degrees in the shade today,' Linda batted back. 'You can fry eggs on the pavement.'

The Old Spice Girls met in Linda's 'party room'. Dino had converted half their enormous garage into an extra reception room so that he and the lads could go and have a game of darts, or watch the football on the sixty-inch screen mounted on the wall whilst partaking of a few beers, and Linda could fill it with her friends on Sunday nights.

'I thought I was having a hot flush to end all hot flushes. Four years I've been having them now and I'm bloody sick of them,' said Gaynor, wishing there was a turbo facility on her fan. 'I must be coming to the end of them by now, surely?' Sometimes Gaynor felt as if nature was against her as well as everything else. 'Can I open a window, Linda?'

'Open the bloody lot of them,' said Linda. 'It's like a slow-cooker in here.' She gave her mother a warning look. 'And don't you dare moan that it's draughty.'

Iris managed to arrange her features into a perfect balance of innocence and disgruntlement.

Caro turned off her fan and put her cup of coffee down on a small glass-topped table with a shelf underneath, She could see a child's book parked there, entitled *Jolly Jellyfish*. She gave a gasp of joy at the sight.

'Oh, Linda, has Freddie been round to see you?'

Linda raised her hand and waved it in a gesture of 'don't talk about it'.

'Has he heck,' said Iris. 'I put that there because Rebecca said she'd bring him round yesterday for half an hour and guess what, she didn't turn up. Again.'

Caro didn't have grandchildren herself, but she could still imagine what it would be like to not be allowed to see them because your ex-daughter-in-law was a controlling cow. She snatched at the nearest passing subject to divert Linda's thoughts.

'We should get some tickets and go to the theatre, make an evening of it. We haven't been for ages, have we?'

'Well, I'm not going this week,' said Linda. 'They're putting on *Rebecca*. No wonder Laurence Olivier drowned her.'

The Old Spice Girls had gravitated to one another to form a friendship group over the years, as women do. Linda was a nurse and had met Stel at St Theresa's Hospice, where the latter still worked as head receptionist. Iris lived with Linda, and they and Gaynor lived on the same sprawling estate in

Dodley. Stel and Caro first met when their children had been in hospital at the same time ten years ago and they'd bonded in the hospital coffee shop as they waited for good news.

'Did Viv get off all right, then?' asked Iris.

Stel didn't answer, because her throat felt suddenly blocked with a ball of solidified tears.

'She'll be all right, love,' said Linda. 'She's a sensible lass, is Viv.'

'She went off to university for three years, Stel. Surely that acclimatised you for her leaving home?' said Gaynor.

'That was different, Gaynor. She was home nearly every weekend and in the holidays. I always felt as if she were on a piece of elastic, but now ...' Her voice dissolved into a croak.

'She's only gone to the moors, not emigrated to bloody New Zealand,' said Gaynor impatiently as she got up from the sofa. 'Think about me. I haven't seen my Leanne for nearly six months.'

Lucky you, thought most of the room. Leanne Pollock had been one of those horrible, spoiled kids who had grown up into an even more horrible, spoiled young woman. She took the art of self-serving to new levels. She had done Gaynor a favour by moving down to London to pursue a modelling career; not that any of them would say that to her, with the possible exception of Iris if the opportunity presented itself.

Gaynor snapped her fingers. 'I knew there was something I had to tell you all. Leanne had an audition for that top modelling agency a couple of weeks ago. You know, the one that Kate Moss used to work for. And they would have taken her, they said, but for one thing, one tiny thing ...' She pincered her thumb and finger together. 'And do you know what it was?'

'Her face?' suggested Iris.

'No, her height.' Gaynor glared at the chippy octogenarian. 'She was one inch too short. Would you have thought an inch made that much difference?'

Caro snorted down her nose and Gaynor threw her a dirty look.

'An inch can make a hell of a difference, Gaynor love,' Linda winked at her.

'Oh, I'm going to the loo if you're going to talk smut,' said Gaynor. The air seemed to lighten by several degrees when she left the room, shutting the door hard behind her. Once upon a time, thought Caro, Gaynor would have been the first to chuckle at the innuendo.

'Your father and I were always very active in the bedroom,' put in Iris, causing Linda to cover her ears.

'Mum, please.'

Iris huffed in exasperation. 'That's the trouble, every generation thinks it invented sex. I used to be a young woman with a figure that your father had difficulty keeping his hands off. We once managed—'

'La la la la.' Linda couldn't hear what her mother and father had managed to do because she was singing and her hands were over her ears. But her friends did – if their widened eyeballs were anything to go by.

'I reckon Gaynor needs a good bonk,' whispered Stel. 'Hasn't Eamonn got any nice friends, Caro?'

'They wouldn't get up there for the barbed wire,' sniffed Iris.

Linda immediately rounded on her. 'Mum, that is mean. Gaynor's struggling and anger is her way of dealing with it.

Even if it wouldn't be yours or my way of doing things.'

All of them wished for her sake that Gaynor could move on, and they knew she wouldn't do that until she stopped denying her Mick the divorce he wanted. She was being as awkward as she knew how, not responding to his solicitor's letters and making her presence felt in any way she could as punishment for leaving her for a girl over thirty years younger than she was. *And a Bellfield at that.* There were some rough renowned families in the town: the O'Gowans, the Clamps, the Crookes; but the Bellfields were considered the worst. Young Danira Bellfield (or de Niro as Gaynor so scathingly called her) was as different from Gaynor as she could be, which wasn't very flattering to Gaynor, and gave a gigantic clue to why Mick had left his wife two weeks after their Pearl Wedding Anniversary. Danira was plump and loud, peroxide-blonde and wanton. But Gaynor, for all her Hyacinth Bouquet pretensions, was a good woman who'd worked hard to make a comfortable home for her family, only to be rewarded with a duplicitous husband and a self-obsessed daughter.

There was the sound of a flush in the background, so Linda quickly switched the subject to the neighbours.

'Annie and Joe next door are renewing their marriage vows in Jamaica next month.'

'I bet he was doing the dirty on her,' sniffed Gaynor as she walked back in and immediately joined in the conversation. 'Couples who renew their vows usually have that story to tell.'

'Actually, you're wrong because——' began Linda, but Gaynor cut her off.

'You mark my words, they won't just be doing it because they're still so much in *lurrrve*.' Gaynor loaded the word with all the sarcasm it could carry. 'It'll come out eventually. He'll have been dipping his wick where he shouldn't have been. He was always too good-looking for her,' she huffed derisively.

That couldn't be said of her own marriage. Mick Pollock was a smart, handsome man but Gaynor more than matched him for looks. She had the same dark colouring, wide mouth and big brown eyes as Sophia Loren. In fact that was the first line Mick had ever said to her: *Excuse me, could I have your autograph, Miss Loren?* Corny, but it worked on her. She had always taken care over her appearance, maybe too much so. Maybe she had been too polished for Mick's tastes, if the slobby Danira was anything to go by. The past year was telling on Gaynor though. Her mouth was set in a downward arc and she radiated waves of resentment. If she had been born a cobra, her hood would have been permanently expanded.

'A fucking Bellfield!' exclaimed Gaynor, sliding into dark, slimy waters in her head. 'Lowest of the low. And what does she see in him? He's thirty years older than her for a start. When we got married, she wasn't even born.' She shuddered as if that somehow made him a paedophile. 'It won't be anything to do with his bank balance, will it? Anyway, he can whistle for his divorce. I burned the last set of papers in our firepit and I'll do the same with the next lot. Bastard. I'll make it as hard as possible for him to get me out of his life.'

The room crackled with Gaynor's electric bitterness. The only sound was Iris's cup hitting the saucer. Then Caro's soft, smoky voice broke through the silence.

'Do you think maybe, for your own sake, you should let him go, Gaynor love?'

Gaynor's lips narrowed until they were almost invisible. 'You are joking?'

Caro prepared to back up her words with more of the same. 'No, I'm not. Look around you, Gaynor. You're in a room full of people who care for you. You're young enough to start a new life, find a new man. All this fighting is damaging you more than it is him.'

'It needed saying,' added Iris, who was never one to miss the opportunity to throw petrol on a fire. 'It's what everyone here is thinking.'

'Is it now?' Gaynor's eyes took them all in.

'Because we're your friends and we love you, Gaynor,' Caro said. She was all too aware that Gaynor thought that she had the Midas touch, and so what would she really know about what Gaynor was going through. Caro had a gorgeous faithful husband, loving children, a big house, a successful business and his-and-hers Mercedes and a motorhome parked in the treble garage. Caro shopped in Waitrose, wore expensive clothes, and had a diamond the size of Poland on her third finger. She and Gaynor had been close friends until Mick had buggered off. His leaving had triggered an irrational envy of Caro which Gaynor knew was both wrong and puerile, but she just couldn't help it. Right now, getting a life lecture from Caro was like pouring acid in Gaynor's wounds.

Gaynor stood up.

'Well, if you've all decided behind my back that I'm a bore and you're all on flaming *de Niro*'s side, I'll go.'

'Gaynor, don't be daft.'

'Oh don't, Gaynor.'

Protests ensued but Gaynor wouldn't be placated.

'I'll show myself out.' She strode out on her long, pin-thin legs and the others knew they had no choice but to let her go when she was in that stubborn mood of hers. They exchanged cringes and shrugged.

'No wonder she's on her own,' piped up Iris.

'*Mum*,' objected Linda.

'We-ell,' said Iris, waving away her daughter's indignation. 'It might do her good to know that everyone thinks she's in the wrong. You've to be cruel to be kind sometimes. She's in a rut and she wants booting out of it.'

'Iris is right,' replied Caro. She hated that there was distance between them and wished they could get back onto a normal footing. The trouble was that the more rain that fell on Gaynor recently, the more the heavens seemed to shine on Caro. If Caro could have stemmed the tide of her good fortune and diverted it to Gaynor, she wouldn't have hesitated to give her friend a break.

'She'll come round,' said Stel, watching Gaynor strut down the road through the window. 'Let her stew for a bit. She knows we are on her side.'

'I worry that Mick will start playing funny beggars,' said Linda. 'Guilt's made him offer a generous divorce settlement, but if she keeps on refusing to cooperate he might start getting as bolshie as she is. I'd hate for her to lose out financially.'

Linda hadn't known Mick that well but she'd been surprised when he'd left Gaynor. He'd seemed such a quiet man, easy-going and settled, even a bit boring. Gaynor had idolised him; and despite her believing that she and Mick had been together for so long that she knew him inside out, she had been the last to discover that he'd been messing around behind her back. The split had hit her hard, but she hadn't yet worked her way through the natural grieving process that might have healed her. Instead she had stuck fast on the 'anger' setting. Gaynor wanted Mick back, and as far as she could see it, clinging on until she had worn down his resistance was her only option.

Linda suddenly leaped to her feet and headed for the bar area in the corner, returning with a bottle of Prosecco and some glasses.

'Bugger tea, let's have a glass and wish Viv well. I didn't know she was that fond of animals, Stel, that she'd want to up and go work in an animal sanctuary.'

'She's based in their office, not actually hands-on with the animals,' explained Stel. 'She wanted a bit of experience working with people in a small business doing accounts and suchlike.'

Linda handed round the Prosecco and poured her mother a Tia Maria, as she didn't drink wine of any description. Iris insisted that all wine tasted of feet, and firmly believed every grape had been trodden by some bloke with verrucas.

'*To Viv*. Here's hoping she enjoys her new home and her new job.'

'To Viv.'

Four glasses were raised in the air. And Stel Blackbird smiled, though inside her heart was breaking because she suspected the real reason why her daughter had taken up that post had nothing to do with getting experience of a small business at all.

Chapter 3

Viv followed Geraldine back into the homely kitchen where the small owl bobbed and squawked at them as if to say 'where've you been?' The kettle was whistling cheerfully on the Aga. Geraldine put some teabags into an old brown teapot and whirled them around with a spoon.

'Is it just the two of you that work here then?' asked Viv.

'Just the two of us full-time now,' echoed Geraldine. 'Though Armstrong likes to come and help out. We pay him in eggs and a bit of pocket money. You'll have guessed we don't have a lot of money for wages.'

Viv had.

Geraldine poured out the tea and put a plate of buttered cake slices on the table. 'Made by my own fair hand. Date and walnut,' she smiled. 'And fresh butter from the farm up the road.'

Viv was touched that a cake had been baked in her honour. Her mother did things like that – made cakes for every occasion, though her efforts wouldn't have exactly had Mary Berry throwing in her towel for fear of the opposition.

'It's not a very big sanctuary, is it?' said Viv.

'You noticed,' said Geraldine. 'Look, I hope you don't mind me saying this . . . I don't want to scare you off but . . . I just want to warn you.'

Viv froze mid-chew. Warn her? About what?

'You're very young . . .' Geraldine sighed.

'I'm twenty-three,' answered Viv quickly. She considered herself more woman than child, but then she had thought that for several years now. She'd had to grow up fast in her teens.

'Oh, bless you,' replied Geraldine. Her eyes were blinking as if there was a lot of activity going on in the brain behind them. Then, as if a dam had broken inside her, she opened her mouth and said, before she could stop herself, 'Look, I'll come straight out with it. Heath isn't the easiest man to get on with, especially at the moment. There's a lot of tension. We're struggling financially and . . . well . . . he can be difficult, blunt, but underneath he's wonderful, lovely, kind.' Then she fell abruptly silent and, as if she had sustained a puncture, her whole body seemed to sag. 'I might as well be honest, Viv, we need someone here, someone who will stay and adjust to him and let him adjust to them without immediately running off.'

'Ok-ay,' replied Viv, wondering what could be so alarming about this Heath bloke. He wouldn't scare her away. She needed to be here, and so she would put up with him, no matter what.

'Don't judge him on first appearances is all I ask.'

'I'm sure everything will be fine.' Viv sipped at her tea, which was strong, just as she liked it. Strong as her resolve not to be intimidated by some old curmudgeon who enjoyed pushing his weight around.

'Once you get to know him, you'll find his bark is much worse than his bite,' smiled Geraldine, relieved by Viv's attitude. 'Now, bring your tea with you and let me show you where you'll be staying so you can get settled in. I hope you'll be all right in the folly. It's compact, but very pretty and you can shut the door on us at the weekends.'

'Do you live on-site too?' asked Viv.

'Yes, my room's at the back of the house, through there,' said Geraldine, pointing to a door in the corner of the kitchen. She sniffed the air. 'I must say, your luggage smells lovely.'

'One of my suitcases is full of oils,' replied Viv, picking up the heaviest one. 'I blend them for companies.'

'Blend oils?' Geraldine questioned.

'I have a neurological quirk,' Viv told her, going on to explain in more detail. 'An acute sense of smell.'

Geraldine was looking at her the way most people did when she said as much.

'The best way I can explain it to you is ... you'll have seen the picture of white light hitting a prism and dividing into a rainbow?'

'Yes,' replied Geraldine.

'That's how I perceive scents. It's like I'm the prism and when I smell something, each component separates itself from the others in my brain. And I also construct formulas; for instance, if a company want me to recreate the essence of an old library or an autumn walk.'

'That's amazing,' gasped Geraldine.

'I know it's weird,' returned Viv, 'but I don't mind it.'

The school bullies used to have a go at her about being a freak, but she refused to feed them with her fear. *Ignore them.*

They're just jealous, because they're ordinary, her mother had said. Stel had always been as brilliant at giving advice as she had been as rubbish at taking it.

'Sometimes the things that make you weird turn out to be your greatest assets, did you know that?' said Geraldine, wheeling the smaller of the two cases towards the door.

Viv smiled. That was such a Stel philosophy it was as if she had just flitted in to join them.

'So who buys these formulas then? People who make candles and those reed diffuser things?' Geraldine went on.

'Amongst others, yes.'

'Goodness. I didn't know such a job existed.'

'I'm not sure it does either,' chuckled Viv, following her out of the door. 'I didn't think anyone would take me seriously when I started, but they did.'

'So it makes you some pin money, does it? It's good that you can supplement your wages, then. It's embarrassing what we offer here.'

Viv didn't say that it made her more money than Geraldine could guess at.

They headed past Viv's car, across the yard to the tall, castle-like folly. Geraldine unlocked it with a long key befitting the heavy arched door, which opened with a characterful creak into a sitting room with rough stone walls and a rich dark wooden floor. There was a two-seater high-backed green sofa and a footstool and a table and two dining chairs. Alongside one wall, there was a run of dark wooden kitchen units, a brown electric oven and hob, a sink and a narrow white half-fridge. Above the sink was a yellow stained-glass window, throwing a golden light onto a welcome-basket of eggs, butter, bread and milk on the draining board. Pretty green curtains hung at the side of a large arched window affording a view of Ironmist hillside and a stone seat was set in the deep wall beneath it. It was certainly 'compact' but on the right side of cosy, rather than cramped.

'It doesn't have a washing machine, but there's one in the cottage,' said Geraldine. 'Obviously, you can use it whenever you want. There's a washing line in the garden and a tumble drier in the cottage kitchen. Let me show you upstairs.' Viv followed Geraldine up the narrow wooden staircase. There at the top of it was the prettiest bedroom ever with white-painted walls and another arched window. There was a three-quarter-sized bed, an old oak wardrobe and a long ornate mirror propped up at the side of a door which led to a very tiny bathroom. A faint smell of unlived-in damp and an artificial rose spray pervaded the air. Nothing that a good dose of fresh air from an open window wouldn't kick into touch, thought Viv.

'It's lovely.'

'It is, isn't it?' agreed Geraldine. 'It was a ruin until three years ago. No one knows how long it's been here or who built it. Heath and a couple of men from the village renovated it. It was my idea to turn it into a little house for whoever we got to help us run things. I thought it might help to attract someone decent because the money certainly wouldn't. Present company excepted, of course,' she added quickly. 'Anyway, the design is very clever. The bed is high so you can store things underneath it and there are secret storage cupboards everywhere. Oh, and it does creak a bit at night as it cools, I do warn you, but it's just house noises, not ghosts.'

No ghost could be as scary as those birds, thought Viv.

'When will he ... Heath ... be back so I can meet him?'

Viv had always preferred to run towards impending disasters rather than from them. That way they were over and done with sooner rather than later.

'I was hoping tonight; tomorrow latest,' replied Geraldine, worry again furrowing her brow. 'I'm sorry, I shouldn't have said anything. Goodness knows what a picture I've painted.' She sighed as if the world and its brother were weighting down her shoulders. Viv put on her best 'look, it's all right' smile.

'I'm sure we'll get on when we meet each other.'

'Bless you for making me feel better,' said Geraldine. 'Words always sound fine in my head but there's a filter in my mouth that makes them come out wrong.' She absently nudged her hair back from the left side of her face and Viv noticed the silvery line of scar tissue crossing her eyebrow and curling towards her ear. 'All I ask is, give us a chance. Now let me leave you to unpack and settle in. Come and have some supper with me when you've found your feet. Nothing flash, just some field mushroom broth but it's a lovely recipe.'

'Thank you, I will.'

When Geraldine had gone, Viv rang her mother to let her know she had arrived safely. Stel picked up after one ring, as if she had been sitting by the phone waiting for the call.

'Thank goodness you've arrived,' she said, as concerned as if Viv had trekked to Base Camp on Everest. 'How is it? What are the people like? Have you eaten?'

'Mum, I am fine. I have a lovely little bijou house—'

'Bijou?' Stel interrupted. 'Estate agents say bijou when they mean minuscule and poky.'

'Yes, well, I'm not an estate agent and I mean bijou in the

very nicest way. It's tiny and sweet, like a miniature castle, and in the prettiest valley.'

Stel opened her mouth to release so many things that were crowded in there, waiting to rush out: *make sure you lock your door, don't let them work you too hard, is your tetanus injection up to date?* Her girl was a woman now and the apron strings were ripe for snapping. It didn't make it any easier that Viv was far more sensible at her age than Stel had ever been. *Funny how we're so different*, thought Stel. But then, it wasn't, really.

'Well, you keep in touch with me and let me know you're doing okay,' was all she allowed herself to say.

'I will, Mum. Has Basil come back in yet?'

'Oh yes, he came back about an hour ago. He's scoffing his dinner now as if he hasn't been fed for a week.'

Stel looked down at the still-full cat food bowl. Basil, their lazy ginger tom, had been out all night, which was unheard of for him. She supposed a lie was forgiveable in the circumstances if it stopped her girl from worrying about him.

'Wonderful. Give him a hug from me. Right, I'm off to unpack then. You take care, Mum.'

'And you. Talk to you soon. Big kiss.'

'Big kiss.'

Stel put the phone down, sank onto the sofa and had a mini-sob. Such was the irony of life that you poured all your love into a child to make them ready for leaving you. With not even Basil to cuddle for comfort, she felt so very, very alone.

Chapter 4

Gaynor poured the last of the bottle of wine into her glass. She was crying. No one had seen her cry for years except the reflection in the mirror.

Time was a great healer, was it? Bollocks. Mick had been gone for eleven months and thirteen days now and every morning when she woke up, she was freshly pierced by the hurt of his desertion, like that bloke in Greek mythology who had his liver ripped out every day. She knew that she would find more sympathy from her friends if she had cried in front of them, crumpled into herself instead of spitting and firing hate bombs; but anger was the only thing keeping her breathing.

She looked around her at the immaculate front room with its palatial-chic furniture, its porcelain seated leopard sentinels either side of the baroque fireplace, its ridiculously priced sofa which looked like something out of Versailles. Mick had denounced it from day one as the most uncomfortable thing he had ever sat on in his life. That sofa summed up her whole marriage. It might have appeared grand, but it wasn't inviting enough to come home to.

Which is why Mick had buggered off to a big squashy sofa he could collapse into with a contented sigh.

Gaynor wasn't a stupid woman. She knew she had spent too much time tending to the accoutrements of her marriage rather than her marriage itself. Okay, Mick wasn't perfect, but she hadn't given him what he wanted and, as much as she hated to admit it to herself, he hadn't asked for that much. He'd told her so many times that he wasn't happy with this or that and she'd ignored him, telling herself he would come round to her way of thinking. It was always him who had to bend to her. Well, he hadn't come around to her way of thinking on the chaise and it had been a hard lesson and one learned too late. She had begged him not to leave her, when he'd come back for some of his stuff, a month after his initial disappearance, but he was impenetrable. It was over. She had been convinced she could mend this. She had cried and crawled after him on her knees, promised to change, promised to mould herself into the sweet, pliant woman he wanted and wouldn't that be easier than leaving and carving up their joint life? Then when that didn't work she had attacked him and ripped into Danira Bellfield and he had walked out to his car, dragging her behind him down the path as she clung onto his calf.

She never realised she had loved Mick as much as she did until he had gone. She missed seeing his shoes in the hallway, she missed him grousing about there being nothing on the TV worth watching, she missed him polishing off every meal she put in front of him because she really was a superb cook. She even missed all the things that used to drive her mad about him: his soft snuffly breathing in the middle of the night, the noisy way he rolled an ice-cube around in a whisky glass, what an unreadable mess he made of a newspaper when he'd read it. Inside she was in pieces; outside she remained upright and brittle, keeping up appearances despite the fact that her husband had left her for a Bellfield – *a Bellfield* – of all families. One who wore crop tops despite the fact she had a belly with more wobble than a half-set jelly. And tattoos. And piercings on her face and God knows where else. And, one day when Gaynor had been out spying on them in her car, she had seen Blobby de Niro and her own husband strolling down the street holding hands like lovestruck teenagers and he had been grinning in a way that she hadn't seen him do for . . . well . . . ever.

Gaynor threw the contents of her glass into her mouth to drown out all the torturing visions; but it seemed that those visions were wearing rubber rings that could float in Shiraz.

Chapter 5

Stel stood on the back doorstep yet again and called out Basil's name. She was getting worried now. Basil liked his home comforts too much to be out at night, or for long during the day. He was fat and lazy and hated the cold and couldn't have found anything to eat to save his life, even if it had been dead, cooked in catnip and served up on a plate with a label reading 'eat me'. He never usually went beyond the boundary of the garden fence, so she had begun to fear the worst.

Stel had adopted him from the Maud Haworth Home for Cats when Viv had been fifteen. Viv had nagged for a kitten for her thirteenth birthday but Stel's then partner Darren had been allergic to their fur. In retrospect, she should have thrown him out and let her daughter have the cat.

'Not turned up, Stel?'

'Oh Al, you scared me daft.' Stel hadn't realised her next-door neighbour was standing on his doorstep too.

'Sorry, love. I've been out and had a look around, but I couldn't see him. Do you want me to ring the council for you in the morning, to see if they've had a report of any animals being knocked down?' Al heard Stel's sharp intake of breath. 'I'm sure they won't have, but I don't mind check-ing for you. Save you doing it. No news is good news, eh?'

'Thanks, Al.' She smiled at him and tried to will back the tears that threatened to flood out of her eyeballs. That was typically kind of Al; he was a good neighbour – and a very old friend. She and Al Thackray had been in the same class all the way through school and he'd lived at the bottom of her street when they were growing up. He'd bought the semi adjoining Stel's fifteen years ago and transformed it from a neglected old person's house into a palace. Some of the kids had been cruel to him when he was young because his mother was useless and had sent him to school in hand-me-down scruffy clothes. Stel's own mum had marched down the street on many an occasion, found Al sitting on his doorstep and made him come to their house for some-thing to eat. She'd also given Myra Thackray some right earfuls of vitriol in the street about it; not that Myra was shamed enough to resume her maternal duties.

Stel knew that Al had always appreciated that she'd never ridiculed him nor made him feel like shit like those other kids – and some of the teachers – at their school had done, but he'd never treated her as anything else but a friend, which was a shame, because she'd always had a soft spot for him. He might not have been academic at school, but he was amazingly talented at making things with his hands. He'd left at fifteen to become an apprentice joiner with a firm that he now owned. He'd had a shouty and childless marriage, which had ended about seven years ago, and there'd been no romance since that she knew of. Al Thackray was a decent man, a good man, a kind man. The sort that never looked at her because the only men she attracted were total knobheads.

When she looked at Al these days, she could barely equate him to the spotty, puny, undernourished boy whose legs were like strings with knots in them. Al was a big fellow now, with shoulders like an ox, a combination of building-site graft and using heavy weights at the gym. He looked after himself, did Al. And he looked after Stel too. If she ever needed anything, all she had to do was knock on the party wall between them and he'd be straight over for her, she knew.

Al handed over a piece of paper with lots of his writing on it.

'I made a list of all the stuff you can do when a cat goes missing,' he said. 'You know, who to leave your details with and all that.'

'Thank you.' Stel didn't want to cry again, not in front of anyone and he must have sensed that because he changed the subject.

'Did Viv arrive safely then?'

'Yes, she's there now. She said it's a lovely place.'

Al's mobile phone went off – its ring tone was the theme tune to *Scooby Doo*. For a few seconds she was back in her childhood house in Holton Road, watching that programme on the TV with him, the pair of them eating Birds Eye fish-finger sandwiches, and her mother looking up the road to try and spot Myra Thackray coming home so she could give her a piece of her mind for 'leaving a bairn locked out in this weather'.

Al took the call and waved a 'bye' at her. She waved back and called one last time for Basil, but there was no miaow of reply.

*

Viv unzipped the smaller of her two cases and took out the faded yellow and black striped knitted bee that was cushioned in the middle of her clothes. EBW went everywhere with her. It had been the first present she ever received, knitted by a nurse at the hospital where she was born. Elke Wilson had worked in the special care baby unit and had hidden a note inside the 'teddy bee'; a note which Viv had found when she was eighteen. Viv had restitched the bee after she'd opened it up to extract the folded piece of paper she'd felt inside it, but the scar was still visible. Viv put EBW on the table at the side of her bed, tenderly as if the toy had feelings, then she unpacked the rest of her stuff; not that it took her long. Her clothes now hung in the wardrobe, her toiletries littered the surface of the dressing table and the deep stone windowsill of the bathroom. Her books and iPad were parked at the side of her bed and her caseful of oils took up the whole dining table. Once everything was out of her suitcases, she almost scooped it back up again and bolted home. She didn't want to be here in this strange little folly in this strange little hamlet. She wanted to be sharing a bottle of wine with her mum, Basil a heavy furry weight on her knee. But she had to be here. She had a job to do which hopefully wouldn't take too long; then she could leave this alien world of three-legged donkeys and mutually dependent owls. Only then.

Chapter 6

'You don't have to knock, love,' Geraldine chuckled, hearing the soft tap of knuckles on the door into the kitchen. Viv walked in to the most beautiful aroma of cooking coming from a black cauldron-type pot on the stove. Geraldine was standing at the work surface slicing a loaf of granary bread into thick wedges.

'Come and sit down,' she said, pointing to the chairs around the table. 'All the animals have been fed and now it's our turn.' There was a half-filled glass of wine at her elbow and a slight slur to her words.

'Can I help?' Viv asked, not used to being waited on.

'You can get a bottle out of the fridge,' she said. 'This is the potato wine but there's beetroot and raspberry as well, if you prefer. Selwyn Stanbury, the barber, makes it. It's the lightest of all his concoctions. I lost three days with his parsnip wine once. And as for his potato vodka . . .' She raised her eyebrows and blew out her cheeks. 'I swore I'd never drink again after that particular sampling session.'

Viv opened the fridge and selected the potato wine from the three bottles that were in the door rack.

'Glasses are in the cupboard above your head,' Geraldine directed, moving over to the pot on the stove and ladling out some soup. It arrived at the table with a swirl of cream on it and a sprinkle of herbs and looked delicious.

Geraldine sat down, then raised her glass.

'Welcome, Viv,' she said, clinking it against Viv's as soon as she had lifted it. 'I hope you're happy here with us. I think Isme would approve of you.'

'I hope I have better taste in men than she did,' said Viv as she picked up her spoon and began to eat. The soup tasted wonderful.

'Do you have a young man?' asked Geraldine, ripping into the bread.

'Not any more,' replied Viv. She noticed Geraldine's face fold in sympathy. 'Oh it's okay. We realised quite quickly we weren't Mr and Mrs Right-for-each-other. I'm in no rush.'

'That's very sensible,' said Geraldine. 'Take your time. And don't settle for anything less than the best just to stave off loneliness. Unless you're ninety-seven and can have both parents at your wedding.' She laughed and Viv decided she liked Geraldine, very much. And likewise, Geraldine thought she and Viv would get on very well and hoped she would stay. It would be lovely to have a friendly female to talk to.

'Please tell me that I didn't put you off with what I said about Heath earlier,' said Geraldine.

'I promise you that you didn't.' Viv reached for some bread and the butter fresh from the farm. She could have eaten the whole loaf. 'You mentioned his father earlier on? Is this an old family concern?'

'Yes, the Merlos have lived at Wildflower Cottage for a hundred and fifty years. Heath's a vet by profession but when he lost his father four years ago, he came back to take over this place. He's still registered, but the sanctuary takes up most of his time.'

He was a vet and yet he chooses to work in the back of beyond, looking after a crippled donkey and a few owls? Surely not, thought Viv.

'The Merlos are one of the three old families of this area.' Geraldine checked off their names on her fingers. 'The Merlos and the Leightons, of course. And the Cooper-Smiths, although their line ended two years ago with the death of poor dear Kate. She was the woman who bred Wonk. It's thanks to her legacy that we're surviving. Just.'

Geraldine emptied more wine into her glass. It was loosening her tongue beautifully.

'Their land adjoined the Leightons', but the two families hated each other because Kate was jilted at the altar by Jasper Leighton, the present owner's grandfather. Kate never recovered from the rejection, especially as Jasper married almost immediately afterwards and brought his new society bride to the family castle. Talk about rubbing her nose in it. So, when Kate became infirm and had to leave Cooper House, she refused to sell it to the Leightons.' Geraldine suddenly realised she might have been talking too much. 'I'm sorry, am I boring you with all this, Vivienne?'

'No, not at all,' Viv protested. 'I want to hear it. It's interesting.' The more she knew about the Leightons, the more it might help her in her quest. 'And please, everyone just calls me Viv. Unless they're annoyed with me, then I get the full three syllables.'

Geraldine gave a small laugh. 'Okay, Viv ... Right, where was I? Oh yes. Well, it wasn't that hard for the Leightons to acquire the land in the end using a third-party agent. They bulldozed Kate's house and nothing could be done about it.' Geraldine sighed heavily. 'Kate was heartbroken by their underhandedness. She hadn't been in the nursing home above a few months when she died.'

'How very sad,' said Viv.

'Ruthless. That's what the Leightons are,' said Geraldine with a snap in her voice that Viv guessed was foreign to her nature. 'Kate Cooper-Smith loved animals though. She knew how much we needed an injection of cash to survive and thank God she gave it to us. She threw us a true lifeline.'

'Have you never opened up to the public?' asked Viv. 'Hawk displays, petting zoos, that sort of thing.'

'No, nothing like that.' From Geraldine's reaction, that wasn't a popular suggestion.

'Don't you get any funding to help you?'

'Not any more, the Leightons have seen to that. They'll be cursing Kate for doing what she did for us because they've tried consistently to cut off our financial blood supply. There isn't much left in the coffers now, but at least it enables us to go on until the bitter end.'

'The bitter end?' Viv queried.

Geraldine's hand flew up to her mouth. She really had said too much. Viv suspected that Geraldine had been starved of company and whatever secrets she was holding were weighing heavy on her. It only needed the slightest of nudges for them all to come tumbling out.

'You can trust me to keep my mouth shut,' Viv said.

'Oh what the hell,' said Geraldine with a resigned shake

of the head. 'It'll all be common knowledge soon, if it isn't already. Heath doesn't own the land here. He leases it and that lease is up in July. It's all such a mess, Viv.'

Viv could see there were tears gathering in Geraldine's eyes. She was confused. She could have sworn Geraldine told her the house had been in Heath's family for generations. 'So, who does own the land then?' Viv asked.

'The Leightons, of course. They own everything around here. The land around Wildflower Cottage is the last piece of the jigsaw for them. And this is land that they know they can make a fortune out of.'

'I'm not sure I understand.'

Geraldine's hands came together with a soft clap.

'Let's go back to the beginning, one hundred and fifty years ago,' she said. 'Cecilia Leighton, the then heiress to Ironmist Castle, was in love with Heath's great-grandfather, Alfred Merlot, but he was only a lowly groom in the stables. She wasn't allowed to sell or give away any of the estate but she could lease some of it out. So she had documents drawn up to give her lover the maximum one-hundred-and-fifty-year lease on this land so he could build them a home to escape to, but for propriety's sake, the house was to be listed as a sanctuary for the animals which they both so dearly wanted to protect. But poor Cecilia died before he had finished building this house, so the estate passed to her impoverished cousin Jasper, who no doubt couldn't believe his luck. Obviously, he tried to claim back the land from Alfred Merlo, but Cecilia had made the lease watertight. So long as there were animals residing in this place that needed a sanctuary, the lease would stand.'

'Poor Cecilia,' said Viv, genuinely touched by her story.

'Terribly sad and romantic, isn't it? The lease, I imagine, was a formality they wouldn't need when they defied convention and married. Or, if that proved to be impossible, they could live out their days in their own little world here. Alfred grieved for her for years. He eventually married a young girl from the next village who reminded him of Cecilia, because she also loved animals.'

'Heath's great-grandmother, presumably?'

'That's right. Nicholas Leighton wants to build a housing estate here, Viv. And once our lease is up, they will do it because they have everyone and their mother in their pockets,' Geraldine continued, her lips tight with fury.

'Why would they want to ruin this lovely place?'

'Money. As if they haven't got enough already. But that's what the Leightons are like. They covet.' She sighed heavily. 'But we have to soldier on. I believe that we have powerful forces of nature on our side because this land was always meant to be a sanctuary and we will fight the Leightons for it. I have never thought that we wouldn't win in the end.'

So the sanctuary might be closing down soon? That didn't leave Viv a lot of time.

'I might have only lived here for four years myself but it's my home now and the only one I will ever want,' Geraldine went on.

'Where are you from originally?'

'Down south. I can't tell you what a special place this is, Viv. You'll discover that for yourself very quickly, I think.'

Viv smiled politely, but knew she wouldn't. She would not be here long enough to let Ironmist get into her system.

'The Leightons have to have what someone else owns,

even if they don't want it themselves. Land, people . . .' She tucked her hair behind her ear and again Viv saw that silvery line of scar. 'I hate them. I hate them for what they want to do to this beautiful valley.'

The phone gave a shrill ring and interrupted Geraldine's flow. It couldn't have been worse timing when they were knee deep in such an involved conversation.

Viv watched with some amusement as Geraldine picked up the telephone reticently, as if she were expecting it to explode in her hand.

'Yes, she's arrived,' Geraldine was saying. Viv guessed this was the mysterious Heath, and he was firing a salvo of questions about her, if Geraldine's somewhat guarded replies were anything to go by.

'Nice . . . very good . . . Yes, a good choice . . . no . . . yes, Armstrong's been wonderful . . . I don't think that would be possible . . . still here . . .' Geraldine was answering yet more questions, aware that she was being listened to at her end of the phone.

'Oh, that's a shame, well, we'll see you when we see you. Take good care. Goodnight and may your dreams take flight.'

What a lovely expression, thought Viv.

'That was Heath,' said Geraldine, coming back to the table and collecting the empty soup bowls. 'He wanted to know if you had landed and were still here.' She gave a little laugh. 'It wouldn't be the first time that someone arrived and drove straight off again.'

Viv was intrigued by him and wished he would hurry up and arrive so she could get a handle on him. She had always prided herself on being easy to get along with. She didn't want any enemies here. She had enough to contend with, without that as a side issue.

'So shall I start at nine in the morning then?' she asked.

'Or thereabouts,' replied Geraldine. 'We don't have that rigid a timetable. The office is next door. I think a clever girl like you will be able to do the job in her sleep. I've made a list of what we need you to do. I'm not very computer savvy but I'm sure you are.'

Viv yawned. She hadn't exactly exerted herself physically today but her brain had been extra busy collecting, storing and dissecting information and it had exhausted her. In mental terms, today had been the equivalent of a double-marathon run.

'You get yourself off to bed,' replied Geraldine. 'I expect I've worn you out with all my talking. I'm sorry if I've spoken too much. You have to forgive me. Today is a date that I like to celebrate . . . Selwyn's wines should be sold to the military as truth drugs.'

'Is it your birthday?' asked Viv.

'Sort of,' replied Geraldine with a soft smile. 'Now, you go and relax and thank you for your company. I so want you to settle in and be happy here.'

'I promise I will do my very best,' Viv said and meant it, albeit temporarily. She wondered what a 'sort of' birthday was.

*

Geraldine washed up the soup bowls and dried them, looking out of the window as she did so. She never failed to be aware of what a beautiful place she had found in this sanctuary for the discarded, the unwanted, the damaged. Was it her birthday, Viv had asked her. Yes, it was. The third of May. Her *birth-day*. The day the new Geraldine had been born, the happier Geraldine, *free* Geraldine. Before that date four years ago, Geraldine Hartley had not existed at all.

Chapter 7

Viv woke to the sound of absolutely nothing. She hadn't realised how much background noise there had been at home because she'd grown accustomed to it, but here there was only silence. She opened her eyes and just for a split second expected to see her own desk and chair, not the unfamiliar furniture of her new home, and her heart felt like a large stone in her chest. She didn't want to be here at all and had to keep in focus that this was likely to be a very short-term appointment.

She swung her legs to the floor, crossed to the window and opened the curtains to see wisps of that low mist snaking around the hundreds of blue flowers. The sun was high and bright and shining on the hillside and on the rooftops of the houses which flanked the road up to the castle and beyond onto the moors. It was like looking at a beautiful picture square-framed by the wood of her window.

It was eight o'clock and her working day was to begin at nine. She had a dribbly shower and made herself some poached eggs and toast for breakfast. Geraldine was already in the kitchen when Viv walked in at ten to nine.

'Morning, sleep well?' Geraldine smiled a welcome. She was wearing another long hippy dress and Viv presumed that must be her usual style.

'Very,' she replied.

'I've just brewed some tea. Would you like some?'

'Yes ple— OH!' Viv shrieked as something wet touched her hand and she whirled around to find the huge dog Pilot standing there, his long tail wafting gently from side to side.

'He's just saying good morning,' chuckled Geraldine. 'He likes to press his nose in your hand. It's just a thing he does.'

Viv noticed Bub in his furry basket, looking at her through the slits of his eyes. The owl was in his ornate white-wire cage, standing on one leg, eyes closed.

'Armstrong is out feeding the animals,' replied Geraldine. 'I'm grateful for his help because it doesn't look as if Heath will be back today after all. Wonk isn't walking right on her new leg yet.'

As if on cue, the door creaked open and in walked Armstrong. Viv liked the smell that hung around him – fresh and innocent, like sweet hay and baby talc.

'I've fed everyone, Geraldine, except the birds. And I've cleaned out Wonk's stable for when she gets back. Oh, good morning, miss.'

'Good morning, Armstrong,' said Viv.

'Good lad. Want a cuppa?' asked Geraldine.

'No thanks, Geraldine. Can I take Pilot out again?' He lifted the lead off the hook on the wall before Geraldine could answer, hoping to force her into saying that he could.

'Only a short one, Armstrong. He was very tired yesterday. You took him a bit too far, I think.'

'I promise.' Armstrong saluted and grinned at Viv. 'You're very small, aren't you?'

'*Armstrong*,' Geraldine reprimanded him.

'It wasn't an insult. Honest.'

Viv laughed, just to reassure him that she wasn't insulted. She'd heard it too many times to be offended. Besides, it was true. Geraldine shook her head from side to side with mild impatience. 'Go on, off with you, Armstrong, and don't wear Pilot out.'

'I promise, Geraldine. Bye, Viv.'

'Have a nice walk. See you later,' she replied.

As soon as he was out of earshot, Geraldine said, 'Sorry about that. Armstrong says what he sees.'

'It's fine,' said Viv. 'I've heard worse.'

'I do hope not.'

'I'm actually a lot taller than the doctors thought I'd grow,' said Viv, watching Geraldine stirring a spoon around in the old brown teapot. 'I was born prematurely and with a curvature of the spine and I wasn't expected to hit four foot six, never mind top five foot. I've had more than my fair share of operations over the years.'

'Oh my goodness, you poor girl,' said Geraldine. 'Are you all right now?'

'Touch wood,' replied Viv, putting her palm flat down on the table. 'I don't need to go back to hospital unless I feel I have any problems.'

Stel had battled every step of the way for the operations and procedures her daughter should have had. She had made Viv do yoga and any exercise class which her research suggested would be beneficial to her – and it had been. Stel was always so much stronger for other people than she had ever been for herself.

'Well, thank goodness for that.'

'Obviously I won't be applying for jobs with any heavy lifting involved.'

'Nor should you,' said Geraldine, putting a mug of tea down in front of Viv. 'You've time for a cup before I show you the office. This is my third. I need to hydrate. I had too much of that potato wine last night. I don't usually turn into an old soak when the moon is out. I hope I didn't give you a bad impression of myself.'

'Not at all,' smiled Viv. 'That soup was lovely. Who'd have thought mushrooms and bread could have been so tasty?'

'The bakery up the hill is wonderful. They supply to a few local hotels and shops, thank goodness, because they'd never make a profit just serving Ironmist.'

'I'm surprised there aren't more houses in this beautiful place,' said Viv, realising immediately that she had said the wrong thing as Geraldine's friendly smile flattened.

'We don't want more houses here. There are just enough houses for just enough people and that's the way the Ironmisters like it.'

'Yes, you're right. It would spoil it,' Viv put in quickly. 'I'll take my tea into the office with me if you like?'

'Come with me then,' said Geraldine, smile back on her face. She opened the door at the back of the kitchen and led Viv through to the hallway, on the far side of which was an office which looked as if it had been burgled. There were papers everywhere.

'As you can see, we need some help.'

'Lordy,' said Viv. What a mess it was.

'I know it's bad. I haven't touched anything because I'm scared to, quite honestly. I don't know what needs throwing away or keeping and I wouldn't know where to start.'

Viv was not put off by the sight at all: she only saw the prospect of kicking this room into shape. She was good at organising and always had been. She'd had to grow up quickly when her mother had found a lump in her breast and her wuss of a partner had run off and left her. Viv had had to take command at fifteen and be the parent.

'Do you think you can do anything with it?' asked Geraldine fearfully.

Viv mentally spat on her hands and rubbed them together and said, 'I'm sure I can.'

Chapter 8

Stel stood by the window in the hospice, looking idly out onto the beautiful tranquil garden, drawing warmth from the cup of coffee in her hand.

'Changed your mind?' asked Maria the head nurse, coming up behind her and looking over her shoulder.

'About what?'

'Ian the gardener, of course.'

Stel hadn't even noticed him there, doing something with a spade behind the hedge.

'No,' said Stel. 'I was thinking about my Viv and wondering how she was.'

'Going out with Ian would take your mind off things.'

'Oh give up, Maria.'

Last week, Maria had told Stel that gossip had reached her that Ian, the new gardener, was asking questions about her: was she married to/living with/seeing a man. It was obvious that he fancied her. Maria had taken it upon herself to interfere. Did Stel fancy Ian Robson because if she did, she would tell him and they could get together with none of the faffing-about time-wasting nonsense.

Maria and Stel had worked together years and were friends, but not quite close enough friends for Stel to tell her the absolute truth. If the head nurse had been Caro or Linda, Stel would have said, 'He seems like a nice bloke but I don't like his eyes. They're too close together. And too high up. As if God had stuck them on his head as an after-thought.' She knew she was being ridiculously petty but it put her off. She just didn't fancy him because of his eyes. Stel knew that her dream man was never going to land in her life now and was prepared to compromise, but still . . . there was no spark when Ian came into the kitchen for a cup of tea or exchanged a few banal, polite words with her. Not one.

'Aw, that's a shame,' replied Maria. 'I had high hopes.'

'Stop matchmaking,' Stel admonished her. 'I can't see me ever going out with anyone again. I only have one sort of luck where men are concerned and it's rotten.'

After her brush with cancer she'd subscribed to Matchmaker.com and had a series of dates that it made her shudder to think about. 'Dating is like finding that needle in a haystack,' Linda had said. Well, she hadn't found the needle but on Matchmaker.com she had certainly found a load of pricks.

'Don't you miss the sex?' whispered Maria.

'Sometimes,' nodded Stel, wishing she hadn't said it as that gave Maria another angle to come in at.

'It doesn't have to be serious. You could be friends with benefits. Every itch needs a scratch.'

'Stop it now.'

'He used to be in the army. He was wounded in action. He got knifed in his side by the enemy. He was lucky to survive.'

'So I hear.' Stel wouldn't be swayed, although admittedly she had been impressed after hearing that.

'And he's got a nice—' Maria snapped off what she had been about to say because Ian walked into the kitchen through the garden door.

'Morning, ladies,' he said, his eyes travelling from Stel to Maria and back to Stel again, where they lingered.

'Morning, Ian,' smiled Maria. 'How's it going?'

'Good, thanks.'

His accent wasn't local. Stel credited the slight sing-song cadence in it to the Derby or Nottinghamshire area.

'Can I make you a cup of coffee?' Stel asked, hoping he wouldn't see that as a sign that she wanted anything other than to put the kettle on for him.

'That would be lovely, thank you.'

She knew how he took it because she'd made him one often enough – weak and very white with two sugars. She wasn't thick, she knew that he timed his breaks to tie in with hers.

'I'll leave you to it,' replied Maria, giving Stel a mischievous wink as she put her upturned empty cup in the dishwasher, and flounced out as quickly as her legs could manage. Stel could have throttled her. She could feel Ian's eyes on her back as she refilled the kettle and plugged it in.

'So how's you then, Stel?' he asked.

'I'm okay thanks, Ian,' said Stel, glancing over her shoulder and throwing him a smile. It was true what they said about watched pots. This kettle was taking an age to boil.

'Daughter all right?'

'Sorry?'

'Your daughter? Has she settled in her new place?'

So he knew about Viv then. Probably through Maria, arming him with information which might get him an 'in' with her.

'Yes, thanks,' said Stel with an absent sigh, which Ian heard.

'That was a big sigh.'

'Did I sigh?'

'Yep.'

Stel swallowed hard on the sudden tears that threatened to come tumbling down her cheeks and embarrass her. Basil still hadn't come back home and none of the local vets or animal centres had had notice of him. One tear escaped the barricade, followed by another which she wiped quickly away.

'Here, let me make us both a coffee.' Ian's hands came gently on Stel's arms and he moved her away from the kettle. 'Sit down.' He took the spoon out of her hand and took two clean mugs out of the cupboard. He remembered how she took hers and didn't need to ask.

Stel sat down at the dining table in the middle of the kitchen and watched Ian preparing the drinks. He had a good physique from the back. Tall, very slim, short dark hair in a military crew cut. She felt shallow that she'd regarded him as unfanciable earlier just because his eyes didn't fit her ideal.

'I haven't got any kids, so I can't talk from experience,' he was saying. 'But I know what a state my mum was in when I left home to go into the army.' He pronounced it 'Ormy'. It made her smile, even though she didn't feel much like smiling.

'Our cat has gone missing as well,' Stel blurted out, not sure why she was taking him into her confidence. 'I've looked everywhere.'

'Oh dear. Maybe he's out hunting, enjoying these lovely summer nights.'

'He's too lazy to hunt anything. He hardly ever goes out and I've got visions of him locked in someone's garage just before they've gone on holiday for a fortnight . . .'

'Hey, hold on, hold on,' he said, pressing his hands down as if attempting to apply a manual brake on her words. 'My mum had a cat that was always going walkabout. She used to get all worked up and then he'd come strolling back in fatter than when he went out. That's what cats do.'

'Not Basil,' said Stel. 'And I lied to Viv and told her that he'd come home.'

'Do you want me to help you look for him? Four eyes are better than two. Or six if I wear my glasses.'

Stel smiled. 'Thanks, but I've looked everywhere.'

'Where do you live?' He put a mug of coffee down on the table in front of her.

'Thank you. Horton Lane, Pogley Top.'

'You've got fields at the back up there, haven't you?'

'And the woods. And a stream. I've walked around them all and called and called and he hasn't returned.'

Ian mused. 'You'll have rung around all the vets and that, won't you?'

'Oh yes.'

Ian scratched absently at his arms, criss-crossed with red lines.

'You should wear gloves,' said Stel.

'What?'

'Gardening gloves.' She pointed at the lattice-work on his skin.

'I know.' He raised up his arms and studied them. 'They look like something off a Frankenstein movie, don't they? I don't think I'd win an arm beauty contest but I'm a gardener, I like to be close to the earth.'

The corners of his mouth twitched upwards. He was quite attractive when he smiled, and that comment about getting close to the earth was ever so slightly sexy.

Stel's eyes flicked upwards to the clock on the wall. 'Oh blimey, I'd better get back to my post,' she said, standing hurriedly and lifting the mug. 'Thanks for the coffee, and the ear. Sorry if I got a bit emotional.'

Ian waved his hand airily to dismiss the notion. 'Oh don't worry. Perfectly understandable in the circumstances. You should try and find something to take your mind off things. There's some good films on at the cinema at the moment.'

Nooo. Alarm bells started ringing in Stel's head. She didn't want to be put in the sticky position of turning him down face to face.

'Never really liked the cinema,' she lied, trying her level best to look as if she hadn't noticed his words were anything other than a casual observation. 'I think I'll get the girls round and have a few drinks.'

'You do that,' he replied, standing up to go. 'Catch you later. And keep that chin up.'

Stel went back to her seat at the reception desk grateful that she had avoided what could have been an awkward situation. Then again, shouldn't she have been flattered that a fine figure of an ex-soldier had taken an interest in her?

Chapter 9

'Please, Rebecca. Please let us have Freddie for an hour. For his grandad's birthday. We're all desperate to see him.'

On the other end of the phone there was a moment's silence, into which Linda read a touch of hope; only for it to be felled by the axe of that one word: 'No.'

'I'm absolutely begging you.' Behind her, Dino tapped her on the shoulder, gesturing for her to hand the phone over to him.

'Rebecca,' he said. 'Just an hour, love. It would be the best present I could have.'

'He's got a swimming lesson.' Rebecca's voice came tinnily down the phone. 'I'll let him run up the path to deliver your card but then we will have to go. I don't want to turn up late.'

Iris was gesticulating madly at Dino so he turned his back on her in order not to be distracted. 'It's not fair,' she shouted.

On the other end of the line, Rebecca huffed. 'Tell her life isn't fair.'

'Look, ignore her,' said Dino with dignity, fighting to

reclaim some ground. 'We will be glad to see you both. You're very welcome anytime.' But he was speaking into the ether as the phone had been put down on the other side.

Iris and Linda both exploded then, Iris with expletives, Linda with tears. Dino put his arms around his wife and pulled her into his shoulder.

'I know, I know, but if I start playing hardball, she won't come around at all. Bloss, you shouldn't have shouted that.'

'Well, it's *not* fair,' screeched Iris. 'It was the sorriest day ever when Andy met her.'

'Then we wouldn't have Freddie at all now, would we, Bloss?' Dino had always called Iris Blossom, which had shortened to Bloss over the years. Even though she was more triffid than delicate flower, the nickname had stuck. 'She said that she'll drive past on her way to Freddie's swimming lesson so he can deliver my card. At least she's bought one to give me. I can't remember her doing that before.'

'I'd better keep out of the way when she comes,' snarled Iris. 'Otherwise I might not be responsible for my actions.'

None of them could understand what their strapping soldier son Andy Hewitt had seen in the older, streetwise Rebecca Pawson. She had a face that could have soured milk but still, they welcomed her into the family since Andy was a grown man after all. A huge flash wedding was hurriedly planned, Rebecca fell pregnant with Freddie then Andy got cold feet and asked for a delay. Rebecca took umbrage – and her newborn – and left him. In a right old financial mess, too. And she'd been punishing the whole Hewitt clan ever since. Rebecca had fought with claws extended, twisted facts and lied until the courts had decreed that the two-hour weekly access between Andy and his son, whenever Andy was home on leave, had to be under her supervision, unless she agreed that he was fit to have Freddie in his lone care. Andy could have fought harder and nastier, but for Freddie's sake he did not want it on public record how much of a bitch his son's mother really was – although Rebecca clearly didn't share his consideration.

Andy could have gone back to court but he didn't have the thousands it would cost in solicitors' fees. Iris would have given him the money gift-wrapped but Dino warned that if they lost, Rebecca would withdraw even the scrap of goodwill she dangled in front of them. They were all trapped under her control until the lad was old enough to make up his own mind.

What worried them most was the way that Rebecca left three-year-old Freddie in the care of the elderly mother whose house she shared. Enid Pawson had never been noted for her reliability, plus she had an ornamental lake in her back garden. The combination of deep water and small boy terrified Linda. She was convinced that it was an accident waiting to happen. She couldn't wait for the day when she could tell the Pawsons exactly what she thought of them. She would make Iris look like Shirley bloody Temple.

'She's not going to let Freddie come around for his birth-day this month either, is she?' said Linda mournfully. 'Just an hour, so he can open his presents here and spend some time with us.'

'It won't always be like this, love,' said Dino. 'Freddie will grow up and come and see us when he wants.'

Linda couldn't help saying, in a low whisper she hoped Iris wouldn't hear, 'That might be too late though.'

Then she felt fingers curl around her own and looked down to find Iris's wrinkled hand there. Linda was a rock-hard matron, in charge of umpteen wards and staff, and whom many doctors deferred to, but suddenly she was whizzed back in time fifty years, feeling the comfort of that same hand, then smooth and plump and warm. She didn't want to let it go, she didn't want to go into that big scary school. Her mother was safe and familiar. Always there when she needed comfort, reassurance, an injection of maternal-strength. Iris was a spiky, loose-mouthed old bugger but she would never let anyone harm the ones she loved. *How dare Rebecca Pawson keep Freddie from her, more than any of us?* thought Linda with a sudden spurt of rage.

Linda closed her eyes and sent a short silent prayer upwards: *Please God, I don't care how You do it, but help us.* She needed to go straight to the top with this one.

Chapter 10

It took Viv three full days to sort out the office, but by the end of them, the files were in order, receipts were sorted and there was a box of old papers which might or might not need shredding – Viv needed the authority of the boss on that one. He had still not made an appearance but she expected him any minute.

Getting the office sorted had taken her mind off being away from her mum and Basil. She liked spending time with Geraldine in the evenings. Geraldine worked so hard both inside and outside the farmhouse. She mucked out the animals and fed them all. Feed was expensive and they were grateful for local donations that helped them get by. The nearby farm sent food, the supermarket in nearby Mawton rang up with offers of fish for the sea eagle and the local police informed them if they'd had to dispose of a deer. The birds loved a bit of venison and playing with the bones.

What Geraldine cooked for herself and Viv was far more palatable. But the previous night Viv had insisted on taking her turn. She had planned pasta cooked with pesto and cream and lots of Parmesan cheese but Mr Mark, the shopkeeper of Ironmist Stores, had asked her what the bloody hell pesto was, so she'd had to leave that ingredient out. It didn't matter – the pasta and the crusty bread from the bakery was perfect. Pilot had laid over her feet under the table as they ate. He was a lovely old fella and despite her initial unease at the size of him, she very soon realised he was as gentle a dog as God could make. Viv liked Geraldine's company. She filled her in on some of the people in the hamlet – who sounded eccentric at best. There was Mrs Macy who knitted teddy bears, all day, every day, and wine-making Selwyn Stanbury who had a forest of Bonsai trees in his barber's shop. Then there was Mr Mark and Mr Wayne, the Ironmist Stores owners who were like psychic twins because they always finished off each other's sentences. Mr Wayne had recently been in hospital to have part of his lung removed and the whole hamlet had rejoiced that he was on the mend. And, of course, Armstrong who was building a rocket in his garden so he could visit his dad in heaven.

Geraldine opened the door with a mug of coffee and a plate of biscuits to find Viv cleaning underneath the desk with a wet sponge.

'My, my, I can hardly recognise the place. Heath is going to be very impressed with you,' she said with a genuine gasp of admiration.

Viv got up from the floor and surveyed her handiwork. She wasn't prone to self-praise, but even she had to admit that she'd done a mighty fine job.

Geraldine dropped a long sigh. 'Oh Viv, I feel so guilty about not telling you when you applied that we don't know how temporary this job is going to be. It was wrong of me, but I knew no one would answer the advert if I had. I'm still surprised you did anyway. But we need to be organised now more than ever. I thought that somewhere in this room there just might be some piece of paper that would help us fight our corner. I don't suppose you saw anything like that, did you?' Her big grey eyes were full of hope.

'I have to say, I didn't,' replied Viv. 'Surely you at least have squatters rights? Surely if this has been Heath's family's home for generations . . .'

'Leighton was going to give Heath one of his new builds, but you can imagine what he said to that offer. Leighton has a team of lawyers costing God knows how much to make sure we're history, because he can afford to do that. There are no listed buildings, no rare species of toad or butterfly living here and needing protection which can save us . . . I'm just hoping that being away from us for a few days has made Heath think of something we might have overlooked.'

'I hope so too, for you all,' said Viv. She hadn't expected this mess when she applied for the job.

Geraldine smiled. 'You're such a lovely girl. I can feel it. Just try not to fall in love with him though.'

Viv's head twisted round sharply and she laughed. 'What?'

'Heath. He's a bit of a mixed-up bunny. I wouldn't want you to get hurt.'

Viv sipped her drink and brought to mind the cranky old man she had pictured Heath to be. Maybe she needed to rethink that image. Geraldine obviously thought him attractive; a big fish in the small pond that was Ironmist. But Viv hadn't come here to fall in love with anyone.

'You can trust me on this, Geraldine, I won't fall in love with Heath Merlo,' she said, taking a biscuit and snapping it in two with her teeth.

Chapter 11

Stel got in from work, looked at Basil's still-full food bowl of biscuits and burst into tears. He was dead, she knew it. Al had come round to tell her that he'd rung the council a couple of times now on her behalf but there were no reports of dead ginger cats being picked up by them, which didn't give her any comfort. What if the binmen couldn't be bothered to file a report? What if he'd been hit by a car but crawled off to die in some undergrowth? He would definitely have been home by now if he were still alive. What was she going to tell Viv when she next called? She wished she could at least know where his body was so she could bury him in the garden. She wanted him home, where he belonged, one way or another. Her lovely big friendly boy. Viv would be heartbroken. The house felt different without him. She wanted to pick him up and bury her face in his fur and hear his pneumatic purr. Her brain had gone into overload: he was lying beside the road somewhere unable to get home; he had fallen in Pogley Stripe and couldn't get out of the water; he had been picked up by scientists for medical experiments; he was suffering, he was cold and hungry and meowling for his nice, comfortable bed.

Stel couldn't face cooking so later she walked to the chip shop at the corner of the road but when she sat down to eat it, even the crisp batter of the cod straight from the fryer couldn't tempt her appetite. Absently she started breaking it up with her fingers to put in Basil's bowl. He always wolfed down leftovers from her fish suppers. Tears pricked her eyes and she let them fall without wiping them up. They plopped onto the table one by one in a sad rhythm.

Then there was an unexpected heavy rap on the front door. Stel hurriedly wiped her hands and cheeks before setting off down the hall. She could see a tall male figure through the frosted glass, and she slipped the chain on just in case before she opened the door.

There on her front step struggling with a blanket that appeared to be alive was Ian Robson.

'Quick, let me in, Stel,' he said. 'I think I've found your cat.'

Stel fumbled with the chain, just in time as a ginger cat wriggled out of the blanket and launched itself from Ian's arms onto the floor. The meow was unmistakable.

'*Basil.*' Stel scooped him up from the floor and hugged him to her. As he rubbed his cheek on her hair, Stel thought her heart would burst with love for him. Ian was still standing outside.

'Come in, Ian, come in.' She pulled him by the sleeve over the threshold. 'Oh, where did you find him?'

'I went looking for him,' said Ian. 'I know that if cats are scared they're more likely to come out at night. I just tramped over the fields at the back and found him looking very sorry for himself up by Elvhurst's farm.'

'Elvhurst's farm? But that must be a mile away.' The farm was at the other side of the thin ribbon of river that the locals called Pogley Stripe.

'Well, he's had time to wander, hasn't he?' said Ian. 'I expect he's ready for a feed.'

'Come through, Ian. Please. Oh my, I can't thank you enough.'

Stel almost bounced with joy into the kitchen where she ripped open a pouch of Basil's food and also gave him the rejected fish which he dived onto immediately whilst she watched him like a proud mother. He broke off only to lap greedily at his water as if he hadn't drunk for a month.

'That is one hungry cat,' said Ian. Stel smiled at him and he smiled back.

'Can I get you a coffee? Tea?'

'No, I don't want to keep you from your dinner,' he said, nodding at the plate of chips on the table.

'I couldn't eat,' said Stel. 'Please, the least I can do is make you a cuppa for finding Basil for me.'

'I'll be honest, I could kill for one if it's no trouble,' said Ian. Stel noticed he had taken off his shoes in consideration for her carpet. *He didn't have to do that*, she thought. She would have forgiven him walking in with manure-covered wellingtons. She scurried over to the kettle.

'Please sit down, Ian. I can't tell you how I feel at this moment. How long have you been out there looking for Basil?'

Ian sat down at the dining table and tilted his wrist so he could read his watch.

'Oh, don't worry about it,' he said.

Stel knew he must have searching for ages. Hours even. What a lovely, kind thing to do. What a lovely, kind man.

'Can I get you anything to eat?' she said.

Ian laughed. 'No, honestly, it's fine.' He could see that she was desperate for him to take something from her, to thank him. His arms were resting on the table as she brought him a mug of her best tea over. One of them was bleeding.

'That looks nasty,' she said. He followed her eyes to the long scratch. 'Did Basil do that?'

'He wasn't happy being cornered by a stranger. You can't blame him. Still, it's worth it now he's home.'

'I am just so happy. You've no idea. I hadn't a clue what I was going to tell my daughter.'

'Well, she need never know now,' smiled Ian.

'I don't know how to thank you,' said Stel, wiping a happy tear as it spilled from her eye.

'I do,' said Ian. 'Come to the pictures with me to see that new James Bond film on Saturday.'

How could Stel refuse?

Chapter 12

Viv's phone rang just as she was about to leave the folly and join Geraldine for a meal. The name 'Mum' showed on the screen. Viv had barely said hello when Stel started bubbling over.

'Viv, I promised myself that I wouldn't bother you but I've got something to say and I feel really bad about it but I lied to—'

'Mum, calm down,' laughed Viv. 'Take a deep breath before you start hyperventilating.'

At the other end of the line, Stel was super-annoyed with herself. That hadn't come out as planned at all. 'I wish I hadn't rung now. I said I wouldn't say anything. Well, to cut a long story short . . .'

'What's up?' asked Viv, sitting down and making herself comfortable on the arm of the sofa. Her mother couldn't cut a long story short to save her life.

'I didn't want to worry you . . .'

Viv's smile dropped and she felt a prickling at the back of her neck. 'Mum, are you all right?'

'Yes, yes, I am now. Totally, perfectly,' gushed Stel. 'I just had a bit of a scare, that's all.'

Viv didn't like the word 'scare'. It made her think of health issues. Her mother had had a major 'scare' eight years ago. In fact 'scare' didn't even touch the surface of it. Stel had been convinced she was going to die and Viv had had to be strong for the pair of them, when she felt anything but.

'When you say "scare", Mum . . .'

Stel heard the tension in her daughter's voice and a fresh wave of self-blame engulfed her. She was making Viv think allsorts.

'No, nothing like that, love. It's about Basil. When I said that he'd come back on Sunday, he hadn't. I was worried sick. That's why I haven't phoned you for a couple of days, because I thought I'd end up telling you that he was still missing and I didn't want you to fret. I'd looked everywhere. But Ian, the gardener at work, went out searching and he found him and he's just brought him back.' And then Stel dissolved into tears of relief.

'Oh Mum, you should have told me. You shouldn't keep stuff from me,' Viv admonished her. 'If you do that, I'll start worrying that you're keeping stuff from me even if you aren't, if you know what I mean.'

'I know, I'm sorry,' replied Stel. 'But Basil's home now and safe and I really wanted you to know.'

'That is good news, Mum,' said Viv, suspecting there might be more to come. She was right, of course.

'And Ian asked me out to the pictures so I'm going on Saturday with him.'

'Ah.'

'He's a nice man, Viv. He was out for hours trying to find Basil for me.'

Viv had to admit that was impressive.

'Well you just take it slow and steady,' she said, adding: 'please.'

'I will,' replied Stel. 'I absolutely promise. Basil's on my knee now, can you hear him purring? He's eaten nearly a whole fish.'

Basil had a very loud purr and Viv suddenly wished she were back on the sofa at home with him crouched on her knee.

'You're all right aren't you, love?' asked Stel. 'I do miss you.'

'I miss you too,' said Viv, fighting the emotion rising inside her. 'I might pop back on Friday night, if that's okay with you?' She wanted to give her mum a big hug, and Basil.

'Oh, that would be lovely,' breathed Stel. 'See you then. Bye!'

Viv put down the phone and blinked away unexpected tears. She hoped this Ian would turn out to be good for her mum. She knew that Stel felt badly that she'd never been able to provide Viv with a loving, caring father figure, though Viv never felt she had suffered from not having one.

'Please make this one be a good one for her,' said Viv, squeezing her eyes tight and offering up a quick prayer. Life however, she knew, was fairer for some folk than it was for others.

When Viv walked in to the cottage kitchen that evening, Geraldine had just finished cleaning the floor. She wrung out the mop and rested it in the drainer of the bucket by the door.

'Vegetable pie okay with you?' she said, crossing then to the tumble drier to pull out the contents. 'I'm just going to put new sheets on Heath's bed first.'

'Want me to help you?' asked Viv, curious to have a nose around upstairs.

'Sure, you can if you like,' Geraldine beamed.

Heath's room wasn't what Viv had expected of an older man. It was all dull neutral colours, sparse and functional. There were no softening furnishings such as cushions or rugs and everything was square and neat and clean – clinical even. It was a big space: two original bedrooms had been knocked into one, and off to one side was an ensuite bathroom. There was no personality to it at all and felt as if it belonged to someone much younger than she had imagined.

'How old is Mr Merlo?' she asked.

'Thirty-two,' replied Geraldine.

'Oh,' said Viv, genuinely surprised.

Geraldine paused from tucking the edge of the bottom bed-sheet under the mattress. 'Were you expecting him to be older?'

Viv nodded. 'Much older.'

'Then you're about to get a nice surprise. Or at least I hope you are.'

The scent that hung in his room did not fit with the one that Viv had imagined for the mysterious Heath either: fusty cologne with a smack of mildew. Instead it was fresh, clean, sandalwood, pine, with a base note of a forest in May when the bluebells were in banks of untamed blue and the raindrops glittered on the branches above. If the receptors in her nasal passages had had eyes, they might have dilated.

She'd attempted to recreate Geraldine's lovely perfume with her oils but it wasn't right yet by a long way. Geraldine had told her that it had been her mother's perfume, but it was now discontinued. She was down to her last quarter bottle, and used it sparingly.

There were no photos on display, Viv noticed. But did men do that? She didn't know. She had framed photos everywhere in her bedroom at home. She had brought a few with her – one of her with her friend Hugo, and one of her mum, and one of Basil as a kitten sleeping face down in his food bowl. Maybe it was a girl thing. But she did notice a gold band on a dish by his bedside. A wedding band.

'Is there a Mrs Heath?' she asked.

'There was,' replied Geraldine. 'Sarah died not long after I came to live here. Breast cancer. Such a young age.' She shook her head sadly.

'Oh, that's a shame,' replied Viv. 'My mum had it too, eight years ago. Luckily they caught it early and she just needed a lump out. It hadn't spread, thank goodness. She's been clear for years now.'

'Sarah wasn't so lucky,' said Geraldine, shaking out the duvet cover. 'She ignored all the signs out of fear and then acted too late.'

There weren't even any photos of Sarah, Viv noticed. But death affected people so differently. At the prospect of it, Stel had crumbled; young Viv had turned into a Viking warrior and Darren had made a bolt for it like the cowardly twat he was. Viv had liked him when he first moved in, even though he never seemed to do much but sleep, eat and watch football. But for him to abandon her mother when she was at her most vulnerable was unforgivable. He hadn't even had the decency to do it to her face but ran off while she was in hospital with cases that he must have been secretly pre-packing for days and left her a perfunctory text that she'd find when she came round from her lumpectomy. Stel had been devastated by his betrayal. Viv might only have been a teenager but she was old enough to realise what absolute pond-life he had turned out to be.

Viv could hear the sound of a vehicle outside. Geraldine crossed to the window.

'I bet this is Heath,' she said. But from the way the smile withered on her face, it was obvious that it wasn't.

Viv looked out also and saw a short convoy nearing the cottage, led by a matt-grey car. Behind that came a silver Range Rover, and following at a canter was the woman on the black horse that Viv had seen up on the hill on her first day.

'Nicholas Leighton,' snarled Geraldine. 'What the hell does he want?'

Nicholas Leighton. Head of the present Leighton clan, thought Viv. Father of the horse rider. The man that Hugo had told her would be useful to get to know and 'she should make damned sure he knew of her'. He was trying to carve a reputation as a philanthropist helping to fund young business people. Who better to recognise the talents of a young fellow Yorkshire person?

By the time that Geraldine had reached the front door, Nicholas Leighton had got out of his car and was standing with another man who was carrying a clipboard and pointing towards the cottage. Geraldine marched out, her long skirt swishing. Viv nudged the mop bucket out of the way with her foot and pushed the door almost closed so that she could watch what happened without being seen herself.

'What are you doing here, Mr Leighton?' said Geraldine.

Nicholas Leighton gave her a cursory glance and then resumed his conversation with Mr Clipboard.

'Get off, you're trespassing,' said Geraldine, in as cross a voice as she could muster.

So this was Nicholas Leighton, thought Viv, momentarily fascinated. He was taller than she had expected and lean with the long legs of an athlete. His hair was thick and black, greying artfully at the temples and in a patch at the front. He'd have a Mallen streak one day, she thought. He looked every inch the country gent in his tweed jacket and expensive boots. His daughter, smoothly dismounting the horse, had the same boots. They probably cost more than the whole of Viv's worldly possessions. She had tight jodhpurs over her slim legs and a beautifully cut snow-white shirt, sleeves rolled up to show off golden forearms. She undid the strap of her riding hat, pulled it off and shook out her long black hair as if she were filming a shampoo advert. She was beautiful and Viv suspected she knew that she was.

'Did you hear me?' said Geraldine. 'It isn't your land yet. Get off.'

'Oh do go away, you stupid woman,' Nicholas Leighton threw over his shoulder, flicking his hand out as if he were waving away an irritating fly. He was talking to the man with the clipboard about the plans for the estate. He wasn't coming across as friendly as his press articles made him sound. Viv could hear giveaway phrases: *There's no problem about extending the existing pipework. Phase one planning permission for two hundred houses has been agreed.* 'Obviously this lot' – he thumbed behind him at the cottage – 'will resort to cheap Fabian tactics, but work *will* commence on the day that the lease expires. Of that there is no question.'

Antonia Leighton strolled towards them, leading the horse. Viv watched her unseen from the kitchen. She was tall and willowy but had the same wide shoulders as her father.

'I'd like you to leave,' Geraldine was squawking at him,

but Leighton wasn't taking any notice of her. She might as well have been one of the hens on the other side of the fence protesting when anyone came within a yard of their eggs.

Viv didn't like how Antonia seemed to be amused by Geraldine's distress. She had full dark pink lips that were twisted into a sneer. She was lovely but it was a very cold sort of beauty, Viv thought. Her eyes were a startling shade of dark blue but there was no warmth in them at all.

Viv watched as Pilot walked over to Antonia, who didn't see his approach, and nudged the hand that hung at her side with his cold damp nose, hoping for a stroke. Antonia jumped and dropped her hat, startling her horse. Then, quick as a flash, she turned, crop still in hand. Viv saw her raise it. Even quicker than a flash, Viv pulled open the door, reached for the handle of the mop bucket, lifted it, stepped out and threw the contents. Most of the dirty water landed squarely on Antonia Leighton, the rest splashed over the full length of her father's expensive sleeve.

The horse threw its head up and shied away, making Antonia stagger. There were a few seconds of the stillest silence ever. Viv's jaw was open more than everyone else's put together. Had she really just done that? What part of her brain had told her to throw a bucket of grimy water all over the shiny white Antonia? She certainly wasn't shiny white any more. Then the silence ended and all hell broke loose. Through the hair plastered over her face, Antonia screamed like a toddler having a tantrum. The horse broke free of her grasp and trotted across the yard, where luckily it halted. Nicholas Leighton, blue eyes blazing, strode angrily towards Viv, his face fixed in fury but stopped in his tracks when Viv grabbed the mop and held it up at his face height like a domestic knight's lance. He stumbled back, almost comically.

'How dare ... Who the hell are you?'

'*Daad* ...' Antonia was standing, arms extended, like the Christ of the Andes. Her face was contorted in disgust.

'My name is Viv. Viv Blackbird,' Viv said. Her voice was strong, belying the massive shuddering underneath her skin. She hadn't imagined the introduction to go like this, but it had and it couldn't be undone.

Glaring at Viv like a vengeful harpy, Antonia screamed at her. 'Have you any idea how much this shirt cost?'

'No,' returned Viv, sounding cockier than she meant to. She hadn't a clue about designer clothes, which she presumed Antonia wore. The most expensive thing Viv owned was a half-cashmere jumper which she'd found in the Debenhams Blue Cross sale last year with seventy per cent off.

'You'll pay for this,' shrieked Antonia. Viv didn't know if she meant literally or metaphorically – but she had no intention of doing either.

'You were going to hit the dog. With your crop.'

'That's assault. You've just assaulted me.' Interesting that Antonia didn't deny the charge levelled at her, thought Viv.

'I saw you raise that crop as well, young lady.' Geraldine stabbed her finger at Antonia.

Nicholas Leighton was still wiping scummy water off his arm and chuntering on to the man with the clipboard. Antonia stomped off to catch her horse and grabbed its reins, too hard for Viv's liking. Retrieving her riding hat, she mounted effortlessly and trotted off as glamorously as her dripping wet hair and clothes would allow.

Nicholas clicked his fingers at Mr Clipboard and pointed to his car; it was a silent and arrogant command that their business had concluded. Then he turned back to Viv and Geraldine, his head swinging from one to the other as he addressed them in turn.

'Tell Merlo that he needs to start packing. I'll have those bulldozers onto this shithole the minute – *the very minute* – that the bailiffs have ejected you. If necessary, I'll have the RSPCA here to remove the animals. Protest all you like but I *will* have you dragged out and this place *will* be demolished.'

He took a step towards Geraldine and glared into her face. 'And after what she did to my daughter this morning' – he gave Viv a brief but murderous glance – 'you can tell Merlo that he will shortly be receiving a letter from my solicitor to cancel the offer of a residence.'

'He's already told you to stick it where the sun doesn't shine so I doubt he'll be bothered, *Mr* Leighton,' Geraldine shot back.

And with that, Leighton and his expensive boots disappeared into the silver Range Rover and he set off at such a pace that his wheels spat earth behind him. The man in the clipboard followed at a more sedate pace in his car.

'Oh Geraldine, I am so sorry,' said Viv. 'I don't know how . . . why . . . I just saw her crop . . .'

Geraldine put her arm around Viv, who was now on the brink of tears.

'Don't you worry, my lovely,' she said. 'Heath was never going to take his hand-out offer. He'd sooner die.' She laughed. 'Oh, I wish I'd had that on camera. It all happened so fast. Come on in and let's have that pie if it isn't burned to a cinder. And thank you, Viv.'

'Thanks? What for? He was furious. Why on earth did I do that?'

'Thank you from Pilot, because he can't tell you himself, can he, but she would have hit him.'

Big, gentle Pilot pushed his wet nose into Viv's hand with expert timing. It was as if he'd said thank you himself after all.

Chapter 13

The next morning, Viv walked up to the shop for some more teabags. Armstrong had rung, nearly crying, to say that he wouldn't be able to take Pilot out because he had a stomach ache and his mother was making him stay at home. So Viv slipped the lead on him and took the big dog out with her.

'Oh, great,' said Viv as there on the hill, atop that beautiful black horse, was Miss Antonia Leighton herself. She was talking to someone in a dusty 4x4 pulling a horse-box behind it.

Viv could feel Antonia's eyes boring into her as she passed and willed her cheeks not to colour. Whoever was in the 4x4 was looking at her too, she could see someone behind the steering wheel. *Probably one of Daddy's posh friends*, Viv thought. She didn't realise she had been holding her breath until she turned the corner and her lungs caved in to the pressure.

From the last conversation she'd had with Geraldine, Viv presumed that it was Mr Wayne who was sitting behind the counter in Ironmist Stores in a wheelchair with a blanket tucked over his knees. He viewed her suspiciously as she swept her eyes along the shelves looking for some tempting biscuits.

'She's working at the sanctuary,' she heard Mr Mark tell him, in a ridiculously ineffective attempt at a whisper. 'She's a very nice girl. Geraldine said so.'

Viv tried not to smile as she walked up to the counter. Mr Wayne gave her a big friendly smile now that she had passed muster. She put down her basket of shopping for him to ring into the till.

'So are you settling in, then?' he asked, putting her purchases into a thick brown paper bag.

'Yes, thank you,' replied Viv, taking her purse out of her bag in readiness to pay. 'It's a beautiful place.'

'Oh, I hope that the Leightons don't get their hands on it,' he sighed. 'No one wants the valley full of new houses. It was never meant for new houses. It's sacred land, you know.'

'Yes, Geraldine told me.'

'What can anyone do though?' said Mr Mark, brandishing his pricing gun. 'The Leightons can buy everyone and everything.'

The doorbell over the shop tinkled and in walked a short, stout woman wearing a bright yellow knitted hat which had a tiny teddy bear as a decoration to the side. Mrs Macy, Viv presumed. Her face broke out in a grin when she saw Viv.

'You're the one who threw a bucket of water over Octavia Leighton, aren't you?'

'Whaat?' Mr Wayne and Mr Mark gave a joint gasp.

'No, I've got it wrong,' said Mrs Macy, chewing thoughtfully on her lip.

Mr Wayne was patting his chest. 'Oh you silly thing, Greta. You had me going there.'

'No, not Octavia. The other one. Everyone's talking about it this morning. You did, didn't you? Last night?'

All eyes were on Viv.

'Erm . . . sort of,' she answered.

'Noooo!' a chorus from the brothers.

'Leighton's daughter was going to hit poor Pilot with her crop, but this young lady here threw a bucket of dirty mop water over her.'

'She didn't!' Mr Mark was open-mouthed. He turned to Viv. 'You didn't?'

Viv gave an embarrassed half-smile. She really didn't want to be famous for upsetting the great Mr Leighton.

'Well, I never,' said Mr Wayne. He reached behind him and took a fat Victoria sponge wrapped in cellophane from the shelf. 'You must have this with your afternoon tea from me and Mr Mark with our compliments,' he said. 'Oh, I wish I'd been there!'

'Some of it went on Leighton,' said Greta Macy, delivering that detail with drama.

'*It didn't!*' A sharp intake of breath from the brothers.

'It did.'

'Oh my.' Mr Wayne's hand was on his cheek.

'What's Heath said about it?' asked Mr Mark.

'He wasn't there. He's only just come back. I saw him driving down the hill about ten minutes ago with the donkey-box,' said Mrs Macy.

Heath was back? 'I'd better go,' said Viv, holding out a ten-pound note. 'And thank you for the cake. There was no need but it was very kind of you and we will enjoy it.'

'I think that news will actually help me recuperate, Mr Mark,' grinned Mr Wayne. 'My my, Leighton and Miss Snotty-Drawers covered in mop water.'

'It's the best thing I've heard in weeks,' said Mr Mark, handing Viv her change. He shuddered. 'Horrible family.'

Viv could feel them all gossiping about her when she left the shop but knew at least that it was complimentary. Geraldine must have said something, or someone on the hill had a pair of binoculars. However they all knew, it hadn't done her reputation as a stranger any harm.

Pilot was still lying patiently on the pavement where she left him, head on his large paws, dozing in the sunshine. He groaned to his feet as she shook gently on his lead.

So Heath was back then, was he? She had a horrible premonition that he wouldn't quite see her in the same heroic light in which the Ironmisters viewed her.

*

Pilot set the pace as they walked back to the sanctuary. It was a pace which Viv wished was faster because she wanted to see the mysterious, difficult, irresistible being that apparently was Heath Merlo. She was surprised to see the same vehicle parked in the yard as the one which had been on the hill when she passed it and Antonia Leighton. It had been Heath engaged in conversation with Leighton's daughter. A strangely lengthy and friendly conversation for apparently mortal enemies.

Pilot seemed to sense his master's presence because his stride quickened as soon as they neared the cottage. He tugged at his lead and when Viv unclipped it he cantered towards the door which was standing ajar, pushing it further open with his long nose.

Viv followed him, more on edge with every step. She picked up Heath's scent before she had entered the cottage:

forest branches, late spring rain, earth and must. She walked in and he was there, standing by the fireplace talking to Geraldine. The miserable gargoyle-faced image that Viv had had of him disappeared forever. She hadn't just got it a little bit wrong, she had it totally wrong.

Her eyes swept up from his big boots to his leather jacket, his cropped black beard, his unsmiling lips, his dark green eyes, his thick, tobacco-brown unruly hair and that was the moment Viv Blackbird felt bombs going off inside her.

Chapter 14

Everyone who knew Viv Blackbird would have told you what a sensible, down to earth girl she was. A girl who was old beyond her years, a strong girl, one who was on course to marry an accountant or at least a steady, reliable man. No one knew that below the surface of the capable, clever, level-headed Viv Blackbird lay a young woman who demanded a much stronger man than any of those she had met so far in her young life. Her wish list was predictable to a point: she would never have been able to fall in love with someone who wasn't kind and respectful or who cheated on her, nor − even more important to her − a man who would desert a woman when she needed him most. But, at the same time, her young heart craved a man who was part wild, who pushed − when appropriate − against convention. She wanted someone passionate who made her pulse throb and set her head into a spin. She wanted to look at a man and for the sight of him to set her whole body quivering with desire. Not that she'd thought this chemical reaction inside her would ever happen, because it was the stuff of Mills and Boon romances, surely? But here she was, standing in front of her new boss and feeling as if her whole blood supply had been replaced by something heady and intoxicating. Then he opened his mouth and that magic tide ebbed so fiercely, she physically had to stop herself from toppling from the force of it.

'So, you're the one who's caused the stir in my absence,' he said in a tone that was edged more with annoyance than welcome. He most certainly didn't sound as impressed as the trio in the shop had been.

'I don't know about that,' said Viv, with a gulp. She came forward with her hand held out. 'Viv Blackbird. Dr Livingstone, I presume.'

It sounded funnier in her head.

He was not the most handsome man she had ever seen in her life. His nose wasn't straight and his cheekbones weren't male-model razor-sharp, but his features were in total harmony as far as the messages that her eyes were hurrying to her brain were concerned. His eyes were the green of an enchanted wood, the lashes around them black and long and thick.

For a moment, she thought he was going to leave her hand frozen in its mid-air position, then just as she was about to drop it with acute embarrassment, he curled his fingers around it and gave it a mild shake.

'Heath Merlo,' he said. 'Dr Stanley.'

If he was echoing her humour, he wasn't accompanying it with the hint of a smile.

'I've just brewed some tea,' said Geraldine. 'Viv, Heath is very pleased with what you've done in the office.'

'I enjoyed doing it really,' said Viv. 'I like making a difference.'

'Oh, you've definitely done that,' said Heath in a way that didn't imply that was a compliment. Pilot was standing at his master's side, his nose in Heath's cupped hand. The big dog's tail was sweeping rhythmically – and contentedly – from side to side. He looked as if he were falling asleep just standing there, breathing in his gorgeous scent.

'I wouldn't have let that girl hit your dog,' said Viv, with tight politeness. 'Especially in an animal sanctuary.'

'I doubt she would have done that,' said Heath, shaking his head.

'She *had* raised her crop,' said Geraldine. 'It looked to me as if she was about to bring it down rather sharply.'

'Thank you for clearing the office,' said Heath, changing the subject. 'I shall sort through the boxes you've left, but at first glance I doubt there's anything in them that can't be destroyed. I'm not sure why we've even set anyone else on, if I'm honest . . .' he flicked his eyes over to Geraldine with a slightly puzzled expression ' . . . but you're welcome to stay until the end, seeing as you're costing us so little. An extra pair of hands will come in useful, to pack up if nothing else.'

'Don't talk like that, Heath,' Geraldine reprimanded him. 'You sound as if you've given up.'

'Given up? You are joking, Gerry,' Heath snapped. If he had been a dragon, he would have been blowing smoke out of his nostrils. 'I'll be hanging from the wrecking ball on the day of judgement, but . . .'

He shrugged, and it seemed to Viv that for all his bluster, Geraldine was right.

'I'll fit in with whatever needs doing,' Viv volunteered.

Heath narrowed his eyes. 'I must say, you're awfully

compliant. I always said to Geraldine that if you pay peanuts you'll get monkeys . . .'

'Heath!' Geraldine protested.

'Oh come on, Geraldine, you can't pretend that anyone else I've employed since you came has been any good whatsoever. At least two of them didn't stay long enough to unpack their bags; two, or was it three, screamed and cried and walked out telling me exactly what they thought about me . . . I threw two out telling them exactly what I thought about them, then I found another one trying to lever the safe out of the wall.' He turned to Viv, his eyes as intense as lasers. 'The crowbar she was using was worth more than the safe contents, incidentally, just in case you were thinking of doing that also.'

Viv held his gaze, her own eyes flashing as she spoke.

'I have never stolen anything in my life.'

'I didn't accuse you,' he replied.

'Viv makes money from blending oils,' Geraldine said, like a mother showing off the virtues of her small child to a headmaster.

'What?' Any attempt to impress Heath fell on very stony ground there.

Viv didn't enjoy being thrown into the spotlight. She felt her cheeks warm with embarrassment and hoped they weren't turning red. 'I blend basic scents together to create more complicated ones. Strawberry and vanilla tarts, summer pudding, moonlit gardens . . .'

'Why the hell would you do that?'

'People buy them from me,' replied Viv tightly. 'For money.'

Heath scratched his head. 'Well, it takes all sorts to make up a world, as they say.'

Viv fought to keep the growl out of her voice. 'It pays a living wage and—'

'Because I don't,' Heath butted in.

'Well, you don't, do you?' Viv butted in back. 'I wasn't moaning. I was fully aware how much the position here paid from the advertisement. I didn't think you'd made a mistake and left a nought off the end. Blending oils earns me good money and tops up my income.'

Heath folded his arms and studied Viv.

'So that begs the question, why would you want to work here then?'

'Experience,' said Viv. It was a well-rehearsed answer and sounded convincing enough.

'Experience.' Heath laughed to himself as he repeated the word. 'That old stand-by, experience.'

Geraldine, feeling that the atmosphere needed lightening, clapped her hands together to get their attention. 'Shall we all go out and look at Wonk and her new leg?'

'Why not?' said Heath. 'Maybe Miss Blackbird could use the *experience* to blend us some oils so that we could recreate "essence of three-legged donkey in her stable" and sell it to raise some funds.'

As Viv followed the others out to Wonk's stable she told herself that her olfactory nerves needed some adjusting. They had been sending false information back to her brain. Heath Merlo wasn't the man of her dreams, he was a rude, snidey, belligerent *pig*.

Chapter 15

The man was large and sweaty and his body odour seemed to reach out and envelop Gaynor as he rapped his finger on the reception desk. 'Oy. When am I going to see the doctor? I should have been seen half an hour ago.'

But Gaynor had dealt with far worse than him in the years she'd worked there and there hadn't been a situation she couldn't handle yet. 'I'm afraid there has been an emergency, Mr Potts. Dr Lyle had to go out and so Dr Gilhooley is seeing his patients. Unless you'd rather reschedule for another day when you can come and see Dr Lyle?'

Mr Potts slammed his large meaty hand flat down on the counter. 'I don't care about excuses. I expect to be seen on time.'

Gaynor locked her fierce, brown eyes onto his bulging, bloodshot ones and leaned her head forward so she had less chance of being overheard.

'I suggest you sit down and shut up, Mr Potts, before I have you thrown out of this waiting room and this practice. You are disturbing people in here with genuine ailments who have been waiting far longer and more patiently than you, so I think you should count yourself lucky, Mr Potts, don't you?'

Mr Potts didn't register that Gaynor was implying his case wasn't genuine. Which it wasn't. There was nothing wrong with his back but Gaynor knew she had stepped over the line in saying what she had. And so did the junior receptionist Janet, who raised her eyebrows and made a mental note to keep out of Gaynor's way today.

Mr Potts shuffled back to his seat, grumbling under his breath. No sooner had Gaynor bent down to get an eraser out of a bottom drawer when a female voice took Mr Potts' place at the reception desk demanding attention.

'Shop.'

Gaynor straightened her back ready to do battle once again but this was a whole different ball game. There, standing squarely in front of her, wearing a too-small denim jacket which hadn't a snowflake's chance in hell of closing over her giant bra-less bosom, was a grinning Danira Bellfield. *What the hell does Mick see in her?* was Gaynor's initial thought. Danira's brass-blonde hair was scraped back into a tight ponytail, pulling her eyes into slits. Her cheeks were already becoming jowly and that red colour on her youthfully plump lips looked ridiculously garish.

'I've come to make an appointment,' Danira said.

Gaynor's second thought was that she wanted to drag Danira over the counter by that ponytail and pummel her face until it was the same colour as her lipstick.

'I'm afraid I can't make you an appointment as you don't belong to this practice,' she replied, outwardly clinging on to her composure, although inwardly she was screaming.

'But h'I am here to register,' said Danira with a fixed

smile and a tone meant to parody Gaynor's rounded tones, a product of elocution lessons she had taken in her twenties when Mick had become middle management and she wanted to hold her own at any of his work functions. 'My lover and I have a house in the h'area now. It's most important that I get hold of the morning after pill. I think you might be able to guess what we've been up to.'

Janet, who had been keeping her eye on Gaynor since she had sent Mr Potts back to his seat, lunged forwards as soon as she saw Gaynor's arm shoot out. She stopped it before it made contact with Danira's face.

'I'll deal with this patient, Gaynor. Why don't you go and take your break,' she said, sweetly and forcefully. She saw the tears in Gaynor's eyes as she gently pushed her into the sanctuary of the small staff room. Gaynor slumped down onto a chair, her hands covering her face, taking refuge behind the shield they afforded her. It felt like an age before Janet came through and shut the door behind them.

'Gaynor, go home,' said Janet.

'I just don't believe that Mick's moved back into the area, *my area*, with *her*,' snarled Gaynor, none too quietly.

'Shhh.' Janet was aware that Gaynor was very much her senior in experience, position and years but Janet liked her. Okay, so Gaynor was frosty and not the girly-chat sort of person, but she was a good boss, brilliant at her job and she'd heard via the grapevine (i.e. the gossipy Dr Gilhooley) what was happening in Gaynor's personal life. 'Please, Gaynor. I've dealt with it. She's sitting and waiting out there. Go out of the back door. You look really tired and you know you aren't yourself.'

'Oh, if only,' Gaynor half-laughed, half-cried as she raised her head up to the ceiling. 'If only I were someone else, anyone else but Gaynor Pollock, I might not be in this mess.' When her eyes drifted back to Janet, it was to see her holding Gaynor's coat and handbag out for her.

'Go home, Gaynor. I can manage.'

Gaynor put on her coat with the weariness of a knackered pensioner and slipped the loop of her handbag over her shoulder.

'I'll see you in the morning,' she said, walking slowly away and through the door. She hadn't had a day off sick in five years but she felt as if the events of the past year had suddenly all joined together and thrown themselves at her in one big lump. As she zapped her car door unlocked, a male voice – a familiar voice – called her name. She turned, and there was Mick.

'Gaynor,' he said. The word hung in the air, as alone and isolated as the owner of that name felt. Mick scratched his head. His hair looked darker and was shiny and spiky. He'd had it cut in a new style meant to offset the thinning and make himself appear younger in the process.

Gaynor didn't say anything. She opened the car door and again he said her name and took a step forwards.

Her appearance shocked him, she could see that. She didn't have a stone and a half to lose and her cheeks were hollow. All her clothes hung loosely on her: the thin mac she was wearing looked two sizes too big. He'd bought her that mac, she suddenly remembered. He hadn't intended to but she'd forgotten her Visa card and he'd put it on his and said it could be part of her fifty-second birthday present.

'Gaynor, are you all right?'

The ludicrousness of the question gave her a quick shot of anger.

'Am I all right? Am I all right?' She opened her mouth to say more then stopped and forced herself to take a breath. He had approached her: she had his attention for the first in a long time and she didn't want to throw it away. She sighed and the breath seemed to take all the strength she had left. 'No, I'm not all right,' she said, her voice a wisp, a croak.

'We could have signed up to another surgery as we're in the middle of two but my records are still here so ... I thought ... I'm sorry.'

'Sorry, for what?' Gaynor asked. She desperately wanted to hear him answer that he was sorry for hurting her, for dragging her through the mud, for turning her into a bitter, envious, miserable cow, so could he please come home.

'For buying a house near you. It was the only one we liked. It was a good price.' His voice tailed off. Even he, with his blunted sensitivities, realised these details were surplus to Gaynor's requirements.

Gaynor wanted to take his hand, press it against her cheek. She would do anything in her power to have him come home. But he had heard her say that at least ten times now and it hadn't changed his mind. She had shown him the full spectrum of her emotional range, all except this empty, hollow shell of herself. She felt as if someone had stuck a spoon inside her and scooped everything out.

'We'll sign up with the other practice. We won't use this one. It's wrong.' Mick's voice was gentle, full of sympathy. No, not sympathy but pity. Pity? She didn't want that. Pity was what you felt for abandoned animals or homeless people, not for wives who couldn't get over losing you. How dare he pity her, the tramp-shagging bastard.

'Yes, you do that,' Gaynor said, straightening her back, reclaiming some dignity. If he hadn't looked at her as if she'd been an injured greyhound that needed putting out of its misery she might have thrown in the towel. Now she'd fight on until the fat lady sang so loudly she damaged her vocal cords. He'd be the one that people pitied, walking about with dyed spiky hair and jeans worn hanging halfway down his arse.

She could have coped better if he had died, horrible as it was to admit to herself. Being Mick Pollock's widow would have allowed her to keep some respectability, whereas being Mick Pollock's ex-wife because he'd run off with a Bellfield scrubber did not.

Mick made no attempt to stop her getting into her car, fumbling with the ignition key, nearly crashing into the car behind because she slipped into reverse rather than first. She did not look into the rear-view mirror and see his expression as she drove away. In her imagination, it would have been one of forlornness that he had made the biggest mistake of his life, and the sight of her there outside the surgery had forced the scales to finally fall from his eyes.

Maybe she would have turned back and drunk in the sight of him looking at her with concern, had she known it was the last time she would see Mick Pollock alive.

Chapter 16

Geraldine threw her arms around Wonk and kissed the sweet grey fur on her head.

'Oh, it's so good to have you home.' Then her face fell. 'What will happen to her if we close? Where will she go?'

'Any sanctuary will have Wonk, she's rich,' said Heath, unable to keep the bitterness from his voice.

Geraldine geed herself up. 'What am I saying? Wonk won't be going anywhere. We have to stay positive.'

'Have you found homes for the animals yet?' asked Viv, thinking Heath was insensitive at best.

'Nope,' he replied. 'We were always waiting for the miracle which was going to fall on us from above. The ancient powers that be would never let this place become a housing estate, everyone kept telling me. We should all dig in our heels and everything would be okay.' His mouth bore a smile, but his words were humourless.

'Something will come up, I know it,' said Geraldine. 'It has to.'

Heath raked his fingers through the tangle of his hair, a gesture of concealed impatience, Viv thought.

'Gerry, we are not living in a Disney film. We have to face facts that it's starting to look unlikely and we should make plans accordingly.'

Geraldine turned and walked rapidly back to the cottage. She was upset, that was evident. Viv stood there awkwardly not knowing if she should follow. Heath was staring beyond Wonk up at the castle.

'I know it might sound a daft question but have you asked them to come to some sort of arrangement?' said Viv, cutting into his reverie.

'What?' Heath quickly turned his head towards her.

'Have you sat down at a table with the Leightons, I mean, and . . .'

'I know what you mean. Taken tea and cakes and asked them to rent the land back to me? No, funnily enough I haven't. Maybe you think I should apply for a mortgage and buy it myself. Have you any idea how much this wonderful stretch of prime building land is worth?'

Viv took a stab at a guess. 'A million?'

Heath gave a dry laugh. 'In your dreams. So no, of course I haven't sat down with them with a cup of tea and a packet of custard creams.'

'Well, isn't it worth a try, then?'

Heath's eyes rounded and his mouth contracted to a grim line. 'You've known me exactly how many minutes, Miss . . . Blackwell and—'

'Blackbird,' said Viv. 'Like your name, only in English.'

'Blackbird then.' Heath's cheeks were colouring with a flush of anger. 'As I was saying . . .' He stopped, breathed out, closed his eyes and shook his head. 'Never mind. It's just not worth talking about. All you need to know is that I have tried everything and it hasn't worked, so I'd appreciate it if you just got on with the job in hand and cut the suggestions.'

'Maybe if you let a stranger take a fresh look at things,' Viv shrugged hopefully.

'By *stranger,* of course you mean you.'

'Well, yes, I—'

Heath folded his arms across his chest. 'Remind me about your law degree again.'

'My law degree?' Viv was confused.

'Yes. Or am I getting mixed up. Did we employ you for your proven record in negotiations in war zones?'

'Oh.' He was being sarcastic. 'I just thought . . .'

'You don't need to think, Miss Blackbird,' said Heath. 'All you need to do is call people from the list I have already drawn up in readiness and ask if they will have any space for my animals in July. I won't let them go until I have to and if I do have to I will thank you for your assistance and send you on your way with a nice reference so you can have some more work "experience". Okay?'

'You seem quite friendly with Antonia Leighton. Couldn't she help?'

'I beg your pardon?'

Uh-oh, thought Viv. *That didn't go down well*, but there was nothing for it but to plough on. 'I meant I saw you talking to her yesterday on the hill, before you arrived here, couldn't she . . .'

Her voice died as Heath turned briskly away from her and stomped back towards the cottage. Viv followed meekly behind. The mention of Antonia's name had obviously touched a raw nerve. *Was there anyone the Leightons didn't have a dramatic effect on?* Viv wondered.

Chapter 17

Caro looked idly out of the window as she waited for her next client to come. Mrs Carnegie was late for her nail infill as usual, but Caro didn't mind today. She had been non-stop since she walked in at eight-thirty and was enjoying a welcome break and a long-belated coffee.

Across the road a minibus had just parked and a group of pensioners were being off-loaded and led into the café there. Someone's birthday, Caro guessed, as one of the last women to get off the bus was wearing a conical party hat. An old man with a stick had taken her arm to help her down the step from the bus and he waited until the next lady had climbed down safely too. A painfully thin woman with a duchess hump and a wobbly head began to alight and Caro froze. Her attention settled on the woman's long, long black flat shoes; they looked disproportionate to the rest of her. *No, it couldn't be.* Her mother had absurdly large feet, the relevant gene passed on to her brother but thankfully not to her. Caro studied her, moving away from the bus as if in slow motion. Her mother would be seventy-seven now: the woman across the street looked older – but then her mother had hardly lived a wholesome life. *Was* it her? Was she in a home now, near the end of her time?

Imagining that it could be her mother, Caro searched inside herself to feel *anything* for the old woman, but there was nothing: no affection, no pity, no interest. As if suddenly aware of her scrutiny, the old lady swung her head towards Caro's shop and it was clear that it wasn't her mother after all. This woman had a long face with a witchy-pointed chin. It was only then that Caro allowed herself to think, *Poor old soul.*

Chapter 18

Heath had gone upstairs to his room by the time Viv reached the kitchen. Piccolo was screeching on the table as if he was telling Viv off in Heath's absence for daring to mention Antonia Leighton. Viv wished she had been brave enough to ask Geraldine what – if anything – was going on between them. *They'd suit each other*, she thought; both of them good-looking and tall, arrogant and feisty. Mortal enemies or secret lovers? They couldn't be both, could they?

'Oh shush, Piccolo,' Geraldine tutted at the owl, not that it did any good. 'I've put the kettle on, Viv. I'll make you a coffee to take into the office with you.'

Geraldine's eyes were puffy and bloodshot. She looked absolutely worn out. Her gaze was on the kettle but her thoughts were a long way away.

'Are you all right?' asked Viv.

'No,' said Geraldine, her voice no higher than a breathy whisper. 'No, I'm not, Viv.'

'I don't know what to say,' said Viv, and meant it.

'I don't either. I can't think about it. This lovely old build-ing demolished and replaced with a housing estate and no one can do anything. Ironmist won't be able to choose who lives here any more if that happens.'

Viv was just about to ask what that meant when the door crashed open and in walked Armstrong, grinning a greeting.

'Heath's back, isn't he? I've just seen his pick-up. Does that mean Wonky is back too?'

'Hello, love,' said Geraldine, pinning on a smile. 'Yes, she's back.'

'Oh that's great,' said Armstrong and clapped his hands together. 'Can I feed her some carrots? My mum sent an apple for her.' He pulled the bright red apple out of his pocket. 'It's a beauty, isn't it? A proper Snow White apple, I reckon.'

'I hope it's not poisoned, Armstrong.' Geraldine gave him a mock stern look.

'No, it's from the garden. It's the first red one on the tree. It's not very big though, is it?'

He hadn't got the joke.

'Would you like to see how much Wonky likes apples?' Armstrong asked Viv.

'Viv's just going to have a cup—'

'I'd love to,' Viv interrupted Geraldine. 'I'll have my coffee in a minute,' she said, smiling at her. Geraldine smiled back. That was kind of Viv to be nice to Armstrong, she thought.

Armstrong skipped out of the door. It should have been an odd sight to see him skip so skittishly but somehow it wasn't. He would always be a boy, however old he became. Viv hoped he would continue to be as happy and carefree as he was now, too, but she suspected that he would take the closing down of the sanctuary very badly.

'Have you met Heath?' said Armstrong, stopping in his tracks and waiting for Viv to catch him up.

'Yes, I've met Heath,' replied Viv, trying to smile as if it had been a pleasant experience.

'Want to see my impression of him?' whispered Armstrong and he stood very tall and stiff and arranged his features into a semblance of exaggerated severity. Viv hooted with laughter.

'He's very stern, isn't he?' said Armstrong, as they arrived at Wonk's field. The donkey had started to walk towards him before he started whistling, tempted by the boy or the sight of the apple or both. 'Except when he's with *her*.'

'Her? Who's her?' said Viv, although it wouldn't have taken Einstein to work it out.

'Antonia Leighton,' said Armstrong, after checking around to make sure there was no one to overhear them. 'They fancy each other.' Wonk nudged Armstrong's hand, the one with the apple in it. He held it out for Wonk to nibble on. She demolished it in two greedy bites.

Viv had a sudden vision of Heath and Antonia naked on the forest floor rolling around together.

'I can tell,' Armstrong confided. 'My mum always says that opposites attract.'

A little current passed through Viv, too quick to ana-lyse what had made her nerves twang. Confusion at that news, if it were true. A pinch of jealousy, maybe. Though really that was ludicrous; Heath Merlo, she told herself, wasn't her type at all – and she sure as hell wasn't his. Her initial reaction to him had been misleading: her damned nose had tricked her. Antonia Leighton and Heath didn't seem a natural pairing though – or maybe her first impressions were wrong there too. Maybe they were like

Romeo and Juliet, star-crossed lovers from feuding families. What a mess, falling in love with your worst enemy's daughter.

She didn't like the way that Armstrong's revelation bothered her. She wanted to ask more but she knew she shouldn't be encouraging Armstrong to gossip, besides which Geraldine was on her way over to them.

'Armstrong, will you help me weigh the birds,' said Geraldine as she neared them. 'Heath's going out to a meeting about some funding.'

As if he had timed his exit to coincide with the mention of his name, Heath's 4x4 zoomed down the drive. He gave Viv the briefest of glances as he passed, loading it with all the irritation he could muster. *I've never made as many enemies in such a short time*, thought Viv, pressing down on the involuntary giggle that bubbled up inside her.

'Yeah, I like weighing the birds,' said Armstrong, beaming a huge smile. 'They sit on the kitchen scales and we work out if we're feeding them all right,' he explained to Viv. 'I know all about the birds.' He was obviously excited about the task.

'I'll leave you to it then,' said Viv and walked back to the cottage. Pilot, standing in the doorway, started waving his long tail as she approached and she was quite touched that he knew her enough to wag at her. Bub was purring and rubbing against her leg as she collected her coffee but she wasn't fooled and he didn't get a stroke. Piccolo was on the floor, comically peering into a hole beneath the kitchen units where the plinth had broken off. The place was a flipping madhouse.

Heath had left a list of animal sanctuaries on her desk for her to ring to see if they could take in his motley family and notes on which animals would be best where. And which could not be separated under any circumstances because they had grown close to each other and would pine. It must have been upsetting for him to draw it up like a will, a sombre but necessary task, she thought. The paper was creased and she guessed he had done it ages ago but hoped he'd never have to use it.

It was a duty that Viv, too, approached with a far heavier heart than she would have imagined. She had been here less than a week and already the place felt *a whole*. To be an agent of its deconstruction made her feel sadder than she wanted to. Her detachment was crumbling more with every wag of Pilot's tail and smile from Geraldine's lips. Coming here, she knew now, had been a monumental mistake and the best thing she could do was get out as fast as possible.

Chapter 19

Geraldine screamed out and sat bolt upright in bed as she broke out of the shell of the dream which enclosed her and suffocated her, and even though she knew she was safe in the cottage, she still felt shaken to the core. There had been detail to the dream which gave it credibility – the way he said her name, the chain he wore around his neck, the smell of his aftershave which he always over-applied. He had always said he would find her and she thought he might because in this digital age it was impossible to hide. It was only in the past year that she had let herself believe he never would; but recently, in the last few days, the dreams had started again. Since Viv arrived.

*

Viv started tackling the accounts the next day. They were in a terrible state. The sanctuary was overpaying on gas and electricity and she negotiated a much better deal on their phone and internet package too. She liked that kind of wheeling and dealing. Stel had taught her that there was always a bargain to be found when you needed to save a few pounds. Although really, if the place was going to be closing, was she wasting her time? Then again, another one of Stel's sayings was 'It's not over until it's over'. Geraldine would have certainly agreed with that philosophy, thought Viv, so she pressed on.

Geraldine was quiet that day. She said she hadn't slept very well and spent hours in the stables, scrubbing them out thoroughly. Stel used to clean things when she had stuff on her mind, thought Viv. It was as if she were trying to scrub away what was gnawing at her by mopping and brushing and blasting things with bleach. She'd done it a lot when she'd been ill, at least when she'd had the energy.

Viv hadn't seen Heath all day, but that was no great hardship. She didn't stop for lunch until nearly three o'clock. She made some cheese and onion sandwiches for herself and Geraldine, who hadn't had a break either. They were both ready for something to eat by then.

'What a treat,' said Geraldine, flopping into one of the chairs around the dining table after she had given her hands a thorough rinse at the sink.

'It's just a sandwich,' said Viv.

'Ah, but they always taste so much nicer when someone else has made them,' replied Geraldine, savouring her first mouthful as if it were a creation conjured up by Raymond Blanc.

'You must be tired,' said Viv.

'Good. I'll sleep tonight then,' Geraldine answered her. 'There's nothing like a bit of stable-clearing for wearing you out.'

'I'm mentally exhausted today,' smiled Viv. 'The accounts will take me an age to get in order.'

Geraldine grimaced. 'I hate doing those and I'm hopeless at them. As you can probably tell.'

Viv broke off a corner of her sandwich, taking care to strip out the onion, and gave it to Pilot who was sitting hopefully at her side. He took it from her so very gently.

'Where's Mr Merlo?' said Viv. 'Shouldn't he be helping you?' *Or me*, she added silently. *Was he the skiving type?*

Geraldine answered as if she could hear what Viv was thinking.

'If you think that Heath is out enjoying himself whilst we are slaving away here, let me tell you that no one works harder than he does. He's been up since the crack of dawn helping one of the farmers up Mawton way. They've been very good to us, sending supplies for the animals, and Heath will always repay a favour.'

'Ah,' said Viv. She wasn't too hard on herself for thinking he was lax though. It would have explained why things were in such a mess.

'What are you going to do with yourself this weekend then?' asked Geraldine.

'I'm going to drive back tonight to . . . er . . . Sheffield and see my mum,' said Viv.

'Well, you get yourself off now in that case,' said Geraldine. 'You've worked like a Trojan all week.'

'Are you sure?' The idea that she could be sitting back on her mum's sofa in less than two hours sounded wonderful to Viv.

'I'm positive,' replied Geraldine. 'Heath will be home soon enough and I'm just about done for the day myself.'

Viv grinned. 'I'll be back tomorrow.'

'It's your weekend,' said Geraldine. 'You spend it where you want, duck.'

Viv didn't say that a flying visit would suffice because there were urgent things she had to do and people she had to see and all of them were in Ironmist. But tonight she very badly wanted to go home and visit her mum and her cuddly ginger cat. She needed to slip back into her old familiar world again before it all changed for good.

Chapter 20

Stel opened the door to her daughter as if she hadn't seen her for a hundred years. She dragged her over the threshold pelting her with questions about her new life at Wildflower Cottage. Basil jumped on Viv's knee as soon as she sat on the sofa and dribbled as he purred and rubbed himself against her cheek and made her face wet and slobbery and Viv thought it was heaven. It would have been easy not to go back and if she hadn't left all her things there, she might not have done.

'Why did you run off then, eh?' Viv asked the cat, stroking his back as he settled down. He'd lost weight. His spine felt knobbly underneath his fur.

'I just can't understand it,' said Stel, handing her daughter a cup of coffee. 'I think he must have taken a wrong turn, lost his bearings and set off in completely the wrong direction. I could have married Ian when he found him.'

'Yes, well, don't,' tutted Viv, making Stel laugh.

'I promise I won't.'

'So he's nice, is he?' quizzed Viv. 'This Ian?'

'Very,' replied Stel. 'He's a gardener at the hospice. And

a really good one as well. He's made an amazing water feature. Very good with his hands.' Then she giggled and Viv heard herself thinking, *Here we go again*. She knew her mother was on course to fall hook, line and sinker after half a film and a bag of popcorn.

'Anyway, never mind about me, tell me all about your job. No, let's order a Chinese first and you can fill me in whilst we're eating. I've got a bottle of Champagne in to celebrate. Well, it's Prosecco really but we can pretend, can't we?'

So, over sweet and sour king prawn, mother and daughter chatted and laughed and drank fizz and tried to pretend they were brave grown-ups and Stel didn't say that she wished Viv would stay home and not go back and Viv didn't say that part of her wished she had never taken the job because it might alter their relationship for ever.

Chapter 21

Stel waved goodbye to Viv at ten the next morning. Storms were forecast at lunchtime and so Viv had driven off earlier than she'd originally intended to in order to avoid them. Once Stel was alone, she had nothing to stop her nerves about her impending date with Ian Robson hijacking her brain. She hadn't a clue how she was going to fill the time between now and seven o'clock. There was no cleaning to do, no ironing. It was too miserable weather-wise to walk around town and Meadowhall was always uncomfortably busy on a Saturday. She tried to read the newly delivered paper but it was no good, she needed to speak to someone and Caro was the first friend who came to mind.

'Morning,' said Caro, seeing Stel's name come up on her mobile.

'Am I disturbing you? Are you with clients?'

'Nope. I'm having a day off. That's the joy of being the boss. Why, are you all right?'

'No. I've agreed to go out with that bloke at work tonight and I'm bloody petrified,' replied Stel.

At the other end of the phone, Caro raised her perfect brace of eyebrows.

'Well, that's a surprise. I thought you didn't fancy him. Not at all, you said. What's changed in such a short time?'

'He found Basil,' replied Stel. 'He went to a lot of trouble for me. It was as if I saw him with different eyes.'

Caro stopped herself quipping that if Ian had had different eyes she might have fancied him a bit sooner. Stel had told them all that the gardener at work had a soft spot for her but that he had eyes she couldn't take to.

'Well, that's great and I can't wait to hear all about it tomorrow.'

'You don't fancy a coffee, do you?' asked Stel. 'It's okay if you don't. I just feel a bit lost this morning and my nerves are in shreds.'

'Do you want to meet me at two o'clock for a coffee up at Well Life? They've just refurbished the café and apparently it's gorgeous.'

'You're an absolute star,' said Stel, mentally clapping her hands together in delight. 'Are you sure though?'

'I'm sure,' Caro said. It was obvious Stel needed some company and after all the times Stel had been there for her, she wouldn't have turned her down. 'I'll see you up there.'

*

Viv was back in the folly by twelve-thirty. There was a lot of fog on the M62 and an accident had caused a further hold-up. It was a very long, miserable journey. She couldn't believe that only three hours ago she had been hugging her mum and snuggling her big purring cushion of a cat. They both felt so very far away.

She made herself a coffee and stood at the folly window looking at the storm clouds advancing across the vast expanse of sky overhead, swallowing up any traces of white. The cottage lights were on and she could see Geraldine standing at the sink talking to someone Viv couldn't see. It could have been Heath but was just as likely to be one of the house animals, because Geraldine talked to them all the time. Beyond the cottage was the garden where the bones of the departed animals lay. They were all at peace now and some digger was going to plough up their final resting place. Viv was as yet undecided whether or not she believed in an afterlife. Old buried bones felt no pain, that she did know. But it still felt such a shame that they'd be scooped out and disposed of like rubbish rather than loved in the ground here.

The mist was thin today, like spider threads weaving through the blades of long grass. Viv tried to imagine what it would be like looking out of the window and seeing houses everywhere. The view of the sun and hill would be the same but the silence would be gone. And the quiet, the calm, was as much a part of this place as the mists and the wildflowers.

Viv, what has all this to do with you? Some reprimanding part of her was wagging its finger at her. She couldn't afford to let sentiment get in the way of what she had to do here.

Hugo had been insistent that being in Ironmist would be to her advantage. Her chance to get an influential business patron on board. She daren't tell him that she had thrown a bucket of dirty water over that potential patron and his daughter.

She felt blessed by the ability she had to replicate scents. Maybe she should have been more ambitious because Hugo constantly nagged her to contact one of the famous perfume houses, and was frustrated by her insistence that she had no wish to join a huge conglomerate. Hugo was a rising star in the London laboratory where he worked. They had stayed good friends; in fact, if Hugo hadn't been gay, he was convinced that they'd have made an amazing dynamic couple. Posh and Becks with test-tubes.

Today presented the perfect opportunity to fulfil the brief for the essence of a summer rainstorm that a major client had requested. And it would keep her thoughts occupied. The windiest, wettest area would be up by Ironmist Castle, she reckoned. So, with her walking boots and old quilted jacket on and her notepad and pen in her pocket she set off to explore. Viv didn't mind the rain. When she was little, on many a rainy day, she and Stel had donned their wellingtons and waterproof coats and splashed in mud. As she grew up, Viv realised it was her mother's way of venting frustration at the men in her life. It saved breaking her fists against a wall.

The main road through Ironmist was deserted except for an old man carrying a paper under his arm and walking a small terrier that was wearing a snug blue coat. He nodded at Viv and she replied with a good morning. When she reached the top of the hill where the breezes blew unhindered, Viv raised her head and inhaled deeply. The wind had picked up the scents of the nearby forest, the last of the May bluebells, the first of the summer flowers from local gardens, a hint of clean linen as if someone's forgotten washing was flapping about on a line. Yes, Viv could put this together in her little makeshift laboratory in the kitchen corner of the folly. As the wind changed direction, she detected something else that wouldn't feature in the mix though: the smell of stables; horses, hay, sweet feed, a middle note of earthy manure. Viv turned and headed towards it, hood up, braced against the gusts. Above, the clouds seemed to be blackening by the second. Light flashed, viciously bright against the sooty sky and immediately after, thunder grumbled. Viv knew that a hilltop was not the most sensible place to be when lightning was on the prowl for a place to earth itself. She would be wise to find some sort of cover. She could either go left and stand under a tree – not the best idea, she thought – or head right past Ironmist Castle where any passing lightning might find something of interest to play with rather than her.

She hurried past the massive closed gates to Ironmist Castle and as the wind dropped for a second, she again picked up the scent of horses – but stronger now – by a path between two hedges. The ground was studded with hoof prints leading in both directions and she figured that this must lead to the stables within the grounds. Out of the corner of her eye, she saw a jagged spear of lightning fork above her head and that made her legs move even quicker down the bridle path. She hoped she wouldn't bump into one of the Leightons on their horses, but at least the weather made it less likely that they'd be riding today.

The rain started to whoosh down; fat drops that fell faster and faster as if racing against each other. Viv was drenched in seconds. The gate at the end of the path was locked, but it was low enough to climb over, especially for someone like Viv who was as fit as a flea. Her mum had encouraged her to exercise and be strong in order to cope with all the operations she'd faced in her life. Viv was on the other side of it in no time – on Leighton land. She half expected an alarm to go off and a floodlight to pick her out in all her trespassing glory, but nothing happened.

The stable block was huge and immaculately maintained. All the wood of the frontage had been recently re-stained by the look of it and the metalwork touched up with shiny black paint. It was evident that the Leighton horses were kept in the lap of luxury. There were four of them, if the number of boxes was anything to go by, but only one was poking its head out over the top of the split doors – a tall chestnut with a long fine head checking out the weather. It nodded at Viv as if greeting her, then blew through its nostrils as if it had taken the salutation back.

Another show of lightning and thunder, so loud that Viv felt it shudder through her. Her hair was plastered to her face despite her hood and her clothes were stuck to her skin. She had never felt as soggy in her life. She huddled under a canopy that jutted above a side door and shook her limbs like a dog. She noticed a security camera above her head but luckily it was trained in the wrong direction to pick her up. She watched the raindrops hit the ground with such force that they bounced upwards as high as her knee and knew she would have to wait it out before attempting to go back to the folly. The canopy didn't afford much shelter as the wind was driving the rain against her. She twisted the handle of the door behind her not expecting it to be unlocked, but it was. Viv opened it tentatively in case all the horses came thundering towards her, but they were enclosed in their own individual boxes. She shut the door behind her and looked around at all the tack, the blankets stored on shelves, the bright rosettes hanging on the walls. Beside the rosettes there were four rustic wooden signs, each one bearing a name scrolled in elaborate pokerwork. Octavia, Antonia, Victoria, Nicholas. And below each hung a hat and a crop. *The whole Leighton family.*

Chapter 22

Stel arrived twenty minutes early at the Well Life Supergym in Dodley because she was sick of walking around the house like a caged tiger not knowing what to do with herself. But she picked up a newspaper and sat in the lovely new café waiting in comfort while the minutes ticked by.

Caro arrived at ten to two looking preened and perfect as always, even though she was only wearing jeans and a long white shirt. She mouthed over to Stel that she'd get the coffees. When she arrived at the table with them, Stel was jittery and apologetic.

'I came early or I'd have got the drinks,' said Stel. 'I didn't want them to get cold though.'

'It's only a coffee, Stel. I haven't bought you a fillet steak,' tutted Caro with a smile. 'If it makes you feel any better, you can get the next one.'

'I will. Thanks for meeting me. I'm just a bit anxious about tonight. I've worn a groove in the carpet walking up and down it.'

Caro slapped Stel's hand which was hovering near her

mouth. 'Don't bite your nails,' she said. 'How long is it since your last date?'

'A year and a half,' Stel replied. 'It was that bloke who sold used cars, do you remember?'

'Was that the one with the really long nasal hairs?'

'No. There was Nasal Hair, then the one who got really nasty when I said I didn't bother voting, then the used-car salesman. He was the one who started crying in the pub.'

Caro clicked her fingers in recollection. 'The one who'd only split up from his wife a few days before.'

'That's the one. Total disaster. I swore after that I'd stay single. Bloody internet dating. I never met anyone decent on that site.'

Caro shuddered. She was so glad she was happily married and had never had to go down the route of signing up to Matchmaker.com.

'But you've changed your mind?' Caro studied Stel's expression. She looked absolutely terrified.

'Yes, Caro, but I don't know why.' Stel lifted her hands up as if she hoped the answer would drop into them from high. 'Scrap that, yes I do know why. Gratitude. I opened my mouth without thinking. So no change there then.'

'Oh, Stel.' Caro smiled at her. 'Then text him and make some excuse.'

'I haven't got his number.'

'Oh hell.'

'No, I'll go,' said Stel. 'I said I would. And he is nice. And kind. I'm just nervous. I tell you, I'm too old for this dating lark. It's too stressful.'

'How's Basil?' asked Caro, changing the subject for a minute before Stel worked herself up into even more of a state.

'Put it this way, I've had to fetch his old litter tray from the garage because he won't go out at all now.'

'Poor boy, he must have frightened himself to death getting lost.'

'I know. I was so relieved that Ian found him. He'd been out for ages looking for him. He was scratched almost to death picking Basil up as well. His arms were a right old mess.'

'Well, you always wanted a knight in shining armour, didn't you? Let's hope this time you've found yourself a good one.'

It made a change for Stel to aim high, thought Caro, though she didn't say it. Stel had had a succession of crap boyfriends when she was younger. Then she took some time away from the dating scene when Viv came along. Then she got lonely and ran back to it with open arms and an open heart when Viv reached school-age. Her luck hadn't got any better for the thinking time. And as for that Darren she'd lived with – ugh. Stel was overdue someone who was as kind and sweet as she was. Such as Al next door. He was big and solid and just what she needed and wasn't it just sod's law that they'd never got together.

'Just be yourself,' said Caro, covering Stel's hand with her own. 'And enjoy it. And don't offer to pay for anything on a first date.'

'He might think I'm tight.'

'If he is a proper gentleman he won't. You're worth being treated. If you don't see your own worth, how do you expect a man to?'

Stel grinned. 'I wish I were as sensible as you, Caro.'

You wouldn't have wanted to go through what I did in order to learn sense, Caro thought to herself, but said instead, 'I have high hopes that one day you will be, Stel.'

Chapter 23

There was little warning of the heavy stable door opening, just the squeak of the iron ring handle being twisted and the judder of the wood as it caught in its frame then a tall, slim woman appeared feet away from Viv. It had to be Victoria Leighton, the mother. She was wearing jodhpurs and an oversized brown jumper, and her black hair had been loosened by the wind from the pins which served to secure it. She looked casual-chic and elegant. Her jaw tightened as she caught sight of the intruder, and with one smooth movement she swept a crop from the wall.

'Who the hell are you?' she demanded loudly.

'I'm sorry, I got caught in the rain. The lightning scared me,' returned Viv. She was soaked through, which lent truth to her account.

'This is private property,' said Victoria Leighton, her hand gripping the crop tightly, ready to use it if necessary. 'The shower has ended so you can get out.' She stood aside so that Viv could pass. 'You're trespassing. There are security cameras, you know.' Even though she spoke with an English public school accent, there was a slight skimming over her Rs, a vestige of her first and formative years in Germany.

'I swear I only came in to escape from the weather. I noticed the stable as I was looking around for somewhere to take shelter.'

Victoria Leighton's blue eyes narrowed as she scrutinised the interloper for a few moments before she snapped, 'What's that in your pocket? What have you taken?'

Viv quickly pulled out the notebook and held it up for her to see. 'It's just a pad. I haven't stolen anything.'

'Why are you even up here in this area? Where are you from?' Victoria's eyes were almost boring holes in Viv's face.

'I was just out walking.' Viv's answer was deliberately evasive. She knew she had to get out fast before Victoria put two and two together and realised that she was the one responsible for throwing the contents of a rancid mop bucket over her husband and daughter.

As Viv took a step towards the stable door, Victoria flicked out her crop, temporarily barring Viv's exit. 'Wait a minute,' she said. 'I want to know who you are.'

'No one,' returned Viv, pushing past her and walking hurriedly away. 'I'm no one at all.'

Chapter 24

Viv now couldn't wait to get back to the sanctuary and half walked, half ran away from the castle estate. She heard a vehicle coming behind her on the road. She gave it a cursory glance over her shoulder and saw that it was Heath in his black pick-up truck. At first she thought he was going too fast to stop, but he screeched to a halt half a metre behind her. She heard the whirr of the electric window being lowered.

'Want a lift?' he called.

'Please,' Viv replied, opening the door and catching a drift of something pungent and metallic. She paused before getting in. The pick-up was clean as a whistle inside and she was wet through with mud all over her boots. 'Have you got something I can sit on and some newspaper? I'm covered in—'

'It's fine,' he said, beckoning her in impatiently. 'Come on, hurry up.'

'Thank you,' she said, clicking her seat-belt into place and hoping that she didn't totally saturate the seat. 'Sorry for any mess.'

'What were you doing up here anyway? Smelling things?' His nose was wrinkled up as he asked. He wouldn't be so *sniffy* if he knew how much *her* nose earned her, she thought with a huff.

'More or less,' she said.

'That's a ridiculous gift to have,' said Heath, slowing down for a sheep to cross the road.

'There are worse ones,' Viv answered, noticing how large his hand was on the gearstick and the dark hairs on the back of it.

The sheep reached the other side of the road and the pick-up began to speed up again. 'It's a very pretty place,' said Viv, trying to fill the silence with some sort of conversation.

'It won't be shortly, when the valley is full of Leighton's houses. Dammit.' Heath growled as he changed gear and it crunched. 'It'll be ugly as hell, totally spoiled.'

Viv realised she had inadvertently put him in a bad mood and tried to rectify it.

'With any luck it won't happen.'

Heath gave a dry laugh. 'We'll need more than luck. And I've never believed in miracles. Gerry's stuck on the spirits saving us and who am I to smash her hopes but someone is going to. And soon.'

'Have you nothing left up your sleeve to try?' Viv asked as they turned into the drive for the sanctuary.

He looked aside at her, his eyes narrowed. 'You're not a journalist, are you?'

'Pardon?'

Heath made a rough spin into his parking space and braked so hard that Viv yelped as she was thrown forwards.

'You heard.' He clipped off his seat-belt and turned to her.

His full-on attention was so uncomfortable that Viv gave a nervous chuckle.

'You think I'm some sort of a spy?'

'Are you?' His green eyes were glittering.

'No, I'm not,' replied Viv. 'Why would you think—'

He cut her off. 'You see, I just don't buy that you're here to work in a sanctuary. For "experience".'

'Well, I am. Why else would I be here?'

She was lying and he knew it. 'I don't know why. I hope I'm wrong with my suspicions about you, but I will warn you, Miss Blackbird, if I find out you're working against us . . .' He left the threat hanging in the air.

He got out of the pick-up, walked to the back of it and waited for Viv to alight.

'Of course, Vivienne, if you really are here for experience, you can help me cut this up for the birds.' He ripped off the green tarpaulin covering his cargo: a dead deer, blood staining its pelt as if it was paint. The wind changed direction and blew across the carcass punching Viv with the full impact of the metallic smell she'd caught a hint of earlier. Much to Heath Merlo's amusement, Viv bent double and threw up her poached egg breakfast on the grass in front of him.

Chapter 25

Back in the folly, Viv changed and gave her hair a blast with her hairdryer and within the half-hour was in her car, driving back up the hill and on the road to Mawton. She had a parcel to send to Hugo and wanted it to get there by the fastest possible service. Ironmist Stores had a post office but the larger one in Mawton had more collections and besides, she didn't want anyone in the village to know what she was doing. She passed the castle again and wondered if Victoria Leighton had gone back to her husband and told him about the intruder she had found in the stables. The more she reflected as she drove, the more she realised that she had probably brought even more trouble to the front door of the sanctuary.

Mawton was an unspectacular town with run-of-the-mill shops. She parked up on the road at the side of a small and very old church built, she suspected, at a time when Mawton had a tiny population which a church of that size could easily serve. She queued up in the post office, paid for her parcel to go by guaranteed delivery and pushed it through the hatch for the counter clerk to take. She felt ridiculously light-headed when she went back outside into the fresh air and thought some carbs might be in order. There was a café a few doors away. The menu displayed in the window showed limited fare but enough for her needs. Inside, the café was clean and Viv sat at the only vacant table in the corner and ordered a pot of tea and a baked potato with cheese and coleslaw.

She took out her phone and texted Hugo.

AM SENDING YOU A PARCEL SPECIAL DELIVERY. POSTED IT TO YOUR WORK ADDRESS. XXX

A text came back within the minute which made her groan.

OH DARLING, AM IN ICELAND. COUNTRY NOT SUPERMARKET. NEEDED HOLIDAY. FOUND A DEAL TOO GOOD TO MISS. WILL RING SOON AS WE GET BACK. XXX

Through the window she could see a post van draw up. A few minutes later, her lunch arrived at the table and she saw the postman load a bag of parcels into the back of his vehicle. The one she had sent to Hugo would be in with them. Viv felt her stomach begin to churn. She looked down at the potato and knew she wouldn't be able to eat any of it.

Chapter 26

Half an hour before Ian Robson was due to pick her up, Stel was so agitated that if she'd had his telephone number, she would have rung to say she was ill and couldn't make it. As the hands on the clock nudged towards seven o'clock, she thought she might throw up. Ian was a nice fellow and she was grateful to him, but once the euphoria of having Basil back had died down, she was starting to curse herself for being so impulsive in agreeing to a date with him.

Her ears registered the sound of an engine and her heart began to thump. A red car came into sight. *Oh God, he's here*, she thought and nervously smoothed down her blouse. But the car drove past, it wasn't him. She glanced up at the clock again. Three minutes had elapsed since she last looked at it but it felt like an hour. Another car, moving slowly then stopping. This time it was definitely him. She swallowed, picked up her summery blue jacket and slipped her arms into it. She dropped the key as she was locking up the front door and as she bent over to pick it up, had a sudden comedy vision of her trousers splitting down the back.

'Hello,' called Ian and waved. He had got out of the car

and was holding the passenger door open for her. He was wearing jeans, a blue shirt and a black leather jacket. He looked smart, as if he'd made an effort for her.

'Hi,' replied Stel. She walked towards him and stumbled slightly as her heel landed on a pebble.

'Steady there,' said Ian, his concern making her feel like a fool. She wished he hadn't said anything, then she could have imagined he hadn't seen her do that. Why the hell had she worn heels anyway? She could never walk properly or elegantly in them like her friends did. Caro always said she'd been born in heels. It was a portent of disaster, she could just tell it was.

Chapter 27

Viv was awoken the next morning by a heavy pounding on the folly door.

She leaped out of bed and peeped through the curtains to see Heath Merlo looking up at her. She jumped back quickly. What the heck did he want at – she checked the time – stupid o'clock on a Sunday morning? Viv threw on the first clothes that came to hand and hurried downstairs. Heath Merlo, she suspected correctly, was a man who didn't like to be kept waiting.

She unlocked her door and opened it to find him standing there, glowering. Behind him, sitting on her black horse which was stomping on the spot as if impatient to be off, was Antonia Bloody Tell-tale Leighton.

'I'll leave you to it,' she said, giving Viv a piercing stare as a parting present.

Heath turned and nodded at her. He made the gesture look like an intimate one, thought Viv with some fascination. As if that nod held the words: 'Thank you, I'll see you later, darling.' It made Viv prickle with something in the ballpark of jealousy.

As soon as Antonia had thundered off on her impressive beast, Heath crossed his arms in front of his wide chest.

'Find many smells of windy willows in stables, do you?' he asked.

Viv felt herself stiffening with annoyance. Whatever happened to being innocent until proven guilty? Even if she wasn't all that innocent really. Not that Heath Merlo could know that.

'If you mean by that, what was I doing up at the castle yesterday then just say it,' she said, with a surprisingly brave snap in her voice.

'Okay, let's try again. What were you doing up at the castle yesterday?'

'I took shelter there. I got caught in a thunderstorm. There was nothing to stand under but a big tree and I didn't think that was particularly sensible. So I climbed over a gate and went into the stables until the lightning stopped. Then I walked down the hill and you picked me up. You saw how wet through I was.' Indignation laced every one of Viv's words. Who did he think he was? She might have had to explain her actions to Victoria Leighton, but why did he have to know?

Heath looked her directly in the eye. 'I don't believe you.'

'I don't give a toss if you do or not. What business is it of yours?'

She was amused to see Heath's mouth drop open with a momentary display of astonishment. Then she saw his Adam's apple rise and fall as he gulped down a huge ball of expletives probably. When he spoke again, his words were slow, deliberate and squeezed out through lips pulled thin by irritation.

'The reason why it is my business is that the Leightons

are looking for any excuse, *any*, to hasten our end here. You are handing them ammunition with which to shoot me.'

'I didn't steal or damage anything,' returned Viv, with the same hostile calmness. 'I didn't sneak a horse out under my jacket or you would have seen it when I got in the truck. I was taking a walk and the rain started and I didn't want to die.'

Heath's dark green eyes waged a silent war with her blue ones. *Who the hell did he think he was?* Was she really going to put up with this crap for a pittance of a wage? She didn't need to be here any more. She had got what she wanted. So when he said coldly, 'I think you'd better pack your things and bugger off, Miss Blackbird,' she replied, 'I will be more than happy to bugger off, Mr Merlo.' And she slammed the door in his face and headed upstairs.

Viv threw everything into her case like a manic Harlem Globetrotter. She didn't bother folding anything, or separating any dirty clothes from the clean ones. She was, however, a little more careful when she came to packing away her mini laboratory. She was just checking to make sure she hadn't forgotten anything when she heard *his* unmistakable rap once again on the folly door. She marched over to open it, presuming he was there to ask how much longer she would be. Her none too polite answer was ready and waiting to be delivered.

But Heath Merlo stood on her soon-to-be-abandoned doorstep with no hint of anger on his face.

'Miss Blackbird. Before you bugger off, may I ask you to hold the fort for a while? Geraldine has fallen down the stairs and I'm going to drive her to hospital.'

Viv looked past him to where his 4x4 stood, engine idling, and saw Geraldine in the passenger seat. She was mouthing the words, 'I'm okay' through the glass, but her face was pale and pained.

'Yes, yes of course,' replied Viv. What else could she say? Once they had gone, Viv went into the cottage, Bub the cat padding behind her, purring as if butter wouldn't melt in his sadistic mouth. But as soon as she knew that Geraldine was all right, she would be off. And that was a definite.

Chapter 28

'Well, come on, Stel, we're all dying to know how it went,' replied Linda, taking the cling film from the plate of goodies which Caro had brought, as it was her turn this week. Waitrose, guessed Gaynor and she was right. Yes, it would be.

'Well,' Stel began, but it was obvious from the width of her smile that good news was about to tumble from her lips. 'It was a lovely evening. He picked me up from the door, almost literally because I put bloody heels on and nearly fell flat on my face. We went to the Imax' – she saw mouths opening, all to ask the same question – 'yes, he paid. And he bought us both a coffee to take in with us. Then afterwards we went across the road to the Chinese. And he wouldn't take a penny. Then he drove me home.'

'Did you invite him in for coffee?' asked Linda, managing to make the word 'coffee' sound both innocent and salacious.

Stel thought back to the end of the date. She'd been so totally relaxed in Ian's company until that last five minutes when she didn't know what was going to happen. Her brain started firing questions at her. *Are you going to kiss him then? Are you going to ask him out to repay him for all the money he's spent on you? Are you going to invite him in for a coffee?* She both wanted him to come in for one, and didn't. The date had been perfect – she should leave it at that. But, as he pulled up outside her house, the compulsion to be polite was overwhelming.

'Would you like a coffee?' she asked. Hoping he'd refuse. Hoping he'd accept.

He turned to her and smiled. 'Thank you, Stel, you're very sweet but I don't want to put you to any trouble. I think I'd just like to drive home smiling and float into bed, if you don't mind.'

Stel mirrored the smile. 'I don't mind at all.' She had walked up the path, aware that he was waiting until she got into the house safely, sure-footed as a goat on her heels. But then, her feet felt as if they were hovering above the ground.

'Well?' Linda's prompt wrenched her out of her reverie.

'He didn't come in for coffee. I did invite him, but he didn't want to inconvenience me.'

'Oh, nice.' Caro sounded impressed.

'Yes, I had a wonderful evening.' Stel let out a Snow-White-at-the-wishing-well sigh, unaware that her friends were exchanging winks and smiles.

'And has he been in touch since?' This from Gaynor.

'We swapped numbers last night and he sent me a text this morning to say that he'd enjoyed my company and he was looking forward to seeing me at work.' Stel's smile was as wide as Linda's party room.

'You might have got a decent fella this time then, instead of a twerp,' said Iris, before slurping out of her cup.

'Oh, I do hope so,' said Stel. 'But I'll take it steady.' She didn't tell the others that the vision of a wedding in Gretna Green had already flitted across her mind. 'Viv came back on Friday night for a flying visit. Oh, it was lovely to see her.' Stel's eyes suddenly blurred with tears. 'Sorry. Hormones,' she excused herself, reaching into her bag for a tissue.

'I was terrible when I went through the Change,' said Iris. 'I was either wailing like a banshee or wanting to murder someone. I once had the window cleaner by the throat for missing my corners.'

No one was surprised by that admission.

'What's your news this week then, Caro?' asked Linda.

'Not much,' replied Caro, uncrossing and crossing her long legs. 'Apart from Marnie's boyfriend finishing with her by fucking text on Thursday.'

She even makes the F-word sound elegant, thought Gaynor.

'Two years they've been together and that's how much he respects her. Poor kid is devastated. He was her first love.'

A mean little part of Gaynor's brain felt a sudden thrill that Marnie Richmond's world had been rocked for once, only for that thought to be immediately driven out by one of shame. *God, what is happening to me? I'm becoming the worst bitch in the world.* Marnie Richmond was a lovely girl. Gaynor stuck her nail into her hand as a punishment.

'What a git,' said Linda. 'Mind you, everything kids and young people do now is via their phones. They don't look up any more, they've always got their eyes glued to a screen. I'd hate to be young today.'

'When my first love finished with me, I thought I'd never get over him,' said Stel. 'I adored him. Can't even remember what his bloody surname was now.'

'Seeing your child go through it is awful,' said Caro. 'They never stop being your babies, do they?'

'No, they don't. That's true, lass,' said Iris, whose heart was breaking for what Linda was going through with the Pawson family. 'Plenty more fish in the sea for Marnie though. I hope you've told her that.'

'She doesn't want any other fish though, Iris. She wants that one. Even if he is a . . . dirt-sucking guppy.'

'A prime bit of halibut, that's what she wants,' said Iris, going off on a piscine tangent then. 'In my day the fish was all cod and haddock and lovely and white. These days they try to fob you off with all sorts of rubbish and tell you that it's just the same. It's not – it's grey. Coley? I ask you. And Pollock. It doesn't even *sound* as if it would taste nice.'

Linda jumped up. 'Quiche anyone?' She thrust the platter into her mother's face, even though there wasn't enough quiche in the whole of the Waitrose distribution centre to shut Iris up.

'Oh, pollock.' Iris realised her faux pas and pointed over at the grim-faced Gaynor. 'Anyway, I should think you'll be glad to get rid of that name when you get divorced.'

'Will you go back to your maiden name?' asked Stel, softening her voice to sound as sympathetic as possible.

Gaynor's lips stretched into a smile-shape, but there was nothing friendly about it. 'I'm not getting a divorce,' she replied, coldly and precisely, with a smile that was more barracuda than pollock.

'How's Leanne doing these days? Has she had any good jobs recently?' said Caro, steering the conversation to safe waters as she knew that Gaynor would jump at the chance to brag.

Gaynor brightened instantly. 'She was at a party with Simon Cowell last week. She had her picture taken with him and put it on Twitter.'

'He follows my friend Doreen Turbot on Twitter, you know,' said Iris, then she grinned smugly. 'We've got a competition at Golden Surfers to see who can hook the biggest-name follower. She might have him, but I've got Ant *and* Dec. Vernon Turbot's got Fidel Castro, but we think that might be a fake account.'

'Anyway, you were saying,' said Linda, looping back to Gaynor before she took umbrage at having her moment hijacked.

'She's doing very well. I'm hoping she'll be up for her birthday in July. It will be nice to see her. And on the subject of celebrations, did Dino have a good birthday, Linda?'

Gaynor turned to her friend then realised immediately that she had said the wrong thing as Linda's eyes flooded with tears. 'Oh God, what's up, Lind?'

'That bloody Rebecca. That's what's up,' snarled Iris.

'I'm fine, I'm fine,' replied Linda, wiping her eyes with one hand whilst waving the other as if to waft away any fuss.

'She said she'd let Freddie see his grandad for five minutes and drop off a card. We waited in all night, on edge, but she never turned up,' explained Iris.

The others shook their heads in sympathy, but couldn't offer up anything to say that might help. Together they had explored every avenue and, unless there was a change in the law – or Rebecca had a frontal lobotomy that rendered her a decent human being – there was nothing that could be done.

*

The clock on the wall made the first of seven chimes.

'Right then,' Linda sniffed, plastered a smile on her face and raised her cup of tea in the air ready to make her usual toast. 'I hope to see you all back here next week safe and well and full of beans. Have a good week, ladies.'

'Chin up, girl,' said Stel, giving Linda a wink.

'Chins you mean,' replied Linda.

'I want all five of yours off the ground this week,' grinned Stel.

'Cheeky cow,' smiled Linda. This Sunday afternoon meeting kept her sane. She loved Dino and she could talk to him, but never with the open heart with which she could talk to the Old Spice Girls.

Gaynor picked up her handbag and fumbled inside it for her house keys. It overbalanced on her knee and Caro reached out and stopped it falling to the floor.

'You should come to the salon, Gaynor,' she said. 'I'll give you a stress-busting massage and a facial.'

'Thanks but I don't do all that indulgent stuff,' Gaynor replied stiffly and shuddered at the thought of it.

Caro shook her head slowly from side to side. 'Maybe you should start, then.'

'I'll think about it,' said Gaynor, annoyed with herself for sounding so brittle. She didn't want to shut out her friends but she appeared to have built a too-strong protective wall around herself. It had sealed her inside a room of poison.

Caro didn't take offence. She knew that Gaynor was an overly proud woman who was finding this public humiliation hard to deal with. Gaynor's problem was that she had spent too much time on her house, her husband and her daughter and not much on herself. She wasn't used to taking. She'd learn in time. *Just like I did,* thought Caro.

Chapter 29

Hours had passed and Viv still hadn't heard anything about Geraldine because Heath hadn't come back or phoned. She found some pastry sheets in the freezer and killed some time by making her signature cheese and onion pie. That was the least she could do before leaving. She wasn't making it for *him*. In fact, she hoped he was allergic to cheese and couldn't have any.

She fed Pilot, hoping she had judged the quantity right, and Bub, who rubbed affectionately against her leg and purred like a machine the whole time she was washing out his bowl and tearing open the pouch of food. Then she made herself a cup of coffee and sat at the dining table. Her mind drifted to Heath Merlo and that morning's exchange. *How dare he sack me because I stood in a flipping stable for five minutes*, she thought, becoming angrier by the second. No wonder past workers left after such a short time. Maybe they'd been thoroughly decent people who deserved better. Maybe the person he'd accused of stealing the safe had been as innocent as she was, too.

Well . . .

Pilot butted against her leg, nearly upsetting her coffee, his way of telling her that he wanted to go out. Viv opened the door so he could wander into the yard. On warm days such as this, he liked to sit on the path, close his eyes and go to sleep. Bub was chasing a butterfly, leaping into the air and darting maniacally. At full stretch he was as long as the draught excluder her mum kept behind the front door. Piccolo was staring into an upturned boot by the kitchen door. The place was mad. Still, none of it would be her concern any more. As soon as Heath Merlo came back, she would be off. Back home. Away from the angry aggressive git with the personality disorder.

She looked at the clock on the wall and hoped he wouldn't be much longer. She was fed up waiting for him. He could have rung and given her an estimated time of arrival at least. She bet he wouldn't have been so inconsiderate had she been Antonia Leighton. What was it about her that softened him, Viv thought, pondering whether the girl had a cousin called Tybalt. *Two households both alike in dignity* . . . Except there was nothing dignified about the Leightons. Or Heath Merlo. If they were a modern-day Romeo and Juliet, then they'd make a very dysfunctional brace of lovers. Viv wondered if Antonia's parents knew about their 'friendship'.

Antonia Leighton was the daughter of his sworn enemy, for goodness sake, and he looked at her with big moony eyes; yet the person who had sorted out his mess of an office and was working for a wage that wouldn't keep her in cup-a-soups for a week, he looked at as if she were something that had just fallen out of Wonk's bottom.

She picked up the tall glass pepper pot and walked it across the table. 'I am Heath Merlo,' she said, in a deep voice. 'I am full of peppercorns as black as my soul.' She tipped it towards her mug. 'And you are Viv Blackbird, a spy. Get off my property.'

The mug waggled back at the pepper. 'No, I am pure and true in heart. You are a nutter.'

'You accosted Mrs Leighton-Snobbery in the stable with the intent of causing evil and nicking a horse,' the pepper accused the mug.

'And how did you find out about it? I suppose it was that lanky, rich Antonia Leighton-Stuckup, dobbing me in.'

She brought the pot full of white salt into play and gave it a posh voice full of plums.

'Yars. Mummy told me over dinner.'

'I bet you were having caviar,' the mug levelled at the salt pot.

'Lobster actually. Daddy wanted to chop off your head but I thought I'd crawl up Heath's bum and stitch you up like a kipper. For then I will get major brownie points from him and we can be married.'

The salt pot was advancing on the mug, trying to drive it off the edge of the table.

'You'll get another mop bucket over you, if you don't watch it,' the mug came back at the salt.

'Oh no, please. You'll ruin my Chanel blouse. Help, help.'

Viv's nose caught a scent. His scent. She spun around in her chair. Oh God, how long had he been standing there listening to her improvised script? Still, on the bright side he was now back and she could be on her way and never see him again.

'I didn't hear your car,' she said. She had been so caught up in her re-enactment that she hadn't heard anything.

'Well, it's there. I didn't fly home,' said Heath, pinching the top of his nose and blinking. *He looks tired out*, thought

Viv. Totally shattered. The weariness of many months of worry was showing. Not that she cared.

Pilot, who had followed Heath in, wandered over to his basket and flumped down with a groan of contentment.

'How's Geraldine?' Viv asked, with chilly politeness.

'She has a badly sprained ankle and a broken wrist. She's staying there for the night to be on the safe side as she gave her head quite a bump on the way down the stairs. She was out cold when I found her.'

'Oh dear,' said Viv and picked up her mug. She crossed to the sink and swilled it out before she left. She didn't want him accusing her of being a slattern. 'Well, do give her my love and tell her I hope she gets better soon.'

'Vivienne . . .' Heath's hand shot out as if to touch her arm, but stopped short of it. 'I'm sorry for what I said. Will you stay?'

The cheek of it, thought Viv. She should have walked out with her head held high, past him and back to the folly to pick up her suitcase, but she made the mistake of glancing at Pilot. His great sad eyes looked up at her through his shaggy fringe and seemed to echo Heath's entreaty. He looked so happy, so settled and yet he would have to get used to another home with nowhere near as much space to wander safely. He wouldn't see Roger and Keith or Wonk or Bertie any more. They'd all be split up, dispersed around the country. They'd fret without the dear familiarity of this which should have been their forever home. Some of the birds were too old to get used to new surroundings.

You can't get involved. That voice again. She should go. Right now. Her affections were already sprouting shoots, reaching out to bind herself to the inhabitants of Wildflower

Cottage, give or take a stroppy vet. If she didn't go now, she was going to find it harder with every passing day. Damn him. Damn them all. Birds and cats and doe-eyed dogs.

'You've got a nerve,' Viv said, suddenly cross. 'You accuse me of all sorts, throw me out and then ask me to stay just because you haven't got anyone else to turn to, which says volumes about how desperate you must be.'

'Doesn't it just,' replied Heath, then held up his hands. 'I didn't quite mean for that to come out the way it did.'

'Oh, I'm sure you did, Mr Merlo. First you think I'm a journalist, then some sort of spy or thief—'

Heath cut her off. 'I've spent a lot of time sitting by a hospital bed today speaking to Geraldine and she thinks very highly of you. I'm sorry. I shouldn't have said those things. I've been rude and thoughtless.' His eyes were beautiful. Like waxy dark green leaves, Viv thought.

She wasn't done with him yet though, despite the genuine-sounding apology. 'How could you think that I was so underhand? If I was working for the Leightons, why did I throw a bucket of water over them?'

'Double-bluff?' Heath suggested, again raising his hands to fend off any advancing aggression. 'Not that I'm accusing you of that. I was just saying that if I was, that would be the conclusion I'd draw. But I'm not.'

'You were doing so well too, Mr Merlo.' Viv crossed her arms, enjoying this feeling of him being in her debt.

'I have absolutely no right to ask you to help me, but I am going to anyway,' said Heath. 'For the animals, if not for me.'

Her thoughts were at either end of a tug-of-war rope.

Go, said a voice. *Go now. This is going to get really messy if you don't. You have no reason to hang around now.*

But what if you need more? Until you know for sure . . . you should stay. You can't leave them like this, Vivienne Blackbird. That's not who you are.

'Okay,' said Viv, dropping a sigh of resignation. 'I'm not used to animals, whatever Geraldine told you. So you might have to bite your tongue occasionally. But I'll do my best.'

She watched a long breath of relief escape from Heath's lips. Heath's really kissable lips. She ripped her eyes away from them quickly.

'There's a pie in the oven if you haven't eaten,' said Viv. 'Twenty-five minutes should do it. Cheese and onion. I've fed the house animals but I didn't know what to do about the others.'

'Thank you,' said Heath. 'I'll see to them.'

'Do you want me to start earlier in the morning than I usually do then?'

'Eight?' He gave her a small expectant smile. 'I'll be up before that but I don't expect you to be.'

She was under no illusion that he wouldn't be so accommodating if there had been anyone else he could have asked. It wasn't as if he was talking to her nicely because he genuinely valued her and wanted to spend time with her. As he did Antonia Leighton. She wished that didn't needle her as much as it did.

'I'll be here on time,' said Viv, walking out of the kitchen and across to the folly to unpack her suitcase for the second time in a week.

Chapter 30

Just before she went to bed that night, Stel rang Viv. She tried very hard not to scream down the phone: *I THINK I'VE FOUND YOUR NEW STEPFATHER*.

'So, how did your date go then?' Viv asked, although she could guess. Worryingly, she recognised that familiar giddy tone in her mother's voice, however much she tried to mask it. Viv knew that her mother was already half in love with Ian Robson and no amount of telling her to slow down would do any good. Viv really hoped that this time her mum had found a diamond; she was overdue a bit of luck in that department and Ian had already earned major brownie points for finding Basil.

When the call had ended, Viv went back to reading about Nicholas Leighton on her laptop. She'd found an article about him that she hadn't seen before, dated a month ago. His star was certainly in the ascendancy. As well as his 'Youth of Yorkshire' business project, intended to cultivate and promote young business people of the county, he had just been made Patron of a children's charity along with a royal Princess and some very high-profile celebrities and – ironically enough – he was in the process of setting up a charity with an international rock-star who, though now at bus-pass age, was still very active in animal welfare issues. The charity was called 'Rockin' Horses' and looked after retired racehorses. Not only that, Nicholas Leighton's fledgling political career was taking off big-time. The new party leader was having a reshuffle and Leighton was about to be appointed as a government Special Adviser to the new ministerial department for Pastoral Care. He was passionate and committed to making a difference for the youth of today, he said in the article. Nicholas Leighton seemed to be everyone's darling – not least the banks who were minding his conservatively estimated wealth of seventy million.

Nicholas Leighton was groomed and handsome in the pictures, on horseback, seated with his family in their baroque drawing room in their 'ancient and atmospheric gothic castle home'. There was a photograph of father and elder daughter standing by a massive stone fireplace. 'Nicholas Leighton, pictured with elder daughter Antonia (22) who helps run Ironmist estate. Antonia was born exactly nine months to the day after Nicholas and Victoria were married.' Antonia looked beautiful, like the human version of an Arabian horse – all legs and swishy hair. She was gazing at her father affectionately, with a smile, as if the cameraman had captured them seconds after one of them had told the other a joke. Viv had never had that relationship with a father. She felt a prickle of tears behind her eyes and willed them back to where they came from, reprimanding herself for being so pathetic. There was a picture of Antonia with her mother Victoria – 'who was born in Kramburg Castle in Germany'. Victoria had spent the first thirteen years of her life there, then her English mother had divorced her German father and returned to her home county of Herefordshire.

There was a beautiful portrait of Nicholas and Victoria, arms around each other, staring into each other's blue eyes. Underneath were the words: 'We knew from the very first meeting at Oxford University that we were meant to be together.'

There was no mention of the estate Nicholas planned to build after demolishing an existing animal sanctuary and ruining the peace for the people who lived in Ironmist. Surely there was something that Heath hadn't tried? The higher Nicholas rose, the further it would be for him to fall. There must be some leverage there?

Viv slept well on the fat, comfy mattress, but her mind was spinning plans in her dreams.

Chapter 31

Viv woke up ages before her alarm was due to go off at seven, her brain rolling with activity. She had a shower and some poached eggs and sat at the dining table making notes for herself. She figured on dressing for physical work today and dragged on her tracksuit bottoms and woolly jumper – the most 'farm-worthy' clothes she had. Then, just before eight, she was striding across to Wildflower Cottage ready for whatever duties Heath Merlo had got lined up for her. The low mist hung on the air in fine curls and tendrils, delicate garlands for the wildflowers. Viv wondered if it would linger when the houses were built, and if the blue-violet love-in-a-mist would continue to flourish, pushing through manicured lawns much to the annoyance of the inhabitants, who would choke it with weed-killer.

Heath was chewing toast with one hand, putting Pilot's food bowl down on the floor with the other. He gave Viv a cursory look up and down and his greeting words were, 'You'll need wellies.'

You're onboard so I can go back to being my usual charming self. Not, Viv read into that.

'I'm not stupid,' she said, 'I've put them on the doorstep. I didn't want to wear them indoors.' She did have some consideration for his home.

'Go and get them on then,' he commanded. 'Unless you'd like me to cook you a full English breakfast first whilst you read the newspaper.'

Viv bit her tongue as she went back outside. Bub purred and rubbed himself against her as she pulled on her wellies, anticipating more wiseguy comments from Heath when he saw them. Unlike his heavy-duty green Hunters, hers were bright yellow covered in bold sunflowers. They'd only had children's wellies left in the shop when she'd bought them for the previous year's rough winter.

'Come on then,' said Heath, appearing behind her. 'Let's get star—. Good God.'

He'd seen them then.

He marched forwards with long strides leaving Viv to follow in his wake. She tried to picture the sleek and refined Antonia Leighton sharing a life with him and found she couldn't. He wouldn't fit in at Ironmist Castle and Antonia definitely wouldn't swap the family seat for a lowly cottage. But, as Armstrong's mum had said, opposites do attract each other. Maybe it was a replay of the story of their ancestors: the delicate refined Cecilia and the rough, handsome, wild Alfred who was in love with her until the day he died. Except Cecilia sounded a lot sweeter than Antonia – and Alfred a lot more gentlemanly than Heath.

With no warning, Heath stopped and whirled around to face Viv.

'What was that you said yesterday about "whatever Geraldine might have you told you"? You were talking about not being very good with animals.'

He obviously hadn't taken it in at the time and it had just come back to him.

'That ... I'm not very good with animals,' said Viv, looking up at him frowning down at her. 'Geraldine didn't ask if I was okay being around them in my phone interview. And as I presumed I'd be sitting behind a desk all day, I didn't think it mattered that ... that ... I'm scared ... of them.' She attempted a smile but achieved a grimace.

Heath rubbed his forehead with the heel of his hand. 'Great,' he said. 'Just great. It gets better and better. When Gerry's fully recovered, I think I'll kill her.'

'Who knows. I might be a natural,' said Viv, convincing neither of them. 'But I'm here and I'm all you've got. And Armstrong. I'm sure he'll help you.'

'I can only trust him with certain duties,' said Heath. 'And when his health is on a level, which, sod's law, it isn't today. Armstrong has very dark days.' He tapped his head. 'I don't know what he'll do when the sanctuary closes. Working here gives him a sense of purpose that he has never found anywhere else.'

Viv dropped a heavy sigh. She and Hugo had been at university with a girl who was bright and beautiful and had everything going for her but mentally had been in a black hole. She'd taken an overdose in the second year. Viv herself had had some depressing times. She'd always been aware that the surgery she'd had on her back could leave her paralysed. And she'd been thrown into her own dark tunnel when she thought her mother was going to die. But always, there had remained that pinprick of light in the distance to focus on that said, 'Follow me, I'll lead you back into the sunshine.' And she had forced herself to concentrate on that, and head towards it.

'Just treat me like a sort of animal idiot,' said Viv. 'Like a kid who's lived on an alien planet and doesn't know . . .'

'Okay, I get the picture,' said Heath, grumbling under his breath. 'Let's give you a crash course in animals then, shall we? We'll start with some easy ones then: the goats. Not even you can be frightened by them.'

The goats were so cute. He was right, no one could be freaked out by them. Ray stayed constantly close to his brother as if they were attached by an invisible thread and because Roy let Viv pet him, Ray did too.

'We'll sort out the horses next,' said Heath, giving the goats a final pet. They butted against his legs when he stopped stroking them as if they wanted more.

Viv started to feel her anxiety levels spike as they entered the paddock.

Heath opened their stable door and turned the horses out into the field. Roger seemed in no rush to venture outside, but the lure of fresh grass worked instantly on Keith. Heath blocked Keith's first steps out of the stable with his body. Even he, with his towering height, was dwarfed by the old horse.

'I need to check his front hoof. He had a stone in it recently and he cut his foot. Never stand where a horse has a chance of kicking you. Even one as docile as Keith can kill you.'

As Heath stood in front of Keith's leg and tapped it, the old horse offered up his hoof for him to inspect. Heath bent down and tilted the foot up so that he could look at the underneath. Keith leaned on him a little, since he was now standing on three legs.

Viv was horrified. 'You don't need me to do that, do you?'

'Er no,' Heath returned, with a note of alarm. 'I can trust

you with a bucket and a tap though, can't I? The horse trough needs filling.'

Viv grabbed the bucket and filled it with water from the tap on the wall. Roger came wandering over to her and Viv flinched.

'Don't make sudden movements, it makes him nervous. Give me your hand,' Heath ordered. Viv lifted her arm gingerly and Heath took hold of it and extended it towards Roger's long nose.

'He won't bite you,' said Heath, reining in his impatience with her. 'Just stroke him.'

Viv placed her hand on Roger's nose, smoothed her hand down the rough hair as the horse stood, head bent, allowing her to do it.

'He'd let you do that all day. But you don't have time,' said Heath. 'Grab those two pitchforks. They need fresh bedding. Move the dirty stuff to the side and I'll load it onto the compost heap later.'

As they forked out the old straw in the stable and replaced it with new, Viv thought she'd tell Heath what she'd read the previous evening.

'I saw an article about Nicholas Leighton in an online magazine. One of those that makes *Tatler* look like *Women by Women*. Did you know that he'd been made a patron of an animal charity?' she said, more than a little part of her hoping that he'd realise a fresh pair of eyes on the matter would help after all.

'Rockin' Horses,' he replied, flattening her expectations. 'Yeah, I know.'

'Doesn't that work in your favour?' Viv stretched a niggle out of her back. 'I mean, wouldn't the newspapers be interested in a story about a man who is allied to . . .'

'. . . an animal charity,' he finished the sentence off for her. 'Do you know, Miss Blackbird, we never thought of that.' He didn't miss a beat as he heaped fresh straw onto the stable floor.

'You're being sarcastic aren't you?' Viv said tentatively.

'Very,' said Heath. 'Trust me, we have tried everything. Every-little-thing. Do you know how much the man is worth? Don't you think that buys editors and favours wherever he wants them? The government is pushing for new housing everywhere; Leighton is seen as a hero for providing it. He's publicly offered to help pay the cost of shifting the animals from the rundown ancient place to shinier, better homes; he\even offered to give me one of his new houses – *give me* – although I told him at the time that he could shove it up—' He cut the sentence off, but it was obvious where Nicholas Leighton could put it. 'He has a PR team working for him that can make the Angel Gabriel look sordid if placed next to him. Tell me, who do you think the newspapers would paint as the benefactor and who the stroppy, selfish ingrate who is digging his heels in?'

'You could bypass the press and flood the truth online,' Viv tried.

'Leighton's solicitors would come down on me like a ton of bricks. Now, I don't have any money, so I'm not worried about being sued particularly, but he could make things very awkward for the people who live in Ironmist. He will crush anyone who threatens his name and good character. He has a lot to lose and sticking a few pins in him is like cutting the head off a hydra: four more grow back in its place. The only way to beat Nicholas Leighton is to kill his plans stone dead – and I can't do it. And, as much faith as Geraldine has in spirits rising up from mists, I think even the supernatural would have difficulty with this one.'

He stuck the pitchfork in a bale of hay as if he'd punctured Leighton's heart. 'Now, let's go and see to Wonk and Bertie.'

Chapter 32

Stel hadn't stopped smiling since Saturday evening. She felt like a seventeen year old again. But then, she had felt like a seventeen year old every time she hooked up with a man – and a seventy seven year old after they'd used her and spat her out at the other end. So this time, she told herself that she really should take things slowly and steadily. Still, something else countermanded that instruction, because Ian Robson could very well be *the one*. She felt there was something special about him, something different to all the others. He'd gone the extra mile for her, finding Basil and treating her like a princess on their first date.

Stella Robson, Stella Robson. It sounded much better than silly Stella Blackbird. It would be wonderful and so respectable to have a married name at last. She had wanted to fizz with excitement when she had spoken to Viv the previous night.

Stel had always enjoyed her job, but she had never been as glad to get into work as she was on Monday. On her morning break she saw Ian through the kitchen window standing talking to Graham, the other gardener, over by the water feature and a few hundred butterflies started flapping in her stomach. How could she have thought he wasn't fanciable? He always smelled lovely and dressed nicely, was tall and slim and had such a wide smile. As if sensing her eyes on him, Ian turned in her direction and Stella raised her hand and smiled enthusiastically. Too enthusiastically – as if she were a fourteen year old waving at Justin Bieber. Her soaring spirits plummeted as Ian gave her the briefest of polite smiles then resumed talking to Graham. Stel felt winded. What had he done that for? Did he see her properly? Had he changed his mind about her? Was he just being polite when he'd said he was looking forward to seeing her at work?

Then, just as Stel was about to slink to her post behind reception, she saw Meredith, the curvy new auxiliary nurse, walk from the kitchen into the garden holding two mugs which she passed to the gardeners and there was nothing polite or forced about the way Ian smiled at her. Stel couldn't hear what they were saying, but Meredith was lingering long after she had handed over the coffee, and didn't seem in a hurry to get back to her duties. Stel watched as Ian talked to her, laughed at something she said. She saw Meredith tuck a stray lock of blonde hair behind her ear – a sure sign of flirting, if that psychologist woman on *Big Brother* was anything to go by. She thought she saw Ian glance towards the window at her again, but she must have been mistaken. Stel gulped as Meredith pushed him gently on the shoulder as if he'd said something cheeky to her.

In the space of five minutes, the temperature of Stel's day had dropped by seventy degrees. She felt like crying as she went behind reception and logged back on to her computer. She knew she was being pathetic and didn't care.

Chapter 33

Bertie liked his belly rubbed. He rolled over when Heath walked into his pen, his hooves waving in the air. Viv couldn't believe what she was seeing.

'He likes ice-cream too,' said Heath, answering her open-mouthed expression. 'This is quite normal for a pig, believe it or not. They're clean and intelligent animals. That's why he has a toy-box. There's a yellow dispensing ball over in the corner. Fill it with these, will you?' He pulled a bag of sliced apples out of his pocket. 'Then open the gate so he can go in with the horses. He likes to sleep by himself but spend the day with them.'

Viv did as she was told. She had a home waiting for the shire horses – a well-to-do place where Roger and Keith would live out a very luxurious life, but they wouldn't accommodate Bertie. The woman on the phone had been quite snotty with her as well. 'I doubt the horses would miss a pig,' she said. 'They don't form attachments like that.' As Viv watched Bertie nose his yellow ball into the neighbouring field so he could play with it in close proximity to his equine friends, she doubted the woman knew as much about horses as she claimed. When Roger abandoned the grass to gently nudge Bertie's head, it was impossible not to see it as a sign of affection.

'He's never actually believed he's a pig, that's the problem,' said Heath. 'He imprinted too much on horses. He was in love with our white foal Sooty when he was a piglet.'

'Sooty?' asked Viv.

'Armstrong named her. Sadly she died when she was three. Bertie was very depressed. But he bonded with the shires. He likes Wonk but she doesn't like him. From her attitude, it's clear she thinks he's not good enough for her.'

Wonk, it appeared, liked to watch the geese. When Viv opened up their wooden houses, they flooded down the ramp, wings a-flapping, hissing at her and forcing her to scream with terror. She noticed Heath stifling his laughter.

'You really are the wrong person to be working in an animal shelter, aren't you?'

'Yep,' said Viv, hopping out of the way of a goose that was taking an unhealthy interest in her legs.

'You didn't ask for a pay rise,' said Heath, crossing his arms in front of his broad chest. She noticed he did that when he meant business. He raised his eyebrows as if waiting for an answer to a question.

'Pardon?' *What did he want her to say to that?*

'I mean, any normal person who'd been asked to double their workload would have asked for a pay rise.'

Viv snorted. 'Would you have given me a pay rise if I'd asked?'

'Of course not.'

She held up her arms in a gesture that said 'well then.'

'You're either a saint or a nutter,' said Heath, reaching into the goose house to retrieve any eggs.

'Only a nutter would work full-time for the ridiculous wage you were offering in the first place,' Viv mumbled to herself as the persistent goose attempted to peck her welly and she made a hasty retreat to the other side of the gate. She'd had enough of the geese. She did, however, find the hens very sweet. As they scratched for bugs in the earth, they looked as if they were trying to moonwalk. She didn't mind collecting the eggs from the hen house. It reminded her of the Easter egg hunts her mother used to set up for her and her friends when they were little.

Then it was time for the big scary birds of prey. She waited near the flying arena for Heath to return with their food.

'Every day we hose down the gravel in their aviaries,' said Heath, grabbing a hosepipe and handing it to Viv. 'You've met Beatrice and know how amenable she is, so let's start with her.'

Heath watched with amusement as Viv started to feed the pipe through the wires.

'You have to actually go in,' he said.

'In?' Viv let out a screech worthy of Frank the vulture.

Heath opened the aviary door.

Beatrice began to yarp. 'Morning, Bea,' said Heath. He held his hands flat out at either side. 'That means, I have no food so there's no point in trying to fly to me,' he said. 'You need to move any old food, bones, casts out of the way first, then we hose, then we feed, which, today, will be some more venison. The birds will see you and associate you with the reward of tasty meat. They'll be putty in your hands in no time.'

Viv would have disputed that. 'Poor deer,' she said, picking up some of the pellets.

'Would you rather we fed them Rice Krispies?' replied Heath with a barely concealed huff. 'Now are you ready to begin? I'm going to switch on the tap. Beatrice will go onto her branches. She will not divebomb you.'

'You're leaving me in here, by myself?' asked Viv. Her heart-rate was through the roof. She jumped as water coursed through the pipe and she quickly directed it onto the ground. Just as Heath said, Beatrice flew up to her branch and watched Viv washing down her gravel with a mix of interest and disdain.

'That wasn't so bad, was it?' said Heath, trying not to chuckle as Viv emerged from the cage shaking. He threw in some meat which the eagle owl swooped on. 'Now I hear from Geraldine that Ursula actually gave you the time of day, which is encouraging, so let me see for myself.' He opened the snowy owl's cage and watched as her head swivelled around to Viv and her beak started to twitch.

'Good. Now, in you go,' said Heath.

Viv's wellies were stuck to the ground. Heath gave her a push and closed the door behind her.

'If she attacks, I promise, I'll be straight in.'

'What do you mean *attacks*?'

Ursula's beak started moving. *Chuck chuck chuck.*

'What does that mean?' said Viv.

'Amazing,' said Heath. 'She's telling you she's fine about you being in there. Give her the sign that you have no food for her,' urged Heath. Viv gave Ursula the full jazz hands.

'Nothing to eat here, birdie,' she said through clenched teeth. 'Honest.'

Viv set about clearing Ursula's aviary, checking on the

position of the bird every few seconds, which made it a very long job.

'You don't have to worry, I did say I was on full chaperone duty,' said Heath, with a smile of impatience which wasn't really a smile at all. 'Although I am impressed that she is letting you get so close to her. She tried to crack open my head.'

'You aren't helping,' said Viv, finishing off the hosing.

'Okay, now you give her food. That will push you up even further in her estimations. Pick some of that up and let her have it. Call her by her name.'

'She can recognise her name?' asked Viv.

'Well, they learn to recognise the sound, which may or may not be the same thing.' replied Heath.

Viv stepped out of the aviary to pull a handful of meat from the bucket. She heaved slightly as she threw it into the far corner. 'There you go, Ursula. Ursula. Ursula. Ursula. Urs—'

'Okay, that's fine.' Heath cut her off. 'I think she's got the gist. Out of there now, let her eat her breakfast. Now for the fun part. Frank. You'll need to take no nonsense from him . . .'

'There is no way I'm going into the pen with a vulture,' said Viv, waving her hands in a definite gesture of 'go stuff yourself.'

'All right, all right,' Heath conceded. 'You did good for today. You can watch this one out.' He walked into Frank's cage with the hosepipe. Frank followed Heath around his aviary as if he were supervising. Then he tugged the hosepipe out of Heath's hand. Heath picked it up and Frank went for it again. They had a gentle game of tug of war and Viv was mesmerised.

'They don't show you stuff like this on cowboy films, do they?' Heath turned to her, a smile playing on his lips. 'They get a very bad press.'

Viv found herself smiling in return.

'You should open this place up to the public,' she said.

'It's a sanctuary, Vivienne,' Heath said, twisting off the tap. 'A lot of these animals have been traumatised by what people have done to them. They don't want to mix with any more strangers than they have to. Although I see your point. But there are other places who do that sort of educating. These guys are here to live out the rest of their lives in peace.' He reached for the food bucket. 'Okay, Frank, that's you done for today. Time for food.'

Frank leaped on the meat and Heath watched him for a while, though Viv wondered if his thoughts were on the bird or far away.

'I'll see to the hawks myself. They need to fly before I feed them today. Why don't you go back to the cottage and do what you have to do there. Can you ring the hospital and let me know if Geraldine needs picking up? They were waiting to hear what the consultant said when I phoned this morning. Will you check the answering machine as well, please. It should flash when there's a message but it's broken and doesn't,' Heath said.

'Yes of course. Shall I put on some lunch? Spanish omelette? It won't take long to make. I can use these.' Viv lifted up the egg basket.

'Thank you. That would be good. Forty-five minutes?'

Viv took the basket of eggs back to the cottage and at the door she turned and looked behind her. The sun was high in the sky, shining down on them all, whilst fingers of mist stole across the thousands of small bright blue flowers springing up from the earth as if preparing to pick them. It was such a beautiful valley. And the man she had moved here to get to know – and had hoped would want to know her too – was the one intent on destroying it.

Chapter 34

Stel had been busy that morning, which took her mind off Ian, but when the rush died down, her mini-depression returned and she sneaked off early for her lunch. Ian always came in at twelve for a cuppa to drink with his sandwiches. She put the kettle on ready for him, her whole body buzzing with anxiety.

She rolled her sandwich around in her mouth but she wasn't hungry. The hands on the clock reached quarter past twelve and he hadn't arrived. He was avoiding her, that was the only conclusion. She took her phone out of her bag and checked for texts and there were none. She turned the phone off and back on again in case there was a problem, but it all looked perfectly normal. Then her head shot up and with it her spirits as the door out to the garden opened and in walked Graham. But no Ian followed.

'Hi, Graham,' said Stel, trying to sound as if she wasn't about to cry. 'Is . . . is Ian coming in?'

'No, he's gone to the nursery. Not sure if he'll be back today.'

'Oh.' The word was full of Stel's sunken hope. She

switched on a jolly smile; she probably went a bit overboard being chatty with Graham to cover up her disappointment. One date and she was totally out of synch: she felt some sensible part within shake its head at her in frustration. Fifty-two years old and she was behaving like a child.

Chapter 35

Linda's cleaner Hilda always arrived half an hour before she was due to start work so she could have a cup of tea and a natter with Iris. It was something they both looked forward to so they could put the world to rights in that time. Most of it, at any rate; but the matter of the Pawsons' hold over young Freddie was one problem too far.

Hilda stole a quick look at the clock on the wall as she sat at the dining table. She had OCD about time and had to start work on the Hewitt kitchen worktops at half-past one. If the house had suddenly burst into flames at twenty-five past, Hilda wouldn't have been dragged out by ten burly firemen until she'd cleaned the granite surface clear of fingerprints.

'When's Andy home then?' asked Hilda, waving away the offer of some Walkers Shortbread.

'Not until next month,' sighed Iris. 'Obviously we haven't told him Rebecca's being a madam because we don't want to worry him. He has to keep his mind on his job, doesn't he?'

'I'm glad my lad is a builder and not a soldier,' said Hilda, shaking her head slowly from side to side. 'I wouldn't be able to sleep at night.' She turned her attention back to the matter at hand. 'But there isn't a force in heaven or hell that would keep me away from my grandkids.'

Iris slammed her hand flat down on the table, making Hilda jump. 'I'm going to have to step in, aren't I?'

Hilda blanched. She didn't want the responsibility of inciting Iris into action. Iris, she imagined, would be a loose cannon in a situation like this. There would be a definite shortage of any tact or diplomacy. 'Now hold your fire a minute, Iris. What I'd do and what you should do are totally different. Leave it to your Linda and Dino.'

'Dino won't do anything. He says that if he goes up there and starts on them, it'll be wrong with him being a man and them being women, and Linda is scared stiff to rock the boat so she won't take the risk.'

'Then you should remember that you could make things a lot worse,' warned Hilda, a note of panic rising in her usually calm voice.

'Aye, but I could make them better as well. I could talk calmly woman to woman to that old cow of a mother of hers.' Iris's eyes were glittering as her brain whirred behind them spitting out sparks. 'She's more my age than Linda's.'

The way Iris's face screwed up as she referred to Enid Pawson didn't exactly inspire Hilda with confidence that any meeting between them would go down well.

'You listen and listen good, Iris Caswell. Stay out of it or you'll regret it. You promise me you will.'

Iris sniffed. 'All right, all right, I'll stay out of it,' she said. 'If you think that's best, Hilda. I don't want to cause any trouble.'

Hilda nodded with relief. *Thank God for that*, she thought. But Iris's gunpowder was lit and fizzing. One was never too old for crossing fingers behind one's back when telling a lie.

Chapter 36

Through the window, as she was washing up the frying pan, Viv watched Heath walking towards the cottage. His shoulders looked huge in the checked shirt he was wearing. But then he needed huge shoulders to carry the burden he presently had to bear. She wondered what he would do when the sanctuary closed. Go back to being a full-time vet in a regular practice, she supposed, which wasn't a bad life. He'd be loaded, for one thing, based on the evidence of what they charged every time Basil needed any treatment. He suited this setting, she could tell that, even after their short acquaintance. But she did wonder if he resented having the responsibility of the sanctuary thrust on him. Maybe having his hand forced might release him from those duties so he could enjoy a life that surely would be a lot less hard work.

Pilot had trotted out to meet him and was now escorting him in, periodically looking up at him like a sheepdog waiting for a command. He too was blissfully unaware that his forever home was a misnomer.

Heath paused by the door to kick off his massive

wellingtons. He filled the door when he stood in it, inhaling Viv's cooking. 'That smells good,' he said.

'It's only a glorified omelette,' said Viv. 'I doubt it's anything of the standard Geraldine supplies.'

But Viv had to admit to herself that she hadn't done a bad job. The ingredients were all from their land: spring onions, the peppers growing in a stone trough at the side of the door, chives standing proud in their pots on the windowsill, the potatoes dug up from the back garden and stored in sacks in the cool cellar, the tomatoes from the greenhouse, and the eggs of course from the rescued chickens. The cheese was from the local farm, a strong nutty cheddar with a hint of sweetness which became stretchy when melted. Heath tucked in hungrily and almost caught Viv staring at him as he ate. He didn't look like a vet, thought Viv. He looked more like a bear-trapper, with his muscular arms and strong frame. She couldn't imagine him giving ear-drops to hamsters.

'So how old are you again?' he asked, reaching for a second quadrant of the tortilla circle.

'Twenty-three.'

'You seem older.'

'Thanks,' and she tutted with dry amusement. She was going to reply that she'd had to grow up faster than a lot of kids, then realised that might lead her into an explanation of her mother's illness, which he wouldn't want to hear about. So she left it at that.

'It wasn't an insult.'

It was hardly a compliment either, to be fair, she thought.

'I'm exactly ten months older than Antonia Leighton,' she said.

He ceased chewing momentarily, then his jaw began to work again.

'What relevance is that?'

Actually, Viv had no idea. She'd just said it without thinking. She thought Antonia Leighton looked older than her age, too. Yes, she was beautiful, but in a couple of years that default setting of a frown and downturned mouth would give her 'lines of misery' as her mother called them. But if she said that to Heath, it would sound like the bitchy comment it was. Viv thought it best to leave it.

'I rang the hospital but the consultant hadn't done his rounds. He was due any minute, the nurse said.' Viv refilled their mugs with more tea.

'Thank you. A hospital minute is at least an hour,' replied Heath, stabbing a square of omelette as if he'd experienced many a 'hospital minute'.

Which led Viv nicely to a gripe that had been niggling her. 'I wish you'd rung yesterday to let me know how Geraldine was. I was worried. I didn't know how badly she'd been hurt.'

Heath's eyes flicked up to her face as if grossly affronted that he'd been rebuked. But some part of him must have taken on board that Viv did have a point.

'I should have, you're right,' he said. 'I apologise for that. My phone battery was flat, and Geraldine doesn't have a mobile but that's no excuse. I could have found a pay phone.'

And no doubt a part of him had still been cross with her, Viv guessed. Okay, so whilst she was in brave mode, she thought she'd ask the big question again. He was hardly going to throw her out for it, because he needed her.

'Can't Antonia Leighton help you?'

Heath's fork clattered onto his plate. 'What?' he replied.

Whoops, thought Viv. Just when it had been going quite well. Maybe she'd strayed too far beyond the boundary asking this one. 'Well, you and she obviously have a . . .' She struggled to find the appropriate word that wouldn't have him picking his fork back up and sticking it in her neck, '. . . a . . . a . . . friendship.'

The timing couldn't have been better. The house phone rang and Heath snatched it up from the dresser behind him. 'Yes,' he barked into it. The poor recipient was copping for his displaced anger, it seemed. 'Yes, yes,' his voice softer now. 'I'll be there in half an hour. Thank you. Bye.' He put down the phone, picked up his empty plate and carried it over to the sink.

'Geraldine's ready to be collected,' he said. 'I'll go and get her.'

'Can I do anything to help?' asked Viv. She didn't want him looking at her with those hostile eyes. She'd rather be facing Ursula than him at the moment.

Heath ignored the question, walked to the door, stopped there, and turned back.

'I'm grateful for your staying on, but a word of advice: you ask too many questions for someone who is "just here to help". You won't make yourself any friends in Ironmist if you pry into the lives of the people here. We don't owe strangers any answers.'

Then he picked up his boots at the side of the doormat and walked out, closing the door so Pilot couldn't follow him, leaving Viv wondering what the hell he meant by all that.

Chapter 37

Stel deleted Ian's number and with it the tinkly ring tone she'd assigned to it so she knew instantly that it was him if he phoned or texted. She wouldn't be messed around, she decided, as she switched off her monitor at home time. Why did Ian fill her up with so much hope that he was looking forward to seeing her at work on Monday, only for him to blatantly ignore her? Once she'd said her 'goodnight, see you tomorrows' and was sitting in her car, the scaffolding holding up her composure fell apart. The tears which had been building behind her eyes all day began to spill over. Hadn't she learned by now that she wasn't destined for a happy ending? Then, as she slotted her key into the ignition, her phone rang in her handbag.

She fumbled to find it, dropped it, picked it up again and looked at the screen to see a number she didn't recognise. But didn't Ian's end in 3-0? She pressed connect just before it went to voicemail.

'Hello, hello,' she said, not even trying to sound cool, calm and collected.

'Stel?'

It was *him*. Her tears dried up instantly as if the car was a giant microwave oven.

'Ian?' She felt as if a light had switched on in her heart.

'Yes, it's me. How are you? I'm sorry I didn't get the chance to see you today. I drew the short straw and had to go and pick plants out in Huddersfield. Normally that's not a short straw, but I'd rather have stayed behind today. No prizes for guessing why.'

'Oh, no worries,' Stel wished she didn't sound as if she'd been crying. 'I presumed you were busy.'

'Have you got a cold?'

'No, no, I've just had a sneezing fit. I think I'm allergic to my new car air freshener.' *Too much detail*, she thought, admonishing herself. *Why didn't she just shut up after the sneezing fit bit?*

'I missed my coffee break with you,' Ian said.

'I missed seeing you for coffee, too,' said Stel, aware that she was gushing and not caring.

'Well . . .' Pause. 'I was going to suggest . . .' Even longer pause.

Oh please, please suggest another date, Stel begged the heavens above. *I can be ready in half an hour.*

' . . . How about having lunch with me in the garden tomorrow. I'll supply the sandwiches.'

'Oh . . . lovely.' That gap between the two words was shouting of disappointment.

'I'm going to spend time with my mum tonight. It's her birthday. Otherwise we could . . . oh well, not to be. Can't let her down.'

'Of course, I understand,' enthused Stel. 'Tomorrow is great.'

'I'll see you in the garden at twelve then. Hope you like home-made cake.'

'I love it,' said Stel. If Ian had said *hope you like raw pig's testicles*, she would have given him the same answer.

'See you tomorrow then.'

'Have a good evening. With your mum.'

Stel put down the phone, a different woman to the one she had been five minutes previously. Yes, girl-power and all that, telling you not to let a man dictate your mood. It was all easier said than done. Cake, home-made cake at that, and a man who spent time with his mother. The idea of Ian Robson as a life partner just got better and better.

*

With Geraldine's arrival came her beautiful floral scent flooding the kitchen. Viv still couldn't put her finger on what that mystery aroma was that hid from her analysis. She'd work it out, it always came to her in the end, but without it, the replica she had created in her mini-lab was lacking.

'Oh Heath, don't fuss,' said Geraldine, hobbling over to the armchair with a crutch under her arm. Her left leg was bandaged up to the knee and she was wearing a strapped medical sandal. Her right wrist was encased in plaster and suspended in a sling around her neck. 'Hello, Viv. How lovely to see you.' Geraldine's smile was warm and genuine. Viv gave her a careful hug of greeting and helped Geraldine manoeuvre herself down onto the sofa.

'Oh my, how wonderful it is to be back,' said Geraldine, patting Pilot's great head with her uninjured hand. 'That's a nice welcome, Pilot. Did you miss me, boy?'

'Sounds like someone else did too,' laughed Viv, watching Piccolo stride up and down the kitchen table with his ridiculous legs, chattering at three hundred decibels. Bub, however, was asleep in his basket and deigned to open his eyes briefly. That was all Geraldine was getting from him for the time being.

'Cup of coffee?' asked Viv, rushing over to the kettle, which had just started to whistle.

'Oh yes please,' said Geraldine with relish.

'The lady at the Corner Caff came down half an hour ago with some buns for you,' said Viv. 'And she brought a card from Mr Mark and Mr Wayne. I think they've put a sign outside that you're okay and were coming home today.'

Geraldine chuckled. 'I hope they didn't put one up yesterday saying what a clumsy idiot I was.' Her laughter dried up. 'Of all times to go and do something as daft as this.'

'Don't worry about that,' replied Heath. 'We'll manage. You do too much anyway.'

'I like things spick and span,' said Geraldine. 'This house has been good to me and I want to be good to it.'

'I'd better go and carry on with my duties,' said Heath, glancing at his watch.

'Yes, yes, don't let me hold you up,' said Geraldine. When he had gone, though, she dropped her head onto her chest. 'Oh, Viv, I could cry. Just when we need all hands on deck.'

'You stop that right now,' said Viv, who'd had more experience of geeing someone up than she should have had in her young life. 'I'm learning. I've helped feed the animals and clean them out . . .'

'But you've got all the office work to do as well,' Geraldine butted in.

'There wasn't that much to do today. I've done some banking and written a few emails. Oh, and ordered some feed.' She could have rung around trying to find an alternative home for the shire horses, one which could have taken Bertie also, but she'd leave that until tomorrow. She couldn't bear that she might fail. 'Are you hungry?'

'No, thank you,' said Geraldine. 'I don't think I could stomach anything. I've been worried sick over this place. What was all that about you being up in the Leightons' stables?'

'That was all a storm in a teacup,' said Viv, delivering a mug of coffee to Geraldine's good hand. 'I really did take shelter to get out of the rain. There's no more to it than that.'

Well . . .

'I did say to Heath that it had to be something like that,' said Geraldine and smiled. *She has such a pretty face*, thought Viv. Geraldine must have been a real beauty when she was younger. Her eyes were bright and shiny-grey and she had sharp, high cheekbones.

'He asked me if I was a journalist,' said Viv. 'It's because I ask too many questions. I'm just naturally nosy; but it's made him suspicious of me.'

With good reason, perhaps? that persistent voice in her head whispered.

'Ironmist is a funny place,' said Geraldine. 'The people who live here are curious about others and at the same time fiercely protective of their own business.'

We don't owe strangers any answers.

'So they want to have their cake and to eat it then.' Viv proffered the plate of Corner Caff buns to Geraldine, but she refused them.

'Ironmist is a safe harbour, Viv. It attracts people who . . .' As if someone had leaned over Geraldine and whispered in her ear to keep quiet, she cut off what she was going to say. 'Oh I don't know. It's just village mentality, that's all.'

Viv wanted to press her, but she knew she couldn't. Not today. It didn't feel right.

'I'll have to sit here with a book today, but tomorrow I'm going to find something – anything – I can do. I refuse to be idle.'

'You should really rest, surely?' said Viv.

'I'll rest in my grave,' quipped Geraldine. 'It's all hands on deck here, even broken ones. Why couldn't it have been my left one, eh?' She lifted up the offending hand and gave it a hateful look.

'Will you need any help getting in bed later?' asked Viv.

'Possibly, if it's no trouble,' replied Geraldine, with a heavy out breath. 'No showers for a while. I'll have to make do with a strip wash and I might need a hand with my bra. Shame you're here really, I could have asked Heath if you weren't.' She laughed and Viv's laugh joined with hers but then Viv had a flash brain picture of Heath Merlo unfastening her own bra and she gulped.

'Well, if you're comfortable, I'll just go and check to see if there are any replies to my emails about the animals.'

'You go, love,' said Geraldine, reaching down for her handbag but her hand fell short of it. Viv retrieved it for her and saw the water swimming in Geraldine's soft grey eyes.

'I could kick myself,' Geraldine said. 'Such a stupid thing to go and do.'

Viv interrupted her. 'Accidents happen. We can't turn the clock back, so we'll have to forge forwards, won't we? Besides,' she smiled, 'kicking yourself will only make it worse.'

Geraldine reached for Viv's hand and gave it a grateful squeeze.

'I wish I'd been as sensible as you at your age, Viv. You wouldn't believe how different my life would have been.'

Viv leaned down and gave Geraldine a small impulsive kiss on her cheek. Then she went into the office in the hope that she could find some miracle online to help the sanctuary stay open. The least she could do for the animals was try her best.

Chapter 38

Heath wasn't very talkative as Viv helped him to put the animals away for the night. The geese had already taken themselves off into their house, though the chickens needed some chasing. Viv wondered if it was because they were worried that once locked up, they might never be allowed into the sunshine again and that they'd wake up back in their old, miserable battery lives. It was a shame she couldn't speak to them in hen language and assure them that wasn't the case.

Any attempt Viv made to initiate a friendly conversation with her boss came to nothing. It was as if he had closed off from her, in case anything he said she might use against him in her role of journalist or industrial spy. Or maybe he was still smarting from her comment about Antonia Leighton helping them. Which was, she considered, a reasonable thing to say in the circumstances. Why was it that the most unmatchable people were drawn together? And why was it that she found herself trying to second-guess what Heath Merlo thought about her, far more than she should?

'I was going to go and get some fish and chips. Would you like some?' Viv asked him, as he shut the stable door on the horses.

'Thank you but no,' he replied. Then, as if he realised he had been abrupt he added in a much friendlier tone, 'I said I'd call in on someone.' He pulled his car keys out of his pocket. 'Mrs Macy's cat isn't well.' He shook his head and sighed. 'Sadly I think she's going to have to let him go.'

'That's a shame,' said Viv. 'Is he very old?'

'At least twenty. No teeth, one eye, arthritis and now a lump in his throat that's stopping him from eating. And still she thinks I'll bring a miracle with me.' Viv thought that for all his bolshiness with her, he'd talk to Mrs Macy as gently as he'd try to treat her cat.

'Have you ever thought about opening your own veterinary practice?' asked Viv. 'You must miss it, surely?'

'I miss it very much, Viv,' he said and she saw his throat rise and fall with a gulp of emotion. 'My dream was to build a practice there.' He pointed to the land at the side of the cottage. 'I wanted it to be a specialist centre for birds. It's where my major interest has always been.'

'You'll go back to being a bird vet then, I presume,' said Viv. 'When . . . if . . .'

'Yes, I will,' said Heath. 'But it will be a lesser dream, doing it somewhere else.' And then he said goodnight and headed off to Mrs Macy's.

'Here, let me give you the money for these,' said Geraldine when Viv returned with the fish and chips.

'Welcome Home treat,' replied Viv, refusing to entertain Geraldine's offer. 'Thought they might spark up your appetite. Just accept and enjoy.'

'You're a very kind girl, Viv,' said Geraldine. 'I shall eat them out of the paper. They taste so much better that way.'

'Someone in the queue asked me how you were,' replied Viv, cutting the long fish in half. The batter yielded with a soft crunch under her fork. 'The shop was full and I knew everyone else was listening so no doubt there will be an update outside the Stores from Mr Mark and Mr Wayne tomorrow.'

Geraldine chuckled. 'The people of Ironmist are good folk.' Then she sighed. 'I'm so lucky I found this place. Or rather it found me.'

'How did you come to live here?' asked Viv, shifting a piece of fish around in her mouth to cool it down.

'I was on my way to lose myself in Manchester and I took the wrong road chasing a short cut. I ran into mist just at the top of the hill there' – she pointed to it through the window – 'so I stopped the car and walked down. I thought that there was bound to be a café or a pub where I could get something to eat and wait for it to pass. I saw the sign in Mr Wayne's shop window for a job at the sanctuary, and the rest is history. Isme led me here. That's why I've always believed she would save us. She does exist, and I don't care who thinks I'm batty for thinking it.'

Lose myself. What a strange way to put it.

Bub's front paws landed on Viv's legs, scaring her half to death as he begged for some fish. Viv gave him a large flake in payment for not digging in his claws and he took it under the table to kill it. Geraldine threw the tail end over to Pilot, who carried it outside in his large jaws to eat in peace in the warm summer night.

'Heath's missing a treat not joining us,' said Viv. 'He's gone to see Mrs Macy's cat.'

'People often ask him to call and check on their animals. He's very kind,' said Geraldine.

'Wouldn't his life be a lot easier if he didn't have to live here?' Viv said and instantly regretted it because it sounded harsh, clumsy.

But Geraldine, to her surprise, agreed with her. At least in part. 'Oh Viv, you have no idea how much easier his life would be. But it wouldn't be a fraction as fulfilling or enjoyable for him. You need to see him in the arena, flying the hawks. Then you'll realise how hard he will find life away from Wildflower Cottage. He was brought up here, the place is part of him. I hope you start to feel it, too. It's a special privilege to connect with a place like this.'

Geraldine reached for the teapot, but she couldn't lift it and Viv took over.

'Heath's mother never settled here. She left them, came back, left them again – many times. It couldn't have helped him form a healthy template for relationships. She left for good when Heath was about ten. He never heard from her again. I can't imagine how anyone could desert their own child. Even the Leightons put their daughters on pedestals.'

The Leightons. Every road led to the Leightons.

'He was a lovely man, Heath's dad,' Geraldine went on. 'Very gentle. A good man. He wanted Heath to go out into the world and enjoy its challenges. He told me how proud he was when his son qualified as a vet and married an animal-loving country girl. Then everything went downhill so quickly, with Heath's father and Sarah passing within months of each other. It was a hard time.' Her shoulders gave a sad lift and fall. 'But have I ever heard Heath rail against his obligations? Have I ever seen any evidence of him not wanting to be here? Never.'

'What was Sarah like?' asked Viv. She pictured someone blonde, fragile and quiet.

'She was . . . a very pretty girl,' returned Geraldine, after a long thoughtful pause. It wasn't much of a description, thought Viv.

'Were they together long?'

'Two years, I believe.'

'And was she from Ironmist?'

'Mawton. Her family have the feed store there. Bernal—'

Geraldine cut the name off short, as if she'd said something she shouldn't have. Viv pretended not to notice.

'There's a feed store there? Why do you go all the way to Fennybridge for supplies then?' Fennybridge was at least fifteen miles past Mawton.

'The feed store at Fennybridge is much better,' said Geraldine. But she appeared to have thought of that answer too quickly for it to be a viable one. *No, there's more to it than that*, thought Viv. Why didn't Heath do business with his in-laws?

But she didn't ask. It wasn't fair to interrogate Geraldine, especially when she had just come out of hospital. Viv made some small talk about fish and chip shops and what a huge range of things some of them sold. The Ironmist one sold fish, chips and that was it.

'I'm glad Heath didn't frighten you off, Viv,' said Geraldine later when she had eaten her fill.

'What's the deal with Antonia Leighton, Geraldine?' asked Viv. 'I made the mistake of asking earlier why she couldn't help him and I don't think he took it so well.'

Geraldine let out a long breath and raised her eyes up to

the ceiling. Then she pointed to a bare lit bulb on the wall. Tiny moths and midges which had been attracted to the light were bumping against it.

'See that, it just about sums it up. Antonia is attracted to Heath because he's handsome and strong and totally illegal so far as her family are concerned. Heath would never encourage the affections of a Leighton: how could that mix of blood ever work? But the mind and the heart are very different. Some creatures are drawn to the things that are destined to harm them.'

Geraldine seemed entranced by the moths, their wings flittering against the hot glass, drawn by the brightness which would burn them, yet they came back for more. 'Look, they're being hurt and can't pull away. Pain becomes their oxygen.'

Geraldine was now looking beyond the moths, as if the light had dragged her into a memory pool of her own. She wasn't talking solely about Heath any more.

'People can be very cruel.' Geraldine snapped out of her mini-trance. 'Promise me, Viv, that if you meet a man who seems too good to be true, you'll keep your guard high until you know him, really know him. Some of them lure you in with the promise of love you so badly crave, and you trust them to lead you to their heart, one sure step at a time through the mists of their charm; but when it clears, you find nothing there but a dried husk.'

She was talking about herself, it was obvious. Someone had hurt Geraldine very much. Is that who she had run from?

'I can assure you, Geraldine, I will. I've learned that one from watching my mum.'

'Watching your mum?' asked Geraldine, with some confusion.

'My mum is lovely,' said Viv. 'But where men are concerned, she has no sense at all. Luckily, she isn't quite at the
stage where she's writing to serial killers in prison, though.'
She smiled and Geraldine chuckled softly. 'She wants to be
loved so much and so she believes everything men tell her,
but she couldn't spot a nice man if he had "nice man" tat-
tooed on his face.' *And the daft thing is, she lives next door to
the loveliest man ever, who is the male equivalent of her*, added
Viv to herself.

'What a shame,' said Geraldine with a sigh loaded with
sympathy.

'Although in saying that, she's just met someone who
sounds nice.'

'Oh, I do hope he is,' smiled Geraldine.

Not as much as I do, thought Viv. *Or at least if he isn't, that
Mum has the sense to get rid of him quick*. Stel was too forgiving.
She gave people far too many chances to redeem themselves.
Darren had leached off her, stolen money from her and
bonked behind her back, and she'd still forgiven him. Viv
could still remember the state her mother had been in when
she found him gone without a word. Her loathing for
Darren had barely diminished in all the years in between.
She thought of what Geraldine had said and added another
promise, one of her own: she'd never give her heart to a man
who could leave a dying woman.

Geraldine's jaw was forced open by a weary yawn. 'I
think I might have to go to bed,' she said.

'Come on then, I'll help you,' said Viv, offering her arm.

In the flowery-scented room down the hallway, Viv
turned back the bed cover and shook out Geraldine's nightdress, whilst she went to the loo. Then Viv helped her undo
her blouse and slip it off. She noticed immediately that

Geraldine's shoulders had crescent-shaped silvery scars on them. *Who did that to you, Geraldine?* she stopped herself from asking.

'I'll wear a vest tomorrow,' said Geraldine with a small laugh. 'I don't really need a bra. I haven't got anything to put in it. It'll make life simpler for us all.'

'Well, you just have to ask if you need any help,' said Viv and with a goodnight, she retreated and left Geraldine to rest. She let Pilot out and when he had done what he had to, Viv locked up the house behind her and walked across to the folly. At her door, she turned to look back at Wildflower Cottage and thought that poor Cecilia Leighton would have loved it. She could imagine her excitedly planning her sanctuary, with young Alfred Merlo telling her what was possible and what was not. Could the kitchen catch all the sun in the morning and the flower garden be to the west? Could he make a large window in the gable end so she could view the expanse of the wildflowers? Every stone and brick would have been in place in her heart, even though she never took one real step inside the finished house.

It couldn't be demolished. The animals couldn't be sent away from their forever homes. It was wrong, wrong, wrong.

As Viv lay in her bed, her eyes fell on the fat knitted bee at her side. 'What can I do, EBW? What can I do to stop this from happening?' But it was a rhetorical question, because she knew.

Chapter 39

Maria had been on a long weekend break and so, that Tuesday morning, she couldn't wait to catch up with what had been happening with Stel's love-life. She forced her to have a tea-break before she started work and relished all the details. Stel had the time to do that because she'd come in to work half an hour early, keen to get in, keen to see Ian.

'The thing with women,' began Maria, talking between mouthfuls of chocolate digestives, 'is that they obsess too much. They think that if a man doesn't ring them straight away then he's cooled off. They don't think it might be because they've got stuff to do. We always have them buzzing around in the back of our minds whatever we're doing and they don't think like that. Men give all their attention to one thing, then they give all their attention to another thing. Women don't do that, we like to juggle twenty balls in the air at any one time. You should read that book, that … you know … "Men are from Mars" thing. It tells you all about men being elastic bands and how woman have to back off whilst their fellas are out stretching. Makes a lot of sense.'

'Anyway, all is well now.' Stel let out a long, contented sigh of relief. 'We're having lunch together in the garden. I would have seen him last night had it not been his mother's birthday and he was spending the evening with her.'

Maria scrunched down her eyebrows in confusion. 'His mum's dead, Stel. I remember him telling us at his interview. She died in a hospice last year.'

'Are you sure?' Though Stel knew that Maria had a memory like an elephant. She felt a cold prickle at the back of her head.

'Absolutely.' Then Maria clicked her fingers. 'Maybe he meant he was going to put some flowers on her grave.'

Stel reached back into her memory trying to retrieve the conversation. He'd said he was going to spend some time with her. He didn't say he was taking her out for a meal. The prickle subsided. He must have meant that he was paying his respects to her. Possible crisis averted. The warning flag dropped.

Maria's pager started bleeping. 'Right, I better get to it,' she said, slotting her mug into the dishwasher. 'Enjoy your lunch in the sunshine. Make sure you don't sit too near to his peonies.'

'You're too dirty to be a head nurse,' laughed Stel, checking her watch. From the expectancy frothing around inside her stomach, she might as well have been back at school again waiting for the school football captain to walk past her in the corridor.

Chapter 40

The morning didn't start off very well for Viv. She walked into the cottage to find Heath stomping from one side of the room to the other with a letter clutched in his hand. He looked like a captive lion who couldn't wait to break out between the bars and claw the zookeeper to death. Her breezy, 'Good morning,' did not go down well.

'Trust me, this is not a good morning,' he said.

At least Pilot was pleased to see her, she thought as the big dog pushed his nose into the hand she had already cupped for him, and Piccolo cawed enthusiastically at her from his stance on the bread board. She'd even have taken her chances with Bub this morning, more than she would with Heath.

Heath explained to her then, in words almost spat out, that a solicitor's letter had arrived by Special Delivery outlining the recent case of assault which Mr Nicholas and Miss Antonia Leighton had suffered at the hands of a Wildflower Cottage employee. Luckily, no action would be taken on this particular occasion but the matter would be reported to the police and the incident would remain on record.

Viv tried to look suitably contrite, but the seriousness of the situation was having the opposite effect on her. She found that she had to work really hard at keeping her face straight.

'You seem to think this is amusing, Miss Blackbird,' Heath snapped at her.

'I don't,' she protested and promptly burst into laughter. The fact that Heath was staring at her with his mouth open and eyes that said, 'you're mad' just added fuel to the flames.

'What on earth is wrong with you?'

Viv's face was in her hands. She couldn't control herself. Boy did she need this laughter. More than he could ever know. When she started drying her eyes she saw that his mouth was twitching. She had infected him, but he was fighting hard against it.

'It's like having a letter from the bank saying you're a million pounds in debt when you haven't got a bean,' explained Viv. 'Then just when you've got your head around that, you read that they've charged you twenty-five quid for telling you. There comes a point when things can't get any worse.'

'That's so comforting,' said Heath. 'Remind me to recommend you as a therapist to the clinically depressed.'

'I'm sorry,' said Viv, recovering. 'I wasn't trying to make light of anything.'

'The Leightons can always make things worse, Vivienne,' said Heath.

The vs were soft, the emphasis on the last syllable. Then Viv realised with some sort of horror she was actually analysing how he said her name. That was something her mother would have done.

Heath looked at the letter again. Viv saw his enchanted-forest eyes follow the words then he ripped the paper savagely.

'Come on. Let's get to work. We'll start with the birds first this morning.'

She waited outside whilst he went to the feed store. Or rather stomped. He stomped in and stomped back out. He was in a very stompy mood, she thought, and because it was her that had put him in it, she would make a determined effort to keep a low profile from now on. She'd be obedient and not-nosy Viv. So she didn't make a fuss about going into the aviaries and cleaning them. Not even scary Ursula's. Viv hoped that Ursula would remember that she liked her. Although why a bird would take to her was anyone's guess. Couldn't it smell her fear a mile off?

Ursula gave Viv her chuck-chuck noise and nodded her head. It looked as if she was bowing in reverence. Heath looked impressed.

'Snowy owls are really belligerent. Bowing her head means she has to take her eyes off you. It's part of her mating ritual.'

'Oh God forbid she wants to mate with me,' said Viv. 'Imagine what the children would look like.'

She had a moment of clarity as if she were viewing the scene from above.

I'm in a closed cage with a huge scary bird and it fancies me.

Heath opened the aviary door and handed her the large glove he'd brought with him.

'Put this on. Left hand.'

'What for?'

'Just do it,' Heath insisted. 'I want to try something.'

He wanted to try and wreak his revenge for that solicitor's

letter, Viv considered. He was going to encourage Ursula to peck out her eyes.

Heath passed her a small piece of meat. 'Just hold it towards her. She's already shown you that she's starting to trust you. No scary eye contact – from you, that is. She can do what she wants.'

Viv had a couple of false starts in extending her hand and keeping it there.

'Good,' called Heath. 'She's letting you get close.'

Viv stretched until she couldn't reach any higher. Her hand was within the bird's reach. Viv watched Ursula's mist-white face lower to her glove, snatch the meat and swallow it and she felt far more moved than she had ever imagined she would, given that it had never been on her list of life's to-dos to hand feed an owl a piece of dead animal.

'Wow,' she said, and the word carried true wonderment.

'Well, I don't know why Ursula has picked you to bestow her affections upon, but she has, so we have to use you,' said Heath, rubbing his chin in amazement.

He hasn't given up, thought Viv. If he had he wouldn't think it worth wasting time on encouraging Ursula to bond with someone.

Wildflower Cottage was worth fighting for. Viv really wished she didn't care about it as much as she was beginning to.

Chapter 41

No man had ever been to the trouble of making a picnic for Stel. She'd got to the stage in her life when she would have sworn that men weren't capable of such thoughtfulness. Women were – her daughter searched high and low to find presents for her that she'd love and her friends were always there for her. Caro once brought her a home-made cake 'for medicinal purposes' when Viv was having another operation on her back. And Caro hated baking. But though she'd been thrilled and touched by it, it hadn't sent cataclysmic pulses through her body the way that Ian Robson's picnic basket did.

She'd been like a jelly when he called into the kitchen at twelve and asked if 'madam was ready for her lunch'. He had crooked his arm for her taking and led her out to the bench in the far corner of the garden where a wicker basket sat. There, individually wrapped in cling film, was a selection of ham and pickle, egg mayo, cheese and tomato sandwiches, sausage rolls and mini-scotch eggs and a small cake that appeared not to have risen very well. He'd brought a couple of bottles of sparkling peach-flavoured water to wash it all down with. Stel hated peaches, but she didn't say that. Actually, it tasted very nice, probably because it was 'Ian's peach-flavoured water' and that seemed to alter her taste-buds so they accepted it.

'Seems ages since we saw each other,' said Ian, giving Stel a wide smile and an unblinking stare that made her cheeks start to heat up. 'I missed you yesterday. It was pretty mad at work.'

It didn't look very mad when you were flirting with Minging Meredith, thought Stel. But then, maybe she had just happened to spot him having the only minute's breather he had all day. *Still, it would only have taken a few seconds to pop in and say hello . . .* Stel forced that thought right out of her brain. It was as if a nasty little imp was trying to spoil things for her. That same imp led her to the subject that had nipped at her all morning.

'Did . . . did last night go all right?' asked Stel. 'With your mum.'

'Well, there wasn't much conversation going on,' said Ian, looking down sadly at his sandwich.

Stel felt ashamed that she'd brought it up to test him. She'd put him off, if she weren't careful. 'This is lovely,' she said. 'Cheese and tomato sandwiches are my favourite.'

'I'm hardly Charlton Heston or whatever that chef's called,' grinned Ian.

'Thank God for that,' smiled Stel. 'He's not my type.'

Ian leaped on her answer. 'Oh, so you're saying I am, are you?'

Stel floundered on a response, not wanting to disagree, not wanting to give too much away. It made him laugh that she stuttered, like the 'yes-no Jim' on *The Vicar of Dibley*.

Ian tilted his head towards the sun. 'I love the sun,' he

said, closing his eyes, letting the heat settle on his skin. Stel studied his profile and thought he was very good-looking from the side. If she could have drawn a picture of her ideal man, it wouldn't have matched him, but it didn't matter. Her ideal man wouldn't have had such a thin mouth, and his eyes would have been bigger and not so close together. He would have had broader shoulders, protective arms, and chunkier thighs, but yet it was Ian who had occupied all her thoughts over the past days.

Without warning, or moving from his position, Ian said: 'I can't wait to kiss you, Stelly.'

He might as well have pressed a detonator for a pile of dynamite in Stel's insides.

'Wha . . . at?'

'You heard,' he said, opening one eye, giving her a glance and then resuming his sun-bathing position. 'Now, when am I going to see you again after this?'

Tonight, tonight, tonight . . . voices screamed inside her. No, she needed to think, to plan. She needed space to get her head together – and clean the house.

'Erm . . .' she pretended to be cool. 'What about . . . tomorrow. I could cook something. Pasta? Or do you like risotto?'

Ian turned his face to her. 'I love pasta,' he said slowly and convincingly. 'I'll bring wine. Do you prefer white or red?'

'Any. White, red, green, brown . . .' Stel trilled a chuckle. Outside she was calm and smiling, inside she was a panicking mess with an overworking brain. Wine? Did that mean he wasn't planning to drive home? Would he get a taxi? Would she let him stay?

Ian stole a glance at his watch.

'I suppose I'd better get back to work,' he said. 'Have you

finished?' He picked up the two sandwiches which hadn't been eaten. 'Do you want a doggy bag?'

'I'm full,' said Stel. 'That was lovely, Ian. A proper treat.'

'A proper treat for a proper lady.' Ian smiled.

Stel floated back into the kitchen where Maria was waiting, hungry for detail. Then she walked back to reception with a clock in motion inside her, ticking down the one hundred thousand seconds to that kiss. It didn't sound so long when she thought of it that way.

Chapter 42

Geraldine had only just woken up when Viv and Heath walked into the cottage. She couldn't stop apologising. Viv told her not to be silly. The bakery had left a basket of sandwiches and a huge tub of soup on the doorstep but Geraldine wasn't hungry. She had a horrible headache and so Viv pushed her back in the direction of her bedroom. She sat at the dining table and ate lunch alone because Heath was outside speaking to someone on his mobile. It didn't look a very friendly call either if his pacing up and down was anything to go by.

She was washing up her plate when Heath came back in.

'Do you think you'll be able to drive the pick-up?' Heath asked her. 'It would help me enormously if you collected the weekly order from the feed store at Fennybridge tomorrow.'

'Yes, I'll be able to drive it,' Viv replied.

'Thank you.'

'Why don't you use the one in Mawton though? It's so much nearer.'

He didn't react to the question other than for his jaw to

give a slight twitch. 'Our account is with Walkers at Fennybridge,' he said. 'You can't miss it. Take the top road over the moors, there's a huge millstone with the word *Fennybridge* chiselled into it and immediately after that, a sign for Walkers Farm. Just sign the docket and they'll load it in for you.'

'Righty-o,' said Viv then she went into the office to check the morning's emails. She opened the window to let the scents of the garden in. It looked as if hundreds more love-in-a-mist had sprung up overnight and she breathed in the delicate scent and felt blessed for the gift that made her so receptive to it. It was a gorgeous sunny day. On days like that, at uni, she and Hugo would laze in the grass quad and they'd bitch about lecturers and just talk about anything from *EastEnders* plots to the end of the world. He'd question her motives for picking a history degree which would be absolutely no use to her at all when she planned to make her fortune from her nose, he said. She'd argue back that she liked history, and if ever her amazing sense of smell dried up, she could always teach it. He could be pushy and though she knew he had her best interests at heart she wasn't as intent on world domination as he was. She missed seeing him every day. He wanted her to move down to London. She had decided that she might take him up on it when she was done here.

A ping announcing the arrival of an email made her snap out of her daydream. It was from a bird sanctuary in Suffolk who were interested in 'procuring the snowy owl'. *Procure* sounded such a cold word. Viv looked the sanctuary up. They seemed respectable enough, but would Ursula take to anyone there? What if they gave up on her straight away and didn't persevere like they had done here? Heath and

Geraldine would have kept trying with her, even though they'd never had a bird so unresponsive to them before.

Viv, you really have to back off here, girl, she said to herself. She couldn't afford to get attached to the animals. Or the birds. She had her own small business that she wanted to develop and her plan was to earn enough money to have her own dedicated laboratory. She loved mixing oils; she had never even considered another profession after she found she could get paid for it.

She'd convinced her regular clients that she could provide them with good service, something that was going to go quickly down the pan if she didn't find some time to fulfil the orders she had on her books. One company – The Little Candle Company which, despite its name, was a massive organisation – had sent her an email that morning asking her to come up with an essence of summer garden. Geraldine's perfume would have been perfect for that. If only she could work out what was missing from the mix.

Viv told the Suffolk people that she'd be in touch. She'd find Ursula a place that didn't use words like 'procure'.

Viv mentioned the bird place in Suffolk to Heath later when they were putting the animals away for the night. She told him that they were interested in 'procuring the Snowy'.

'Procuring?' he asked and muttered something like 'over my dead body' and that was all he said on the matter.

Viv took Pilot for a short walk up the hill after all the animals had been tended to. It was a beautiful evening. The full moon sat in a velvety blur of different blues sandwiched with Turkish Delight pink. There was a warm breeze in the air that had ruffled through the thousands of love-in-a-mist flowers. Viv sucked it into her lungs and knew that

she would mix this before she went to bed and call it
Summer Moon. She knew her customers and Jeckson and de
Vere would love it. They paid good money to a short freak
with an oversensitive nose, she chuckled to herself. She
might have had a childhood full of too many hospital
appointments but she was certain that whatever had gone
wrong in her mother's womb and caused her twisted spine
had also given her payback in the form of her enhanced
senses. It would earn her a fortune over the course of her
life. She might even end up in that glossy magazine herself,
seated on a buttoned sofa; a narrative running underneath
the photo about how rich and accomplished she was. Just
like one of the Leighton girls.

Chapter 43

The next morning Viv found herself sitting in Ursula's aviary doing nothing but holding out a piece of meat.

'Are you sure you want me to do this?' she asked Heath. 'I feel a bit guilty doing nothing whilst you're cleaning out the cages.'

'It's important,' said Heath, as he tended to James, the great grey owl who had a huge round moon of a face. 'And don't worry, if you feel guilty you can turn over the compost heap later on. I wouldn't want you to feel as if you were missing out.'

'Why don't you ask Nicholas Leighton if he'll build you a new sanctuary?' asked Viv.

Heath stared at her as if she were mad. It was a look she was getting used to seeing.

'That way all the animals would stay together, wouldn't they?'

'You don't get it, do you?' said Heath. 'He wouldn't give us a penny more than he has to. His "people" offered to help find the animals new homes – which I obviously refused to let them do because how can those corporate ... *idiots* be trusted – but if you think he'd build a whole sanctuary for us, then you're ...' he rotated his finger at the side of his head. 'Besides, even – *even* – if he had a mental aberration and offered to do that, it still wouldn't be here, would it, *here* on this land where it should be.'

'So you didn't ask him?'

Heath gave a weary sigh.

'If you must know, yes I did ask.' His voice was tight and Viv could tell that it pained him to admit he had. It must have taken him a lot of effort to swallow that amount of pride.

'He said no, then?'

Heath gave her a look not unlike the look Ursula was accustomed to giving him. 'Surprisingly enough, Miss Blackbird, he did refuse.'

But you asked because you'd do anything to keep this place together, Viv said to him silently.

'He's very rich isn't he?' she asked him.

'Very.'

'Why would he want to build a housing estate here? You'd think he'd prefer this area to be quiet, wouldn't you?'

Heath blew out his cheeks. 'To answer your first question: because people who lived here would want things and he'd supply the shops and restaurants and make even more money. To answer the second question, the valley bowl is far enough away from his estate not to cause him a problem.'

'But what if —'

Heath was obviously tired of her questions. 'Look, Ursula isn't playing ball today so why don't you go and pick up the feed. I can finish off here by myself.'

She had broken her promise not to press him, so Viv didn't argue. She walked obediently back to the cottage, changed out of her wellies and into her ankle boots and set off in the pick-up.

It was a lovely drive on the top road. Even flooded in sunshine, the moors looked bleak, mysterious and full of secrets. In August they would be a sea of purple heather, but she would be long gone then. And so would Wildflower Cottage.

A pheasant ran across the road, cutting off her train of thought. Viv stamped on the brake and the vehicle lost control, stopping just short of a ditch. Her heart jumped into her mouth. *Concentrate, concentrate*, she snapped at herself. She needed to clear her mind of everything but driving. Which was easier said than done.

She picked up the feed and headed back, but decided to call in at Mawton en route. She pulled into the car park near St Francis Church, as she had done last time she was here, and walked down the main street, intending to have a sandwich at the café, but it was full. They did have a selection of takeaway sandwiches for sale though, so she bought an egg mayo, a bottle of fizzy orange and looked for somewhere to sit and eat it in the sunshine. Some people were sitting in the pretty grounds of the church: a man in a suit tearing into a baguette, two old ladies sharing a flask of tea. She walked past them and sat at the next available bench, which was tucked away in a corner out of the way. She unwrapped her lunch and began to eat it. Gentle scents drifted to her on the fluttery breeze: freesias, violets, sweet peas. She tilted her head back and let the sun warm her face. It felt as if it was leaning down close to her, holding her cheeks in its hands and, like a caring parent, was telling her that everything was

going to be all right. Her mind emptied of all but the feeling
of heat on her skin and she could easily have drifted off to
sleep. A breeze stirred its fingers in her hair and wafted more
floral perfume towards her, this time a dense rich scent
which she recognised immediately: grand prix roses. Huge
velvet-headed roses with tightly packed petals that pulsed
out a bouquet of myrrh, musk and wild fruits with a dis-
tinctive shadowy note of spices. Viv pulled it into her
nostrils as if she were savouring the breath of a rich, deep
wine.

As she stood to go, the scent of the roses drew her, chal-
lenging her to find them. She walked steadily down the
path, trying not to look like a bloodhound on a quest. She'd
walked too far, the scent had dissolved; she turned back and
it was there again. Forwards now, leaving the path, passing
ranks of stones until she saw them three rows up, five across:
tied in a bunch, their perfect blood-red petals facing the tall,
grey headstone, bright against the darkest green leaves, their
long stems laying across the heart of the person who lay
beneath. Viv had impressed herself being able to pick them
out from so far away. *In Loving Memory of Emily Sowerbridge,
Precious wife.* Viv looked at the dates and worked out that
Emily had died on her seventieth birthday. Today she would
have been eighty. Hence the beautiful birthday roses with
the card amongst them in an old man's scratchy scrawl.
Emily. You are missed every day. What must it be like, thought
Viv, to meet someone who came into your life and never
left it, even after death separated you. She wondered if Heath
thought about Sarah or if Antonia Leighton had supplanted
her in his affections.

Viv strolled back to the path viewing the different-shaped
stones and reading the inscriptions. Some were very old,

dating back centuries, the writing weathered and barely readable. One had a cameo photo of a smiling old gent. The sight of a small, white stone carved into a heart pulled her to a halt. Apart from the dates of the incumbent's birth and death days, there were just four words:

SARAH BERNAL
BELOVED DAUGHTER

She died aged twenty-five, four years ago. Was this another Sarah who had died at such a young age, or could this be Heath's wife? But if it was, why wasn't it her married name that had been chiselled into the stone?

Viv's brain started to spin with the intrigue of it all. Heath, Geraldine, the animals ... she had to stop them slipping into her heart when she wasn't looking and making her care about them. Because she had the potential to be their worst enemy of all.

Chapter 44

Stel buzzed around cleaning the already immaculate house. She was so jittery about the evening to come that she had to use up all the adrenalin-fuelled nervous energy or she would have exploded. Then she changed outfits four times because her jeans looked too casual, her dress looked too dressy, her trousers made her bum look big – leggings and long top it was then; flat shoes, hair up and dangly earrings. She gave herself an appraisal in the mirror and wondered if she should have chosen the jeans ensemble instead, but time was moving on.

The pasta was ready for the oven, the table was set, she had decanted a bottle of Merlot like a proper wine buff. She'd even dropped an old penny in the bottom because she'd read at the weekend in the *Sunday World* supplement that it made it taste more expensive. Then she sat on the sofa and waited and wished she had never invited Ian Robson to her house. She was so tense that an evening in her pyjamas watching an old *Columbo* seemed a much more sensible idea.

She thought she heard a car and jumped to her feet. She

opened the front door and peeked out to see Al from next door walking up his path, holding his biker's helmet in his hand. He'd had a mid-life crisis and bought himself a Harley Davison. Mid-life suited him though – he'd never been as happy, as well-off, or as fit.

'Hello Stel,' he smiled, but then Al was always smiling. Ever since he ditched that bitch of a wife anyway.

'Hello Al,' she smiled back.

He sniffed. 'Not half a nice smell coming from your house. You cooking me dinner?'

'I've got a date,' bubbled Stel, with a childish giggle.

'Have you? Well, good for you, pet. Hope he's treating you well.'

'He is,' she nodded.

'He's a lucky fella. I hope he knows that. You look lovely, all sparkly.'

Stel was just about to say that he didn't look bad either. He was dressed in his biker's leathers and he wore them well. She wondered if he'd ever thought, when he was sitting in their front room eating fish finger sandwiches and trying his best not to appear as if he hadn't eaten for a week, that one day he'd own his own business, live in a lovely house and ride around on a piece of metal that would have grown men crying with envy. But he started talking again.

'I'm glad I've seen you, Stel, because there's something I probably should mention ...'

Then Ian's car drew up and Stel cut him off. 'Oh, he's here. Sorry, Al, you were saying?'

'Ah, it's nothing. There's your man,' he said as Ian got out of the car. 'I hope you've got a good one this time, Stel.'

'I hope so too,' replied Stel. 'You know me though, Al, too much of a dreamer. I've stopped waiting for that knight in shining armour to come riding up the road on his white steed.'

'Well, you shouldn't have. If you aim low, that's what you get. As you know only too well.'

Inside, Stel cringed a little with embarrassment that Al knew so much about her shit love-life. He'd seen off one of her dates a few years ago when he arrived drunk as a skunk at the door demanding that she let him in. But she never felt as if he judged her, though she suspected he might have fondly despaired of her a few times.

Ian walked towards her carrying a bunch of pink flowers and a carrier bag in one hand and a jacket over the other arm. He was wearing a smile of greeting, but, had Stel been looking at a photograph of him at that moment, the caption underneath would have read: 'what is wrong with this smile?'

'Hello mate,' said Al, pulling off his leather glove and extending a big paw. 'Nice to meet you I'm Al, Stel's neighbour.'

Ian's hand came out but slowly, dragged into position by politeness. 'Hello,' he returned, his tone flat.

If Al noticed that, he didn't show it. 'Have a good night, you two,' he said, slipping his key into the lock and pushing open his door. 'Don't do anything I wouldn't.'

'Can I take your jacket?' asked Stel, once they were in the house. She was trying to stay calm but failing. There was an awkward interchange as Ian passed over the flowers just as Stel was reaching for his coat. They both laughed and when the coat was hung up and Stel had cooed over the flowers, she led him through to the kitchen.

'It looks bigger than the last time I was here,' said Ian, looking around. 'Oh, there's my friend. Hi Boris.'

'Basil,' corrected Stel, as Ian bent down to give Basil a

stroke, though Basil darted off out of the room and up the stairs.

'He's a grumpy old sod,' said Stel, excusing him and then she felt a little ashamed of herself for lying, as if Basil could hear her, because he wasn't really.

'He probably remembers me as that bloke who threw his coat over him trying to catch him,' said Ian, taking four bottles of wine out of the carrier bag. 'Two red and two white. Do you think that will be enough?'

Stel trilled a laugh. *So he's brought his car but he's drinking. That means he's probably going to drive home in the morning.*

As if he heard the workings-out in her head he put out his hands as though to push those deductions back. 'Just in case you're wondering, I've brought the car because I don't like leaving it on my street if I'm not in. I'll get a taxi and come back for it in the morning.'

'No worries,' said Stel, feeling a pang of disappointment. 'Dinner will be ready in fifteen minutes.'

'Is that garlic bread I see?' asked Ian. 'Our breath is going to be nice and stinky then.'

Stel closed her eyes against her own stupidity. Just the very thing to cook when she was hoping for a snogging session. And there was loads of it in the pasta sauce too.

'What a total ...' Stel sighed. Ian chuckled and caught hold of her hand. A second later she was in his arms.

'We better have that kiss now then, hadn't we?' he said.

Stel gulped but didn't have time to say anything because Ian's lips were already descending. His gentle kiss made Stel feel light-headed and warm, young and desired.

Half an hour after they had eaten pasta, Stel was pulling him upstairs and neither of them seemed to care that they were engulfed in a fug of garlic.

Chapter 45

Stel drifted back to consciousness after a wonderful, satisfying night's sleep, to find Ian propped up on the pillow, studying her. She was horrified.

'Don't look at my morning face,' she said, covering it up with both hands. She hoped he hadn't been staring at her for long and seen her snoring or slavering out of the corner of her mouth. She dabbed it to check if it was damp and found, to her relief, that it wasn't.

'Don't be silly,' said Ian, peeling her fingers away. 'You're lovely. I actually like you better *au naturel.*'

'You should get yourself to Specsavers,' replied Stel with a dry chuckle.

'No, I shouldn't. You've got beautiful skin, why would you want to cover it in disgusting gunk,' he said, stroking her cheek gently with a crooked finger. 'And your lips are lovely and naturally pink.' He leaned over and kissed them softly. 'Let me tell you, women look a lot more attractive with natural eyelashes than with big clumps of mascara stuck on them. Women like men to be as they are, but yet men aren't allowed to think the same, are they?'

Stel opened her mouth to say that she couldn't even bear to look at herself in a mirror without make-up on, never mind go outside and show her face to the world. People would think Halloween had come early.

'Tell me, would you prefer George Clooney with his natural hair or dyed dark brown?'

Well, that was easily answered. 'But he's a man,' said Stel. 'You lot can get away with the natural look.'

'Okay then, imagine Judi Dench with Chelsea eyebrows and bright red lips.'

'Yeah, but she wouldn't go to those measures, would she? She might just use a bit of enhancement; so you hardly notice.'

'So then what's the point?'

He had her there. She opened her mouth to argue back but couldn't.

Ian stroked her hair back from her face. 'How pretty you are,' he said. 'I'm going to make you a cup of coffee and bring it up for you.'

'Oh.' Stel's gasp was in proportion to a declaration that he had bought her Elizabeth Taylor's big diamond. But it was a big deal for her because no man that Stella Blackbird had ever been out with had brought her a cup of coffee up to bed. It was one of those small considerations that her ideal man would afford her.

He hopped out of bed with enviable confidence in his nudity and Stel saw again the scar on his side where he'd had the knife wound when he'd been in the army. She also saw his little flat bum and wished she hadn't. What was wrong with her? Why, after a lovely night with an attentive man – and he had made sure she had been more than satisfied – was she being so judgemental?

Hearing him pottering about downstairs, Stel sneaked across to her dressing table and opened the curtains slightly for some light. She looked at herself in the mirror and knew that there was no way she could go out in public without make-up. She would rather not wear knickers. But, she supposed she could tone it down a bit. She had worn bright lipstick for thirty years, maybe it was time for the subtle fairy to wave her wand over her make-up bag.

*

As Viv was driving back from replenishing stocks of teabags and milk at the village shop, something pink darted across the road ahead of her. Intrigued, she pulled up, got out of her car and tried to spot where it had gone, and what it was. She saw it almost immediately; it was some sort of animal, resting in the long grass that grew against the fence. Viv approached it tentatively and it pressed deeper into the foliage. She wasn't an expert on British wildlife but she was pretty sure none of it was pink. And it was too small to be a disorientated baby flamingo, if indeed the things flew. Whatever it was, was now trapped between the fence and her presence. Viv leaned over and moved aside the grass coverage. It was a rat, a giant rat. She stepped back and squeaked in horror. But it wasn't the right shape for a rat, it was like a furry ball. Its mouth was twitching. Viv bent down and saw that it was a small rabbit, with no ears. A straight line crusted with blood traversed where they should have been. Someone had cut this little bunny's ears off and sprayed him bright pink.

Viv didn't know what to do. She couldn't leave him there, but she couldn't pick him up either. *Well, you'll have to do one or the other,* she said to herself. She peeled off her cardigan, aware that her heart had quickened in pace. She really wasn't looking forward to this at all.

'Come on, Viv Blackbird, you can do this.' She danced on the spot as if she were gearing herself up for the starting blocks of an Olympic sprint. She'd had a psychotic owl's claw in her hand. This should be a doddle. *One-two-three.* She threw the cardigan over the rabbit and scooped the animal up. It wriggled furiously in her arms and she fought against the urge to drop it. She held on with one hand, opened her boot with the other, and placed it in. Then she shut the lid quickly. Her whole body was shaking.

She floored the accelerator down the drive and flew into the cottage kitchen. Geraldine was up, dressed in one of her floaty frocks and was at the sink, washing up. Heath was just ending a call, probably to the bank because Viv heard his last words just before he slammed the old phone back down on its cradle: 'Why don't you shove your temporary over-draft facility up your arse.'

'Heath, I've got an injured rabbit in my car,' said Viv quickly. 'I found it down by the gate. I think someone's cut its ears off.'

Heath followed her out. Viv opened the boot carefully and there she saw the creature properly for the first time, sitting in the wrap of her cardigan, its little white body cruelly dyed with something that made its fur stiff and matted. It was shaking so much it looked as if it were sitting on a power plate.

'Bastards,' he said. 'People are bastards.' Then, as he leaned over to pick the rabbit up, his voice changed imme-diately to a calm, low tone. 'Come here little fella. That's it, nothing to be scared of.' Viv watched his long fingers close around the rabbit's body and it didn't attempt to struggle as he picked it up and placed it next to his chest, talking to it all the while.

'Oh no, who the hell would do such a thing?' Geraldine moved out of the doorway to let them in. She limped over to the table. She was close to tears, but Viv was closer.

Heath gave the rabbit a careful check over. 'He's an unneutered male, hard to tell the age but I'd guess not very old. He's very thin and these ears have been cut off with scissors or a knife. This isn't an injury from another animal,' said Heath. 'This has been done in the last couple of days, by the look of things. How nice of them to dump him and let nature finish him off.'

'Or he's come to us because he's meant to,' put in Geraldine. 'Animals gravitate towards those that have a home and a heart for them. And so do people around here. It's not as if it's an uncommon occurrence in Ironmist, is it?'

She reached behind her to the dresser drawer and pulled out a camera.

'We'll take some pictures for the police,' Geraldine explained to Viv. 'Not that they have any chance of catching whoever did this. And even if they were prosecuted, they'd get a slap on the wrist. Oh, I hate this world sometimes.'

'What the hell will happen when we're not here, eh, Gerry?' said Heath, soothing the little bunny with strokes and soft sounds.

'Don't talk like that, Heath,' Geraldine replied. 'Just don't.'

'I think I'm going to have to sedate and shave him when he's a little stronger. We don't want him swallowing that stuff. But we need to get some fluids into him. Viv, can you do as much as you can with the outside animals?'

'Yes of course,' said Viv. Heath had switched into vet mode, Geraldine into the role of his assistant, one she had played so many times and was at ease with, and would miss with her whole heart. She slipped off her shoes and threaded her feet into her flower-patterned wellies.

'Viv.' Heath's voice arrested her first steps towards the door. 'Thank you.'

'No worries,' she said. She didn't ask him what precise thing he was thanking her for. It didn't matter.

*

When Stel walked into work that day, Maria did a double-take. Stel with toned down make-up? Was she ill?

'I know what you're going to say,' said Stel, holding up her hand in a silencing gesture. 'I've just decided to start acting my age a bit more.'

'What do you mean?' asked Maria. 'Did you ever see photos of Barbara Cartland? She had full slap on always.'

'Precisely,' said Stel, taking off her jacket and hanging it up on the coatstand. 'And how bloody ridiculous did she look with Towie eyelashes at her age.'

'Whose mad idea was this?' asked Maria, resting her bosom on her crossed arms.

'Mine, of course,' Stel replied. 'I haven't quite gone bare yet, I've got a light covering of foundation on and a bit of mascara, but think of all the time I'll save in the mornings not having to tart myself up. Not to mention the expense. My lipsticks are twenty quid each. You'll get used to the new me in no time.'

'Well, as long as you don't expect me to join you,' said

Maria. 'I've got a complexion not unlike corned beef. If I didn't wear make-up, this building would empty of people because they'd be running into the streets screaming.'

Stel chuckled. Then she caught sight of her reflection in the window and thought she looked like a ghost. Still, Ian would be pleased that she'd made the effort for him. And that's all that mattered.

Chapter 46

Iris had told Linda that she was catching the bus into town to go to the library. She had lied. Iris wasn't disposed to fibbing, seeing as she found most of her fun in telling the truth, but on this occasion, she thought it best to be economical with the facts.

She put on her confused-old-lady act at the bus station. It worked and the bus driver escorted her to the 367 to Maplehill. She then asked the driver of the 367 where she would need to get off for Tennyson Lane and he assured her that he would shout up when it was her stop.

He was good as his word. He even pointed out the bus stop where she should get back on and informed her that they ran every twenty minutes. Iris gave him her best daft-old-biddy grateful smile and got off the bus ten houses down from her destination.

Before knocking on the door, she peeped in the front window. The house was open-plan and the lounge at the front was empty, but she could see Enid Pawson in the kitchen beyond. Iris opened the tall gate that guarded the back of the house as quietly as possible so as not to announce her arrival and stole down the path. She halted before she turned the corner to look with disgust at the ridiculous garden with its ugly bushes clipped, very badly, into various animal shapes. There was a pair of armless romantic nude statues covered in moss and gnomes nestling in amongst plants everywhere. The Pawsons thought they lived in bloody Downton Abbey by the look of things. Tackiest of all was the huge pond complete with a central island where an enormous gnome stood open-mouthed spewing water, pumped up through the middle of him, onto the backs of the Koi carp below. The vomiting gnome was holding a jailer's bunch of metal keys in one hand and a stone heart in the other with a keyhole carved out of it. *Who in their right minds would have that monstrosity in their garden*, thought Iris. Well, she'd answered her own question there.

She's seen enough, it was time for action. With steel in her spine, she turned the corner and rapped on the large glass French door as a matter of courtesy, because it was ajar, then she walked straight into the kitchen.

'Enid. I thought it was time we, as matriarchs, had a little chat. All right to come in?'

Enid Pawson was wrong-footed. It was easier to agree than to disagree so she shrugged and said, 'Well, you are in, aren't you?' Even if she wasn't best pleased about it.

Iris noticed immediately that Enid had placed herself between Iris and the worktop, blocking her view of what stood on it. Not much got past Iris though. But even if she hadn't seen Enid turn quickly and smuggle the bottle of gin from the worksurface into the cupboard below, she could still smell the perfumed chemical smell hanging around her.

'I'm not stopping so no need to put on the kettle,' said Iris, which made Enid's drawn-on eyebrows shoot up her forehead because she'd had no intention of doing that anyway. Iris pulled out a chair and sat at the smoked-glass dining table. It was all very stylish and cold, she thought. And the glass table had sharp pronounced edges. Not that child-friendly for a three-year-old boy.

'I've come to talk to you about Freddie.'

Enid wasn't going to join Iris at the table, it seemed. She stood leaning against the worksurface, arms folded across her skinny chest.

'What about him?'

'Have you ever stopped to think what you would feel like if you were denied seeing your only grandchild?'

Enid's mouth held fast to the cat's-arse-like pout on her lips.

'You're not being denied.'

'Who are you trying to kid, Enid? Because it's certainly not us and you can't honestly believe that the present set-up is fair.'

'It's what the law says.'

'No, the law said that Rebecca could change the arrangement in our favour at any time. Wouldn't it make it easier on everyone if she did? You and I both know that in court she made Andy look like something he most definitely isn't. Was that really fair?'

'It's none of my business.'

Iris was fast losing patience. 'Of course it's your business. And it's ours. That bairn is as much our flesh and blood as it is yours. We want to spend time with him. I want to spend time with him before it's too late. You're robbing him of memories.'

'You should be talking to Rebecca about this, not me.'

Iris wanted to slap that tight little moue of smugness off her face.

'You know as well as I do that Rebecca won't discuss it. I was hoping you would talk to her. As a fellow grand-mother. As someone with some perspective on the matter, a bit of wisdom and sense. Ha!'

'Rebecca doesn't trust Freddie with his father.'

Explosions started to go off in Iris's head. It took every bit of effort she had to keep her tone level as she asked, 'Why?'

'You hear these stories, don't you, our Rebecca says. Men kidnapping their kids and running off to Palestine.'

Iris's eyebrows Mexican-waved across her forehead as the brain inside tried to compute this and failed. She tried to sound puzzled rather than sarcastic and failed on that front too.

'You think Andy will run off to Palestine with Freddie?'

'You hear stories.'

'Usually when the father is from Palestine. Andy's from South Yorkshire. He's a decorated soldier. Why the hell would he run off anywhere?'

'Revenge.'

There was a large pepper grinder on the dining table. Iris had a sudden image of herself bludgeoning this stupid woman to death with it. She rubbed her temple with her fingers.

'Look, Enid, you know perfectly well that Andy isn't going to run off anywhere. He wants to be able to take his son off for the day, to the seaside. He wants Linda and Dino to put him to sleep in the bedroom they've decorated for him. Dino's painted jellyfish all over it. And spaceships. You should see it, it's like the Sistine Chapel for boys. We just want to have some precious time with *our* little lad.'

'He's not *your* little lad though, is he? He's ours.' As Iris watched that puckered-up little mouth change shape into a thin-lipped sneer, the brake on her mouth which she had tried so hard to keep wedged on snapped.

'He won't belong to either of us if you get pissed on gin and let him drown in that bloody fish pond, will he?' Iris pointed to the glass door leading out to Enid's garden with the dreaded uncovered pond in it.

'I beg your pardon?' Enid's mouth now fell open in a long O of indignation.

'You stink of bloody gin,' accused Iris. 'You hid the bottle as soon as I walked in. I saw you. You and your snooty-knick-ered daughter talk about us running off with a little boy to the Middle East, well, let me tell you he'd still be safer with us in the middle of Beirut High Street than he is here with you.'

Iris knew that she would be told to leave as soon as Enid could get a word in, so she stood up so that at least she could jump before she was pushed. 'And I'll tell you this, Enid Pawson: if anything, *anything*, happens to that child whilst he's in your care, I will personally swing for you. You aren't fit to look after a stuffed parrot. Gin-soaked with an uncov-ered pool ... Freddie would be safer with King Bloody Herod as a childminder.'

'Get—'

Iris cut short Enid's low growl. 'I'm going. But I warn you. No more Mr Nice-Guy. I'm reporting you to social services. And the police. If you want to box dirty, Mrs, then you better get your gloves out ready.'

Iris snatched up her handbag and walked as fast as her

arthritic knee would allow her. She didn't want the adrenaline flooding through her to stop because it was blotting out everything but her fury at the Pawson Two. Once it subsided, she would realise what she had done. Linda was probably going to put her on the first plane to Palestine.

Chapter 47

Stel looked through the window to check if Ian had arrived yet. This time there was no doubt that he would be staying the night because they'd had a cheeky kiss in the hospice garden at lunchtime and he'd asked if he could come over that night, with fish and chips, and he'd cook her breakfast the next morning. He'd also said that she looked so much better without 'all that gunge' on her face.

And, 'Next stop you need to sort out your wardrobe.'

She'd replied to that with a laugh of confusion.

'What do you mean?' she'd asked, thinking that it was a bit harsh for a joke, and he'd rubbed his mouth with embarrassment.

'Stel, I am so sorry, I shouldn't have said anything.'

But he had, and she needed to know what he meant. She looked down at herself and wondered what was so wrong with her black trousers and blue shirt ensemble.

'It's just that ... no, no, ignore me ...' he had said, but she'd pressed until he answered.

'Okay, on the line, I just like to see women in skirts, that's all. You've got a cracking figure and you cover it up.'

She'd hooted with laughter then. 'Cracking figure? Me? Don't be so ridiculous.'

'Don't laugh at me,' he'd said and just for a second, a split second, before his smile broke out, Stel's sensors picked up something that flashed the briefest amber alert.

'Look, forgive me. What do I know about women's fashions, eh? I'm a leg man – I can't lie.' He held out his arms at the side of him, a gesture of *what you see is what you get.* 'And a bum man and a breast man,' he carried on and she giggled. Then he kissed her and said he would see her at about seven and she grinned all the way through the afternoon.

Now she was standing by the window in a skirt and a V-necked top, peeping from behind the curtain and watching him get out of the car. Al from next door had pulled up on his bike and raised his hand in greeting. Stel saw Ian walk towards Al and talk to him. That was sweet, she thought. Friendly. They must have been talking about her because Ian thumbed backwards towards the house. He isn't letting Al get much of a word in, she thought. She backed away from the window in case they saw her spying, and she checked her face in the mirror. She thought she looked bloody awful without make-up.

'Hello, hello,' called Ian, letting himself in through the front door. 'Delivery for Miss Blackbird.'

'Oh lovely,' said Stel, feeling her cheeks colour as Ian took in her outfit and mouthed the word 'wow.'

'Come through.' She bashfully kissed him on the cheek before teetering down the hallway in her heels, letting her bottom swing a little. She did feel quite sexy, especially as he obviously approved of what she was wearing.

'I saw you talking to Al,' said Stel.

'Yeah, we just said hello,' replied Ian, opening up the

parcel of fish and chips. 'He was asking me how we were getting on and I told him that things were getting pretty serious.'

Serious, after a week? thought Stel, though that was immediately replaced by a rush of excitement. *A whirlwind romance.* How could that fail to make her feel special.

'What did Al say to that?'

'Just good luck,' replied Ian. 'Anyway, I don't want to talk about your fat neighbour, Stel. Come on, lass, chop chop. Get the cutlery out.'

Stel scurried to the cutlery drawer, cursing herself for not having it ready. Al wasn't fat, but something stopped her making the point. She wouldn't like it if he started talking about Minging Meredith, would she? *Minging Meredith.* She'd given her a derogatory nickname because a little part of her was jealous. Meredith was blousy and blonde, curvy and confident and all too aware of the effect that she had on men. That's why Ian had called Al fat. He was jealous. Stel sighed. Ian was falling for her. She'd given up hope of that ever happening to her again.

Chapter 48

'Geraldine, will you please sit down and rest,' said Heath, watching Geraldine attempting to wash up. 'You're a nightmare. Do as you are told.'

'Oh Heath, I'm not used to doing nothing. There must be some way I can help,' said Geraldine, conceding. Her bones must be knitting together, as her mother always said, because that was when things became painful. Her hand was especially tender today. Her leg just felt tight, although when she positioned it right, she gained some respite, but her hand ached constantly.

'Let me make you a cup of tea,' said Heath. 'And you can look through the new feed catalogue. You can work out how much their prices have gone up for me. Will that make you feel better?'

'Lots,' said Geraldine, brightening immediately.

She watched him as he strode across the kitchen with the kettle. If she'd ever been lucky enough to have a son, she would have wanted one just like Heath Merlo: a hard-working, honourable lad with solid values and a good heart that she thought sometimes beat for everyone but himself. It crippled her to think of him wrenched from this place, the house he grew up in. Like her he would be lost, floundering. He'd get by because he'd have to but it wouldn't be the same. How could it be? Wildflower Cottage was built on land protected and watched over by spirits. It was special.

Heath put the kettle down on the Aga and sat at the table with Geraldine. He slumped into the chair as if bowed down by all the weight on his shoulders. Geraldine could have cried for him.

'Why did you choose Viv, Gerry?' he said, as if he had been pondering the question for some time.

'She answered the ad I placed in the paper. We weren't exactly snowed under with applicants,' Geraldine chuckled.

'Why her?' he pressed.

The smile faded from Geraldine's mouth 'Blackbirds,' she replied.

Heath shook his head. He'd expected no less ridiculous an answer. Something ethereal and airy-fairy. 'Blackbirds,' he repeated.

'Serendipity. She was a Blackbird and your name means blackbird. It was a connection I couldn't ignore.'

Heath gave her an indulgent grin.

'You can look at me like that all you like, Heath Merlo, but blackbirds are a symbol of determination and also gentleness. They are a good bird to associate yourself with in times of trouble. I think I made a good choice. We need all the spiritual help we can get.'

'I wish I had your faith, Geraldine,' he said.

'I won't give up hope, Heath,' she replied. 'I've always believed in old magic and forces of nature. Isme has never left this place, and she never will.'

Heath crossed to the sink to retrieve two cups from the draining board. Through the window, he spotted Viv walking towards the cottage carrying a basket of eggs. Pilot was strolling alongside her. There was a thicker than usual ground mist today and they appeared to be floating towards the cottage. The sun was high in the sky and pouring its light over the valley, picking out the golden threads in Viv's hair. She looked like one of Geraldine's faery folk.

She was a strange one with her fascination for scents and smells and her ridiculous fear of animals, thought Heath. Not someone he himself would have chosen to work in a sanctuary had he been the one doing the telephone interviewing. Then again, how much bravery had it taken her to capture the poor pink-painted rabbit. And then there was the connection she had with Ursula. The stroppy, bad-tempered snowy owl had chosen Viv to extend the claw of friendship to. He couldn't ignore the intuition of animals. He only wished he'd been blessed with the same gift.

Geraldine watched him staring out of the window: whatever he was thinking about was making him smile. She hadn't seen his features soften like that in a long time.

Chapter 49

The next day Viv cleaned all the aviaries out single-handed because Heath had taken Geraldine to the hospital for her check-up. And she'd even been in the feed store herself for the meat. She'd retched a bit but she'd done it.

It was the first time she had been properly up close and personal with Frank the vulture but she steeled herself before going in. Vultures were dominant – even playful Frank – so she needed to stand her ground and show him that she *was* going to clean his aviary and he'd better behave. She imagined how Antonia snotty-cow Leighton would do it. Even if her insides were rotting with fear, Antonia wouldn't have let anyone see it.

I am a Leighton girl, I am a Leighton girl, Viv repeated to herself. She imagined that she had dark flowing locks and a minuscule bum. She imagined that she had long new-born-foal thin legs and she was so beautiful that Heath Merlot's pupils dilated when he looked at her. And then she realised that she had imagined too far because she was straying into dangerous territory.

What must it be like to have his arms around her, she

thought. What must it be like to breathe in the scent of his neck? What must it be like to know that she was on his mind? Well, if his type was Antonia Leighton, she would never get to find out because someone who liked skinny, leggy, dark-haired beauties was hardly likely to find her attractive.

Frank eyed her cautiously, but he was getting used to seeing her hanging around by now so he must have figured she passed muster. She moved slowly around his space, picking up his debris and, because there was no one around to hear her attempts, she made soft clucking noises which she hoped weren't vulture for 'Let's fight.' He pulled on the hosepipe whilst she was using it and it shot out of her hand and sprayed on them both before she picked it back up. Viv chuckled. He was playing with her.

She left Ursula till last. There was no hesitation on her part now as she slid open the latch and walked into the snowy owl's aviary and was greeted with a soft *chuck chuck chuck*.

Viv hosed down the gravel, then took up position in the corner. She held out a rabbit's foot in her glove; Ursula would have to work for this one. It didn't take long for the hungry owl to be tempted. She flew down to the floor of the aviary on her gorgeous glider wings, not too close, then walked tentatively towards the food as if she was playing Grandmother's Footsteps. Then Viv held tight as the bird started tugging on the meat. Ursula had a claw on her glove to get purchase on the snack. Then she placed the other one on it too. Viv lifted her hand ever so slightly to feel the weight of her. She was a fine lump of owl. Viv adjusted her position causing Ursula to fly off, but it didn't matter because this was a game of little steps, for both of them. She was learning to trust Ursula just as Ursula was learning to trust her.

Chapter 50

It was Saturday before Hugo rang Viv. She had slept through her alarm due to go off at eight, and his call dragged her from the pit of an exhausted sleep at half-past.

'Didn't wake you did I, Viv darling?' he said. 'You sound a bit groggy.'

'Yes you did,' she replied, 'but that's okay because I've overslept.'

'Overslept on a Saturday?'

'It's all hands on deck. We're a man down,' explained Viv. 'Anyway, how was Iceland?'

'Oh. My. God,' began Hugo with drama. 'You have to go and swim in the Blue Lagoon. It's a must. We went whale watching and saw geysers and the Northern Lights. I thought we would be there too late for those but they honoured us. The scenery was fabulous and Icelandic men . . . oh so sexy. I have to go again. Next time you must come with us. I want to know what the Northern Lights smell like.'

Viv chuckled, but she could feel a nervous tension creeping up on her.

'Darling, I just thought I'd ring and tell you that I'm back at work on Tuesday. I checked at the lab to see if your parcel had arrived and it has.'

'Good.' *Or was it.*

'So how's life with you?' asked Hugo. 'Have you made contact with Nicholas Leighton yet?'

Viv swallowed. 'Oh yes.'

'Fabulous. Tell me he's asked to see your business plans and thinks you should hook up with Chanel.'

'Well . . .'

'I tell you, this guy will be running the country in five years. It's totally fortuitous that he happens to live in the same place that you're staying.'

Hugo would be very disappointed in her when she told him that Nicholas Leighton had considered suing her for assault. He was about as likely to champion her as Wonk was to win the Grand National.

'I'm going to have a meeting with him soon,' said Viv, glad they weren't on Facetime and he could see her cringing.

'Oh my God, that is brilliant. Well done you.'

'Thanks.' She'd burst his hope-filled bubble later. But for now, blissful ignorance would be best. 'So, how long do you think it'll take to . . .'

'A few days. I'll keep you totally up to speed. Promise.'

'Thank you.'

'Then it's up to you, my lovely.' She could hear his swallow at the end of the phone. 'Look, Viv, I am so sorry if I pressurised you into this. I was thinking about you on the plane. What would have been right for me might not necessarily be good for you.'

'No, it's what I want,' Viv said. And she had wanted it. Now she wasn't so sure. 'Talk soon, eh?'

Hugo blew her a kiss down the line. 'And good luck with Nicholas Leighton. Let me know the moment you come out of the meeting. I bet he tells you to get your sweet arse down to London. I'll have your room ready.'

Viv rested her phone on the table next to her bed where EBW, the knitted bee, sat upright and alert, looking at himself in the mirror opposite. Five years ago, when Viv first found the note with Elke Wilson's details written on it, she had gone to see her. Elke was seventy and retired by then, but she remembered clearly the baby who'd weighed as much as a bag of sugar, the tiny girl with the deformed spine who fought for her right to breathe and grow and survive. Elke Wilson had a huge part to play in why Viv was now living at Ironmist.

*

The rabbit was doing better than expected. He was in a hutch in the kitchen and eating hay as if he were in training for a Man vs Food competition. Most of his hair had had to be shaved off in case he groomed himself and ate the paint, but it didn't seem to be giving him a problem. Understandably though, he shied away from anyone touching his ears. Or lack of them. As expected, the police filed the case and liaised with the RSPCA but no one was holding their breath for a prosecution. Armstrong was back at work and loved the rabbit, whom he had named Jason Statham. Despite his large lumbering frame, Armstrong was incredibly gentle with small animals. The little fella was doing well and he wasn't at all perturbed when Piccolo squawked at him. Bub didn't deem a mere rabbit to be worthy of his interest and lovely old Pilot sniffed in the direction of the hutch every now and then, but that was the limit of his attention.

'Aren't you going back to see your mum this weekend, Viv?' asked Geraldine, as Viv rustled up an egg salad for their lunch.

Viv hadn't wanted to leave Geraldine in her incapacitated state, but there were also other reasons why she thought she'd stay at the sanctuary.

'I thought I'd give Mum some space. She has this new man in her life and he's taking her mind off me not being there,' Viv said. 'It'll do her good not to miss me so much.'

She had rung Stel the previous night to find that she was just waiting for Ian to arrive. They were having a takeaway and watching a film. She sounded as fizzed as a teenager and Viv was glad for her.

Geraldine smiled fondly at Viv. She'd lost a daughter many years ago. She should have left *him* then but she was caught up in something so dark she couldn't see any light to aim for. He'd taken away her chance to have a girl who might have grown up to be like Vivienne.

'What will you do if the sanctuary closes, Geraldine? Will you go home?' asked Viv, sprinkling some spring onions over her culinary creation.

'This is my home, Viv. I have no ties to anywhere but here.'

Viv didn't press her on what she might have to do if the bulldozers came trundling over the land. Geraldine was still clinging onto that eleventh-hour reprieve.

'Do you think you'll stay here, Viv? I bet this place doesn't feature in your long-term plans but I'd like to think it did.'

'My friend wants me to go and live in London.' Viv cut some hunks of bread. 'His parents have money and they've helped him buy a flat. He's offered me a room in it.'

'Oh Viv, I can't see you in the big city somehow,' said Geraldine, hobbling across to get the plates and cutlery. 'I lived in a town in my old life but I was always a country girl at heart. I don't know how I survived without the space and the quiet and the vast expanse of sky above me. Sometimes, when I'm up on the hill and look down across the valley, it's like the whole focus of the sun is on Wildflower Cottage. It's as if it's been here forever, and the building has risen up from the mists and is part of the land. That's why I know, *I know,* it will stay here.'

Viv brought the salad and bread over to the table. She didn't reply. She couldn't bring herself to puncture Geraldine's hopes, all invested in smoke.

'Oh that looks like a piece of artwork,' said Geraldine, viewing her plate.

'Ach, it's hardly Jamie Oliver.' Viv dismissed the praise.

'Don't bat back the compliment, young lady.' Geraldine wagged her fork.

'Well, thank you, then,' smiled Viv and sat down to eat.

'You were saying, about your friend in London. Will you go, do you think?' asked Geraldine.

'I don't know,' Viv replied. *I'm not sure what I do want any more.*

Later, as Geraldine watched Viv cleaning up the dishes, she wondered why she was really here, though she didn't say it. She'd had time to think about many things since her accident, Viv's presence here being one of them. Heath had been right when he said that if you pay peanuts, you get monkeys, but that's all they'd been able to afford, so it was inevitable what sort of people would be attracted to the job. Then along comes a sharp, accomplished young woman with initiative and drive and no real plausible excuse why she had applied for a job which was now breaking her back for nothing extra in her wage packet. Geraldine knew about running. *What was Viv running from?*

Chapter 51

Heath watched as Viv held up her glove near to the branch on which Ursula was sitting. She had food in her hand, but it was out of the owl's reach. Ursula leaned forward and nearly claimed it, so Viv inched back.

'Steady,' said Heath, advising from the sidelines. 'Don't go too far away. She needs to make just a little hop.'

They both watched in thrilled silence as Ursula's claw lifted as if she was working out the possibility of her hooking the meat with her foot, before deciding that was a ludicrous idea. Then she flew from the branch, landed on the glove, considered it too scary and returned to her branch.

'Did you see?' shrieked Viv, then clamped her right hand over her mouth. 'She came to me. Oh my God.' Viv felt as exhilarated as she did when the examiner told her she'd passed her driving test. More so. She was shaking. Heath could see the glove quivering.

'I never thought I'd see the day,' said Heath, standing with his hands on his hips, moving his head slowly and incredulously from side to side.

Heath laughed with her and at her, but kindly. She looked

ridiculous standing there grinning like a loon, wearing a glove that made her arm look like that of a Fiddler crab. She reminded him of someone, just for a moment, then it was gone before he could grab the name.

From what he could remember, his mother had long brown hair with streaks of sunshine and caramel. He would cry when she left and cry when she returned until he got used to the pain and it became part of him.

She blamed him for tying her to this place, he knew. The guilt at leaving him kept her springing back to this life that she hated. *Why were you born?* she had once screamed at him. Then she had kissed him and soothed him and said she was sorry but all the affection in the world couldn't erase the words; they had been branded onto his brain. He knew that this template of a relationship had damaged him, made him love women destined to hurt him because that was all he knew. Sarah had made him love her and then left him forever. Antonia was haughty, unlikable, manipulative but there was a time when he would have pushed aside their family enmities to quench their obvious thirst for each other and damn the consequences. It had just been a narrow window, but it disturbed him that it might have happened, that he had been so messed up that he would have allowed it.

So why was his heart warming to Viv Blackbird if it had no sense? She was infuriating with her thousands of questions, arrogant with her suggestions that she could really find something they hadn't tried to stop the closure of the sanctuary. And how idiotic was it to work in a place like this when you were afraid of animals? Not to mention that he often caught her lost in a moment when she was obviously smelling things, dissecting them in her head into a list of ingredients. Viv Blackbird was odd. But harmless. And

Heath didn't do harmless. It worried him that his heart knew something he didn't. That Viv Blackbird could hurt him.

'I think that'll do for today,' said Viv, cutting into his thoughts and taking off her glove. 'I'll feed her and then nip up the hill for some shopping. Anything you want me to pick up whilst I'm there?'

Generous, hard-working, she was too good to be true, thought Heath. Really she was. He couldn't help but be suspicious.

Viv rang her mum before she set off to Ironmist Stores. It made her happy that Stel had a smile in her voice. A smile that only a man could put there.

'Well, how's it going with Ian, then?' asked Viv, after she had assured her mum that she was fine, happy, well-fed and not overworked.

'Oh, it's wonderful,' gushed Stel. 'We get on so well. We like all the same things. We had a lovely meal at the Star of India last night, he chose for me like they do on those romantic films and it was perfect. He's even trimmed the privet in the garden to look like a snake.'

Viv stifled a giggle.

'No one has ever done anything like that for me before,' sighed Stel.

'Well, that's true,' grinned Viv.

Stel opened her mouth to tell Viv so much more, then held it back. She didn't want her daughter to think she had fallen head over heels so quickly, even though she had. She knew she had found her soul-mate; the big prize that had always eluded her. She'd thought that Darren had been *the one*, because they were so close that they could finish off each other's sentences. But he'd turned out to be more arse-hole than soul-mate.

It was only when Stel heard herself speaking aloud about how well suited Ian and she were together that she realised how many of her wants he met. She had told Ian about Darren, of course, and he'd been disgusted at how anyone could treat a woman with such disrespect. He told her that he would have looked after her, had he been her man at the time. His mother had had breast cancer years ago and he'd been there for her every step of the way. They both liked Indian and Chinese food, they liked the same type of films. They liked walks, drives in the countryside, lazy Sunday mornings and pub lunches. They liked cats and Greek holidays, even read the same newspaper. It was almost as if Ian Robson had been manufactured to a specification that Stel had supplied.

Chapter 52

'Jesus, Stel. Is it trick or treat night already?' Linda opened the door to the last-to-arrive Stel devoid of foundation, eye-shadow, extended lashes and that familiar red lipstick of hers.

'Oh cheers,' replied Stel with a disgruntled click of the tongue. 'Do I look *that* bad?'

Linda felt slightly guilty for her over-reaction then. 'No, don't be daft. It's just a ... a shock. I don't think I've ever seen you without the full slap on.'

Stel passed over two plates of sandwiches and small cakes. It was her turn to do the catering today. 'I thought I'd have a change. New man, new image. He likes me better like this.'

'Going well, is it?' asked Caro, thinking that Stel didn't look like Stel today, in her tight skirt, pin-heels and a pale, bare face.

'Wonderful,' grinned Stel.

'Well, I'm glad somebody's had a good week,' said Linda with a sigh and a very pointed sideways look at Iris, who was the picture of innocence as she sat on the sofa drinking tea.

'Sounds ominous,' Stel answered. 'What's up?'

'Ask Kofi bloody Nannan over there,' and Linda tilted her head towards her mother.

'What have you done then, Iris?' asked Caro, on tea-pouring duty.

Iris opened her mouth to speak, but Linda spoke over her. 'She took it on herself to go and see Enid Pawson. You can guess how it went if I tell you that we are now totally banned from even speaking to Freddie on the phone.'

'Oh, Linda.'

'She stunk of cheap gin,' snarled Iris. 'That woman and that bloody fish-pond and that giant vomiting concrete gnome combination is an accident waiting to happen. I thought I might be able to talk reason to her. Grandma to great-grandma.'

Every other woman in the room exchanged telling glances at the notion of Iris Caswell as a diplomatic force.

'Now, of course, we are totally knackered. Rebecca screamed at me down the phone. I've got a pile of presents ready for Freddie's birthday but she'd smash them and return them if I deliver them, she said.' Linda felt herself close to breaking-point, but she took a deep breath and pressed her hands down as if pushing on a physical plane of rising distress. 'I am not going to cry today, I am not going to cry today,' she recited, a mantra she was unfortunately too familiar with.

'I don't know what to say. Words fail me,' said Gaynor. 'The . . . the bitch.'

'I can't blame Mum for trying,' said Linda, sinking to the sofa. 'I think Mother Teresa would have ended up throwing C-words at the Pawsons if she was in our shoes. I think they actually enjoy the power trip. I just can't wait until Andy gets home.'

'Won't be long,' said Stel, reaching over to give Linda's hand a tender squeeze.

Linda allowed herself a further moment's sadness then shook her head. 'Look, I refuse to pull the mood down. Someone tell me something nice. Gaynor – anything good to report?'

'No.'

They all thought that Linda probably shouldn't have relied on Gaynor to lighten things up.

'These are lovely,' said Iris through a mouthful of tuna sandwich.

'I've got the magic touch,' chuckled Stel. 'I've switched to diet mayo though.'

'Good,' said Linda. 'I can't understand why I'm putting weight on but not eating any more than I usually do.'

'That's the menopause for you,' said Iris, reaching for a miniature pork pie. 'I went from a size twelve to having an arse the size of Russia in six months. I was all right once I cut out bread and potatoes. I lost it easily.'

'Thanks for not giving me your genes then,' tutted Linda. 'I'm built like Dad.'

'Your father had a very sweet tooth, Linda. I was never that bothered about cakes, although I am very partial to those macaroon things that look like little biscuits.'

'*Macarons*,' Gaynor corrected her with an over-egging of French accent that made them all want to giggle. They decided against it though as Gaynor was super-sensitive at the moment.

'I never had a sweet tooth before I hit the menopause,' said Stel. 'Now I could mainline chocolate for a living.'

'I hate the bloody menopause,' spat Gaynor. 'I'm sick of waking up at night and having to change the sheets; I'm sick of interrupted sleep; I'm sick of feeling on edge all the time.'

'And being so stiff after sitting down for a bit that you can't get up without making that *Ooof* sound,' chuckled Linda.

'And my memory has shrunk to the size of a peanut,' said Stel. 'I can't tell you how many times I've gone upstairs for something, forgotten what, had an automatic wee, come back downstairs and then remembered what I'd meant to do in the first place.'

Linda slapped her hands together. 'Sod tea, I'm having a vodka. Anyone care to join me?'

'Not for me, thanks,' said Gaynor.

'Count me right in,' said Caro. 'I'm stressed to hell today.'

'Here, Caro.' Linda got up to fetch a bottle of Grey Goose. 'What do you want in it – orange, tonic?'

'Another bloody vodka,' replied Caro. 'Eamonn has decided that the kitchen needs tiling and he's turned the house into a building site. He can't believe I'm moaning about it. Splash of tonic please, love. His idea of relaxing is to start renovating things. The man cannot sit still. He always has to be "doing".'

'They have no idea,' said Stel. 'Although I could have put up with that after having Darren, who listed his hobbies as stagnating and vegetating.'

'What about the new fella, Stel?' Caro gave her a wink.

'Totally the opposite. He's perfect,' Stel smiled.

'Thank God we have this group on a Sunday,' said Linda. 'I'd go mad without it. Dino drives me bonkers with his untidiness. He thinks he's faultless.'

'Tell me about it,' said Gaynor with a curled lip.

'Come on Gaynor, what did you hate about Mick?' said Stel, unsure whether she should ask, but then Gaynor would get the hump if she were left out.

Gaynor thought for a few moments before answering. 'He used to make a noise with everything he did. He'd chink ice in glasses, constantly crinkle newspapers when he was reading them, drop things. He couldn't do anything quietly. He couldn't shut doors, he had to slam them. And he couldn't whisper to save his life.'

So many things had annoyed her about Mick but they were everything she missed about him now. If he came back to her she'd never moan at him again. He could chink and crinkle and slam to his heart's content.

'Have a vodka, Gaynor,' urged Linda, and wouldn't take no for an answer. So Gaynor drank it and along with the men-bashing and buffet her pain was dulled for an hour or so and it galvanised her into thinking positively. She'd always felt Mick would come back, when he worked this temporary madness out of his system. She just wanted to touch his face and tell him that she loved him.

*

Viv was totally and utterly flaked out that night. Her eyelids felt as if there were lead weights tied to them, but she had decided that there was no way she was going to bed without finding the missing component of Geraldine's copy perfume. She made herself a strong coffee, which might give her half-an-hour's spark at best, and sat at her makeshift lab on the folly's dining table. She pulled the bung out of one of the test-tubes resting on the rack with the Geraldine's Perfume labels on them and inhaled. It was some sort of herb. Her mind scurried over the files of aromas stored in her head: *thyme, sage, basil* – no, all wrong.

Something caught her eye outside the window. It was the

bedding she had put out on the line to dry and had forgotten about. She downed tools to unpeg the sheets and bring them in. They'd been hanging up since the morning and were loaded with all the scents that the breezes had picked up. As Viv pressed her nose into them, a thousand-watt lightbulb switched on in her head. How stupid of her not to know. She'd fixated on that missing part being something far more complicated and exotic, but it was simply cut grass. She threw the sheets down on the sofa and opened up her box of phials. She had three cut-grass oils in her box, uncomplicated base scents made by people who had the same devotion to their jobs as herself. She chose the May grass: green fat blades plumped by sunshine and warm summer rain. And that was all it took, just two drops added to the mix and Geraldine's perfume had been replicated perfectly.

Chapter 53

As Gaynor was hunting for her keys the next morning, the postman slipped a letter through her door and it slid to the floor addressee upwards. Just what I bloody need to start off the week, she thought, recognising the solicitor's stamp at the top. She snatched it up, ripped it open and read it.

> *Dear Mrs Pollock*
> *Can you please contact us at your earliest convenience to discuss a matter of great urgency and delicacy.*
> *Your sincerely*
> *Edgar Leadbetter*

Well, there were no prizes for guessing what that was all about, Gaynor growled to herself. She'd changed her email address, home telephone and mobile numbers the previous week to make things even more awkward for Mick and his solicitor to bully her into signing the divorce papers. She could make a detour on her way to work, call in to Cripwell, Oliver and Clapham, Solicitors at Law, and give that snidey little shit Edgar Leadbetter a piece of her mind. She had knickers in her drawer older than him, so she would tell him face to face once and for all that SHE. WAS. NOT. SIGNING. ANY. DIVORCE. PAPERS. FULL. FRIGGING. STOP.

Gaynor seized her keys, locked the door roughly and drove aggressively into town. There were no vacant spaces outside the solicitor's office, which didn't help her mood. She flew into the reception area and announced herself to the young receptionist with all the regality of the Queen of Sheba.

'Mrs Gaynor Pollock for Edgar Leadbetter. I do not have an appointment but he'll see me.'

'Right, right. Would you like to take a seat. I'll ... I'll ring through to him.'

Gaynor was too wound up to sit and chose to pace up and down instead. She expected Edgar Leadbetter to keep her waiting but he didn't; he arrived quickly, holding out his hand in readiness to greet her.

'Edgar Leadbetter, Mrs Pollock, how good of you to come in,' he said. Gaynor shook the hand, but not very enthusiastically. She managed to convey in the action that she was extremely pissed off. 'Please come into my office.'

She followed Edgar Leadbetter out of reception and across the hallway. He didn't look old enough to be a fully fledged solicitor. Actually, he didn't look old enough to be a school prefect.

'Please, have a seat,' he gestured towards one of the two chairs at the other side of his desk. He appeared nervous. As well he should, thought Gaynor.

'It's good of you to come,' he said, running his finger between his thin neck and collar. A blotchy rash was pushing up through his skin there.

'Isn't it,' replied Gaynor sarcastically.

'Can I get you some tea?' asked Edgar.

'No thank you,' said Gaynor, her tone clipped. It would take more than a cuppa and a sodding jam ring to make her play the game, if that's what he was thinking.

He cleared his throat before speaking next. And his chair creaked as he rocked nervously back and forwards on it. She remembered those little details later. That the chair needed an oiling, that his fingernails were bitten to the quick and there was a slight brown smudge on his shirt as if he'd spilt a drink on it and dabbed off the worst of it.

'I've been trying to ring you, but without success. I er . . .'

'Mr Leadbetter.' Gaynor pushed down on her rising fury and started calmly, intending to build up to a crescendo he wouldn't forget in a hurry. 'I think you might be fully aware by now that I have absolutely no intention of cooperating with you or my husband. If he wants to divorce me then he will have to do it without my consent and I will fight—'

He cut her off. 'Mrs Pollock, I—'

She cut him off back. 'I will not be persuaded, cajoled, blackmailed, pushed, forced or otherwise into making this easy or pleasant for Mick Pollock and his scruffy, stupid, common little tramp of a girlfriend. However, I do have every intention of costing him as much money as possible, of causing him as many sleepless nights as I can. I will not acquiesce. I will make these divorce proceedings feel as long as my thirty-year marriage if I can. I will cause him expense and frustration. I will rejoice at every new grey hair he sprouts as a result of his stress. I will do everything I can to reduce the perfidious bastard to rubble. I will rip the innards financially and emotionally out of him and cause him so much destruction that they will name the next hurricane in

Mexico after me. Now, what do you have to say to that, *Mr Leadbetter?*'

The aftermath of silence rang in the air. Mr Leadbetter's fingers threaded together in a tight ball and he gave Gaynor a strained smile of sympathy.

'Mrs Pollock, the reason I needed to get in touch with you was that Mr Pollock died on Friday. I am so sorry.'

Gaynor felt a *ping* noise in her head, as if something that kept her from feeling that the world was spinning had stopped working and the full impact of its movement hit her like a wrecking ball. She put her hand out on the desk to steady herself.

'Mr Pollock had a massive heart attack,' said Edgar Leadbetter, his voice sounding echoey as it bounced off the inside walls of her head. 'He died instantly. He didn't suffer at all.' His fingers made an absent click as if that's how long her husband had taken to die. Gaynor's brain was telling her this wasn't true, that she was dreaming, to buy her time to compute all this, but simultaneously she knew she was conscious and that it was real and that it had happened.

'He had changed his will to make Miss Bellfield his next of kin but I thought you had a right to know.'

More words. Something about Danira arranging Mr Pollock's funeral service and Gaynor was expected to respect her wish that she was not to come to it. That she didn't have to worry about not being financially secure because Mick had made sufficient provision for her in his revised will. Words that floated around in her head, refusing to be pinned down and absorbed, except for three which thundered and flapped and looped and took up the whole space in her skull. MICK IS DEAD. MICK IS DEAD. MICK IS DEAD.

'Is there anyone I can call for you?' asked Edgar

Leadbetter, his voice soft, bringing her back into his office, as if drawing her from the depths of a trance.

'No, no, I'll be all right,' Gaynor said, wondering why she wasn't crying. She wanted to, she wanted to howl and scream but her eyes were dry, her insides were dry. She felt hollowed out by grief from this revelation.

She remembered writing down her new contact details for Mr Leadbetter. There was a blank after that, then she was in her car, putting the key precisely into the ignition. Then she was setting off, pressing the button that connected her phone to the car by Bluetooth. Then she was speaking to Janet, her fellow receptionist, and telling her that she wouldn't be coming into work today because she had just become a widow. The word belonged to old women in black veils. It lent respect and dignity. But all Gaynor could feel, as she drove on automatic pilot, back to her house, the house she had shared with her husband for thirty years, the house he had carried her into as a young bride, the house she now moved around in like a ghost looking for him, was pain.

Chapter 54

The weather started to change that Monday and it was not the only change that was happening in Ironmist. As each hour passed, the air cooled more, the clouds thickened, their soft whiteness muddied and the sunshine over Wildflower Cottage faded. The ground mist formed into discernible swirls and the colours of the love-in-a-mist seemed to intensify to an almost electric violet.

Heath rested from brushing Keith to look over at the next enclosure. The big horse blew out a shudder of breath as if telling him to hurry up and start again. He stood there patiently waiting for the scratch of the bristles to resume. Viv was showing Armstrong how to groom Wonk, avoiding her front flank as Wonk didn't like the feel of the brush near her false leg, and how to put her at ease. She'd found all this out herself as Wonk wasn't usually very tolerant of the brush, but when you talked any old rubbish to her in a soft voice, she allowed it.

Viv had come far in matters of animal care since she'd arrived at Wildflower Cottage, thought Heath. She didn't even flinch now when walking through the geese to lift their eggs. And as for the growing relationship between herself and Ursula, it was touching to watch. More than touching – beautiful. One minute, Viv was throwing up on the grass at the thought of cutting up meat for the birds, the next she was flying nearly as high as they did on the wave of their acceptance.

Maybe he had been wrong, maybe she really was here 'for experience' as she put it. He had to give it to her, she was a damned hard worker. She had cooked, she had washed, she had dealt with the paperwork and helped with the animals without a single murmur of complaint and then gone back to the folly at night probably to mix her potions, like a white witch. He noticed that the folly lights were still on past midnight sometimes.

She was the same age as Sarah had been when they first met, yet Sarah was like a skittish colt, girly and giggly. Antonia Leighton was serious, dark and moody. He knew that a large part of her allure was that she was so different to Sarah, or so he thought, but then similarities began to surface. Sarah was pretty, knew it and used it. Antonia was all too aware of her beauty. Both of them were adept at attracting people to them but once he had seen past their polished veneer, what remained was not enough to hold him.

Viv was laughing, reaching behind her, securing her caramel hair back into the band from which it had escaped. He rarely saw her without a smile playing on her lips, a light dancing in eyes as blue and warm as Antonia's were blue and glacial.

Talk of the devil and he's sure to appear. Or rather *she* in this case.

Antonia Leighton was riding down his drive. She was

dressed in black and looked as if she were part of the horse, as if she had ridden out of a dark fairy tale, a wild malevolent spirit with bad powers. The horse slowed to a trot, her body rising and falling in rhythm with it. There was no smile on her face, there never was. Antonia Leighton's beauty was one which sat best on a scowl and Heath wondered what madness could have ever persuaded him to think of her in romantic terms.

'Hello Antonia,' he greeted her politely enough though. 'What can I do for you?'

'I was just passing,' she shrugged nonchalantly. 'I thought you might like to know that I've persuaded my father to re-offer the house to you, the one that you so recklessly refused.'

'There was no need,' replied Heath, resuming his brush-ing. 'I don't want it.'

'There's gratitude for you.' Her eyebrows quirked in sur-prise at his obstinance. 'I see *she's* still here.' She nodded towards Viv. *She's jealous*, thought Heath. She wasn't used to having other young females around taking the limelight away from herself. That had been part of the confusion; he'd been viewing her primarily as a young woman and not as a Leighton. He'd been temporarily blinded by her sex.

He tapped Keith on the rump and the horse walked off towards his stable-mate. Then he turned fully towards Antonia and said: 'Will you please remove yourself from my land.'

There was a curve of confused amusement on Antonia's dark pink lips.

'What?'

'I said, get off my land.' His voice was calm, hard, devoid of any of his past civility. 'It might have escaped your attention but you're a Leighton and you're as unwelcome here as the rest of your clan.'

'I beg your pardon?' Antonia obviously didn't believe what she was hearing.

'Just go. I don't even know why you ever thought I'd be interested in one of your father's poxy little new-build boxes. We aren't all money-grabbing, egocentric, selfish bastards.'

Humiliated and rejected, Antonia swung immediately into damage-limitation mode.

'To think I actually tried to help you. I felt sorry for you.'

'You and I both know that isn't true,' Heath said. 'A Leighton hasn't done anything for anyone else in one hundred and fifty years that didn't benefit himself first.'

She closed her heels on the horse's sides and it circled, keen to be off.

'I'll be first in the queue to watch you being thrown off our land, you ignorant *fucker*.' She was spitting, trying to wound; he expected nothing less so didn't react other than to turn his back on her, saying, 'Goodbye, Miss Leighton,' over his shoulder whilst walking into the stable to put the horse brush away.

'Miss Leighton, Miss Leighton.' Running towards them was Armstrong, waving his hand still looped in Wonk's brush strap. 'Look, I've been brushing the donkey.'

Antonia nudged her horse forward towards him. Armstrong leaned on the fence, exhausted from his burst. 'That's very good,' she said to him, 'very clever.'

'Can I brush your horse? I won't stand behind him because you can get kicked but I can reach your horse because I'm very tall and he's very tall.'

'That's right, Armstrong.'

Her voice was pure sugar, sweet and gentle. Heath suddenly realised where this could go, but was too late to stop it.

'So what will you do when this place closes in a couple of months, Armstrong? Did they tell you that all the animals are going to be slaughtered and the sanctuary is going to be knocked down? You won't have anywhere to go, will you?'

Viv was running towards them now.

'They're all going to die, Armstrong. The horses are going to be meat for dogs. That stupid donkey will be made into burgers. There's really no point brushing her is there, it won't make her any more tasty. Yum yum.'

Armstrong froze, then his whole body started to tremble as if there was an engine inside him that was revving up.

'You bitch.' Viv wished she were taller and could drag Antonia Leighton off that damned horse.

Then Armstrong began to wail, a siren of a noise, a keen of pain and panic and Viv threw her arms round him but she was too short to pull his head onto her shoulder and he threw her off and started darting here and there, screaming for his mum. Antonia Leighton cast a hateful stare at Heath and coursed off down the drive, the horse's hooves kicking up dry dust behind it.

'I'm okay, just see to Armstrong,' cried Viv as Heath stepped towards her. He chased the sobbing boy, forced him into his arms, held him tight, talked to him, told him over and over again that the animals were all going to be safe, that Antonia was joking, very badly, that she was cross, but no harm would ever come to the animals. It took all Heath's considerable strength to hold Armstrong until his panic subsided as his body emptied itself of tears.

Viv wasn't okay, he noticed, because she'd had to struggle

to her feet and looked drained of colour. She'd been winded and too embarrassed to show it.

'I'm going to take him home,' mouthed Heath over Armstrong's shoulder. 'Are you all right, Viv?'

'I will be,' said Viv. 'Don't worry.'

Geraldine was hobbling towards them now at speed.

'Gerry, can you look after Viv,' called Heath.

'Viv, darling, lean on me,' said Geraldine, supporting her and leading her inside, as Heath gently led the still sobbing Armstrong to his car.

'That poor boy,' said Viv.

'Those Leightons are evil,' snarled Geraldine. She lifted her head. 'Isme, if you're here, for goodness sake don't let them get away with it.'

And as if the old earth spirits had responded, the breeze suddenly lifted, bringing with it the scent of a thousand blue flowers.

Chapter 55

Monday passed in a blur for Gaynor. She rang Leanne, but as expected there was no answer. She texted – RING URGENTLY. I HAVE TO SPEAK TO YOU, MUM and left three voicemail messages. Then she rang Eastman's funeral parlour, because they'd looked after Mick's parents and he always said if anything happened to him, he'd have them look after him, too. She didn't believe the lady who answered that he wasn't there. Gaynor accused her of hiding him and screamed down the phone at her. The lady shamed her with her patience and Gaynor sat on the carpet and yowled like a wild animal. She was still in that position when Leanne rang in the afternoon. Leanne was at a swim-wear photoshoot and she said she'd get a train from London when she'd finished for the afternoon.

Gaynor couldn't remember ringing her mother, but suddenly she was there, pulling her daughter up from the bouncy, expensive carpet, holding her tightly, being a mum.

*

When Stel came back from work, she couldn't believe her eyes. Outside Al's house there was a For Sale notice. She was absolutely gobsmacked that he was selling up but more so that he hadn't told her. They'd been living next door to each other for how many years and yet he hadn't mentioned it? It shocked and upset her.

He was out, otherwise she would have knocked on his door. She would have to go round when he was in and find out where he was moving to and why he hadn't said anything.

She wished she weren't seeing Ian later. She fancied climbing into her fleecy pyjamas and catching up on soaps. They'd quickly fallen into a pattern where he came around every night at seven and stayed and it was lovely, but it had been eight years since she'd had that sort of intensive relationship. He hadn't invited her round to his place yet and that slightly grated on her, if she was honest. He'd given the excuse that he was having a lot of work done in his house so it was in a bit of a state, but she wondered if that was true. She'd taken a sneaky peek at his personnel file and found his address: 43 Crompton Street. It wasn't in the best area of town, but surely he didn't think she'd bother about that, did he?

Stel fed Basil and cleaned his litter tray. She noticed that he didn't jump on the sofa to snuggle up on her lap when Ian was there, sulking probably that she had a boyfriend. As she was peeling potatoes, she saw, through the kitchen window, that Al's electric garage door was sliding down. He was home. She darted to the door and stuck her head out to find him there on his path.

'Oy you,' she shouted. 'What's with the For Sale notice?'

He turned and said, 'Hello Stel,' but she saw straight away that his customary grin was missing. 'Yeah, I was going to tell you, I've part-exchanged against one of the houses on the new Roselaine estate. Couldn't turn the deal they gave me down really. It'll be ready for me first week in June.'

'The Roselaine estate?' Stel blew out an impressed breath of air. 'Wow.'

She'd seen those new houses advertised in the *Barnsley Chronicle*. There were only ten on the plot and the smallest of them had four bedrooms.

'I can't believe you didn't tell me, Al,' said Stel, trying to keep it light. 'All these years we've been friends.'

'Yeah,' he said, an unreadable flat expression on his face. 'All these years we've been friends, Stel.' And with that he walked into the house and shut the door firmly behind him.

*

Leanne Pollock arrived in a haze of designer perfume carrying a very good copy of a Louis Vuitton case. Her mother and grandmother threw their arms around her as soon as she walked in and they all cried on each other.

'I'm sorry but I had to finish that job, Mum, or I wouldn't have been paid,' explained Leanne. 'I mean it's not like Dad was on his deathbed and I missed his final minutes, was it?'

Gaynor's mum Paula had rung around all the local undertakers but they couldn't find which one held Mick's remains. Paula was incensed that they'd been asked to stay away from the funeral.

'Me and you will drive round tomorrow until we find out where your dad is, Leanne,' she said to her granddaughter.

'I can't, Nan, I've got to get the ten o'clock train back. I've got work commitments,' replied Leanne.

'Eh?' shrieked Paula.

'I'll come back for the funeral. But what can I do?'

'What about be here for your mother?' snapped Paula. Leanne might have been her grandchild, but she was under no illusion what a selfish little madam she was.

'Mum, I'm here for you, you know that,' said Leanne, taking her mother's hands between hers. Gaynor noticed the long perfect acrylic nails, the tiny gold charms pierced through those on her little fingers. She noticed the tell-tale knots of expensive extensions in her daughter's hair, and the flawless frozen forehead.

She wondered how long it would be before Leanne asked about the situation with her father's will. It was ten minutes.

Chapter 56

Viv sat with a hot water bottle on her back against the chair, as Geraldine insisted. She'd panicked initially because her back was her Achilles heel, but really she knew she was fine although she'd probably have a beauty of a bruise tomorrow. She wasn't hurt half as much as Armstrong must be; she felt so sorry for him.

'Do you want Heath to run you up to the hospital when he gets back?' asked Geraldine.

'No, I'm okay,' said Viv.

'That poor boy,' sighed Geraldine, 'I could weep for Armstrong.' Pilot nudged his nose under her arm for affection. 'I don't know why Heath ever gave that Leighton girl the time of day in the first place. Attraction or no attraction, it couldn't go anywhere, could it?'

'It worked for Alfred and Cecilia,' Viv smiled gently.

Geraldine huffed. 'Cecilia was a lady, the last decent Leighton to live in the castle. I bet she's turning in her grave at what's been going on.'

'I heard Antonia say she'd tried to help,' said Viv. She had been trying not to listen in on their conversation, but admittedly not very hard.

'Poppycock,' humphed Geraldine. 'She thought she had Heath right where she wanted him.'

'He was sort of allowing her to think that though,' Viv countered.

Geraldine turned her gentle grey eyes full beam onto Viv.

'Oh my love, sometimes you haven't a clue how far you've become trapped in a spider's web until you try and leave it.' She shook her head as if revisiting an unpleasant memory.

'Is that what happened to you, Geraldine?' asked Viv.

'Biggest spider of them all.' Geraldine pushed her fingers through Pilot's fur. His head was nodding as his eyes shuttered down. 'When my mum died I was a wreck. There had always just been me and her, no brothers or sisters, and I never knew my dad. Oh, I loved her so much and then she was gone. I felt completely lost and alone. I wanted someone to love me again.' Geraldine's lips puckered. 'Some people can smell your vulnerability from miles off. I was ripe for picking by this ... *man*. Oh he was so kind, so gentle in the beginning. He was everything I wanted, everything I needed as if he'd been made especially for me. He drowned me in love and affection and flowers.' She laughed. 'He swept me off my feet, Viv. It was a mad wonderful whirl. Nothing was too much trouble. I was the centre of his world. I was supposed to think that. I was supposed to feel safe. So when little things started to go wrong, I shooed them away because they didn't belong in my perfect picture of him. I put any blame on my own judgement. It's hard to imagine you walk into that web yourself with your eyes open and have disabled all your own alarm bells because you want to trust and believe in someone. And even when that spider's back is turned and you think you've got a chance of leaving, you don't. Because he's got you on a string and you'll only be able to go so far before you feel him pulling you back.' Geraldine placed her coarse hand over Viv's softer, smaller one. She couldn't open up all those boxes in her head again. So many of them filled with all the things he had done to her. He'd killed their baby when she'd been growing inside her. He'd made her life a living hell and he followed her into her dreams. There was no respite from him, not even in sleep. She didn't want Viv to think badly of her, for what she'd had to do in the end.

'I took some pills, Viv. It was the only way I could think of to escape. And then I woke up in hospital with him beside me, holding my hand. I hadn't got away from him.'

Viv felt her squeeze. 'But you did get away, eventually,' she said.

Geraldine swallowed. She wanted to tell Viv so she did. 'I tried to kill him in the end. The night I went to prison was the first time in years that I slept properly.'

She turned to Viv hoping not to see condemnation in her eyes, but all that was there was warmth and the gloss of tears.

Ironmist is full of people like me, Viv, Geraldine wanted to say but she wouldn't because she couldn't give up the secrets of other people who lived here, the ones tortured by mistakes, the ones who had been accused of things they hadn't done but were never able to escape the shadows, people who had helped their loved ones in pain. They'd all been led here by something outside their

understanding. She didn't think they could survive anywhere else.

'People make mistakes, I know that,' said Viv. 'Sometimes
they do terrible things when they can't see a way out.'

She knew it only too well. It was why she had come here.

Chapter 57

'I've been thinking,' said Ian, as he switched off the bedside light. 'I could turn that other bedroom into a dressing room. How do you fancy that?'

'The other bedroom?' exclaimed Stel. She didn't even know he'd been in it. 'That's Viv's room.'

She felt Ian's hands slip around her back and start stroking her and she knew he was starting his sexual routine. She was tired and didn't want to tonight. And that encounter with Al was sitting heavily with her. Too much had changed in a short time and she wasn't sure she liked things moving so fast any more.

'Viv's gone. Are you going to be one of those mothers who keep a shrine to the children?'

He started caressing her breasts and kissing her neck.

'Did you notice the For Sale notice outside next door's house?' asked Stel.

Ian stopped his ministrations and flicked on the bedside light.

'Stelly, have you noticed that I'm trying to make love to you and you're rabbiting on about For Sale signs? Talk about a passion killer.' He laughed. 'Now, I'm putting the light off and we'll start again.'

'Ian . . .' she pressed her hand against his naked chest. 'Not tonight, eh. I'm a bit tired.'

'I'll make it quick.'

'No, not tonight.'

'What's this about?'

'Nothing, I'm just not in the mood.'

He stared at her, eyes roving over her face, then his eyebrows lifted in realisation.

'Oh, I see,' he nodded. 'You're upset about Al.' His tone was soft, understanding so she presumed it would be all right to be honest.

'I am a bit. He was so . . .'

Ian swung his legs out of the bed and reached for his underpants.

'I'll go home,' he announced gruffly.

'No, I . . . don't do that.'

'I should go.' He pulled on his socks quickly, grabbed his shirt.

'Why?' Stel scrabbled on the carpet for her dressing gown.

'Look. I really like you, Stel, really like you,' said Ian, fastening the buttons up on his shirt at full speed. 'I thought that maybe, just maybe, you were feeling the same way about me that I was about you. Yes, it's early days but I want to be with you. I think about you all the time and I'm sorry I suggested that a space that no one uses any more would make a lovely dressing room' – he pulled up his trousers so fast that he slightly toppled – 'for you, not for me, for you. When you're our age, what's wrong with moving a bit faster?'

'Nothing,' said Stel. She didn't want him to leave her. 'I was just tired . . .'

'No you weren't, you were thinking about him next door.' Ian's voice raised as he sneered at the dividing wall.

'I wasn't,' Stel protested. 'Oh please, don't go.'

'I am going to go and I'll see you tomorrow at work. It'll be hard but we can be civil to each other.'

He was finishing with her. She jumped out of bed. 'Oh Ian, don't end it. What have I said?' She felt panic claim all her limbs, they felt shaky and numb.

'Look, it's fine. You can move on to Al next door and I'll take Meredith up on her offer.'

'What do you mean, what offer?'

Then despite her sobbing and pleading, Ian raced down the steps and out of the front door. He'd had four large glasses of wine but still he zapped open his car and drove away whilst Stel stood in the doorway with tears coursing down her face.

Why did she have to mention Al? Why couldn't she just have had sex with him and then gone to sleep? It wasn't as if it would have been the first time she'd laid back and thought of England.

She cried herself to sleep like a distraught teenager, replaying the night in her head where she kept her mouth shut and had sex and a nice cuddle and then she woke up still in a relationship.

Chapter 58

Stel was late for work because it took her half an hour to get rid of the puffiness under her eyes which had resulted from a night of little sleep. She plastered on a smile at the hospice door, marched in wearing the outfit that Ian said she looked her best in and hoped she could hold it all together. She just wanted to see him and tell him she was sorry. She couldn't bear it if he went off with Meredith. What was it he'd said, that she'd 'made him an offer'?

'Have you seen ... Ian this morning?' she asked Maria casually, when the nurse passed by the desk.

'Meredith was chatting him up in the kitchen five minutes ago,' laughed Maria, not realising the effect her words would have on Stel. 'You want to watch that minx.'

Stel's heart plummeted right down to her toes.

'I'll tell him you're looking for him, shall I?' said Maria.

'Please,' said Stel, the smile shaky on her lips.

It was lunchtime before Stel managed to get a break on that very busy morning, to learn that Ian was taking his lunch at the pub. With Meredith.

*

Viv's arm was extended, food in her hand. Ursula was in one corner of her aviary, Viv in the diagonal opposite. There was an impasse though; nothing was happening.

'What do I do? She's not coming,' said Viv.

'Whistle,' said Heath.

'I can't whistle.'

'Oh for goodness sake just try. She needs some encouragement.'

Viv put her lips together and blew.

'That's pathetic,' said Heath.

'I told you I couldn't.'

'Good grief, woman. Why the hell did this beautiful bird pick you?'

Viv chuckled and Ursula's head cocked to the side.

'She can recognise your voice. Try again.'

Viv blew. It was easier if she made a staccato sound. 'Ursula. *Phew-phew-phew-phew-phew.*'

After a few whistling attempts, Ursula eventually responded. Her wings lifted as her feet pushed off from the branch. For a moment the feathers fanned behind her like an angel's. Her eyes fixed forward and she dropped down with a bump on Viv's glove, beak to the meat, pulling it, gulping.

'Try walking slowly,' said Heath, advising from outside.

'She weighs a ton,' replied Viv with a grin, putting one foot slowly forward in front of the other.

'That's it, that's it,' said Heath, excitement rich in his voice. 'She's eaten. She has no reason to stay on your glove other than because she wants to.'

Viv did a full lap of the aviary and Ursula only flew off when Viv started to move too fast.

'I just don't get it,' said Heath, scratching his head. 'The most awkward, ridiculous, arrogant bird in the place . . .'

'What about Ursula?' Viv barked with laughter.

'Her as well,' replied Heath, opening the door for her. Viv stretched her back. It was aching.

'Armstrong hurt you, didn't he?' asked Heath.

'Not as much as Antonia Leighton hurt him,' said Viv. He hadn't come that morning to help them. He was in one of his dark places. In fact, there was a depression that seemed to have settled over them all since Antonia's visit. A stagnant weight that even chased off the lovely mist.

The hawks and the eagles were in the arena, sitting on perches in the sun.

'Come on, Viv, help me,' said Heath. He was all too aware that the events of the weekend had left them under a cloud. 'There is only one way to cheer things up on a miserable day. Bathtime.'

There were a stack of deep trays at the side of Frank's aviary. Heath dragged them out, distributed one next to each bird. They began squawking and dipping.

'They know what's coming. Get one of the hosepipes, Viv, and fill them up with water.'

Viv unwound the pipe and started to fill up the tray at the side of Heath's hawk Sistine. She tried to claw the water, stamping in the stream, pushing her head into it.

'They love this,' replied Heath. 'Far more than owls, who are notorious for being scruffy sods.'

'Don't you call my girl a scruffy sod,' said Viv and flicked the hosepipe towards him.

'Oy,' he said and laughed.

When all the baths had been filled, Viv sat on the bench and watched the floorshow. The birds loved the water, tossing it over their heads, settling their beautiful feathers into it, savouring the cool respite from the warmth of the day.

Viv recalled that she had just referred to Ursula as *my girl*. The bird might have started bonding with her, but had Viv not realised how much she was bonding with Ursula? She was growing close to them all: Geraldine, Armstrong, Wonk, Bertie, the horses ... She looked across at Heath holding the hosepipe so that Sistine could play in the spray and she wished she could stay in this beautiful bubble of an afternoon where the world was good to this place and the people and the animals that lived here. Heath could be stroppy and bossy and rude but he was fundamentally a good man, a kind man, a gentle man. Unfortunately, she had bonded with him too.

*

Stel was operating on two levels that day. On the surface she was performing her duties, directing people to where they needed to go, answering phone calls. She was the model of efficiency. Underneath was chaos, a mess of insecurities, jealousies, rage and sorrow. And as much as she went over the events of the previous evening, she could not for the life of her work out why the situation had flared up like it had. It had to be because she admitted to thinking about Al whilst Ian was touching her. Did he think she was trying to make him jealous? Was he hurt because she didn't want to have sex with him? Annoyed with himself that he had invested too much too soon in their relationship? Her brain was telling her that these were signs that he liked her a lot. So then why was he avoiding her and making no secret of the fact that he had taken Meredith out?

Five o'clock could not come fast enough. But beyond that yawned an evening of loneliness and mental torture. Internally she was black and blue from beating herself up, for being the catalyst of her own misfortune. What woman starts talking about one man when she's having sex with another? No wonder he was cross.

As she was about to climb into her car, someone came up behind her and placed a hand over her eyes.

'Guess who,' said a dear, familiar voice which didn't only flood her earholes but filled her whole body with a wildly disproportionate joy. She turned round and there stood Ian, a big bunch of flowers in his hand.

'I didn't know where the florists were round here, so Meredith volunteered to show me where the best one was at lunchtime.'

So that's why they'd gone out. Stel burst into happy tears.

'What the hell are you crying for, Stelly?' chuckled Ian. 'I tell you, that Meredith would have me if I let her. But I made it clear, there's only one lass I fancy.'

'Did you?' She would have liked to have seen Meredith's face when he said that.

'Stelly, I've been thinking. About us.'

'Me too. All day. I am so sorr—'

'Shhh.' He placed a finger over her lips. 'I love you. I want us to live together but if I'm freaking you out by moving so fast, let's call it a trial period. If it doesn't work, I'll move out, but I'll warn you, I'm an all or nothing guy. We do this or finish. So what's it to be?'

Stel didn't want to finish, especially if Meredith was waiting to jump into her shoes. If it didn't work out, they'd have to split up, but she couldn't think long term, only about now, the time that mattered and governed her emotions.

She was so relieved that he still wanted her, she thought she'd blown it and so she nodded.

'I love you,' said Ian, throwing his arms around her. 'I'll come over at seven with a suitcase. Let's do this. We could have an amazing life together.'

'Let's do this,' echoed Stel, pushing down all those little anxieties that were fast-sprouting like cress-seeds on speed in her head.

Chapter 59

Caro was just locking up her shop when she heard her mobile phone ringing. She had the shock of her life when she saw on the screen that it was Gaynor calling. Gaynor hadn't called her for months. She pressed connect, lifted it to her ear and said cheerfully, 'Hello, Mrs. This is a nice surprise.'

'It's not Gaynor,' said an older woman's voice. 'It's Paula, her mum. Look, she doesn't know I'm doing this but she's mentioned your name to me in the past and I think she needs her friends at a time like this.' Then Gaynor's mum relayed the awful news that Mick Pollock had died.

*

Linda, Caro and Stel were outside Gaynor's door within the half-hour. Paula greeted them with a sad smile and led them through to the lounge where Gaynor was slumped on her French sofa with a fleecy blanket wrapped around her. A cup of coffee and a sandwich sat on a table at the side of her, neither touched.

'Gaynor, love, your friends have come to see you,' said Paula, her voice soft and lilting as if she were speaking to a child and not a fifty-three-year-old woman.

Gaynor lifted her head. Her Sophia Loren big brown eyes were slits from crying on and off for a day and a half.

'You sit down,' fussed Paula to the group. 'I'll make us all a nice cup of tea.'

'Oh, Gay ...' began Linda, but couldn't even finish her name. She enveloped Gaynor in a hug and kissed her cheek. 'Oh love.'

The others followed suit, whispering in her ear that they were there for her, that they were so sorry.

Gaynor folded up the blanket and placed it on the back of the sofa, as if she didn't want to be seen as vulnerable. She patted her hair, trying to plump some volume into it. 'I must look a mess,' she said.

'You never look a mess,' said Stel.

'Why on earth didn't you ring us?' said Caro.

Gaynor shrugged in an 'I don't know' way. 'I can't find out where he is,' she said, the words scraping on her throat. 'That bitch de Niro wants to keep me away from the funeral.'

'You're joking,' said Linda. 'She can't do that. Can she?'

Caro shook her head in annoyance and disbelief. 'When did it happen ...?'

'Friday apparently. Heart attack. I found out yesterday. Mick's solicitor sent me a letter.'

'A letter?' Stel was incensed.

'I'd changed all my numbers,' said Caro. 'They didn't know how to get hold of me.'

'One of them could have bloody knocked on the door,' called Paula as she walked in with a tray of china teacups and saucers. Gaynor didn't have mugs.

'Mick wrote a new will and named *her* next of kin.'

'What about Leanne? She's got a right to know where her father's body is.' Caro was furious for her.

'Our Leanne came up last night but she had to go back this morning,' said Paula, with an involuntary sniff of annoyance.

'I loved him so much that I hated him,' croaked Gaynor. The pain in her heart was so fierce it was almost a physical one. She couldn't believe she could survive it for much longer.

'It's so wrong,' sighed Paula, pouring tea from an ornate teapot and inviting everyone to help themselves to milk and sugar. 'But he has left our Gaynor financially secure so he must have still had some feelings for her, mustn't he? But that trollop won't let her go to her own husband's funeral. Oh if I could get my hands on her, I tell you . . .'

Caro looked over at Gaynor. She might have been broken into bits by Mick's death but Danira Bellfield's thoughtless-ness was no small thing at the side of it.

'I know what music he would have wanted,' said Gaynor, letting tears drip down her cheeks unchecked. 'I know what words he would have liked. Thirty years I was with him. We have a child together. How can she not let me say good-bye to him? He was the love of my life.'

*

Eamonn was at home by the time Caro got back and she filled him in on where she had been and why. He poured her a glass of wine as they talked at the dining table.

'I'm going to see Danira first thing in the morning,' she said.

'Caro . . .' There was a warning appeal in his voice.

'Eamonn. It's the right thing to do, you know it is.'

Eamonn Richmond heard that tone in his wife's voice, the one that wouldn't brook any argument. He had married a good woman and he had no reason to argue when she was adamant that she was right. He squeezed her hand. And she knew that he understood.

Chapter 60

When Stel pulled up outside her house, Ian was already there, sitting outside in his car. He'd come early. He got out and dragged two suitcases roughly out of his boot, a strained smile on his face.

'I thought you'd be in cooking tea on this special night,' he said.

'I had an emergency,' replied Stel.

'An emergency?' He laughed, as if he didn't believe her.

'Yes. A friend's husband died,' she said.

'I'll need a key,' said Ian, ignoring her words. 'I've brought us a bottle of Champagne to celebrate. Hurry up, Stelly, these are heavy.'

Stel was piqued at his insensitivity. Even if he didn't know her friend, she thought he might have asked about her. She saw Al's head pop into his front window for a brief second and knew that he must have seen Ian and his suitcases. He would be thinking, *What the hell is she doing? Again.*

What the hell *was* she doing? Why was she letting a man whom she first went out with less than a fortnight ago move in? This wasn't her best idea.

She really should say something, slow all this down. She opened her mouth to try. He opened his at the same time.

'I'll bring the rest round tomorrow. There's not much because I'm leaving the furniture in. Pal of mine has just split up from his wife and so it's a perfect arrangement. I've just left him happy as Larry watching my TV.'

'Already?' Stel squeaked.

'Yep. He can't back out now, it's binding. Rent book signed and first month paid up-front, hence the Champagne. Let's get it on ice and drink it in bed.'

It was a rough Cava and it hadn't had the chance to cool properly. It made Stel feel slightly sick.

Chapter 61

Stel was woken up by the weight of Ian's arm swinging over her body and coming to rest over her neck. Her eyes snapped open to her alarm clock reading 5.36 a.m. and beyond, Ian's clothes hanging over the door of the wardrobe because there was no room inside for them.

What have you done? she asked herself. How could she have been so stupid?

She liked Ian but she hadn't wanted to move this fast. And she couldn't change her mind because now someone else was living in his house.

I thought he was having loads of work done to it? That's why he wouldn't invite you round.

She groped around in her brain trying to recall if that's what he'd said. Yes, she was sure of it. So he had been lying about that, as she suspected.

Outside she heard Al's motorbike start up. He was on an early one this morning, she thought. She suddenly longed for the life she had just a few weeks ago: being on the best terms with Al, Viv in the room across the landing and sole occupancy in her bed.

Stel moved Ian's arm and tried to get up without disturbing him but he woke up anyway. He stretched, leaned up on his elbow and saw the illuminated digital display of large letters projected onto the wall.

'Stelly, love, are you all right? It's only half past five. Come back to bed.'

'I can't sleep,' she said. 'I'm going to make myself a coffee.'

'Okay, love. I'm going back to sleep. I'm taking you out for a celebratory meal tonight by the way.' He pulled the covers over him. 'That sparkling wine was awful last night. I thought I'd picked up Champagne, I'm so sorry. I'll make it up to you. I'm an idiot.'

'No, you're not. Easy mistake,' said Stel, dismissing his need for an apology.

Downstairs in the kitchen, she put the kettle on, her mind a tug of war.

You're just pulling back because you've been out of the game too long.

Don't you think you've been manipulated here a bit, 'Stelly'?

Your mum and dad met and married in four months, Stel – and stayed married for fifty years, didn't they?

Yeah but that was four months, Stel, not two bloody weeks!

He's a kind man. They aren't all knobheads, you know.

You gave him an inch and he was in like Flynn.

You're just scared, Stel. It'll be all right.

It would be all right, she decided, dropping a sugar cube into her cup. He loved her and he was good to her. He was taking her out for a meal, wasn't he? When was the last time she'd met anyone who liked to treat her to things like that? Of course it would be all right.

It would be all right. Really. It would.

Chapter 62

Caro pulled on the handbrake of her gorgeous Mercedes but didn't get out of the car immediately. She sat and studied the brand new house on the estate. It wasn't one of the extra-large ones, but it was detached, with a neat garden and a new blue Mini parked on the drive. Danira had done very well for herself. There weren't many in her family as financially solvent as she was.

Caro flicked her long legs out of the car and smoothed down the creases in her coat before walking down the short path. The white front door could have done with a wipe down, she noticed. It had a brown mark on the bottom as if someone had nudged it open with a muddy shoe. Danira had only been in this house a couple of months, hence its relatively good state. Caro wouldn't have liked to have seen what it would look like this time next year. It would be the eyesore of the estate.

She pressed her finger onto the doorbell button and heard the long buzz deep in the house. She could see a head bobbing about through the frosted glass in the door. Two heads, but no one came. Caro buzzed again. She had no intention of moving away until she had confronted Mick Pollock's mistress. After the fourth persistent buzz, Caro saw a figure stomp towards the door, heard the lock turn on the inside and it was yanked open. There in a grey-white towelling robe and grubby pink slippers stood Danira. The furious look on her face softened immediately on seeing who the visitor on her doorstep was.

'Auntie Lena. God, what are you doing here?'

'I've come to see you, dear,' said Carolena Bellfield, as was, stepping into the house.

*

Hugo's name on the screen of her mobile sent Viv into a panic. She was all fingers and thumbs when she pressed the connect button.

'I haven't got any news yet. I'm on it but I'm going to need more time,' he said all in one breath. 'I bet you saw my name on the screen and had a fit, didn't you?'

'Something like that,' said Viv.

'I'll be back to you as soon as I can,' Hugo replied. 'Promise.'

*

'Er, come in,' said Danira, when Caro was already inside. 'I ... er ...' Danira scratched her head in embarrassment as a scrawny young male with a crew cut and a hand cupping his naked crotch appeared in the doorway which led to the kitchen.

'Who is it?' he said.

'It's my auntie,' said Danira. 'Get some fucking clothes on, Ash.'

Ash strode towards them. 'You're going to have to shift, then. Me clothes are upstairs,' he said. Danira squashed herself against the wall to let him pass. Caro didn't move an inch and he had to squeeze past her, muttering expletives not quite under his breath.

'Didn't take you long, Danira,' Caro said, when Ash had reached the top of the stairs.

'He's just a friend. I said he could kip down here for a bit.'

'You can make me a cup of coffee,' said Caro.

'Er, yeah, come in,' replied Danira, clutching the neck of her robe and scuffing the soles of her abnormally long slippers on the carpet as they entered a very untidy kitchen. She'd inherited the family's bigfoot gene, it seemed. With pincered fingers, Caro lifted an empty condom wrapper from the table and held it out to her niece.

'Just a friend then, Danira?' said Caro, as it was snatched from her hand and stuffed in the bin in the corner. Caro sat stiffly down on the chair and looked around at the work-surfaces littered with all sorts. This lovely new house would be a dump in no time. 'I think Ash should go. I want to talk to you in private.'

There was a flash of protest in Danira's eyes, but she quickly extinguished it. At that moment, Ash's footsteps could be heard on the stairs. He swaggered into the kitchen in jeans and a T-shirt emblazoned with a blasphemous slogan and was just about to take a seat at the dining table when Danira barred his way with her arm.

'Can you leave us for a bit?'

'Eh?'

'I want to have a talk with me auntie.'

Caro gave him a smile. Not a nice one. A smile that said, 'you heard what she said, so do one.'

'Who the fuck is this telling you what to do? I could hear you upstairs, you know.' Ash jutted out his chin as if he was about to square up for a fight.

'Do you really want to know who I am?' said Caro, unruffled, crossing her long elegant legs and sitting back in the chair.

Danira pushed him out of the kitchen and Caro listened to her whispering to him in the hallway, warning him. Seconds later, Ash had crashed out of the front door.

Danira came back into the kitchen. She thumbed behind her. 'Sorry about that,' she said. 'He wouldn't have talked to you like that if he'd known who you was.'

'Lucky for him you told him then, before he said anything else, isn't it?' said Caro. 'I like my coffee with no sugar and just a dash of milk, please.'

Danira jumped to the kettle and Caro tried not to let the amusement show on her face. Danira was a gobby little slapper but she wouldn't have crossed 'Auntie Lena'. Nobody would.

Young Carolena Bellfield had been the apple of her father Johnny's eye, not that she'd seen much of him growing up because he'd been in prison after taking the rap for a top London hardman, Carolena's godfather. Even now if she needed a favour from their family, all she had to do was ask. Carolena's brother was a total embarrassment to Johnny, getting banged up in a young offenders institution for mugging pensioners, but he revelled in how lovely his Lena was growing up, despite being in the care of a pathetic drunk of a mother. Johnny died in Belmarsh when Carolena was fifteen and she left home on her sixteenth birthday. She ended up working all over the world as a croupier until one day in Monte Carlo, stationed at the roulette wheel, she met the handsome Eamonn Richmond from West Yorkshire. She married him within two months and it was the best gamble she had ever taken.

Carolena had never told her friends her full history. She might one day, if it ever came up in conversation, but it hadn't so far. She had lied only once to them, when their little club started two years ago, and told them that her maiden name was Hampton. She knew them well enough now to know that, with the obvious exception of Gaynor, they would think no less of her for her connection to the Bellfields.

Danira delivered two cups of coffee to the table and then sat down opposite her aunt.

'So what can I do for you then? Is it about my dad?'

'I haven't seen your father for three years, nor do I want to,' said Caro. 'I came to talk to you about Mick Pollock.'

'He's dead,' said Danira. 'I'm a widow.' She had a smirk of pride on her lips as if the word was the equivalent to a damehood.

Caro corrected her. 'No, you aren't his widow. His widow is Gaynor Pollock, who is still married to him and has a child with him.'

'He left her. He loved me.'

'I'm sure he did find you exciting and fresh,' said Caro, throttling back on the sarcasm as much as she could. 'But you know that he would have gone back to Gaynor in the end, given time.'

Danira's jaw dropped open. 'He wouldn't of,' she said. Caro shuddered at the clumsy grammar and Danira assumed her aunt's reaction was at her protestation. 'He wouldn't of left me. He was divorcing that cow and he'd asked me to marry him.'

'In bed, presumably,' sighed Caro. 'In the post-coital glow of sex.'

'Yeah, after we'd done it,' nodded Danira, presuming that's what 'post-coital' meant. 'He said he adored me. He couldn't keep his hands off me.'

'And did you love him as well?'

Danira opened her mouth to answer, saw in her aunt's eyes that she would be able to tell a lie from a mile off and shut it again. Then re-opened it to deliver the truth this time.

'I liked him a lot. He was good to me.'

'He bought a house, which I presume is now yours.'

'Well, yeah.'

'And you have a car. And a cash card to a joint bank account that you'll have emptied by now, just in case Gaynor had a claim on it.'

Danira didn't need to say yes, the flush rising to her cheeks said it for her.

Caro lifted the mug of coffee, saw the traces of lipstick on the side which weren't hers and put it back down again.

'I want you to do the decent thing and let his wife arrange the funeral.'

'Eh?' Danira's black-dyed eyebrows sank into a deep V of confusion in the middle of her forehead.

'You heard.'

'It's been sorted already. I had to go and see the funeral bloke . . .'

'Unsort it. It's Gaynor's job. She's known Mick for thirty years, you haven't known him for thirty months. She is his wife, you aren't. And you're already sleeping with someone else.'

'I'm . . .' Danira started to protest then shut up.

'You've done very well out of this, Danira. You've got a new house and a new car all for few months' work. I don't doubt that Mick Pollock left this mortal coil with a big smile on his face but he would have got tired of having Pot Noodles for tea and living in a pigsty eventually.' She cast her eyes around the room. 'I want you to pick up the phone and tell Gaynor that you think it's only right you should step back and let her take over the reins of her husband's funeral because he was about to leave you and go back to her. He told you that he'd made a mistake.'

Danira dropped her cup of coffee all over her dressing gown. She swore, jumped to her feet and pulled the material away from her skin, then grabbed the kitchen roll and blotted herself with it, and all the while Caro sat and watched her, cool, detached and emotionless.

'No way, no fucking way,' Danira said. There were tears in her eyes, a combination of frustration at not being able to give vent to her temper and pain from the burn.

'I'm not asking you, Danira, I'm telling you. Gaynor Pollock is a good woman and it would cost you nothing to do this. But it would cost her everything not to be able to grieve in public for him as his wife. Sit down. I heard he changed his will.'

Danira sat, covered in coffee. 'Well yeah. He still left her loads though. He had stacks of insurance policies and pensions and stuff.'

Caro picked up the bling-covered mobile, which was face down on the table, with her lethal red nails and handed it to her niece. 'Ring Gaynor now.'

Danira looked at her aunt's hand and noticed the arthritic bump on her third finger and that observation recalibrated her thoughts. Who exactly did her aunt think she was? She was nothing! Johnny Bellfield – the bigshot – was dead and Lena lived a soft life in a big house and she was getting on a bit. What could she do if Danira said 'no'? So she tried it.

'No.'

'I beg your pardon?' Gaynor said, though she wasn't shocked really. She'd been prepared for this word since before she stepped over the threshold.

'No, I won't do it.'

'Fine,' said Caro, with a dangerous smile. 'Then I'll make a call, shall I? To a certain Vic Briggs. Do you know him? Yes, you do, don't you? You and one of your dodgy friends burgled his dad's house of two thousand pounds when Vic was doing time. And it was all on CCTV. But your dad paid Mr Briggs Senior five thousand pounds to forget it, didn't he?' Caro really was enjoying seeing Danira's face drain of colour. 'He bought the tape with the evidence on it from him, but guess who gave him the money? And guess as well, who has that tape in her safe at home?'

'Yeah right,' said Danira, cockily but with a tell-tale nervous gulp.

'I thought you'd say that,' said Caro. She took her phone out of her handbag and clicked onto the stored videos. She pressed play and held it up so Danira could see herself. The video was grainy but she could clearly see that it was her face tilted to the ceiling in perfect view of the camera which Vic Briggs had fitted in his dad's house.

'Alas they can't see the face of the other person but there is absolutely no doubt that it's you, wouldn't you agree? You remember Vic Briggs? My goodness, can that man hold a grudge. You know, he always said that burglary contributed to his dad's death.'

Danira was now as white as her dressing gown would have been had she ever washed it properly in Persil.

'You wouldn't. You're family,' tried Danira in a lame attempt to wriggle out of this trap.

Caro leaned over the table and put her head very close to her niece's. Danira did her best for a moment to stare the 'old woman' out, but there was a light in her aunt's eyes that was blinding. And nasty. It was like staring into the sun and she had to turn away. 'I might not have the Bellfield name any more, love, but I can scrap like one and I will. For those I love and I care about and that includes Gaynor Pollock. Your dad begged me to lend him that money to get you out of the shit. I gave him seven thousand pounds and he handed over five and I'm still waiting for a penny of it to be paid back. He stole from me, his own sister, so don't you *family* me, lady.' She thrust out her hand with the phone in it. 'I'll give you the number. Put it on hands-free so I can hear. Now ring Gaynor.'

Chapter 63

Gaynor was sitting in her kitchen wearing a pristine fluffy white towelling robe. On the table beside her was her mobile, a cup of lemon tea which had long gone cold and an ashtray. It had been ten years since she'd had a smoke, but she'd found a packet with five cigarettes left inside on Leanne's bedside cabinet and that morning had smoked them one after the other.

Her mobile rang on the table. She didn't recognise the number. She answered it hoping it would be someone telling her that she was due some PPI compensation so she could give them both barrels of fuck-off and feel justified in venting her spleen.

'Hello,' said the voice. A rough woman's voice. A young common voice.

'Who is this?'

'Don't hang up, it's Danira.'

Gaynor didn't hang up but she was throttled into silence by the cheek of her.

'I want to tell you something that I think you should know.'

Gaynor's finger was now hovering over the end call button ready to cut off Danira at the first sign of venom.

'Hello, you there?'

Gaynor swallowed. 'Yes, I'm still here.'

Now there was silence at Danira's end of the line for a few seconds before the blurted sentence was delivered. 'Mick was coming back to you.' She bared her teeth at her aunt, hating her for making her do this.

Gaynor gasped. 'What did you say?'

A huff. 'I said Mick was coming back to you, okay?' The words were like razors in Danira's mouth. 'He said he'd made a mistake. He said it had been fun but he missed you and he was going to go over to yours and beg you to take him back.'

'When?'

'What?'

'When did he say this?' Caro could hear the thirst for details in Gaynor's voice.

'I don't know.' Caro mouthed the correct answer at her. 'Thursday night.'

'The night before he died?'

'Yeah. The night before.'

Hearing those words it was as if there had been a crack in the black clouds above Gaynor's world and the sun had come pouring through.

'He was definitely coming back?'

'Oh for fu— Look, he'd packed to leave me, all right? I didn't tell you before because ... because I was hurt. He wasn't mine when he died. I think you should ring the funeral home and take over the arrangements. Co-op in Hoymoor. He said whatever happened, this house was mine, okay?'

Gaynor didn't care about the house. She didn't care about anything but the revelation that Mick had intended to come back to her. She broke down into sobs.

'Did he say he loved me?' she said.

Caro nodded slowly and menacingly. The inference was that Danira better get this right.

'He said he'd never stopped loving you,' she said through gritted teeth before ending the call.

There was a long moment's pause before Caro spoke.

'Well done. Now that wasn't too painful, was it?'

'It was a load of bollocks.'

'Did Mick ever mention what he felt about Gaynor?'

'He said he felt sorry for her,' said Danira. 'He said that he couldn't remember when he'd fallen out of love with her but it was a long time ago.'

'But only you and I know that,' said Caro. 'Besides, words are cheap. Infatuated men speak with their dicks.' She stood to go and picked up her handbag.

'You'll give me the tape, right?' said Danira.

'No, I won't give you the tape, Danira. I don't trust you but you can trust me on this: if you ever, ever mention what we spoke about today then I will hand over the tape to Vic Briggs and the police – in that order – without even warning you and that's a promise. All you have to do to remain safe is to believe that what you told Gaynor today is the truth.'

'That's not fair.' Danira screwed up her face.

'Life isn't fair. If it were, old people wouldn't get burgled by young scum, would they?' She tilted her head at her niece who had the decency to lower her eyes in submission because she didn't want to prod her aunt into action.

'You know, Mick Pollock has given you the chance to have a change of life, Danira. Just because you have the

Bellfield name, don't let that dictate your fate. Ditch the plankton you hang around with, take some pride in yourself and this lovely house. You're a young woman with your whole life in front of you.'

'Like you did, you mean?'

'Yes, like I did.' Lena Bellfield died many years ago; Caro rose from her ashes and made a very good life for herself. 'But no one gave me the advantage of a house and money to christen a new life, I had to work bloody hard to get it.'

'My nana is still alive, you know,' Danira said, with a shrug of her shoulders. 'Just saying.'

Caro showed no reaction to that. Her mother was consigned to the dark vaults in her head where she belonged.

'Goodbye, Danira, and thank you for doing the right thing. Who knows, you might get used to it,' said Caro. She walked regally out of the kitchen, down the hallway and out of the front door and back to her lovely life as Mrs Richmond, even though she knew that if ever push came to shove, she would always be able to fight like the alley cat that Lena Bellfield had been.

Chapter 64

The tug of war in Stel's head continued all morning until she was so sick of it that had she been able to cut the top off her skull and pull the two warring parties out, she would have grabbed an electric saw immediately. She only had respite when Gaynor rang Stel at quarter to twelve to give her something else to focus on. A miracle had occurred. Danira had not only rung Gaynor to tell her that Mick was going to come back to her but she was handing over the arrangements for the funeral. Gaynor sounded as ecstatic as if she was organising a wedding. She asked if Stel would mind telling the others for her.

It would give her an excuse to drive off and sit in her car for her lunch hour instead of spending it with Ian. She sneaked out five minutes early and told the other reception-ist that she had to go out to the shops if anyone asked where she was. It was with some relief that she made it out of the car park unseen.

She left a message on Linda's voicemail because she always had her phone switched off when she was in the hospital; Caro picked up though.

'You'll never guess,' said Stel. 'De Niro rang Gaynor this morning and told her that she and Mick had been on the brink of splitting up. He wanted to go back to Gaynor, apparently.'

'Well, that was always going to happen,' said Caro. She would have been rubbish at acting surprised so plumped for the 'not surprised' reaction.

'Do you really think so? I mean, he changed his will.'

'And signed it with his impulsive prick,' replied Caro. 'What's happening with the funeral, did she say?'

'Gaynor's now in charge. She's moved everything from the Co-op to Eastman's.'

Caro let out a long whistley breath. 'That'll be a relief for her. I wish she'd let me give her a hot stones treatment. It would work wonders for her.'

Stel, greatly in need of some stress relief said, 'I might book in for a massage.'

'Do. Have one at lunchtime tomorrow. I'm free,' said Caro, scanning her appointment book.

'Lovely,' said Stel, aware that she was making an excuse to fill another lunchtime. She couldn't keep doing that every day though, could she? And how the heck was she going to tell Viv that Ian had moved in after a fortnight? She doubted that Caro would get the stress knots out of her back with a few warm pebbles. She'd better get a sledgehammer ready to dip in her aromatherapy oils.

Stel rang Viv just before driving back to the hospice. She wanted to hear her daughter's voice so much. How could she have raised such a wonderful, sensible girl when she was an emotional train-wreck of a woman? She hoped she'd been a good mother. Viv had always had the best of everything she could afford to give her, and her time. Stel's mum had always said that the most valuable thing you could give a child was that. She'd only ever moved one man into the family home and that was Darren. To be fair, he hadn't been a bad man, just a bloody useless one. Then Stel had discovered a lump and all the cards had been flung up in the air. Suddenly Viv had become the parent, propping up her useless wimp of a mother and she'd been doing it ever since.

'Helloo, Mum.' Viv's lovely voice flooded into her ear and Stel could have wept at the sound. 'How's things?'

Stel told her about Mick Pollock dying and Al moving. Viv had never met Mick so though she thought it was sad for her mother's friend, it was the news about Al that really gave her a punch. It was smashing that he could afford a nice new house but he'd been their neighbour for ever, or so it felt like. She was very fond of Al.

'It's all change for you, isn't it, Mum?' she said. 'Me moving out, Al moving out and your new man.'

Moving in, Stel added secretly to herself. There had been too many changes, thought Stel, swallowing down her emotion. She wished Viv would come home and sort her out yet again but this time she knew she had to do it for herself – and she would, and then she would never be so stupid again. She could not keep expecting her daughter to manage her problems, it wasn't fair. Plus Viv needed time and space to sort herself out. Part of Stel dreaded what Viv might discover in Ironmist, both about herself and . . . other things, but she had to be brave, step back and let her daughter get on with it, even if it meant things might not be the same between them afterwards. And it wasn't fair of her to distract Viv from what she had to do. Stel had got too used to being pathetic. Well, no more. She had a plan.

'Talking of change, Viv, I've decided to have the house redecorated so I'm just letting you know that you might be as well not coming back for a couple of weeks until it's all done.'

'Wow. When did you decide all this then?'

'Last night. You know how impulsive I am.' At least her biggest fault would work in her favour here.

'Er, slightly,' Viv chuckled. 'Are you sure you don't want me to help you move stuff . . .'

'Nope, it'll keep me busy and the decorators will lift the heavy things, I'm sure.'

Stel knew that Viv believed her. That was good. It would buy her time.

'Well, I can't wait to see it,' said Viv. 'How are you and Ian?'

'Oh we're fine,' replied Stel, her composure starting to slide now. 'I'll let you get back to whatever you were doing.'

'Hand-feeding a three-legged donkey carrots.'

There was a smile in Viv's voice, she was happy, thought Stel.

'I love you, Viv.'

'Love you too, Mum. See you soon.'

Stel hoped that she would, too. As soon as she'd extricated herself from the glue pot she'd landed herself in and proved to her daughter that she could be a grown-up.

Chapter 65

Ian had booked a table at the Tarnview pub in the Town End. It was nice enough, waitress service, plenty of choice on the menu, although the chef only needed to be able to throw frozen food into a microwave. He ordered a bottle of house Champagne so they could properly toast their cohabitation. That gave Stel the opportunity to bring up something which had been niggling her.

'Didn't you say you were in the middle of having a lot of work done to your place?' she asked, trying to make it sound conversational, and not as if she were leading him into admitting a lie.

'I am,' he said. 'But Pete's desperate and the house he's just left was a total shit-hole so mine is a palace by comparison.'

That sounds feasible, so why do you assume he lied? Her own head was giving her a talking to. *You gave him the wrong signals so all this is your fault. Just tell him that the living together thing is too much and he'll be fine about it. Then you can carry on at a slower pace. He'll just have to tell his mate that there's been a change of plan.*

'Anyway, look, cheers,' he held up his glass and when she followed suit, he chinked it against hers. 'I want us to be happy.' And he looked at her with such tenderness that she was overcome with guilt that she thought any ill of him.

'Me too,' said Stel. She didn't want it to end. They were good together. They liked so much of the same stuff and he couldn't keep his hands off her which meant he fancied her like mad. These were all things she had wanted in her ideal relationship so what was wrong with her?

Ian picked up the menu and studied it. His eyes remained fixed on it whilst he asked her about earlier. 'By the way, I was a bit surprised that you didn't tell me you were going out for lunch today,' he said.

'I had some phone calls to make for my friend. The one whose husband died.'

'Did you have to drive off to make them?'

'No, but I wanted some privacy.'

'Okay.' He tapped the menu with the back of his hand. 'So, what do you fancy, apart from me of course?' He laughed. And Stel laughed but she wasn't sure she did fancy him and she didn't want to admit that to herself. She'd tried to force herself to find him attractive, but she still didn't like his eyes and she wished she did. She really did. Talk about screwed up!

She chose scampi and chips and he had soup and a steak and kidney pie. The portions were enormous and they struggled to finish them.

'My old mum would have loved this,' said Ian, wiping his mouth on the paper serviette.

'Mine too,' said Stel. 'She'd have had the pie and then moaned that it wasn't as good as one she could make, but she'd still have eaten the lot. She did it every time we went out.'

'Mum gets fed through her stomach now,' said Ian, with a sad smile. 'She can't eat solids any more.'

His mum's dead, Stel. I remember him telling us at his interview. She died in a hospice last year, Maria had said.

Stel felt as if someone had tied a knot in her throat. She tried to cough it away but it stayed put.

'Oh,' she said, 'I must have got it wrong. I thought your mum had . . . you know . . . passed over.'

Ian raised his head and though his smile was still in place, it looked as if it had been glued on.

'I told you I went to see her on her birthday the week before last, not that she knows who I am. Or anyone for that matter. It's my step-mum who's dead. She was the one who brought me up.'

'Oh, oh.' Stel shook her head as if she was stupid and the action might jiggle some sense into it.

'Bit confusing,' said Ian. 'I wasn't close to my real mum until about two years ago. She left my dad when I was a baby.'

'That's a shame,' said Stel. She couldn't get her head around a woman walking away from a baby. But she knew they did.

Ian stopped chewing as if a sudden thought had just locked his jaw. He swallowed and said, 'So, if you thought my mum was dead, what did you think when I told you that I'd been to see her?'

'I just thought that you'd been to her grave with flowers.'

'Christ, I wouldn't have given that old cow flowers when she was alive, never mind dead,' he laughed coldly and it shocked her.

'You weren't close to your step-mum then?'

'She was a fucking bitch,' he said, too loud, his lips contorted with hate. He dropped his voice and offered an apology. 'Sorry, Stelly. Let's not talk about mothers, eh?' He reached over the table and grabbed her hand. 'It upsets me. I've not had the best experience with them.'

So which one had breast cancer then? The one he was there 'every step of the way' for? Something wasn't adding up, or maybe she was remembering that wrong.

'Maybe you should tell me something else about yourself. I don't really know that much about you, Ian,' said Stel, thinking again how ridiculous it was that the man opposite to her had a key to her house and she didn't even know if he had any brothers or sisters. She knew lots of unimportant stuff about him, such as he liked peanut butter, Lacoste polo shirts and his favourite film was *The Shawshank Redemption*, but what did she know about his history, other than his name was Ian Robson, he came from Nottingham, he was a forty-eight-year-old gardener who had once been a soldier and he'd just rented out his house in Crompton Street to his mate Pete? It wouldn't fill a postcard.

'Stelly, just look forwards, eh, love? Why rake over old bones? We have our whole lives ahead of us. Why should we waste time looking back?'

Stel thought of all the things she'd rather he didn't know about her: the Matchmaker.com years, the older married man she'd once had a fumble with when she was young and drunk, so many daft things she'd done and she realised he was right; it wasn't necessary they knew everything about each other, was it?

The waitress came over and cleared the plates and asked if they'd like to see the dessert menu. Ian said no at the same time as Stel said yes.

'We'll just have the bill,' Ian said, giving the waitress the definitive answer, then he addressed Stel. 'I think we've eaten enough tonight so we'll just go home.'

It's not your home, it's mine, Stel mumbled in her head. But she rather thought she was a bit late to the party with that information.

Stel was cross on the way back but she didn't want to say anything, especially as Ian was well over the alcohol limit but insisted he was fine to drive. *How dare he decide when I've had enough to eat*, she thought. She'd been saving a space for an Eton Mess, that's why she hadn't had a starter like he had.

She'd feigned being very tired when they got in the house.

'I've got something that will wake you up,' Ian had said, kissing her neck.

'I've eaten too much,' protested Stel, using his own argument against him. She pulled away from him but he wouldn't let her go.

'I'll help you burn it off,' he insisted.

'Ian, I'm really tired. I got up at five thirty this morning.' Stel's polite smile was laboured now.

'Well, that's not my fault you couldn't sleep, is it? Come on Stelly, just a quickie. We've had a nice evening, make it extra special for me. Don't spoil it. I've bought you a nice meal and Champagne.'

And because Stel didn't want to spoil the evening, because she didn't want to seem like an ungrateful cow, she let him do it. But she hated herself for it.

*

Gaynor went to bed that night as happy as someone who had newly acquired the status of widow could go. She had been to see the new funeral director that day and asked him to change the casual clothes that Danira had chosen for Mick's interment. He would want to leave this world with dignity and that wouldn't be achieved with 501s and a sweatshirt. She supplied one of the suits he had left behind, the only one that she hadn't cut out the crotch from. It was the suit she had bought him for their Silver Wedding Anniversary and she couldn't quite bring herself to deface it.

She had chosen a poem and the hymn 'Love Divine' which had been played at their wedding, although she hoped it wouldn't be the same organist who had massacred it with bum notes. Her dad had brought the house down by remarking in his father-of-the-bride speech that he was sorry Les Dawson couldn't join them at the reception, but he had another wedding to play for. And she had written a glowing obituary for the *Chronicle*, leaving out the part about Mick pissing off with a woman younger than his daughter and buying her a house. She had ordered the flowers: a simple cross of white and red roses, because he was born in Lancashire and she was a Yorkie and so that's what she had had in her wedding bouquet. Danira hadn't booked any catering for after the crematorium service – *wanting to save her money for drugs no doubt*, thought Gaynor – but she secured the function suite at the Farmer's Arms between Dodley and Maltstone where she and Mick had often gone for Sunday lunch. She paid for the luxury buffet with sparkling wine on arrival.

Then Gaynor spent a couple of hours sitting by Mick's

side in the funeral parlour and she talked to him and relived old precious memories. She touched his face and said that she forgave him and loved him, had always loved him and would always love him. And she hoped that heaven would give them a chance to do it all again, properly, with a sofa that you could slump into next time. She promised him he could have first pick if there was a DFS in the clouds.

Chapter 66

Once again, Stel took an early lunch break, sneaking out before Ian noticed she had gone. She knew she hadn't said a definite no to sex the previous evening, but she still felt violated. It was all going terribly wrong. She needed the massage that she had booked with Caro; but not as much as she wanted to talk to someone and ask them for help.

When she was laid face down on the massage table, Caro whistled as she started kneading her muscles.

'There are some serious knots in this back, lady, what's the matter with you?'

Stel looked down through the head hole and saw a tear bounce on the floor tile below.

Just tell her. This is your friend, screamed a voice inside her.

'I'm not sleeping too well,' she said.

'I'll work some magic,' promised Caro, spreading more warm oil onto her skin. 'I was going to use stones, but I think you need my hands. Jesus, it's like someone's put cornflakes under your skin. Can you feel that crunching? You should get your man working on these for you every single night until they're gone.'

'Ow.'

'Stop moaning. This will get worse before it gets better. I'm going to get my elbows in on the act in a minute.'

Caro worked on Stel's shoulders. It was like trying to soften concrete.

'How's Viv doing?' she asked. 'Have you seen anything of her this week?'

'She's really busy,' said Stel. 'The woman she works with has had a fall so she's taken on a lot more duties. She's doing very long hours.'

'You could always drive over to her, I suppose.'

'I will, when she's got more spare time.'

'You must miss her.'

Like you wouldn't believe, thought Stel. She wouldn't have gotten into this mess if Viv were here. But she would get out of it and Viv need never know.

Caro rotated the tip of her elbow into Stel's shoulder blade.

'If this doesn't loosen you up, I'm going to use a hammer-drill,' chuckled Caro.

Stel groaned. 'It feels good in a sort of agonising way. I might need hospital treatment after this though.'

Caro kept the pressure on. 'Only seems ten minutes, not ten years, since we were sitting in that waiting room in the hospital, doesn't it, Stel? How the years fly by.'

They had been two strangers, both waiting for news of their children. Marnie had meningitis, Viv was having her most serious back operation. Both women were terrified. Both were drinking coffee on a continuous loop and ended up sitting in the hospital restaurant together. They had bonded instantly through their pain. They cried, they shared their lives, they held each other's hands through black hours.

Then, when the news became good, they both rejoiced with and for each other, clinging to each other with relief.

'We've both had some shit, haven't we, Caro?'

'Haven't we just. So come on, tell me then, how's the love-life.' Caro felt Stel's muscles contract instantly.

'All good,' replied Stel. She wanted to pour everything out, share it, let someone tell her what to do.

'Is he treating you well?' asked Caro. 'You've gone all tight again.'

'Sorry. He took me out for a meal last night. Tarnview. It was very nice.'

'Good. It's about time you had someone who looked after you.' Caro applied her elbows again. What the hell had happened to make Stel's back as pliant as a gravestone?

Stel dared to open up a little. 'I'd forgotten what real sex was like. You know, the cramp when you get in the wrong position, the mess. I think I've been watching too many romantic films.'

'Plenty of sex then, eh?'

'Plenty.' Too much, Stel wanted to say. He wanted it every night. Even when she didn't.

Cajoled. She wasn't even sure if it was the right word but that's what came into her head yesterday when they were in bed. He had *cajoled* her into sex.

'He must fancy you rotten then.'

'He says he does.'

Caro reached for a bamboo stick. 'Let's see if I can roll some of that tension out. That's lovely to hear. I'm so pleased for you, Stel.' Caro knew how much Stel wanted to be part of a couple. A good couple, like herself and Eamonn. A couple who loved and respected and looked out for each other.

'He wouldn't let me look at the dessert menu last night,' Stel blurted out. 'He said we'd eaten enough.'

It sounded puerile when the words were spoken, so it came as little surprise when all Caro said was, 'Cheeky sod.'

Stel tested her. 'Would Eamonn have ever done that?'

'He's committed his fair share of faux pas. Men can be very clumsy,' laughed Caro, remembering once when he forbade her from having a dessert. But then again, she had been doing the Atkins diet and had warned him before they went to the restaurant that he must, under no circumstances, allow her to cave into temptation. He couldn't understand why she didn't talk to him until the next morning.

Stel lay still as Caro rolled the bamboo stick around her muscles and considered her situation. She had landed a loving man who fancied her like mad, took her out – and paid for her – loved her company and wasn't selfish in bed. He hadn't forced himself on her last night. If she'd said no and sounded as if she really meant it, he would have left her alone. *Must be taking a bit of getting used to though, dating again*, Caro must have thought. And even wonderful, considerate Eamonn had told Caro that she shouldn't have a dessert. *Oh Stel Blackbird, you are so stupid for worrying.* Did she want to split up and for Ian to move on to waiting-in-the-wings Meredith? No, of course not. Then she just needed to stop pressing her panic button and relax.

She felt so much happier as she left Caro's salon, less crunched up physically and mentally lighter. *What better start for a relationship could there be than a man who was kind and nice to her?* had been the lesson for today. She walked back into the hospice with a less troubled smile on her face.

Chapter 67

'Okay, Viv, this is the big one,' said Heath, clapping his large square hands together. 'Today you are going to stroke Ursula.'

'What?'

Viv, securing the rabbit leg between the fingers of her stiff glove, looked round at him with an Elvis lip of disbelief.

'She'll let you. I think she trusts you enough now. Call her over.'

Viv made her ridiculous parody of a whistle. She didn't flinch when Ursula flew to her glove and started picking at the meat.

'Okay, try,' said Heath.

'I can't,' said Viv.

'She needs to learn that she shouldn't be afraid of your hands,' explained Heath.

'Will it hurt if she bites me?' asked Viv, looking at Ursula's beautiful but cross face.

'Yes, very much,' replied Heath.

'You aren't selling this to me at all,' mumbled Viv. She looked round to see he had a twinkle in his eyes.

He likes and trusts me, she knew. He had no idea.

'Touch her wings, Viv. If she lets you do that, try the chest.'

Viv's right hand made a tentative journey to the bird. Her fingers smoothed down the freckled soft feathers of her wings and Ursula allowed it without missing a beat from eating.

'My God, look at me, Heath, I'm doing it.' Viv reined in the shriek that was threatening to burst out of her.

Viv's hand touched the bird's breast.

'That's my girl,' she said, her voice trembling, and Heath realised that tears were rolling down Viv's face. He didn't need to ask why she was crying. He knew the swell of emotion she must be feeling; it spread like a warmth in the chest and flooded outwards. He felt so proud of her. He wanted to gather her up in his arms and tell her so and would have, had he the slightest inkling that she would have wanted him to. Ursula hadn't got it wrong, she had picked someone special to put her faith in. Viv Blackbird was lovely.

Chapter 68

Stel called in at the supermarket on the way home from work. Ian had gone back to his house to collect some more of his belongings. After the weekend they'd both be able to use his car to travel to work and save petrol, he'd said. She batted away any ridiculous suggestions that she'd have her wings clipped if that happened. She'd have to ask his permission to borrow it if she wanted to go out at lunchtimes. She didn't consider that she wasn't being silly and that her intuition was spot on.

She picked up an extra bottle of wine and a card because it was Al's birthday and they always bought each other a little something. They usually shared a glass in each other's kitchen too, but that couldn't be the case this year. She didn't think Ian would like that.

Ian's car was parked up when she got home and so was Al's bike, so she knew he was in. She left the shopping in the boot until she'd delivered his card and present. She rat-tatted on his door knocker and saw his silhouette through the frosted glass of the door. When he opened it, his face wore the same expression as the last time she'd seen him to talk to: uncharacteristically chilly.

'All right, Stel,' he said. There was no invitation to come in. But then he probably felt that would be inappropriate now that she was with Ian.

Stel extended her hands, with the card and the present in them, towards him.

'Happy Birthday, Al.'

There was too much distance between them for her to give him the customary birthday kiss on the cheek. And he wasn't making any attempt to bridge it.

'You shouldn't have,' he said, accepting them with reticent politeness.

He's never said that before, thought Stel.

'Well, it's your birthday. I always get you a bit of something.' She smiled, wondering why he was acting so oddly with her.

Al's head cocked towards her door. 'I see he's moved in then.'

'Well, it's a trial run,' Stel said, relieved that he was at least conversing with her.

'Bit quick.' Al's expression remained impassive.

'Well, we're not getting any younger,' she said with an awkward laugh.

He looked down at the card and the bottle. 'Thanks anyway,' he said and stepped back inside to close the door. Stel instinctively put her hand flat on the glass to stop it.

'Al, what's up? Have I upset you in some way?'

An expression of gobsmacked disbelief took over his features. 'After all these years, Stel and . . .' He broke off what he was going to say. 'Forget it, just forget it. I hope you're really happy.'

And with that he shut the door firmly in her face.

Stel stared at it as if she expected it to open again and for Al to appear and tell her what was going on, but instead it was her own door that opened and Ian appeared.

'What are you doing, Stelly?' He didn't look amused.

'I was just giving Al a birthday card. I'll go and get the shopping in.'

'I'll get it,' he said. 'You make a start on tea.'

Stel stepped over the low fence separating her garden from Al's and she walked into a house that she barely recognised. There were cardboard boxes everywhere, black bin liners and battered suitcases. There were old electrical appliances covered in dust that looked as if they had been dragged out of a loft after being stored there for years, a stained ironing board, five pairs of big boots, a stack of sheets and towels and a cheap-looking quilt covered with blooms of stains.

'Don't panic,' said Ian, carrying in the Tesco bags. 'I'm going to car boot a lot of this stuff but for now I'll store it in the spare bedroom.'

Stel bristled with annoyance. 'You mean Viv's room,' she said, making the point that she didn't have a spare room. There was Viv's bedroom across the landing and Viv's workroom in the attic. And that's how it would be until she said she didn't want them any more.

'It *was* Viv's room,' said Ian. 'I'm going to need it now, unless you want to live like this forever.' He put the shopping bags down on the kitchen floor and pulled out the packet of slow-braised beef. 'We'll have this tonight,' he said and tossed it across to Stel.

*

Geraldine insisted on making everyone a simple tea. Oven chips, tinned peas, fried eggs and hunks of doughy white bread and they opened up a bottle of Selwyn Stanbury's parsnip wine which was as sweet as the afternoon had been, and strong enough to take the edges off the reality of their situation. Pilot sat at Heath's feet as they ate and laughed and talked at the table, Bub was curled up on the sofa imitating a furry black cushion, Piccolo sat with his eyes closed in his cage, balancing contentedly on one leg and Jason Statham was safe from harm in his hutch. There was such a feeling of contentment in the cottage that Geraldine's hope that all this would come right in the end powered up again.

Goodnight and may your dreams take flight, she whispered as she lay in bed later and blew a kiss upwards to Heath in his room and across to the folly for Viv.

Viv watched the sun melt into the sky from the downstairs window in the folly. She had been blending oils to remind her of this perfect day. The tang of her leather glove, the snuff of Ursula's aviary, Geraldine's perfume, soft bread and sweet wine, the ever-present love-in-a-mist, the sunshine over Wildflower Cottage – and him. It would bring his green eyes to her mind when her business was completed and she was gone. If only she were someone else who could stay.

*

In bed, Ian pulled playfully at Stel's nightie. They'd both had wine but Stel felt far drunker than she should be. She should have some water and a couple of ibuprofen; she knew she'd have a headache in the morning otherwise.

'What's this, a suit of armour?' he laughed. 'Get it off.'

'I'm cold,' said Stel, making a fake shiver. *All you have to do is say no.*

'What was all that about earlier with Fat Al then?' He was pushing up her nightie, his hands were everywhere.

'I told you,' said Stel. 'I was giving him a birthday card.'

'Why didn't you just post it through the letter box?'

'I wanted to say Happy Birthday in person.' It came out as *happy birdie*. She couldn't talk properly.

'He fancies you,' said Ian. 'He's got the hump now that I'm on the scene.'

He had manoeuvred her nightdress nearly over her head. Her limbs felt too heavy to stop him.

'Don't. I don't want to.'

The room was spinning. There was something wrong. This wasn't normal drunk.

Ian's hand cupped her face. 'Just a word of warning, Stelly. I don't share.'

His fingers were as tight as a clamp on her cheek.

'Ian, get off.'

'I don't think so, Stel,' he said.

Chapter 69

Stel swam to consciousness the next morning with the hangover from hell. She felt as if someone had emptied out her head and replaced her brain with rocks that crunched painfully together at the slightest movement. Sound hurt her ears, light hurt her eyes, her mouth was bone dry and her breath smelled foul when she exhaled.

Her eyes focused on Ian standing at her side holding a mug of tea.

'Morning, love. How do you feel?' His voice was smooth as honey.

Stel didn't answer. How could he behave as if nothing had happened?

He laughed. 'What are you looking at me like that for with your lip all curled up?'

'You . . .' she coughed up something thick and nasty. She reached over for the box of tissues on the bedside table.

'How very attractive,' Ian tutted. 'Now, what were you saying?' He sat down on the side of the bed.

'I didn't want sex last night,' said Stel.

'I know, you said,' he replied.

'So why did you ...'

'Why did I what?' He looked as if he had absolutely no idea where this was going.

'You made me,' Stel yelled and then wished she hadn't because her head thrummed as if someone was hitting it with a drumstick.

'I beg your pardon?' said Ian crossly.

'You heard,' said Stel.

He put the mug down on the cabinet so roughly that the tea slopped over the top and into the tissues.

'Now wait a minute. What exactly can you remember about last night, Stelly?'

'I remember you stripping me,' she hissed, her voice gravelly in her throat.

Ian snatched the bedclothes down. 'You've still got a nightdress on.'

Stel smoothed her hand down and felt her pants were in place too.

'Do you remember being sick, Stelly? Do you remember me holding your hair back and you screaming at me to get off? Do you remember doing this?'

Ian stuck his cheek next to her eye and she saw the long red scratch. 'It bloody hurt as well.'

She couldn't remember any of that.

'It was like you were having a nightmare,' Ian said. 'You came for me like a fucking tigress shouting, "I don't want sex tonight, I don't want sex tonight."' His parody of her voice make her sound pathetic. 'And I'm sorry but I didn't want sex with you anyway in that disgusting state.'

Could she have got all this mixed up? That scratch on his face looked nasty but her nails were bitten down. Her head hurt when she thought. She wanted a drink so badly.

'Stelly, I'm going to tell them at work that you've had a migraine.' His finger came out to tenderly nudge a wave of hair out of her face, then he handed her the cup of tea. 'You drink this and get back to sleep. I have to say you shocked me last night.' His eyebrows rose and he shook his head as if recalling a particular incident. 'I'm not used to being labelled a rapist.'

The word hung in the air and felt too big for the room.

'I didn't say that,' said Stel.

'It's what you meant,' Ian barked. 'Remind me next time you're chucking up your guts to leave you to get on with it. I think if you can't handle your drink, Stel, that you should give it up. You've obviously got a problem with it. I didn't recognise you last night.'

Stel was horrified. There were big holes in her memory. She could remember being in bed, but she couldn't remember climbing up the stairs to get to it, or putting on her nightie. She usually had a shower, but she couldn't remember taking one. She certainly couldn't recall being sick or scratching him. After insisting that she didn't want sex with him and trying to fight him off, her mind was a total blank.

Ian stood up. 'I'll see you after work,' he said and left the room after giving her a look of such revulsion that she felt ashamed. And when she struggled out of bed to shout after him and caught sight of herself in the mirror, she slipped further down into a well of self-loathing – baggy, panda eyes, whey-face, hair like a busted sofa. She looked like the sort of feral woman who would have attacked a man.

'Ian,' she called. 'Listen. I am so sorry. I don't know what happened. I don't usually drink that much.' She suddenly felt sick, really sick. Her hand flew up to her mouth.

'Into the bathroom,' ordered Ian, appearing at her side, pushing her quickly in there where he managed to flick up the toilet lid just in time. Wine-red vomit pumped out of Stel's stomach and Ian held her hair, rubbed her back and said, 'This is becoming a habit.' She felt turned inside out at the end of it and she sat on the side of the bath hunched and limp whilst he patiently wiped the loo seat and floor tiles with toilet paper. Then he ran a cold cloth under the tap and pressed it to her forehead and it felt like heaven.

'Get some sleep, Stelly,' he said and led her like a child back to bed. Stel felt as near death as she had ever been.

Ian kissed her cheek and checked his watch.

'I've fed Basil and changed his litter. I've got to go because I'm late so I'll see you later, okay? I'll ask Pete if he'll get out of my house and I'll move back over the weekend because this obviously isn't going to work, is it?'

Stel's brain went into reverse thrust. She must have got this whole situation wrong. A man who treated her as lovingly as this could not have done what she thought he had. She'd had too much to drink and it had all become distorted. She couldn't bear that it would end like this and that he'd tell people they split up because she was an unhinged, violent drunk. What was going on inside her head? Was she having a mini-breakdown because of the mixed bag of things that had happened to her in such a short time: Basil's disappearance, Viv leaving home, the romance with Ian?

'I don't want that,' she said. 'I really don't.' She felt drained. Tears were sliding down her face, and her head and her stomach were aching so much.

'Just get some sleep,' he said. 'I'll have a good think about it all at work and I suggest you do, too.'

She heard him talk softly to Basil just before he left: 'Look after your mum, Bassy, because she's a bit poorly in the head today.' And Stel thought there wasn't a better description to suit.

Chapter 70

Linda stared at the pile of cards and presents wrapped up in jellyfish- and spaceship-themed paper and the tears sprang to her eyes. It was Freddie's fourth birthday today but they wouldn't be able to see him till Andy came home. Whatever Dino said to pacify her, Linda *knew* that at some point in the future, Freddie would recall how he didn't end up with his birthday presents from his paternal grandparents until well after the event. She hadn't been able to sleep thinking about it and she woke up in the sure and certain knowledge that she *had* to see her grandson today. It was a compulsion that would not be put to bed.

'I can't stand it,' said Linda, pacing up and down her lounge carpet. 'How dare Rebecca deprive that little boy.'

'Look love, he'll enjoy the presents when Andy takes them over. It'll be like a second birthday for him,' said Dino, sounding diplomatic, but it was killing him, too.

'It won't be his birthday though. He should have his presents on the actual birthday,' said Linda. 'Kids remember stuff like that.'

Iris looked at her daughter brushing the tears away from her cheeks and she felt awful that she'd further soured relations between the Hewitts and the Pawsons.

'I'm so sorry, Linda. I'm just an interfering old bat.'

'Yes you are, Mum,' said Linda, wagging her finger at her mother, 'but you did what you thought was right and I'm not blaming you. In fact, I wish I'd done it myself instead of waiting for any scraps they chose to throw us from their bloody table. They were never going to play ball so I might as well have done. In fact . . .'

Linda marched out of the room and came back with her jacket. ' . . . Dino, get me a carrier bag. Mum, get your shoes on. We are going to see our lad for his birthday. Freddie is having his presents today and if that pair of bitches decide to take them away from him then I'd rather he remember that than not getting them from us at all.'

Linda had her *do not argue with me* face on. Dino got the carrier bag and Iris put on her shoes.

Linda's face was set in steely determination as she drove to Maplehill. She pulled up on the quiet, leafy Tennyson Lane and whilst Dino helped Iris unfold herself from the car, Linda grabbed the huge bag of presents from the boot.

'Steady now, love,' warned Dino. 'Enid's liable to call the police on us.'

'Let her,' said Linda. 'Let Freddie see the police drag his nana away for the crime of loving him.'

She swaggered up the path and hammered on the front door with her closed fist. There was no response. In her mind's eye, Linda saw Enid Pawson sitting tight until her unwanted visitors went away. Well, they weren't going to. Whatever had pulled Linda Hewitt here today would keep her here until she saw Freddie. Linda tried the door but not surprisingly it was locked. She battered on the glass panel with the side of her hand until it hurt.

'You're going to break that bloody thing in a minute,' said Dino.

'Good, she might come out then. I would have thought she'd have made an appearance by now, if only to stop the neighbours talking.'

'Last time I went round the back,' said Iris. 'She wasn't expecting that.'

'Dino, get round to the back,' barked Linda. She stepped over something horrid and prickly in a plant pot in order to look through the front window. Snagging her tights on it didn't help her mood. She shielded her eyes from the sun and peered in.

'The side gate's locked,' said Dino.

'Huh. They'll have done that in case I ever came back,' huffed Iris.

'Can you climb over?' asked Linda.

'Linda, it's six foot high. There's no chance of me doing it, love.' Dino was off work with sciatica as it was. He could barely lift his foot to get up a step.

'Not you specifically, but you in general. I mean: can it be climbed?'

'Yeah, by Edmund Hillary.'

Linda adjusted position to make sure that what she could see through the window wasn't a trick of the eye.

'Dino, I think Enid's lying on the floor.'

'What?'

'I can see a part of her leg, I'm sure.'

'Part of it? Has she been cut up?' enquired Iris, then she sniffed. 'Hope so.'

'Something isn't right,' said Linda, brow furrowed in escalating concern. 'I felt it this morning. Dino, let's err on the side of caution. Ring an ambulance.'

'Linda . . .'

'Just do it. Where the hell is Freddie?'

Iris's hand leaped up to her throat. She went to the side gate and shouted his name.

'Shit. That bloody French door is open,' yelled Linda. She stepped back over the snaggy plant and laddered her other leg. 'I'm going to have to climb over that gate.'

'How the hell are you going to do that? No, no, you can't,' Dino protested but Linda was insistent. She might have been eighteen stone but she had to get into that back garden.

Iris's cry alerted them. 'Linda, Freddie's here, on the other side of the gate.'

'Oh thank God,' said Linda trying to see through the wooden slats, but there were no gaps. 'Freddie, are you all right, love?'

'Nana's fallen,' said Freddie. 'I can't wake her up.'

'It's okay, sweetheart. It's Nana Hewitt. I'm here to help her. Freddie, do you know where Mummy keeps the key for this gate?'

'Hello, can I order an ambulance . . .' Dino was saying into his mobile. He sounded as if he was ordering a Chicken Bhuna from Edwina's Curry House, thought Linda, as she scouted around for something either to bash down the gate or enable her to climb over it.

'I know keys,' Freddie said, his voice shrill with excitement. 'Shall I get them?'

'Yes please, my lovely. Then I want you to try and throw them over.'

'There's a step-ladder resting against next door's wall,' said Iris, pointing over the hedge.

Linda strode as fast as she could down the path, out of the gate, up next door's path and back again with the ladder.

'They're sending an ambulance,' replied Dino, coming forward to take the ladder. He propped the ladder against the gate and said to his wife, 'How the bloody hell are you going to get up there?'

'Freddie,' Iris called. There was no response. Then a picture loomed in her head of that hideous gnome, and what he was holding . . . 'Oh, please, no,' she said.

'What's up, Mum?'

'There's a statue in the middle of that pond. A big ugly gnome with a set of keys in his hand. You don't think that—'

'Dino, hold that ladder,' shrieked Linda.

'Freddie, don't go near the pond, will you, love?' Dino thumped on the gate.

Linda started to climb up the steps.

Dino groaned. 'You'll break your bloody neck.'

'Good job there's an ambulance coming then,' said Linda, as she managed to haul herself over somehow and scraped down the other side. 'Stand back. I'm throwing a brick over. Bash the bloody gate in, Dino.' She picked up a loose brick from a stack and threw it as gently as she could over to her husband then hurried round to the back of the house, scanning for Freddie. He wasn't in the garden, thank goodness. He must be looking for keys somewhere inside. Enid Pawson was lying on the kitchen floor unconscious. Linda dropped to her side and checked for a pulse in her neck. She found it and it was strong. And so was the smell of alcohol on her breath.

Behind her Dino and Iris poured into the kitchen.

'She's pissed,' growled Linda, checking Enid for immediate signs of damage.

Enid's eyes fluttered open but she couldn't seem to focus.

'Where are you, Freddie mate?' Dino went to the bottom of the stairs and called for his grandson. When there was no answer, Iris scurried back outside to double-check that Freddie wasn't there.

'Bloody hell, Linda, come quick,' cried Iris, 'There's something out here in the water.'

Linda was on her feet like a flash and running past her mother. She pushed her way through the plants and headed towards the pond, heart in her mouth, blood pounding in her ears. There at the base of the statue was Freddie, floating face down, arms resting on the water at either side of him.

She couldn't remember jumping in, but she must have done because she was wet through when it was all over. Suddenly Dino was there too, helping pull their precious little Freddie out and laying him on the grass. Then Linda set to work.

Pulse. Check airways, sweep mouth, tilt to side. Some water comes out – not much. Angle neck, seal mouth with her own, blow. He was so cold, so pale. She still couldn't feel a pulse. She'd performed CPR on many patients in her life, but never had to pull one back from drowning. *This is my little boy. Commence chest compressions. Count to thirty. Check pulse. An ambulance siren. A pulse. Thank You God.* Freddie was retching, crying. He was alive.

Dino was talking to someone behind her. 'She's a matron at the hospital. If anyone could save him, she could.'

Iris's voice. 'She's pissed on cheap gin and in charge of this boy on a daily basis. And no, I don't know where his

bloody mother is, but his father's a decorated war hero serving his country. Now you tell me, officer, which side of the
family would you give the babysitting to?'

The police were here as well, it seemed. Linda thought
that a better person wouldn't have relished her mother's
indiscretion, but today . . . sod it. Rebecca had gambled with
her son's life and nearly lost him because of it. No, Linda
would have no compunction at all about using what had
happened today as leverage if it would mean that Freddie
was safe. Life wasn't fair – as Rebecca so often said, and some
words just came back to bite you on the bum.

Chapter 71

Stel had been feeling awful all day. The headache had been cured with two lots of ibuprofen and copious amounts of water but it couldn't take away the shame of behaving as she had in front of Ian. She believed his recollection of events more than her own. There were too many holes and inconsistencies in her memory for it to be relied on. She promised herself that she would never let him see her like that again and set about the process of making amends. She cooked a one-pot chicken stew for their tea which she hoped he'd like. He returned home from work with a bunch of flowers cut from the hospice garden and a bottle of Lucozade. He'd given her a big kiss and told her that he hoped they could put the last day behind them because the last thing he wanted was for them to split up. He had worried himself stupid all day that she thought badly of him.

How could Stel have doubted such a considerate man?

*

Hugo rang at 5 p.m. just as Viv was refilling Wonk's water trough. His call confirmed what she already knew, really. He said he would email her all the technical jargon but filled her in verbally on the main points. She'd tried to talk matter-of-factly, which she managed, until she put down the phone. Then she'd thrown her arms around the little grey donkey's neck and she had cried because now it was all real and she had a choice to make. And whichever one she picked would hurt her.

*

That night Ian got into bed, said goodnight to Stel and rolled over.

'No goodnight kiss?' Stel had asked, blinking back tears of disappointment.

'I'm not being funny, Stelly,' he said over his shoulder, 'but I don't think I'd be able to raise a smile tonight. Being accused of rape doesn't do much for the libido.'

He was asleep in minutes. It took Stel much longer than that.

Chapter 72

Viv wouldn't have thought it would be possible to function as normally as she had on the Saturday.

She had seen to the animals, collected the eggs and done two loads of washing. She had walked Pilot up the hill, food shopped, conversed normally with Mrs Macy and complimented her on her new hat. She marvelled at her body's ability to mask the activity sparking in her brain, but Ursula had picked up on her stress. She would not fly to Viv's glove. Not even for a chunk of her favourite venison.

Viv felt like a Dalek, as though a different person was driving her outer shell with levers and buttons: *wash those plates, delete that spam from the mail file, talk politely to Mr Wayne about the nice weather we are having.* She was the same person she had been only one day before, but also she was very different because *she knew* now and there could be no undoing of that.

Viv picked up the knitted toy bee from her bedside table. She wished she had never opened the box and lifted it out. She wished she had never cut the seam when she felt the paper inside it. But she had made the decision to do so. And each of the choices that spun from that moment had been harder and bigger and more complicated than the last.

Chapter 73

'Are you ready to go then?' asked Ian.

Stel looked round from brushing her hair in the kitchen mirror. She checked the time on the wall clock. She didn't usually set off to meet the Old Spice Girls until quarter past five. Why would she set off at quarter to?

'Bit early,' she replied.

'It's not. It starts in half an hour.' Ian lifted his jacket from the back of a chair and put it on.

Stel was confused. 'What does?'

Ian rolled his eyes. 'The film.'

'What?'

'The film,' he repeated the word but increased the volume. 'I told you that I was taking you to the cinema.'

Stel couldn't remember him mentioning it at all. Besides, she wouldn't have agreed to go on a Sunday early evening. That was her Old Spice Girls slot.

'When did you say that?'

Ian looked at her with open-mouthed disbelief. 'Yesterday.'

'I can't,' said Stel. 'I'm going to Linda's. I always go to Linda's on Sunday. It's set in stone.'

Ian laughed dryly. 'You are joking. We could have gone yesterday but I thought you might need a rest after the ... incident. You said we'd go today instead.'

Stel shook her head. 'I didn't. I wouldn't have said that I'd go on a Sunday.'

'Stel, trust me, you did. You really did. We had a whole conversation about it. You said you wanted to see that new Tom Hardy film – I said I'd take you tomorrow. You said great, you couldn't wait, remember?'

'I remember saying I wanted to see the new Tom Hardy film ...' Stel did. But she couldn't recall them arranging anything. She was sure of it. Or was she?

'So what are you saying?' Ian's hands-on-hips stance was one of clear annoyance.

'Well, I'm going to Linda's.'

Ian threw up his hands. 'I honestly think you're losing it, Stelly.' He ripped his coat off and threw it across the kitchen. 'Right, you fuck off to your friend's then,' he said with no veil drawn over his anger.

'Ian, don't be like that. I go there every Sun—'

'I bend over backwards for you, Stelly. I bring you flowers, I clean your sick up, I forgive you when you gouge half my face off and then accuse me ...'

Stel clamped her hands over her ears. She couldn't bear to hear what a mess she was. 'I'm sorry, I can't remember,' she said, tears threatening. 'Look, we'll go and watch the film. I'll text Linda and tell her I don't feel very well.'

'I mean, who spends Sunday evenings with their friends every week?' asked Ian with a mirthless laugh.

'We've done it for years,' said Stel, wiping her running nose. 'We let off steam.'

Ian handed Stel a tissue and put his arms around her. 'You

shouldn't have any steam to let off. I don't want you to be stressed. And if you are, you can talk to me now, okay?'

He lifted up her chin, despite her protest. She didn't want him to see her with red eyes and a snotty nose. He'd seen enough of her imperfections in the past few days, but he held her face firmly and stared fixedly at her as if she were beautiful.

Then he said, 'Go and brush your teeth because they look a bit yellow and we'll go.' And he kissed the tip of her nose.

Chapter 74

In Linda's party room, Gaynor was filling everyone in on the arrangements for the funeral. No one said it, but she looked happier than she had all year.

'One o'clock at St Jude's Church and then on to the crematorium. Then refreshments at the Farmer's Arms. I'm expecting a good turn-out.'

'You coming with us, Caro?' said Linda. 'There's not a lot of parking at the church so we might as well go together. I've texted Stel and told her to be here for just after half-past twelve.'

'Thanks, Linda. Did Stel say what was up with her exactly?'

'She'd been sick and was going back to bed,' replied Linda.

'Probably be one of those twenty-four-hour bug things. There's something going around,' said Iris. 'They do a good spread at the Farmer's, Gaynor. That'll have cost you a bob or two.'

'Well, nothing but the best,' said Gaynor, giving a sniff,

although she didn't feel like crying one bit. The knowledge that Mick missed her and had never stopped loving her would carry her through the rest of her life like a warm current of air. 'He's left me well provided for. House is paid off now and we had a couple of life insurance policies. *She* did all right as well. A bloody house and a fat bank account. And God knows what else.'

'Stop thinking about her now,' said Caro. 'Mick was coming back to you. We all knew he would in the end. He had a mid-life crisis and regretted it. You'd have got over it and had many happy years together.'

'You should go to one of them mediums,' said Iris, spraying egg mayo on her lap. 'Mick might send you a message.'

'They're all rubbish, Mum,' scoffed Linda. 'I don't believe in any of that psychic bollocks.'

'You can laugh but Joan Fleetwood went to see one when her Judd passed over because she couldn't find his wallet. Pat Morrison in Horcroft, she's called. And he came through for her.'

Linda rolled her eyes. 'And did he say where his wallet was?'

'No, but he said she should buy a new fridge freezer.'

Caro coughed to cover up her involuntary giggle. Linda threw up her hands in exasperation. 'And?'

Iris looked at her as if she were daft. 'And what? That's it. She bought a fridge freezer.'

'What about the bloody wallet?' said Linda impatiently.

Iris shrugged. 'I don't know, I forgot to ask her.'

'You'd have thought that if he'd taken all the trouble to come through, he'd have had something more relevant to say, wouldn't you?' said Caro, trying not to laugh.

'As it happens, Pat Morrison's nephew dealt in electrics, so he got her a really good deal.'

The penny dropped for everyone but Iris.

'Charlatan,' said Linda. 'See what I mean? Out to fool people.'

'I don't think I'll bother with a medium, I think I'll catch up with Mick when I see him,' said Gaynor. One day they'd be together again, she knew. He'd be waiting for her and she wouldn't have to spend eternity by herself. She'd been comforted by that more than anyone could ever know. Obviously, when they met at the Pearly Gates she'd give him what-for first and get it out of the way. Then they could go furniture shopping and she wouldn't pick anything he didn't like.

'He'll have a good send-off tomorrow, Gaynor love,' said Iris, with a warm smile. 'That's all you can do for him now.'

'Talking of psychic stuff, what about you with your super-intuitive powers then, Linda?' said Caro with a grin. 'Hero of the hour or what? How is Freddie?'

Linda puffed out her cheeks. 'I never want another day in my life like that, I can tell you. Freddie's fine, thank goodness. They kept him in hospital for the night but we've got him now. He's watching TV with his grandad. Social services were going to place him in temporary care but I said over my dead blumming body. Rebecca kicked up a proper stink about that, but she cocked up when she admitted knowing her mother had a drink problem. She said there was no one else who could look after Freddie whilst she went to work. Well, there was – us – and social services weren't very happy that she "demonstrated a lack of regard for her child's best interests", as they put it. Rebecca was more concerned with hurting us than she was with protecting her own child and that came across loud and clear to them.' She gave such a deep exhalation of breath, it seemed to have been dragged up from her toes. 'It's wrong, you know, how grandparents have no rights. Our boy almost had to die for us to be able to spend time with him.'

'What about long term, Linda?' asked Caro.

'Well, social services are keeping their eye on us to make sure Freddie hasn't gone from the frying pan into the fire and there will need to be a full assessment of the whole family situation. When Andy comes back next month, he won't be lying down for her like he did when they split up, I can tell you that for nothing. We're not after taking the lad away from his mother but she could do with some help and we can give it to her. With any luck she might learn to defrost that bloody face of hers as well.'

'I'm surprised you haven't had the local rag sniffing round.'

'Oh I have,' chuckled Linda. 'But I don't think it's fair on Freddie to have this splashed all over the papers. Ooh' – she did a little dance and rubbed her hands together – 'I could eat him. Those big blue eyes.'

'She might not believe in the supernatural, but she had a message that day,' Iris insisted, stabbing her finger upwards. 'Sure as God is up there.'

'It was intuition, Mum. Or coincidence, or just plain and simple luck,' Linda replied with a shiver. 'Whatever it was, I thank it. What if I'd have ignored it? What if I hadn't looked through the window and seen Enid on the floor and we'd gone back home because we presumed they were out? I couldn't sleep on Friday for what-ifs.'

Iris wouldn't have that it was chance. 'I bet you your

father had something to do with it. He had psychic lean-
ings, I know he did. He used to feel things when we were
in bed.'

A moment of intense lip-biting ensued.

'When we buried him, a robin flew into the church. Do
you remember, Linda, I said "That's your father, that is".'

'I remember,' nodded Linda.

'It flew all around the church and then landed on the
coffin.'

'Really?' said Caro, tears bursting from her eyes from the
effort of keeping herself in check.

'Oh aye,' said Linda. 'Then it flew up again and crapped
on the organist.'

Caro couldn't hold it back then. She unleashed her laughter and the others followed suit.

'All down his black jacket. There he was, happily playing
away "The Lord is my Shepherd" with half a pint of robin
shit down his back.'

Caro gestured for Linda to stop because she couldn't
breathe.

'I knew it was your father because he hated that song. He
said it always reminded him of funerals,' said Iris.

'Well, why did you pick it then, Mum?'

'I shouldn't have. I got persuaded into it by the priest.
Your father wouldn't have wanted any hymns, least of all
that one. That's how I knew he was that robin. It's the sort
of thing he would have done.'

'What, crapped on an organist?'

'Linda, don't be so disgusting. This is your father you're
talking about!'

Even Gaynor was laughing so hard that her stomach
muscles ached. For a minute or so the room was engulfed

in a cloudburst of much-needed tension-releasing mirth.

'Oh, it's been a mess this week for us, hasn't it?' said Linda, recovering now. 'All of us laughing one minute, crying the next. I've felt like I'm on a bloody roller-coaster; I think I'm going to book in for one of your stress-busting massages, Caro.'

'Just ring me when you're free,' replied Caro. That brought the subject back round to Stel for her. 'Hey, has anyone seen Stel's new fella yet?'

No one had.

'She came to see me this week for a massage,' said Caro, tapping her lip as she reflected. 'I didn't pay much attention to it at the time but later, I wondered if she was sounding me out.'

'What do you mean?' asked Linda.

'I might be overthinking this but . . . well . . . something she said . . .' she rubbed her forehead as if it were a magic lamp and would bring the words to the front of her mind exactly as Stel had put them. 'She said that he wouldn't let her see the dessert menu when they went out for a meal. She wanted to know what I thought about that and asked me if Eamonn had ever done that sort of thing.'

'What are you getting at, Caro?' said Gaynor.

'She was stressed to hell. It was like trying to massage a bag of breeze blocks. Add to the mix that nonsense about not wearing make-up . . .'

'Hmm,' said Linda, putting that all together. 'Do you think this Ian might be a bit controlling?'

'I have no idea,' replied Caro. 'But maybe we should keep our eye on her. You know what Stel's like where fellas are concerned. She couldn't pull out a good one in a bucket full of Liam Neesons.'

'We'll ask her some subtle questions when we're all together tomorrow,' decided Gaynor. It might have been her husband's funeral but she couldn't help him any more. She could, however, help a friend if she were in need.

Chapter 75

Ursula still refused to come to Viv. She was happy enough to grant permission for Viv to be in her space, but she sat steadfastly on her highest branch and wouldn't budge. It was early evening; Viv would have liked to have thought that it wasn't the usual time for interaction and that was disorientating the Snowy too much for her to play ball, but she couldn't fool herself. Ursula somehow could see into her soul and knew what she was and hated her.

'Any chance of some advice, Ursula?' said Viv. 'I'm stuck. I'm stuck in the middle of a right old mess.'

Ursula fixed Viv with her bright yellow eyes.

'You see, I came here to do one thing. I thought that would be the difficult bit, but I can't tell you how easy it turned out to be. Just being here, this is the hard part, the *really* hard part, and I didn't expect that.' She tried to whistle the sound that Ursula would recognise. Viv blinked because she couldn't see any more. Tears were dripping down her cheeks, down her chin. She could smell the salt in them as they slid past her nose.

'I never wanted to fall in love with you all,' sniffed Viv.

'I've got to think of myself though, haven't I? I don't want anyone to hate me.'

Ursula bowed her head. Was she offering her consent? There was no warmth in those sunshine-yellow eyes though.

'I don't know what to do. And I can't ask anyone. Which is why I'm sitting in a cage and talking to an owl.' She laughed at the absurdity of it.

She wouldn't even talk to Hugo about it. He thought she'd told him the whole story, but she hadn't. She couldn't.

Viv's head dropped onto her chest and she sobbed. Heath had driven up to look at Mr Mark and Mr Wayne's poodle Douglas; Geraldine couldn't have walked as far as the aviary. There was no one to hear her but the animals.

Then Viv felt a soft whoosh. Ursula had flown to the floor in front of her. Viv raised her glove and Ursula hopped onto it. There had been no food to entice her, she had just come because she wanted to. She didn't feel threatened as Viv touched the back of her head, her fingers smoothing over the thick, soft, deep plumage. A Snowy's colouring was her camouflage, so she could disguise herself against the snow to strike without warning.

Strike without warning.

Those words gave Viv a Eureka moment. She not only knew what she was doing to do but, more importantly, how she was going to do it.

Chapter 76

Stel didn't really enjoy the pictures. She hadn't been in the mood for going and would rather have seen her friends but she put on a show of gratitude for Ian. She'd had to pay for the tickets because he'd left his wallet at home – because they'd argued and she'd made him forget it, he said. Anyway, he said, it was about time she stuck her hand in her pocket for something because he was always buying things for her. He made Stel feel mean and so she over-compensated to prove that she wasn't and bought popcorn and drinks and nachos. She could have bought a small house for less.

He was quiet on the drive home and when they got back and put on the TV, she could tell his mind must have been chewing on something because he had a faraway look in his eyes. Even though they were focused on the screen, he wasn't in the room.

'Would you like a cup of coffee?' asked Stel tentatively at ten o'clock.

He turned his head slowly towards her. 'No, but I'd like to see your phone,' he said.

That came from left field. She gave a small laugh of confusion. He fluttered his fingers at her in a 'give me' motion.

'What do you want to see my phone for?'

'If you don't have anything to hide from me, Stelly, you'll show me what's on your phone.'

He sounded like an automaton.

Stel didn't have anything to hide so she got it out of her bag and handed it to him.

'You've got a passcode on it. What is it?'

Stel felt an odd swirl of anxiety inside her.

'2-5-1-2. Christmas Day,' she said.

His thumb moved deftly over the screen. 'Who's David?' he said.

'David? I don't know a David,' said Stel.

'Just testing,' he smiled. But there was an unpleasant twist to his mouth.

He was scrolling down her messages. She had loads of them because she hardly ever deleted them. She tried to think if there were any that she wouldn't want him to see. Had she texted any details about him to the Old Spice Girls? Or were there any ancient emails from Matchmaker.com still lurking in her files? She felt her heart flutter with apprehension and when he tossed the phone back to her, she felt a ridiculous surge of relief rush through her.

'Why would you think I was hiding something?' she asked.

'Women always hide things from men,' he replied flatly.

The atmosphere in the house felt as if it had been doused with petrol and one incendiary word would have blown the walls apart.

'You do remember I'm going to a funeral tomorrow,' she

said, quietly, tentatively, 'so we'll have to travel in to work separately.'

'Convenient,' he replied, clicked off the TV and marched up to bed without another word. She found his cold back waiting for her and she was glad of that.

Chapter 77

Viv said that she needed a couple of hours off the next morning to go and see the doctor in Mawton. She was slightly worried about her back, she said. After what had happened when Armstrong knocked her over, no one had grounds to disbelieve her. Heath offered to drive her but she said she was fine. There was no need for any fuss.

Viv drove up the hill but took a left instead of a right. She parked her car on the grass verge and took from the boot a tin of white emulsion and a brush that she'd found in the maintenance stores at the sanctuary. She walked down the bridle path that she had taken the afternoon of the storm, climbed over the gate and made sure she swung past the eyes of the security cameras. One had been adjusted to cover the stable door now, probably after her last visit.

Viv opened the can, dipped in the brush, painted a message on the stable door. And she waited.

Chapter 78

It took ten minutes for the Range Rover to arrive. It crunched over the gravel with angry tyres and an even angrier driver at the wheel: Nicholas Leighton. Viv noted that Victoria was in the passenger seat. She and her husband had come alone. They'd understood. And they were taking her seriously.

Nicholas Leighton threw open the door of the car and marched silently over to Viv with fire blazing in his eyes. He had a golf club in his hand and as he was steps away from her, he swung it aggressively. Viv covered her head with her hands and shrieked, expecting to feel its impact. Instead she heard a crunch and realised that he had smashed the security camera that covered the defaced door, but his action had been intended to intimidate her also.

'What the hell do you think you're doing here?' Victoria Leighton got out of the car. She appeared elegant and assured with her long dark hair falling around her shoulders, but her arms were crossed defensively across her chest and her movements were twitchy.

Nicholas was blasting the door with water from a nearby

hosepipe. The six large numbers written in white paint were melting away into the water. She knew that message would have them coming to her as soon as they saw it. No security, no police, no Antonia in tow.

'Answer me,' demanded Victoria. 'What are you doing here?'

Viv hadn't realised she had been holding on to her breath until her lungs overrode the manual control. She exhaled long and slowly before she told them: 'I'm your daughter.'

*

Heath opened the door to clean Ursula's aviary and the owl immediately got on her high horse with him. He grinned.

'No use griping at me, Ursula,' he said. 'Viv is otherwise engaged this morning.' He looked up at the snowy owl, lifting her wings, making herself appear like an avenging angel.

'What is it that you like about her so much, eh?' he said. 'What has she got that I haven't?'

Ursula pinned her great yellow eyes on him, watching his every move.

'I've fed you for years and do I get as much as a head bow? Nope.' He smiled at her. 'And yet along comes a woman who would probably have fed you Trill if I hadn't been here to teach her and you're all over her like a rash.'

He cupped his hand around his ear. 'What's that you say? She does a really entertaining play with condiments? Okay, I'll give you that one. And her cheese pie is good? How did you know that, Ursula? And of course, as you say, she's a mean shot with a bucket of dirty water. These are all important things to you, are they?'

*And she hasn't stopped working since she got here and it feels
like she's been here forever. And she threw her arms around a boy
whose heart was breaking and got hurt for it. And that's why you
love her, Ursula.*

And Heath Merlo thought he could see where the bird
was coming from.

*

There was a pin-drop silence to end all pin-drop silences
and the only sound was the hosepipe falling to the floor.
Then Victoria Leighton started to hyperventilate and her
husband ran to her side.

'You recognised my birthdate then?' said Viv.

'I knew, when I saw her. I knew there was something . . .'
Victoria was borderline hysterical. Nicholas pulled her
around the corner and started talking to her in a growling
whisper. He returned alone, leaving his wife out of sight to
calm down, recalibrate.

'We have no idea what you're talking about. Can you
please explain yourself.' He looked in total command, not
ruffled at all. He was used to holding his ground though and
he had an army of people who could get his own way for
him. He was not in the habit of being at a disadvantage.

He smelled of very expensive cologne, oakmoss, cedar, a
bold pop of lavender in the mix that bloomed into the air
when his skin heated, as it was doing now if the rising colour
in his cheeks was anything to go by.

As she started to speak, Viv was aware of her left leg
shaking, as if it was the pressure valve to the rest of her body.
'You had me on Saturday, March the twenty-first 1992 in
Hallamshire Hospital.'

Victoria appeared at the corner. Viv caught the drift of her scent and it was of a woman much older than she was: a drench of cinnamon with a heavy dust of powder. Viv lifted no sweet notes from her at all.

'I've had plenty of time to imagine what might have happened but let me see how close I am. Scans showed you were carrying a very imperfect baby when it was far too late and dangerous to abort. The only real option was to go through with the birth.'

Nicholas Leighton said nothing but his hand was clenching and unclenching at his side.

'The labour started earlier than you expected. You had to get to a hospital, but not the nearest one in case you saw anyone you knew. The Hallamshire was just far enough away to dump *it*, then you could get on with your lives. The baby was so premature that chances were it would die anyway.'

Victoria Leighton was clinging on to her husband now, thirsty for his comfort and protection.

'You spoke in German to each other, called each other by false names to disguise who you were.'

Victoria Leighton blanched. 'How could you—?'

Nicholas cut her off quickly. 'Be quiet, Tori.'

Viv was in full control of what details to give them. They didn't need to know everything, just enough to convince them of who she was. She would drip-feed the information as and when it was required.

The nurse on duty that night, Elke Wilson – Elke Baumgartner Wilson – happened to be a naturalised German. She knew immediately something was strange about the guarded couple masquerading as German holiday-makers who didn't speak much English, because the man spoke her language with a discernible English accent. So she listened and remembered. The patient had said her name was Kristina but Elke heard her husband refer to her by mistake as Tori.

The couple had left secretly less than two hours after the birth. It wasn't the first time a sick baby had been abandoned. She was so poorly that her chances of survival were slim, especially when compounded by the spinal deformity.

Elke wrote down all the details she could remember: the man's expensive shoes and his watch and that the woman's wedding ring was silver in colour. She recorded their physical descriptions and that 'Kristina' should have had a blood transfusion but she refused.

'I read an article about you both in February,' Viv went on. 'You' – she pointed at Nicholas. She didn't know what to call him now – 'Mr Leighton, you were encouraging people to donate blood. Because your wife and your elder daughter are both AB positive. You needed blood after the birth.' Viv levelled this at Victoria. 'But then they would have discovered your blood group. It's not the most common sort, is it?'

Victoria Leighton was sobbing against her husband's Barbour. 'Make her stop, Nick.'

'How can you possibly know all this?' he hissed, the words squeezed out between his clenched teeth.

'One of the nurses wrote down everything she could remember about that night on a piece of paper and stitched it into a knitted bee, a soft toy which she gave me, in case it was found and destroyed. They called me Baby Bee, you see, on account of my blood group. Social services stored the box of my belongings away until I was eighteen and old enough to decide if I wanted to see it or not. There wasn't much in it to be fair, the wrist and the ankle tag that said *Baby Bee*. And a tiny hat plus a couple of cards that people had sent, wishing me love and hopes that I'd recover. Which obviously I did.'

Victoria was burying her head in her husband's coat as if the material would serve to cushion the words. Nicholas looked like a statue, stiffly bearing this most alien of situations because he had no idea what else to do but adhere to his stoic demeanor.

Viv went on. 'I went up for adoption. Plenty of people want babies but those with physical problems and a lot of operations to look forward to tend to be a bit harder to find homes for. Luckily for me, South Yorkshire had so many kids on their hands that they had a brainwave in the early nineties and encouraged loads of single people to come forward.'

And along came Miss Stella Blackbird who had a nice steady job and was solvent, kind, clean, warm and keen to give a child the loving upbringing she'd had. She might have been rubbish at romance, but she was a hell of a mother.

'I was adopted immediately as it happens,' Viv continued. 'Stel was . . . is a wonderful woman. She was there every step of the way for me; after every operation I woke up to find her holding my hand. She made me do yoga, exercise, swim. She battled with doctors when she had to, she wouldn't take no for an answer ever where I was concerned. Thanks to her, I'm kind of normal height and I'm strong and I'm fit and I'm alive.'

Nicholas Leighton was glaring at her still; his eyes were cold as Arctic ice, his face an emotionless mask.

Victoria Leighton had stopped sobbing now, but she kept

her face against her husband's chest. Viv noticed the wet patch on his shirt. It was funny what silly little details you picked up on sometimes. That's what Elke Baumgartner Wilson had said when Viv went to visit her. But all those many little details put together and added to over the past five years had eventually led her here.

'I read that you were married nine months before Antonia came along. There are photos on the internet of the very grand occasion,' said Viv. 'But that was just a blessing ceremony, wasn't it? A PR smokescreen because you really married months before that, didn't you? A hastily organised registry office wedding between realising I was on the way, and finding out I was damaged goods. Was that to secure your first-born's legitimacy? Makes all the inheritance stuff so much easier, doesn't it?'

Nicholas Leighton's jaw was tightening on the beat, like a pulse. Every time Viv opened her mouth, she could almost hear his brain recalculating her damage potential.

'You see, that would be me then. As the first-born of legally married parents.'

'Look, where is this going?' asked Nicholas Leighton brusquely. He'd been tortured enough now. He didn't do dangling on the ends of strings. He called the shots, not the other way round. But the woman in front of him had this wrapped up in a nice neat parcel with a bow on top. 'Are you some sort of journalist?'

'No, I'm exactly who I say I am. Oh, and just in case you aren't totally convinced, I have DNA evidence.'

'Wha-at?' Victoria Leighton's large blue eyes widened to full stretch.

'She doesn't have it,' Nicholas said to his wife.

'Actually, I do,' said Viv. 'Hairs on your inside of your

riding hats. That day you caught me ... Victoria, I really was sheltering from the storm. I hadn't worked out how I was going to get hold of your DNA until the opportunity just landed in my lap. I was lucky to get a couple of hairs with the root still attached.'

She had sent them to Hugo: a sample from the mother, one from the father and one from each girl. He had his work cut out, but there was enough to prove she was full sister to one, full daughter to Nicholas.

'You don't have my permission,' snarled Nicholas Leighton.

'No. You're right, I don't,' smiled Viv. 'But I had to find out who I am.'

Hugo worked in a DNA analysis lab in London. He was adopted, too. It was one of the things that had brought him and Viv together. Hugo had traced his birth mother to discover she had died; he'd convinced Viv that she'd regret it if she left it too late to search for her own parents. When she discovered where the trail led to, she'd misled him slightly. She told him her suspected family were in Manchester, so she was basing herself at a safe distance in a hamlet called Ironmist. When Hugo looked it up, he found that she'd be in the vicinity of someone who could springboard her career. She didn't tell him that Nicholas Leighton, the great advocate of young business people, and her father were one and the same.

Nicholas and Victoria looked at each other, as if they were communicating on a psychic level. Then Nicholas Leighton turned slowly to Viv. She saw the Adam's apple rise and fall in his throat before he asked the obvious question.

'So what do you want?'

If he had asked this question when she first arrived she

would have answered that she wanted nothing other than just to see them. Maybe, if the chance presented itself, to let them know that she had survived, absolve their old guilt if they had any. She wasn't a gold digger, her prime objective really had been to put her curiosity to bed. But a tiny part of her had held on to the hope that her parents might have wanted to get to know her, draw a line under the past and find a way to build a tentative new relationship.

But then Viv started to fall in love with the people whom the Leightons were trying to destroy. What had begun as an uncomplicated task became a dichotomy. Whichever side she picked would alienate her totally from the other.

But then again, Stel Blackbird had brought up Viv to be a decent human being. In the end, there was only one mast to which she could pin her colours.

'I want Wildflower Cottage,' said Viv. 'And the sanctuary.'

Chapter 79

Stel looked at herself in the full-length mirror and thought she looked bloody terrible in black with no make-up on. She went into the bathroom cupboard and got out her box of tricks and sat down at her dressing table. She applied the full works: foundation, eyeshadow, eye liner, blusher, mascara, eyebrow pencil and finally red lippy – and only then did her reflection throw back the real Stel. She didn't feel like that Stel any more. That Stel smiled and wasn't jumpy. That Stel didn't think that everything she did was wrong. That Stel didn't get drunk and forget things. That Stel wouldn't have searched for her wet-wipes to put in her handbag solely for the purpose of removing her make-up before Ian saw her later.

She checked her bedside cabinet drawer, but they weren't there. Then she looked in the other one on Ian's side of the bed but he'd emptied it and put his own things in there.

In the drawer he had some dental floss, a box with a signet ring in it, a pen, some watch batteries and her own spare car keys. She'd thought she'd mislaid them, as happened often, and they'd turn up eventually. *Why would they be in here?* She opened the cupboard below, checking instinctively over her shoulder to make sure he hadn't suddenly materialised behind her. There was a toilet bag and a notepad, the pages bound at the top with a spiral wire. She opened it and saw a long list of dates, numbers and symbols.

59750 ✓
59772 ✓
59772 ✓
59790 ????
59820 ✓.

Halfway through the pad were more dates and next to each, letters and symbols – some sort of code. On the back page he had written: 2512, her phone pin.

Basil wandered upstairs on silent paws and jumped up on the bed. Stel shrieked, throwing the pad up in the air and realised that she was a nervous wreck. She put the pad back where she thought it had been, but then wasn't so sure she'd got it right. Oh God. What if he'd left it there in a certain way to test if she'd looked through his things?

Stel closed the cupboard and just prayed she'd positioned it correctly. Then she set off for Linda's house at speed because she was running late.

It was when Stel switched on her ignition and the mileage flashed up on the display as 59826 that the numbers in Ian's notepad made sense: he had been recording her car mileage.

Chapter 80

Nicholas and Victoria Leighton stood in open-mouthed amazement. Viv prepared herself because she knew this was when things were likely to get nasty. Cornered rats struck out. Nicholas Leighton would throw every piece of ammunition he had at her now. He'd try and discredit her, make her feel like an opportunist, threaten her, play indifferent, appeal to her better nature. In the game of psychological warfare she was a cadet up against his Brigadier.

'Imagine what the newspapers would say about all this.' Viv tried to remain focused, firm. She was acting against her nature, she was preparing to blackmail him. But she had entered a game of crush or be crushed and had to see this through to the end. 'Not to mention all those charities you're associated with. And' – she tapped her lip tauntingly – 'you're going to inherit a title from your childless cousin one day, aren't you, which you might be able to pass onto your eldest child. Oh, hang on, that's me.'

Nicholas's face crunched up in rage. That piece of information stung him right where it hurt.

'I mean, you just might have managed to do a PR spin on bulldozing a crumbly old animal sanctuary, what with all those lovely new houses being built on the land, but I'm not sure that being Special Adviser to the Department for Pastoral Care would be appropriate for a man who abandoned his own child, do you? And we really must talk about my share of the estate . . .'

Leighton had decided he had heard enough. 'What the fuck do you really want, you ridiculous . . . You . . . you . . . freak. You nearly killed my wife.'

'I told you. I want the land that Wildflower Cottage stands on. I want the valley,' said Viv. Her confidence was returning because he was lashing out now, flailing. That was a portent of weakness not strength. It might have been a good sign, but his words still wounded her.

'How can I possibly *give* you that?' he scoffed with a hard disbelieving laugh.

'I don't want you to give it to *me*. I'm asking you to give it back to the Merlo family. Sign it over to them for ever. The sanctuary must remain, and Heath must be allowed to build a veterinary practice, but never a housing estate. If you do that, you'll get off really lightly because I'll never pursue you for an inheritance or any other favour. Not even a kidney. Your daughters will never know that their parents had another child. You'll be a hero, the animal-loving rock stars will love you even more and you'll be able to rise through the ranks as a celebrated man of the people who put local interests first. Or . . . '

She left the word swinging in the air like a creaky motel sign in a horror movie.

Nicholas was stock-still, belying the chaos taking place in his brain. The wires in his head must be sparking like fireworks, thought Viv. He couldn't exactly leave this one with a team of advisers.

Victoria Leighton's eyes locked on the stranger in front of her.

'You don't look anything like us,' she said.

'That will make it easier on us all,' said Viv. She meant it kindly.

'You should have died,' said Victoria.

The words plunged into Viv like a cold-steel knife; their impact caused her a moment of real physical pain. She turned her head to the side, focused on the view of the gate to let the sudden rush of tears sink back to their resting place.

'What possible guarantee can you give me that I will never hear from you again if I do as you ask?' said Nicholas.

Victoria looked at him in total disbelief, 'Nick, you can't seriously—'

'Be quiet, Tori.'

'I can't offer you any guarantee other than my word,' replied Viv.

'Your word?' Nicholas's eyebrows rose in disbelief. 'The word of a blackmailer?'

'The word of your daughter,' Viv said.

'You aren't our daughter,' he replied. His lip curled at such a disgusting thought.

'I think you'll find the DNA analysis says I am. A legitimate heir, too, if I chose to announce myself.'

Something came to Nicholas that confused him. 'Wait a minute. So, let me get this right. What do you get out of all this?'

'Nothing,' said Viv.

She didn't want anything. Well, okay, millions of pounds would be good but in order to get them she'd have to either destroy the Leightons' reputation or resort to extortion and she wasn't that sort of person. Her blood might have made her a Leighton, but in her heart she was all Blackbird.

'I will give you my word and my guarantee, as God is my witness, that if you agree to let Heath Merlo keep the land and' – *this just came to her, but she was glad it had* – 'as a worthy charity cause, you encouraged donations to it for the animals since, after all, it would make sense for their local friendly Ironmist estate to support them financially . . . I will forget that I was born with your name. If you attempt to destroy my friends at Wildflower Cottage, then I will destroy you.'

The Leightons considered her words then Nicholas exploded. 'This is preposterous.'

'You have no choice, is what I'm saying,' said Viv, her tone firm but quiet, cement and velvet.

Nicholas Leighton rested his hands on his hips and stared hard at Viv. But she'd been stared at by worse. Ursula for one.

Then he exhaled and on the breath he said the words, 'All right.'

'Nick . . .'

'What can we do?' Nicholas rasped at his wife.

'I want you to visit Heath Merlo within forty-eight hours . . .' Viv chose that time-scale because they always said it in films. Then she looked at her wrist and only just stopped herself from laughing as she thought of saying, *let's synchronise our watches*. ' . . . Let's make it twelve noon on Wednesday, and tell him what action *you've* decided upon. You'll get all the credit for it. I will pretend that it is as big a surprise to me as it will be to them. Feel free to get the press involved for your benefit. It will make you a community hero. The people of Ironmist are lovely, you know.

It wouldn't do you any harm for them to think better of you.'

Nicholas stared hard at the young woman in front of him. He did not recognise her as one of his own but if he had, he would have commended her ability to checkmate him so absolutely. She had reminded him of someone when they first met and now, after this prolonged encounter, he knew with certainty who it was. Her summer-blue eyes and her bronze-golden hair were just too similar to Cecilia Leighton's for comfort. He thought that he would have the portrait of her that hung on the grand staircase removed with immediate effect.

Nicholas opened the car door for his wife and she clambered in. He turned to Viv, punctuating each word with a stab of his finger, 'If you ever ... ever even think of ...'

A full threat display, thought Viv, likening him to one of the birds of prey at the sanctuary. But this ruffle of his feathers had no effect on her. Her family honour had been her shield today. The Blackbird honour.

'If I have nothing to fear from you, you have nothing to fear from me,' she returned.

Nicholas crunched over the gravel to reach his side of the car.

'Now get off my land,' he said and sped off the same way he had arrived.

Chapter 81

Mick Pollock's internment arrangements were typical Gaynor Pollock-style.

'Bloody hell, have we got the wrong church and turned up at Winston Churchill's funeral?' asked Linda, as the hearse arrived at the church draped in a Union Jack flag. The others bit their lips and tried to stay sombre. There was something about the solemnity of a funeral that spawned a breeding ground for inappropriate humour.

What Gaynor called a 'simple cross' contained half the blooms of the Chelsea Flower Show. Gaynor, Leanne, Paula and Mick's brother and his wife followed in a black Daimler so shiny that it looked like a huge beetle. Gaynor emerged from it in a stunning black ensemble and a hat the size of a spaceship. Leanne's longline jacket was at least a foot longer than her skirt and her heels were so high that Linda's feet ached just looking at them.

Inside the church, a local opera singer in a long black frock sang a moving rendition of 'Bring Him Home' which set off a Mexican wave of handbag-opening for tissues. Then the vicar began the service. The organist played 'Love Divine' in too high a key so that everyone either mimed or stretched painfully for the notes. Mick's brother read the eulogy – a glowing and tender tribute to a dear brother, husband and father. A flawed man, but essentially a good one, with a love of home comforts, David Bowie and football. Then the Old Spice Girls clambered into Linda's seven-seater and set off for the crematorium.

'You know, your face is so much better with make-up on it, Stel,' said Iris. 'You've looked like death warmed up these past couple of weeks.'

'You're subtle, Mum, I'll give you that,' sighed Linda.

'You feeling better, Stel?' asked Caro. Stel didn't look right to her. Her eyes were dull and there was a cold sore at the side of her mouth which she'd attempted to cover up with foundation.

'I'm improving,' said Stel with a fluttery smile.

They had to skim past Ketherwood to get to the crematorium. Ian's house was somewhere around here.

'Linda, where's Crompton Street?'

'It's coming up on your right.'

'Have we time to drive up it?' asked Stel.

'I can do a loop,' said Linda. 'What do you want to go up there for?'

'There's a house for sale that took my eye in the *Chronicle*,' lied Stel.

'You wouldn't want to live here, surely?' said Iris. 'You've got a lovely house. And that nice lad next door to look out for you.'

'Al's a bit off with me at the moment,' said Stel. 'I don't know what I've done wrong.'

'Ask him then,' said Linda. 'You've only known him

forty-odd years. What number do you want? God, I wouldn't have one of these houses given to me.'

'Forty-three,' said Stel.

'He's a lovely man is Al,' said Caro. 'I wish you and him would have got it together. He'd have looked after you and you'd be living in the lap of luxury now.'

'Any decent man is blocked by her radar,' said Iris. 'Only the idiots get through. Apart from now maybe?' She cast a sideways glance at Stel. Stel didn't reply.

'Forty-three,' Linda pointed. 'Ugh.'

Forty-three Crompton Road was a shabby mid-terrace of five. The left end one had its windows boarded up and a large rectangle of chipboard nailed over the door.

'I can't see a For Sale notice,' said Caro.

'Just stop for a second. I'll be quick as I can,' said Stel.

She got out of the car, hearing a female chorus of 'what the hell's she doing?' behind her, and peered through the front window of forty-three. There was a grotty black sofa in the middle of an otherwise empty lounge, and it had the air of an abandoned property. The door to forty-one opened and a painfully thin man, who looked much older than he probably was, appeared on the doorstop.

'Who you looking for, love?' he asked.

'Er, John,' Stel picked a random name. 'He's renting the place from the owner.'

'You've got t'wrong place. Housing Association own all these,' said the man. He had no teeth, Stel noticed. He couldn't have been over twenty-five. 'Last bloke left a couple of weeks ago.'

'Are you sure? I could have sworn he said he was staying here.'

'Someone called Ian had it last.'

So there was no friend who had been staying here then. Ian had lied.

'Thank you.' Stel felt slightly sick.

'Who's your new friend?' asked Linda, when Stel got back in the car.

'I think the *Chron* put the wrong picture in,' she answered.

*

Lots of Mick's present and ex work colleagues had gone straight to the crematorium rather than join the church service. Gaynor was glad that plenty of people had turned out for him, it made her proud that he was so well thought of. Everyone was respectful to her, shook her hand and said that they were sorry for her loss. No one said 'I thought he'd left you and buggered off with a young lass.'

Gaynor had held up very well all day. Her brain had resolutely stuck in organising mode, making sure that everything went as planned with neither hiccups nor unwanted Bellfield guests. But as the vicar said his final words, his Irish voice soft and rich and gentle, Gaynor's composure began to slide.

'As we say goodbye to Mick, take a moment to remember the best of him. Keep that memory in the scrapbook of your heart. Let the Mick you know, go on, with your love.'

The final music choice started up: 'Ashes to Ashes', Mick's favourite Bowie track. Gaynor remembered him trying to dance to it at a wedding during his New Romantic days and making a total pig's ear of it. He was such an appalling dancer, but he did carry the frilly white shirt off well.

Let him go on with your love. She imagined him floating up to heaven in that shirt, looking like Adam Ant's more substantially-built brother. The further up he floated, the more like an angel he appeared.

She felt her mother's arm slide around her shoulders as the guests began to file out, dropping notes and coins which would be sent on to the British Heart Foundation onto the plate at the door.

'Come on, love. You've done him proud,' said Paula to her daughter.

'I need a drink,' said Gaynor.

Chapter 82

For so long now Gaynor's focus had been either on getting Mick back or kicking him in the bollocks. Then after he died, arranging his funeral absorbed all her attention and now it was done with, there was just a void in her life. Today, she filled that void with wine. A lot of wine.

Gaynor was washing her hands in the ladies when Leanne appeared at her side, all hair extensions and spray-tan, towering over her mother in skyscraper heels.

'Mum,' said Leanne with a sad smile and put her arm around Gaynor's shoulder. Touched, Gaynor turned her head into her daughter's shoulder and stood there, breathing in her daughter's Dior Poison perfume. She had her father's square shoulders and his hazel eyes. Gaynor squeezed her tightly, knowing that as long as she had Leanne, she would always still have Mick, too.

A few seconds later, Leanne asked, softly and tentatively, 'Mum, any chance of having my share of Dad's money sooner rather than later?'

Gaynor pulled away. 'What?'

'He did leave me some money in his will, didn't he?'

'Well, he left some in trust—'

'It's just that I could really do with a cash injection. Everything is so expensive in London.'

Alcohol muddies brains, but it can also unlock zones where clarity reigns supreme. Leanne might have looked like her dad on the outside, but inside was a very different story. There was no softness about Leanne at all. Selfishness oozed from every square millimetre of her. For all his faults, Mick had been a giver, not a taker. He had a great capacity for tenderness and love and in all those things they had been a true match. Leanne Pollock was not the sum of both parents. Gaynor felt as if someone had thrown a bucketful of disappointment over her which drenched her down to the bone marrow.

'Do we have to talk about this now? On the day of your father's funeral?'

'Well, I'm leaving in about half an hour. I've got a taxi booked so I can go and pick up my suitcase from the house and—'

Gaynor's mouth had dropped open in an O of incredulity. 'You're not staying with me? I've aired your bed. I've bought food in . . .'

'No. I'm working. I'm doing some catalogue shots on Friday . . .'

'But this is Monday.'

'I've got to prepare, Mum. You don't know how these things work. My car is getting old. It's not worth repairing. Dad would want me to be safe on the roads.'

'Your car's less than three years old, Leanne.'

She knew that because Mick had bought it new for Leanne's twenty-first birthday, a neat little Toyota Aygo. It couldn't have had above twenty thousand miles on the clock. She hardly drove it around central London.

Gaynor suddenly understood. 'You mean you want a bigger car. A grander car.'

'Image is everything in my work. People look at what you wear, what you drive. I need it. Dad would have wanted me to benefit from his death.'

Gaynor looked at her daughter, really looked at her and she felt ashamed. How had Leanne turned out to be such a self-obsessed little cow? Yes, they'd given her the best of what they could afford, but they'd tried to make sure she appreciated how lucky she was, too. They'd hoped to instil good values in her and thought they'd led by example. They'd given her freedom to grow but within reasonable boundaries. They'd made sure she knew she was loved. But still she had managed to grow up a cold fish, making sure she was all right Jack and sod everyone else. Gaynor thought her daughter had been crying in church but her eye make-up was immaculate. The dabbing of her handkerchief at her eye had been just for show – just like everything Leanne Pollock did. There was nothing below that orange tan but greed and more greed.

Gaynor straightened her back and asked, 'What happened to the twenty thousand your dad gave you when your nan died last year?'

Leanne tutted. 'It just went, on things.'

'Do you still have her jewellery or did you sell it and that went "on things" as well?'

'Oh for God's sake. Look, can I have some of Dad's money, please? Now, when I need it, not later when you're . . .'

'Dead.' Gaynor filled in the missing word for her.

Gaynor noted Leanne's pouty, inflated lips, the Hermes

scarf at her neck and the ridiculously expensive handbag over her arm. She'd spotted the scarlet-soled shoes earlier. These were the essential 'things' of her daughter's life. Trying to keep up with Victoria Beckham. The fur coat and no knickers brigade, as Iris would have put it.

'I think it's about time you stood on your own two feet, don't you?' said Gaynor.

'Legally I think . . .' Leanne shut up as quickly, realising that she was in gross danger of overstepping the mark.

Gaynor laughed and the hollow dry sound echoed off the tiles. 'Don't tell me you're thinking about suing me. Not on the day of your own father's funeral.'

'No, of course not. I didn't mean . . .'

'Oh I know exactly what you meant,' said Gaynor, strong and angry. 'You'll get your money when you're thirty or when I'm dead and buried, whichever comes first. Don't you worry, you'll be able to waste everything your father and I worked all our lives for on fish lips and Stella McCartney frocks but you're on your own for a few years now. And if that takes me off your Christmas card list then so be it.'

She glared at her daughter, fire spitting from her eyes. Her daughter glared back: their eyes battling for dominance.

'Oh for fu—' Leanne huffed like a frustrated four year old. 'There's no point in hanging around, is there? I've said goodbye to Dad so I'll just go.'

'That's up to you,' said Gaynor, her voice brittle.

'Bye then.' Leanne paused, giving Gaynor the chance to change her mind. She knew that behind the flint expression, her mother was on the brink of begging her to stay for the night. They'd talk and make friends and look at old photos, have hot chocolate and cry a bit.

And she was right. Gaynor did want all those things, but

the alcohol in her system was serving to strengthen her resolve rather than weaken it at the moment. So Leanne Pollock strutted out, heels tapping an angry, spoiled tattoo on the tiles. The door crashed against the wall and as it made a thump back into its wooden frame, Gaynor could feel the reverberations rattle all the way down to her heart.

Chapter 83

'Everything all right, Viv, duck? What did the doctor say?' asked Geraldine, as Viv walked in through the door.

'Yep. Back's just bruised, that's all,' Viv answered. 'Nothing to worry about.'

Heath was sitting at the table reading the newspaper. He had Phantom the young barn owl sitting contentedly on his glove, acclimatising to people and noise. She clacked her beak and flapped her wings when Viv got too near for comfort.

'Steady,' said Heath.

'Doing a spot of *manning*, I see,' said Viv, with a smile.

'Oh very good,' said Geraldine, clapping her hands together. 'She's picking up the terminology.'

'More barn owls in captivity than there are flying wild,' replied Heath, with a grumble. 'I wish I could teach everyone about bird care as quickly.'

'Crikey, was that a compliment?' Viv gave a dramatic mock-gasp. 'Tea, anyone?'

'Yes please,' said Geraldine, wondering why Viv was so perky after a visit to the doctor.

Heath's thoughts were otherwise engaged. There were

exactly six weeks to the end of the lease on Wildflower Cottage. Nothing was going to save them now and he needed to start moving the animals out to new homes. There could be no more delaying of the inevitable. The sooner they settled in, the better. He'd had a call from the Owl Sanctuary near Northallerton. They presently had a place for the snowy and the great grey owls and gave him first refusal. If he didn't take those places within three days, they would offer them to someone else. It was a good sanctuary, Heath couldn't afford to pass it up. He'd made an appointment to take them up there on Wednesday morning but he'd kept that to himself. He knew Viv would be devastated but she'd be leaving here herself when they all had to move out of Wildflower Cottage. He couldn't bear to think of what state Geraldine would be in. She would cry, he wouldn't, but a piece of his heart would break off with every creature that left its home here.

Viv left the others under the pretence of catching up with some paperwork in the office. She needed to be by herself for a while and she'd find it difficult today making polite chit-chat, even with the lovely Geraldine. The events of the whole morning were churning around in her brain. One minute she felt shining and triumphant, the next grubby and manipulative.

Her actions had been a necessary evil, but she hadn't felt good about wielding a staff of power over the Leightons, however they'd treated her, and others she cared for. She was the sanctuary's only hope and she had to save it or she would never again have been able to sleep at night.

And she knew that she'd given the Leightons the chance to earn a zillion points of goodwill and likability. She imagined they'd play the press like a cheap guitar. They would continue to reign as the perfect, gorgeous family with everything. No one need ever know about the oddball in the closet.

There had been not one note of warmth sounded in the symphony of their showdown. Not one shadowy memory of a vulnerable little girl had crept over their hearts in the whole twenty-three years, she knew that.

You should have died.

Viv switched on the ancient computer and read the emails. She wanted to hit delete on all of the correspondence that related to finding the animals new homes, but she forced herself to wait for the final clearance. Leighton's brain would be working like every department in GCHQ simultaneously. If anyone could find a loophole, he would. Why the hell hadn't she said twenty-four hours instead?

Chapter 84

A little old lady holding a serviette, points gathered together in one hand to form a knapsack, squeezed Linda's hand.

'I'm so sorry for your loss,' she said.

'Oh it's not my husband,' said Linda, scanning the room for Gaynor. 'I don't know where she is.'

'My mistake,' said the old lady. 'You look so much alike.'

Stel snorted down her nose. Gaynor and Linda couldn't have differed in more ways: one dark and slim, the other blonde and rotund. Linda and Stel watched the old lady return to the buffet table, where she picked off some quiche and added it to her serviette stash.

Mavis Marple loved a funeral. This was her favourite place for a buffet as well. They made the best salmon and broccoli quiche at the Farmer's Arms. She had a black book in her handbag to remind her what to choose and where.

'Ghoul,' tutted Linda. 'I bet she hasn't a clue who Mick was and is just here for the bloody sausage rolls.'

'Do people actually do that?' chuckled Stel, swiping another glass of white wine from the tray of a passing waitress. Oh, she really shouldn't. Look what drink had done to her the last time she'd indulged, but somehow she didn't care today. She wouldn't be able to drive back from Linda's as she was over the limit already, so she might as well have a few and pick up the car tomorrow. She'd drunk just enough to feel relaxed and on the right side of fuzzy and she was ever so glad to be in the company of her friends again. She wanted to get hammered and tell them all that she didn't know what the hell was going on in her life and that she felt as if something heavy were pressing down on her chest and she couldn't breathe.

'You all right, Stel?' asked Linda. 'Really all right?'

'Well, apart from that bug ...'

'Stel, this is me you're talking to.' Linda said sternly. 'I'm a bit worried about you if I'm honest. You just don't seem yourself lately. It's not this new man of yours, is it? You've not gone and landed another arsehole, have you?'

Stel wanted to spew it all out. But here was not the place and if she started talking she might not be able to stop. *Another arsehole.* She was so predictable, she thought, with an internal shake of the head. Everyone would think her such a fool for having walked into it. She was fifty-bloody-two, for Christ's sake. For once, she would act like a grown-up and sort out this mess herself. No one need ever know she'd been taken in yet again.

'Everything's fine, love. Honest.' Stel raised her glass before sipping from it. 'I promise I'd tell you if it wasn't.'

*

Gaynor noticed a slight shift in the shadows under one of the cubicle doors. Seconds later, that door opened and out walked Caro, who flinched.

'Oh Gaynor, I thought you'd gone out,' she said. She'd been trapped in the cubicle for the whole of that exchange between mother and daughter. She genuinely hadn't wanted Gaynor to know she'd been party to it.

Gaynor groaned. Of all the people to have heard. It would have to be *her*. Caro Richmond with her Mercedes-bloody-Benz, her successful business, A-star engineer son, perfect fucking husband, and her smartarse gorgeous daughter.

'I'm sorry,' Caro went on. 'I covered my ears so I wouldn't hear . . .'

'Yeah, course you did,' laughed Gaynor dryly.

'I really didn't want to be in on that conversation, Gaynor.'

'No doubt you found it all very amusing.'

'Not at all.' The sympathy in Caro's voice was like a fork down the blackboard of Gaynor's pride.

'Of all people to hear first hand what a bitch of a daughter I've raised, it had to be you, didn't it, Caro?'

Gaynor's hip bumped into the sink and the pain blossomed. Everything hurt. She felt pain in every part of her. She felt as if someone had flayed her and then thrown vinegar and salt on her.

'Gaynor . . .'

'Oh don't Gaynor me,' came the growled reply. 'I bet you were thinking, "Oh I'm so glad my Marnie isn't like that".'

'I wasn't thinking that at all, Gaynor. I was thinking what a shit day you were having—'

'Oh please spare me the nicey nicey act,' shrieked Gaynor. 'Why do some people get all the luck and others don't?'

'I don't know,' said Caro. 'It's just life, isn't it?'

'Just life, you say.' Gaynor gave a dry laugh. 'Must be marvellous being you.'

Caro knew that Gaynor was spoiling for a fight. She
was upset and half-drunk and she needed something to
pound.

'I do know what today must be doing to you. I know
you're in pain, so please, let's just leave it at that and go back
out into the bar.' She took her arm and pushed her gently
forwards. Gaynor shrugged her off.

'How the hell could you possibly know what I'm going
through? You've never had a moment's pain in your bloody
golden life.'

'Gaynor. Don't. Really.'

But Gaynor's resentment was a springy jack clown that
wasn't yet ready to go back into its box. It was having too
much of a good time, squeezing out all that built-up fester-
ing anger.

'Pain? What do you know about pain? The only pain you
know is when you break your frigging fingernail opening
a tin of caviar.'

Despite the humourless situation, Caro laughed and
threw back her head as if addressing the ceiling. 'What do
I know, eh?'

Gaynor stabbed her finger at Caro. 'You're the sort who'd
win the lottery without buying a bloody ticket.'

'Have you ever stopped to think, Gaynor, that some of us
have had our shit early on?'

'Shit, you? What, did you fail an A-level and your mother
bought you a pony to compensate? That sort of shit?'
Gaynor was laughing hard now. This is what being mad
must feel like, she suddenly thought. It was liberating not
having a conscience, just hating and spitting.

But Caro had had enough. Ever since Mick had run off
with Danira, Gaynor had fermented this absurd resentment

against her. She'd even started to feel guilty that she had all the things that Gaynor was missing out on. It was going to end today, she decided.

'Grow up in a nice house, did you, Gaynor? With a nice loving mum and dad? Food in the cupboard, nice bed to have nice dreamy sleeps in?'

'Lovely,' smirked Gaynor. 'Not by your standards though. I didn't get foie gras in my lunchbox.'

'What do you know about me, Gaynor? What do you really know about my life before I met you? I'll tell you, shall I? You know nothing. You've presumed a lot, but you know nothing.' Caro stared right into Gaynor's brown eyes. 'I'm a Bellfield, Gaynor. A fucking Bellfield.'

The name was too big for Gaynor's head to absorb it in one. It took a while for her brain to compute and then it consigned it to spam.

'Yeah, right,' she humphed.

'Oh, I'm a Bellfield all right. Scum of the earth. Father in prison, hardly knew him. Mother bringing back men at all hours. Try sleeping in a house where you pray that she doesn't pass out and those men come into your room at night. Then imagine being dragged to a struck-off doctor paid extra to keep his gob shut because my dad would have killed her if he'd found out what she made me do. Knackered my insides. I could never have children of my own after that. When I met Eamonn he was a widower with two little kids. So don't you tell me about pain, Gaynor Pollock. And don't you tell me that I don't deserve some love and security because I'm fucking well overdue.'

Caro exhaled as if it were the breathy equivalent of a full-stop. Gaynor's mouth was moving, but no sound was coming out. But plenty was coming out of Caro now.

'You've had plenty to say in the past, is that it now? Are you going to fucking shut up?'

Caro sounded like a Bellfield. There wasn't a trace of her usual refined accent.

'I had no idea,' said Gaynor then, numbed by shame.

'I didn't want you to have an idea,' said Caro. 'I don't want anyone knowing what shit I came from. It's not a badge of honour being a Bellfield.'

Gaynor's head fell into her hands and she sobbed. 'I am so sorry. I've been such a cow. A jealous, nasty, horrible cow.'

'Yeah, you have,' said Caro, stepping forwards to put her arms around Gaynor. She felt the hold reciprocated. Gaynor had had an awful year where things just got a bit mad and distorted. A true friend could handle that but sometimes a hard word was the kindest one.

Together they walked out of the toilet and back into their friendship.

Chapter 85

Stel was full of boozy bravado until Linda rounded the corner of her street and she saw Ian's red car. Then any nerve she had built up toppled like a stack of fog cemented with dust. As she waved Linda off with a smile, inside she was screaming for her friend to turn back and help her. She had to persuade Ian to leave. The fact that she was shaking as she walked up the path because she hadn't taken her make-up off told her everything that was wrong about this relationship.

Ian didn't look up as she walked meekly in to her lounge. He was studying something on his phone.

'Had a good time?' he asked.

'Well. It was a funeral,' she said. She mispronounced it *foo-neral*.

'Had some wine, have we?' he joked. He sounded normal and with some relief she felt her guard ratchet down a notch.

'Just a couple. To be sociable.'

'You know what happens when you have wine, Stelly,' said Ian. 'You do stuff like this.'

He lifted up his phone and showed her a photo. It was her. And Ian.

Stel's whole body was overtaken by a shockwave of panic; it felt as if something nasty and harmful had been injected into her bloodstream.

'It's what you did the last time you were drunk. Your idea, not mine I hasten to add. Can't you remember? Look, here's another.'

More pictures, each one more sordid than the last.

She couldn't remember any of it.

'Delete them,' a shock of tears blinded her. 'Please.'

'Ah ah,' Ian laughed. 'Don't worry, they're safe in the *cloud*.' He looked up and rotated his head as if they were floating in the air above him.

'Please,' Stel begged him. 'I don't do that sort of thing.'

'You did that night.' And he laughed again.

'No . . . no. That's not me.'

'Trust me, Stel, it's you. You can tell it's you.' He enlarged the image so she could see a close-up of her face. 'See?' She looked totally out of it. He was grinning at her terrified reaction. It was like being in a nightmare.

She'd read about things like this in newspapers. Kids doing stupid things for sadists who controlled them like puppets using strings of their own shame. She knew now why some of the people in the reports ran straight to bridges and threw themselves off. Who could bear the horror of knowing that people you worked with, lived beside, your children, saw you doing *that?* She didn't even have the excuse of being a young kid who should know better.

'Look, don't get upset,' said Ian. 'It's not as if I'm going to do anything with them. They're just for us to enjoy, Come on now, Stelly.' He stood up and opened his arms and she walked into them hoping to appeal to him. 'I love you. I wouldn't do anything to hurt you.'

'If you loved me, you'd get rid of those photos,' sobbed Stel. 'I look horrible on them.' She thought of an idea. 'Delete them and we'll do some more.'

He pulled her gently away and lifted up her chin with his finger and his deep crescent of a smile felt like a further assault as he said, 'But I like these ones.'

Chapter 86

It was six o'clock on Tuesday afternoon. There were eighteen hours to go before the deadline. Nicholas Leighton was not giving up without a fight, thought Viv as she sat at her dining table in the folly. She was mixing oils, something that usually relaxed her, but her head felt like a jar of bees.

Not hearing anything is good news. It means he hasn't found a loophole.

Ah, but it also means bad news because he still believes there might be one.

Her mind strayed to Heath. The strain on him was telling today. She was sure there were more lines on his face than there were yesterday. Tomorrow, with any luck, they would smooth out like magic when Leighton arrived to deliver his proposal. Heath would be able to plan for the future and never have to worry about his, or the animals', security again. She wanted him to be happy. She liked him so very much.

Once the deeds were handed over, there was no reason for her to stay any more. She'd told Hugo that it was enough she knew for definite who her parents were and she wouldn't approach them; it was the end of the story. He'd told her to get her ass down to London then, now that she'd done what she had to do on the 'wild and spooky' moors.

But they weren't spooky, they were beautiful and Viv had grown to love the sight of them dark and dramatic under glowering skies or bright and magnificent beneath the sunshine. She was not sure she could easily trade the caress of this valley for the assault of the city.

The great expanse of sky over Wildflower Cottage was the bonniest shade of blue that early evening, with not a single wisp of cloud to blemish it. It would have been a perfect one for Viv to fly Ursula, thought Heath, imagining the white and speckled wings sailing across such a perfect backdrop. Neither of them were ready for that but this was to be the owl's last evening at Wildflower Cottage.

He knocked on the door of Viv's folly. She opened it and escaping scents engulfed him.

'"Dancing Sunshine", in case you're wondering,' explained Viv. 'Lovely scent – obviously – because I made it, but not my choice of name. Sounds more like a racehorse to me.'

'Or a Native American,' smiled Heath, resting his arm on the lintel. He was so tall and broad he filled the doorway. 'Wife of "Dancing with Wolves".'

He was wearing a blue shirt. *He looks as if he's made of the sky*, thought Viv, feeling her cheeks colour slightly. She couldn't imagine him belonging anywhere else but in this valley. She hoped to God there was nothing Leighton had found that could prevent that.

'I thought you might like to try and fly Ursula in the

arena,' he went on. He held up a cord. 'She'll be wearing this, so she can't fly off more than twenty-five metres.'

Viv didn't need to be asked twice.

'Just let me stick the bungs in the test tubes and wash my hands. Come in.'

Heath walked into the folly. He watched Viv as she turned on the tap and soaped her hands. She was wearing a yellow shirt and the light from the stained-glass window cast a gilt glow over her and Heath thought, just for a silly moment, that she looked as if she were made of sunshine.

They walked together down to the birds, passing Wonk who was standing asleep, her face to the last rays in the west, and the horses chewing contentedly on grass.

'Isn't it a gorgeous evening,' said Viv, willing herself to pump out positive thoughts. An evening like this had to be a good portent. She wished she could tell Heath. Her secret felt so huge and heavy inside her.

Heath didn't answer. It would indeed have been a beautiful evening if he could have viewed it merely as artwork, but emotion was bleeding too much into the scene. This was the last night that the family of Wildflower Cottage would be complete, and he was the only one who knew that.

They entered Ursula's aviary.

'When she comes to you, I will attempt, very quickly, to attach this cord,' said Heath. 'She might try to kill me. If she does, please do not alert the authorities. Being murdered by an owl would ruin the good name of the sanctuary.'

He was trying too hard to be jovial, he knew.

With Ursula eventually on her glove, Viv walked into the arena. Heath led her to a post and coaxed the owl over to perch on it. She turned her back on them as if in disgust. Heath led Viv halfway across the space.

'Now this is going to be strange for her and she's not hungry so don't expect miracles. Glove out, meat proffered and call her.'

To their joint surprise, Ursula responded immediately. She pushed off the post, her delicately-peppered wings moving as if in slow motion towards Viv and then she landed precisely on her glove.

'Oh my God, oh my God,' said Viv. 'That was amazing. Can we do it again?'

'Of course. I haven't dragged you out just to do it once,' he mock-barked at her.

Heath watched the faultless repeat performance. The bird had absolutely bonded with Viv. And Viv's face was lit up with so much joy that he knew he'd made a bad call. She was going to be even more devastated tomorrow when Ursula left.

He had to turn away when Viv returned the bird to her aviary. Then he walked with her back to the folly.

'Thank you,' she said. Had she been taller she would have leaned forwards and kissed his cheek.

'You're very welcome,' said Heath. He wanted to lean down and kiss her cheek but he stepped backwards out of her space because if he had done it, he would have felt like Judas Iscariot.

*

Whilst Ian was in the bath, Stel went outside to put the bin out. She opened the door and gulped at the air as if she'd been starved of oxygen. What was preventing her from walking out of the door, not stopping to look behind and starting a new life where no one knew her, like one of those people in witness protection on police dramas? she thought. It was the only way she could think of to escape the mental torture Ian Robson was putting her through.

Al had just rolled his bin onto the pavement.

'Stel,' he said in stiff greeting as he passed her.

'Al. Al, stop a minute, please,' called Stel. 'What have I done to upset you?'

Al turned back to her in a slow half-circle.

'I've always liked you, Stel. Always respected you but I never knew you had such a problem with that. You should have just told me to my face.'

'Pardon?' said Stel.

Al held his large hands up. 'It's okay, I got the message loud and clear. You want me to stay away from you and I will. I'm sorry if I have ever embarrassed you. I'm sorry that you felt the need to be polite to me when all I do is make you feel awkward. I'm sorry that you feel obliged to buy me a birthday present. You didn't have to send your bloke round to do your dirty work, Stel.'

'Al, I . . .'

'Just leave it, will you.'

As Al strode back into his house, he muttered loud enough for her to hear that he couldn't wait to get out of this bloody street.

Chapter 87

The last thing Viv remembered thinking at one in the morning was that she had about as much chance of sleep as growing an extra foot in height, but she did. A solid, dreamless sleep from which she snapped awake just before seven. She had a bath to try and quell the nervous tension that was inhabiting every capillary in her body, then she made herself some poached eggs for which she had no appetite in the end.

The weather was odd this morning. She had opened the curtains to fog so thick, it appeared as if a layer of cotton wool had been glued over the windows. It felt clammy on her skin when she walked out into it and she had to turn back for a sweatshirt. There was no sunshine over Wildflower Cottage today.

Through the thickness of the mist, Viv could just make out a ghostlike Heath loading two black boxes into the back of his pick-up. They looked like rectangular safes. She called out good morning.

Heath returned the greeting but under his breath he was cursing. He had wanted to have left with the owls before

Viv was up, but the fog was too thick to drive in. Occasionally the bowl of the valley filled up like this and cleared in a couple of hours, but the weather forecast had given an alert for the whole area. Freakish conditions, and drivers were advised not to make unnecessary journeys. There was nothing for it, he'd have to tell Viv where he was going.

'Are those safes?' she asked, trying to work out what they were. 'Are they the ones that the ex-employee tried to jemmy out of the wall?'

Oh God. 'They're bird carriers,' said Heath.

'Oh?' said Viv, feeling a prickle of suspicion. 'I hope they're empty.'

He had to tell her. He swallowed. 'Look, Viv . . .'

'Heath, there's a call for you,' called Geraldine from the door of the cottage. 'Mr Wayne wants to ask you something about Douglas.'

Heath was grateful for the temporary reprieve. 'I'm coming.'

'Morning, Geraldine,' Viv called to the fuzzy shape, thinking it was odd that the fog had muted vision but sounds were clearer.

'Morning, Vivienne. Would you like a cup of tea?'

'I've just had one. I'll make a start,' she returned. There was no way she could sit still at a table. She felt as if she were full of crickets. She checked her watch. Every minute was one less to have to wait. The best thing she could do was keep busy so she gave the stables a really good clear-out and turned over the compost heap and filled up a bath of water for the geese. Her stomach was in knots.

Geraldine called over to her at eleven, insisting she take a break. Viv walked back, smiling at gentle Pilot as he stood wagging his tail in greeting at her outside the cottage door. Again she looked at those boxes in the back of Heath's pick-up and wondered what they were doing there.

'This is a message from Isme, you mark my words,' said Geraldine, standing at the kitchen window and studying the fog.

'I hope so,' grinned Viv. When Leighton turned up doffing his Austin Reed cap, Geraldine would be totally convinced it was Isme's doing and she'd be extra happy. Then Bub suddenly jumped up onto Viv's knee and settled, kneading his claws into her jeans, but she was so taken aback that she let him, despite the pain.

'Now, look at that,' gasped Geraldine. 'There's something very strange going on this morning.'

Heath didn't join them. Viv hoped he might. She'd had such a wonderful evening and it had left her with a perfect memory. She thought about him saying goodnight to her on the doorstep of the folly. It would have been a perfect opportunity for him to kiss her if he was ever going to. That told her that she really ought to kill any hopes she had on that score. Still, she hadn't 'negotiated' with Leighton because she thought Heath would fall in love with her and ask her to stay so she could benefit from the arrangement. She'd done it because it was the right thing for Geraldine and Heath and whoever he ended up kissing at the folly door. Hopefully not Antonia Leighton though. She imagined he would be a wonderful kisser.

At twenty-five to twelve, Viv swilled out her cup and noticed that the sun was at last managing to push through the fog. At the top of the hill, the castle stood like a black smudge and she wondered what activity was going on inside its walls now.

The crickets in her body had turned into giant grass-hoppers. By twelve they'd be kangeroos. Viv doubted that her nerves would ever sit still again. When she went back out to collect the eggs, the first thing she noticed was that the two black boxes had gone from Heath's pick-up. Why had he come for them without bobbing his head into the kitchen unless he was avoiding her? There was something he wasn't telling her, which was ironic really, seeing as she was probably winning by a country mile on the 'something I'm not telling you' front.

Her feet gathered pace the closer she got to the bird com-pound. She saw Heath closing Ursula's aviary carrying one of the black boxes. He had fresh scratches on his hands. The aviary was empty.

'What's going on?' she asked. But she knew. 'Oh don't.' Her face crumpled.

'Viv . . .'

'This is why you wanted me to fly her last night, isn't it?'

'Oh Viv.' Oh, he wanted to put his arms around her so much, but he knew that if he put his arms around her at this moment, she would fight him just like Ursula had. 'I've found her such a good home. The best. I planned to set off this morning before you got up so you wouldn't have to see her go. I wanted last night to be the goodbye you'd remem-ber. Bloody fog.'

Viv took a quick look at her watch. How could she delay him for twenty minutes without him smelling a rat.

'You can't go yet. The . . . fog hasn't cleared,' she said.

'It's just in the valley now. If I take it carefully up the hill, it'll be clear on the top road.'

'I need to see her.' Viv dropped to her knees. The box had no window in it, just discreet air-holes. 'Please take her out.' Crying would help manipulate him and she tried to force tears out. They came too easily.

'Viv, that wouldn't be fair on Ursula. It's taken me ages to get her in and it would stress her.'

Heath felt like crap. Viv's distress was genuine and wounded him. It mattered to him that her memories of this day would be stronger than those of last night.

'Who's in the other box?' asked Viv, unable to wipe the tears away as fast as they flowed.

'James,' said Heath, head bowed. James the gentle great grey owl had been completely the opposite to Ursula – so easy to put in, but it didn't make Heath feel that he had betrayed him any the less, in fact probably more so because James trusted him.

Why the hell doesn't Leighton come? Viv wanted to scream. What difference could a quarter of an hour make? He was trying to claw some power back. She had a good mind to ring and tell him that she was going to the newspapers NOW and see his sorry backside spin into action. But she knew she couldn't, because she had made a deal and if she moved the goalposts, he would assume she would move others.

'Can I have five minutes just sitting with her then?' asked Viv. 'Please.'

'Course. I'll go and ... do something.'

He wanted to reach out and touch her arm, just make contact but he knew she would pull away. He walked off and Viv sat on the floor between the two boxes. She placed a hand on either one, hoping they'd know she was there and that they'd be all right. James was deathly still in his box, Ursula was trying to flap inside hers.

What if Leighton doesn't *come?* A wave of nausea rose inside Viv's stomach and she felt physically sick. Then she really would have to say goodbye to Ursula today. Teardrops carried on rolling down her face and felt like they were dragging her skin with them.

Her five minutes were up and more; he'd let her have extra time. She saw Heath heading back. She didn't get up from the floor until she had to but made a pretence of struggling, rubbing a pain in her back that didn't exist. Anything to delay him by seconds because she needed every one of them.

Heath lifted the boxes and carried them too easily, despite their weight. Viv followed him, slowly, hoping her pace dragged him back and it did, but only a little.

It was minutes away from noon and Leighton hadn't come. And there was no sign of him either because in the stillness of this strange fog, a car's engine would probably be heard from the bottom of Ironmist Hill. Viv's lip started to tremble. Leighton must have found a way to forge ahead with his original plans. A picture of him sitting smug on a throne, phone in his hand, waiting for her to call so he could deliver his death stroke, flashed into her head.

Heath was talking to her, saying something about the sanctuary in Northallerton being fabulous, but her brain had no room for it.

Heath hadn't told Geraldine either that he was letting Ursula and James go. She came out of the kitchen to find him loading the boxes on the back seat of his pick-up and her hands shot to her face.

'We have to,' said Heath, getting into the driver's seat. 'You both know that.'

It was after twelve now. Heath slammed into first gear and Geraldine and Viv held onto each other watching the pick-up and its beloved cargo disappear into the fog.

Chapter 88

Maria walked up to the reception desk and knocked on it because Stel looked miles away.

'Earth to Stel.'

'Sorry, I was er . . . in a world of my own there.' *Oh, how I wish I were*, she thought.

'Ian sent me round to say that lunch is prepared in the garden.' Maria winked and followed it with a grin.

'Oh I'm too busy,' Stel replied, with a regretful smile. 'Would you do me a favour and tell him that you've asked me to work through my lunch because there's so much to do?'

'I certainly will not,' tutted Maria. 'Get yourself out there and have a break. The union will be down on us like a ton of bricks if we start doing stuff like that. Come on, up and out with you.'

'Maria, I'm not hungry,' replied Stel in as loud a whisper as she dare. 'But I don't want to hurt his feelings.'

Maria brought her hands to her hips. 'Stel Blackbird. How long have you waited for a considerate fella and now you've got one. So just go and sit in the flaming sunshine with him even if you don't want to eat anything.'

'Please. It's really ... sweet of him but I've got a work head on and I want to do all this whilst I'm in the mood.' She picked up a conveniently nearby file.

'Really?'

'Really.'

'Tsk. Okay then,' said Maria and set off back to the kitchen area, hips swinging as she walked.

Stel closed her eyes and wondered how long she could go on like this. She'd lost nearly half a stone in a week from stress. She'd thought about going to the police but then imagined Ian finding out and pressing a nuclear-type big red button that sent those photos EVERYWHERE.

Maria came back.

'I told him you insisted on working through your lunch because you're too conscientious for your own good ...'

No, I wanted you to tell him that YOU *insisted I work.*

' ... he said you can make it up to him at home,' said Maria, giving her eyebrows a saucy raise.

Chapter 89

As Heath reached the end of the drive, a silver car came speeding out of the fog down the hill. It was Nicholas Leighton's Range Rover. Heath's lip twitched in disgust as he turned left but Leighton was blasting his horn, demanding his attention. Heath braked and lowered his window. Leighton leaned out of his and said, 'Merlo, I want to talk to you.'

'Leighton, I've got nothing to say to you.'

'If you want to make an eleventh-hour deal, I suggest that you turn around now.'

'Are you joking?' replied Heath.

'Just turn the fucking car around and I'll follow you up the drive.'

Leighton sounded hacked off. As Heath negotiated a three-point turn he had no doubt that whatever 'deal' Leighton might have come up with had nothing to do with altruism and everything to do with how any change in his plan might benefit him first and foremost. But he'd listen because any straw was worth grabbing at.

*

Geraldine wiped her eyes on her sleeve. They had held back the tide as much as they could, but James and Ursula's leaving was the klaxon that they had failed. Their safe little world was starting to crumble.

Just as Viv was about to go into the kitchen, she cocked her ear as the sound of Heath's pick-up engine was increasing in volume, not decreasing.

'He's coming back,' said Geraldine, as the shape of the vehicle punched into the fog. Neither of them saw the Range Rover following until it was nearly in the car parking area as it was camouflaged by the mist.

'Who's that?' said Viv, realising what a crap actress she was, as she knew perfectly well whose car it was.

'Leighton,' said Geraldine. 'What's he doing here?'

Thank You God. Thank you Isme. Thank you Buddha, Vishnu, Allah, Cleopatra, General Custer . . . whoever sent him, thank you, said Viv inwardly.

Heath got out of the car and lifted the two owl boxes into the kitchen, closing Piccolo's cage so he didn't fly out and freak Leighton, though he was tempted to loosen the catch on Ursula's box.

Nicholas Leighton stalked into the kitchen blasting out vibes of arrogance and carrying a gusset folder. He did not deign to acknowledge Viv, other than with a cursory glance as his eyes swept from one side of the room to the other, like a war-time searchlight.

'Bloody fog,' he muttered. 'Couldn't make out the road.'

Was that said for her benefit, thought Viv. Had he tried to regain some control in the situation by leaving his visit until the last possible moment, then not realised how bad the weather conditions were?

'What's this about, Leighton?' Heath folded his arms across his broad chest.

'Can we talk in private?'

Viv made to go, but Heath stopped her.

'Whatever you have to say, you can say in front of all of us.'

Viv daren't make a fuss. She had to act as naturally as possible.

'All right,' Leighton said. 'I've got a proposition. Keep the land. I'll sign it over.'

Geraldine gasped. Viv thought she'd better do an open-mouth thing too.

Heath stared unblinkingly at him waiting for the catch. The silence in the room was thicker than the fog outside until Heath smashed it.

'Just like that?'

'Obviously not "just like that".' Leighton gave his lip a nervous or aggressive chew, it could have been either. 'It would be more in keeping with my long-term strategies to abandon the project rather than revitalise the valley.'

Heath let this sink in and his brain worked on what Nicholas Leighton really meant by it.

'So, cutting through the bull, you've discovered that philanthropy is a better way to power you further into orbit than by demolishing your local animal sanctuary. Is that what you're saying? Because if it is, I could have told you that. In fact, I think I did, quite a few times as I remember.'

'Maybe . . .' Nicholas's lips formed into a grim line. It appeared as if this conversation was ripping his soul out via his throat. 'It has been suggested . . . that if you were to comply with the theory that I resisted pressure to develop the valley because ultimately I consider this land best serves the immediate community as an area of natural beauty, animal welfare and English heritage, that would be . . . help-ful.' He paused, waiting for Heath to respond. He didn't so he carried on. 'It could also be seen as a gesture of magna-nimity to honour an historic contract between two families which should never have expired.'

There was a long electric silence then Heath nodded slowly. Leighton couldn't have been more transparent if he tried.

'My legal team have put together this which outlines everything.' Leighton handed Heath the folder. 'There are stipulations. The land must never be sold or given away for building development. It must remain as a sanctuary and a centre for animal welfare. A veterinary practice would be permitted.'

Viv swallowed down the cheer bubbling up in her throat.

'You will not defame me or my family, publicly or pri-vately. You will let it be known, if asked, that we reached this agreement mutually and cordially, though my initial motives for utilising the land for much-needed housing were understandable. In return, I will agree to recommend fund-ing for you from third-parties and . . .'

This bit is really going to stick in his craw, thought Viv as he coughed the words out.

' . . . upon signature of contract, I will direct some reve-nue to you from the Ironmist estate charitable funds. I will need you to submit accounts and my office will work out a sum of suitable remuneration.'

The room was sucked into a vacuum. Nothing moved. Even Jason Statham didn't scuffle around in his straw.

Then Heath blew out his cheeks and smoothed his hand down the back of his unruly dark hair.

'This isn't a joke?'

'Don't be obtuse,' snapped Leighton.

'When do I get my guarantee that you won't change your mind?' asked Heath.

'Now,' said Leighton. And he held out his hand.

*

Viv walked with Heath down to the bird compound. He was obviously still in shock and Viv did her best to display the same depth of amazement. She would never have won an Oscar for best actress.

She'd shared no eye contact with Nicholas Leighton, not even on his exit. But then he had not acknowledged Geraldine either. She had called him a male chauvinist pig when his car set off down the drive then immediately clamped her hands over her mouth because she had broken the terms of the contract already.

James flew straight up to his branch. He was none the wiser or the worse for being shut up in the bird carrier. He took the conciliatory mouse as adequate recompense for his inconvenience and carried on with his comfortable exist-ence. Ursula, contrarily, had to be tipped out of the box, after almost severing Heath's wrist to be put in. She too accepted the peace-offering and that was that.

'Viv, I cannot go back into that kitchen,' said Heath, coming to a sudden halt on the path. 'Geraldine will go into Isme overload.'

'Can you blame her?' smiled Viv.

He looked so big and strong and happy and as if someone had ironed the furrows from his forehead.

'I daren't go to sleep tonight. I'll wake up and find it was all a dream,' grinned Heath.

'Just watch out you don't find Nicholas Leighton having a shower in your bathroom,' said Viv, tilting her face to look at him.

'I just can't believe it.' Heath laughed as the joy rose up in him like a geyser and he grabbed Viv up from the ground and whirled her round as if she were as light as air. Her face was on a level with his and he smelled of cedarwood and a deep forest in early summer and his eyes were green and shiny and suddenly his lips were on hers and her arms were round his neck and it felt as if a million birds were fluttering in her stomach. The kiss lasted seconds yet it would take her hours to come down from it, even though she knew it had only happened because of a momentary surge of euphoria.

'I can't believe it either,' said Viv as he set her back down and she tried to act normal but there was a fat chance of that when her brain was sparking like a Catherine Wheel.

They walked back to the house where Geraldine was waiting for them with the kettle on and a heartful of supernatural theories.

Chapter 90

At five o'clock, Ian wandered over to the reception area to meet Stel who had been fretting all afternoon about the possible repercussions of Maria telling him that she had snubbed his lunch invitation. He smiled in greeting, he helped her on with her coat and crooked his arm so she could link him on the way out. He talked pleasantries on the drive home and asked her what she wanted to watch on the TV. He ordered a Chinese for them both and asked her if she felt all right because she hardly touched it, but he did not mention anything about lunchtime. The house felt as if a massive thunder cloud had filled it, choking every room with dread because Stel wasn't fooled by his friendly, chivalrous demeanour. Stel wanted to scream at him to bring on whatever he was intending to do and get it over and done with because she knew that this black cloud was aching to let rip with thunder and lightning and sheet rain.

He did not touch her in bed but she would have let him if he made a move on her, just to keep the peace. She craved the oblivion of sleep but her brain refused to rest. Eventually, through sheer mental exhaustion, her eyelids shuttered down and she dreamed of the tension cloud bursting and the rain falling hard on her face, saturating her and she woke up with a start to find that her face really was wet. And that was because Ian was standing over her slowly pouring a beakerful of cold water on her head and she daren't move and he didn't stop until it was empty.

Then he climbed back into bed without saying a single word.

*

That night, Viv had a terrible feeling that she had turned into her mother. She lay in bed replaying that kiss over and over again, picking at the detail, hoping that somewhere in her brain she might recover the missing moments just before their lips came together. Did he pull her towards him, did she swoop on him? Who pulled away before the other? For the first time she had an insight into Stel's Mills and Boon of a brain and understood her a little better for it.

Now she had some space to think of things other than the future of the sanctuary, her mind returned to the subject of her mother. As Viv waited for her breakfast eggs to poach the next morning, she thought how odd it was that Stel had put her off going back home for a visit. They were due a chat. She'd ring her after she'd eaten, she decided, and ask if the decorators had started yet. Something was niggling her and she didn't like it.

But Stel didn't answer when she saw Viv's name pop up on her phone; she couldn't. If she'd picked up, she would have broken down at the sound of her dear, sweet, lovely voice.

Viv had left her a voicemail saying she had just rung for a chat, nothing else. Stel sent a text five minutes later.

SOZ LOV. JUST GIONG IN TO CUSTMR RELS COURSE SHEFFIELD TDAY. X

There were just enough errors and shorthand for it to appear genuine.

Chapter 91

Viv had brought the sanctuary accounts right up to date and she volunteered to hand them personally to Nicholas Leighton. She wanted to prove to him that their business had been consigned to a private history book that only three people had ever read.

So her mother was on a customer relations course in Sheffield, was she? Viv had no reason to doubt that was true. Her mother didn't keep secrets very well, she wore her heart too much on her sleeve. Course or no course, if Stel had something on her mind that she wanted to talk to her daughter about, she would have picked up her phone. So Viv decided that her niggly worry about her was probably nothing then so she carried on thinking about Heath Merlo who had occupied a lot of her grey matter since the three seconds she spent in his arms yesterday. Her business at Ironmist was done, she could go back to Yorkshire now, or to London but she wanted to do neither. Heath Merlo's kiss had anchored her to Ironmist for the foreseeable future. She hadn't turned into her mother and started looking up wedding dresses, but she wanted to linger in the perfect orbit of

Wildflower Cottage for however long it extended its welcome to her. It had become home.

This time there was no need for illegal entry via the bridle path and vaulting over the gate; she drove straight to the main entrance of the Ironmist estate.

You could have inherited this, she thought to herself.

It's not mine. It doesn't even flash up on my radar as having anything to do with me, she countered.

She parked up on the gravel circle in front of the impressive centuries-old building and felt a nervous stirring in her stomach which intensified with every step she took towards the heavy wooden door. She pulled down on an iron lever to activate the bell and heard it ring deep within the belly of the castle. Eventually the door opened with a wholly appropriate horror-film creak and a girl appeared. She had the same dark hair, high forehead and large blue eyes as Antonia, but her lips were much thinner, cheekbones sharper, nose longer, skin paler. Her willowy height amplified her reed-like figure. This must be Octavia, thought Viv. There was definitely no chance of them ever being identified as sisters.

'Can I help you?' Octavia asked with a strained smile. Viv would have put money on her knowing exactly who she was though. Well, maybe not *exactly*.

'I've brought these,' she said, holding out a carrier bag full of files. 'They're the accounts for the Wildflower Cottage sanctuary. Is Mr Leighton in?'

'No he's out,' said Octavia, taking them from her.

'Ah, well would you ask Mr Leighton to return them to us when he's finished with them, please.'

Behind Octavia, her sister appeared.

'I'll deal with this, Otty, I know about it.' So 'Otty' handed over the bag then went back inside.

'I'll make sure Dad gets these,' Antonia said to Viv, wearing a suspiciously pleasant smile.

'Thank you,' replied Viv, with cool civility. She hadn't forgotten how Antonia had upset Armstrong. The sooner she was out of her presence, the better.

'Do give Heath my love,' Antonia called as Viv stepped towards her car.

'I will,' Viv threw over her shoulder.

'I liked him very much,' added Antonia with an exaggerated sigh. 'I do hope we can all be friends now.'

Viv didn't say anything.

'I liked his ruthlessness.' Antonia walked out onto the gravel. She had those expensive riding boots on again and Viv wondered if she slept in them. 'Do you know what I mean?'

'I'm afraid I don't,' said Viv, getting into the car.

'I like bad boys.'

'Oh, do you?' *What was she on about?* Heath wasn't a 'bad boy'.

'Not with animals, obviously. With people. Women,' Antonia went on.

'I wouldn't know, I just work there,' said Viv. 'Bye then.'

But Antonia had a point to make. 'Well, you know about his wife, of course.'

It was a remark meant to pique Viv's interest. And it worked.

'His wife?' Viv delayed closing her door.

'Sarah, the one who died of cancer. Sarah Bernal. "Beloved Daughter". That's what it says on her gravestone. She's in a very pretty churchyard in Mawton.' Antonia raked her long hair back from her face with her fingers. 'I don't blame the family for insisting that the headstone didn't have her married name on it. The first one did, but they ripped it out. Replaced it after what happened.'

Antonia was being deliberately tantalising. She was trying to press Viv's buttons. Correction, she *was* pressing Viv's buttons.

'So, what happened?' Viv asked, annoyed that Antonia had got to her, but she needed to know.

'Heath abandoned Sarah when she was dying. Didn't you know? How wonderfully callous is that, to break the heart of your terminally ill wife?' She sighed with twisted admiration. 'Ask the family if you don't believe me. Bernal's food store in Mawton. Just don't tell them you're shagging him.'

'You really are a bitch, aren't you?' said Viv and slammed the door on Antonia's poison. She was shaking as she accelerated away, hands locked on the steering wheel. *No, no, no, he wouldn't have done that.* She thought of Darren deserting Stel. There was no way that Heath could have done the same to Sarah. But why didn't her gravestone bear the Merlo name? Why was there only the word *daughter* on it and not *wife*?

Should she drive to Mawton and ask? *Excuse me but could you tell me what happened between your daughter and Heath Merlo that made you rip out her first gravestone?*

Everything she knew about Heath Merlo, everything she felt about him had been torn up and thrown in the air. She couldn't be around him if what Antonia had said was true. There was no excuse that she could think of that would absolve him of that.

Someone much closer, and honest, would know.

Geraldine.

Chapter 92

How emotions could change like the weather, thought Viv as she sat through a lunch of fresh garden spinach, fried potato cakes and eggs with a beaming Geraldine and the man she had woken up smiling about and now could hardly bear to look at. Just as the foggy day had given way to bright sunshine, the sun in her heart had been swallowed by cloud. At the table, she existed in a dark bubble as all around her was lightness and jollity

Even Pilot seemed to have been rejuvenated. He was shaking his tuggy toy for all it was worth.

'You okay, Viv? You're quiet,' said Heath, leaning over and bumping her arm gently with his fist. Had he done that two hours ago her skin would have sighed at the contact. Now she felt numb. In the same way the kiss had been tumbling over and over in her mind, Sarah Bernal's imagined last hours had now taken their place.

'I think she's still in shock,' chuckled Geraldine.

'True,' said Viv, plastering on a fake smile.

'I'm going up to Selwyn's and I'm bringing back wine,' said Heath, decisively scraping back his chair as he got up from the table. 'I'll call in at Fennybridge first, pick up the order and tonight we will knock our glasses together and celebrate. You all right with that, Geraldine? Viv?'

He was studying her. He had picked up on there being something not quite right because she couldn't sustain eye contact with him.

'Sounds good,' she said, flicking her eyes upwards.

He was so handsome, and happiness radiated from him today, but until she knew the truth, the portcullis on her emotions remained down. Despite all the good he did for animals and the considerate way he treated Geraldine, whatever heaven his kiss tasted of and however much his scent set explosions tripping along her nerves, she would never be able to see past his weakness, his cruelty and his selfishness if he had deserted his wife as she lay dying. She could not stay here. Not even for Geraldine's sake. Not even for Ursula.

When he had gone, Viv cleared the table, wiped it down, acted as normally as she could.

'Whilst the cat is away, the mice will play,' she said, preparing the ground in case she had to go. 'I'm taking a long lunch break today.'

'And so you should,' said Geraldine.

'I think I'll have a leisurely wander around the shops.'

She crept up to the subject of Sarah. Word association, a stepping stone closer to her with each one. Moors. Mawton. Graveyard. Roses. Sarah Bernal.

'She never lived here then?' asked Viv.

'Only for a little while,' replied Geraldine. 'When his father started to fade, Sarah moved here with Heath so he could take over the sanctuary. I'd only been living here a few months myself. It was chaos.'

'So when did Sarah become poorly then?'

'Before Heath's father died. Heath was in an awful state. I think he blamed himself for not realising how ill she was, because he'd been concentrating on his father so much. But no one knew. She covered it up.'

'Did Sarah die here at the cottage?'

'No. Not here. She'd left by then.'

'They split up?' Viv felt mean press-ganging Geraldine for answers, but she carried on regardless.

'Well,' Geraldine cleared her throat, suddenly aware she'd given out some information that Viv didn't know. 'She ... things weren't working out between them so well.' She delivered the line sing-songy, as if setting the words to a melody made them more acceptable. 'There was a lot of pressure on Heath. As I say, she hid it from him ... He wasn't to know ...'

She's defending him, thought Viv. She pressed on with her questions.

'Where did she go?'

'Mawton.'

'Is there a hospital in Mawton?' Quick fire questions, not giving Geraldine time to fabricate answers.

'No, no. She must have gone back to her family. I think.'

'I've seen her grave. It says Sarah Bernal, not Merlo.'

'Her family ...'

'They were angry with Heath?' Of course they were. That's why they didn't want his name on the grave. How could it be any more obvious?

'They weren't normal circumstances. Heath's dad had just died, you see and, well, Viv, as I know only too well, things aren't always as straightforward as they appear ...' Viv knew that Geraldine must feel as if she were caught in a storm of questions, but she couldn't stop – wouldn't stop – not until she heard it all.

'Geraldine, just tell me so I don't ever put my foot in it,' said Viv, ignoring her conscience's protest that she was manipulating her friend. 'You told me your story, I didn't make you feel judged, did I? When I took the accounts up to Ironmist, Antonia Leighton told me that Heath had abandoned Sarah. I want to be able to stand up for him if I hear anything like that again.'

Lulled into a deceptive sense of security, Geraldine told her.

'I was there when he said that she should leave.'

'Where? Here?'

Geraldine turned her head towards the fireplace. She didn't even know she'd done it. A picture of a fragile, distressed Sarah Merlo arguing there with Heath flashed into Viv's brain.

'Why would he say that?'

'He couldn't look after her, he wasn't in any fit condition ... He was empty.'

'Geraldine, what did he say? The actual words.'

'I can't really remember the ac—'

Geraldine was lying. She knew what they were and Viv needed to hear them. She wanted Geraldine to prove Antonia wrong and give her the ammunition to blast away the doubts that sat in her heart like gangrene.

'I *need* to hear them, Geraldine.'

Geraldine sighed. '*She* said that she needed to be with a man who loved her. *He* said he was sorry it wasn't him.'

The impact of her words showed clear on Viv's face. She could see that, however much Viv had said otherwise, she hadn't been prepared to hear the truth at all. Geraldine tried to pat the words into a digestible shape and ended up distorting them further. 'He didn't mean it. I know he didn't. She was nearer the end than he knew ...'

Viv nodded as if she accepted that he had made a mistake; although she didn't. A mistake was forgetting to put the bins out, or setting an alarm clock for the wrong time; not telling the woman you'd married – for better or worse no less – that it would be too much trouble to help her die in peace.

'Heath never forgave himself,' said Geraldine. 'He's a good man, Viv.'

'I know that,' was all Viv said.

Pilot nudged under Viv's arm for affection and she took his big shaggy face in her hands. His great sad eyes looked up at her as if he understood that she had to go. And she kissed him on the nose and she knew she had said goodbye to him for all of them.

'Okay, well,' Viv jumped enthusiastically to her feet, 'if Heath's gone for wine, I think I should bring a cake home with me. A huge chocolate one.'

'You are all right, aren't you, Viv?' asked Geraldine as Viv opened the kitchen door to go out. She wished she could have rewound the last five minutes and said that she didn't know anything. One reveal had pulled another with it, like a constant stream of magician's tissues.

'Of course,' said Viv.

As soon as Viv entered the folly, she started scrambling together everything she had into her suitcases, half-blinded with tears.

Geraldine realised she had gone an hour later when Heath came back and asked why the folly was empty.

Chapter 93

Viv booked herself in at a Travelodge for two nights. She didn't want to go back to Stel immediately. She didn't want to talk or think or feel. She texted her mother to say that she'd be home on Saturday morning and then switched off her phone. She had both the numbers of Wildflower Cottage and Heath's mobile in her phone, but they didn't have hers. They had a false address for her on file so they couldn't contact her. They owed her a week's wages but she could stand that. She wouldn't ever go back for it; she couldn't ever go back.

*

She arrived at Stel's at ten on Saturday morning, but sat in the car looking at the house for a minute or two, before getting out. From the outside, everything was the same as she'd left it last time, but it didn't feel like her home any more. She'd never looked at it differently when she came back for holidays from University, but she knew this time that she had moved on. Her heart had found a new place to settle but she'd had to wrench it away and now she was adrift. She didn't know where she belonged any more.

Stel opened the door and stood there with her arms held wide ready to close around her daughter and squeeze her. Her mum felt distinctly thinner than Viv remembered. Then Ian came out and he gave Viv a kiss and said that it was nice to meet her. He smelled of Paco Rabanne and it suited him. But it was ladled on and masked all the other layers of scents that would have given him dimension.

Stel led her upstairs to the attic, twittering like a nervous bird that Ian was storing stuff in her room and staying for a bit, just until he got his place renovated and that's why she'd had to postpone the decorators. Viv wasn't daft, she knew her mother was scared to tell her that she'd moved him in. Once again, she'd hardly let the grass grow under her feet but maybe this time it was the right decision for her. It didn't matter anyway because Viv wasn't coming back here to stay. It was time she made her own life. And it was time for her mum to lift her wings and fly.

Viv tipped out her suitcases and loaded the washing machine with every item of clothing from them – clean and dirty. She needed everything to smell of Persil and Comfort and not misty morning flowers and hay-scented air. Basil sat on her bed like a fat ginger cushion as she carefully removed her mini-lab and set it up on the table by the window. She found a bottle of the oil-copy of Geraldine's perfume and realised that she had never given it to her. She'd send it to her in the post without a covering note. Viv picked up Basil and cuddled him and smelled her mother's scent on him. And salt, as if she had been crying into Basil's fur recently.

Viv went downstairs to make a sandwich. She hadn't had

anything for forty-eight hours but she could have eaten all day and never filled her hungry heart.

Stel insisted on making her a toastie. She was fussing too much, as if she were a battery-operated doll and someone had tweaked up her speed. Viv ate it quickly, less so because her stomach was empty and more because she felt in the way of her mother's new set-up. Ian was sitting opposite her at the table with the paper held in his hands but Viv noticed that he wasn't reading it because his eyes weren't moving across the words and his finger was tapping beats of impatience on the edge. He was killing time until she left them alone, that much was obvious.

'I think I'm going to have a drive to Meadowhall,' Viv said.

*

Stel felt Ian's outward breath fill the room when Viv left the house.

'You can't have her staying here,' said Ian, flapping the paper as if that gave special emphasis to his words.

'She's my daughter,' said Stel with quiet defiance.

'Well, she's not mine,' said Ian. 'Get shut, unless you want *your daughter* to be the first to see what her mother gets up to behind her back.'

Chapter 94

Just as Viv reached her car, she heard someone calling her name and she turned to see Al jogging towards her, bear arms extended ready to envelop her.

'I shouldn't do this because I've just done a five-mile run but I'm not missing out on a cuddle,' he said, nearly breaking her ribs. 'When the bloody hell did you get back, lass?'

'This morning,' said Viv, smiling. But then Al was one of those blokes who had always made her smile.

'Are you here for good now?'

'No, I'm just parking for a bit until I can work out where I'm going next.'

'I'm off as well, did you hear?' said Al, thumbing behind him at the For Sale notice. 'June the seventh I leave, so I've started packing up.'

'I had heard, and I hope you're very happy in your new home, Al. You deserve to have a fancy house. My mum will miss you though.'

Al stroked his stubble and it made a scratchy rasping sound against his hand.

'Me and your mum had a bit of a falling out,' said Al.

'You and Mum?' Viv wondered if she'd heard that right. They'd never fallen out. 'What about?'

Al checked over his shoulder to make sure there was no one spying out of Stel's front window.

'That new fellow of hers more or less told me to back off. He said that your mum had complained to him that I'd pestered her for years and she didn't know how to stop me.'

Viv screwed up her face in disbelief. 'Al, Mum would never have said that. You don't pester her at all. She's really fond of you and she likes living next door to you as well. I can't tell you how many times I've heard her say that she always felt a lot safer knowing you were only a knock away through the wall.'

Al put his hands on his hips and shook his head.

'He said your mum couldn't stand the sight of me ...'

'That's absolute rubbish, Al.'

'I tell you, I was so embarrassed, Viv. I felt sick ... I felt hurt. I've never overstepped the mark with your mum. I was so upset when I'd heard she'd said that. I went over and over in my head conversations I'd had with her in the past ...'

Viv knew her mother, and Stel wouldn't have pulled Al down like that. She wouldn't have been disloyal on that scale, even if she had thought it. But she also suspected that Al might have believed it because deep down a part of him was still a little skinny kid with no self-worth in a constant state of amazement that a lovely woman like Stel would bother to give him the time of day.

So why had Ian lied, then? That was the burning question, because it *was* a lie. Viv would have put her life savings on it.

'I don't like him, Viv. I didn't from the off. You keep your eye out for your mum,' said Al, reaching over and giving her shoulder a squeeze. 'And you can tell her from me that talking or not talking, if she needs me, I'm still just a knock away through the wall.'

Viv walked around Meadowhall, tried on some clothes, looked at some books but she didn't want to be there. She bought herself a coffee and sat in the Oasis food court and felt as if she were moving at a different pace to the rest of the universe. She felt dry, faded as if she were made of dust and the slightest single breeze would send her scattering into the air as a trillion motes. She might have cried had she had any tears left inside her.

*

Stel walked into her attic bedroom with an armful of fresh sheets to make up the narrow single bed for Viv. She sat next to the ginger curl of Basil and stroked his fur. He was always up here these days, and hardly ever came into the lounge any more. She wondered if that was because he could sense what a sadistic bastard Ian Robson was.

Stel had agreed to take Viv to one side and tell her that she had to find somewhere else to stay. But though she'd nodded submissively at Ian's instructions, inside she had reared up at last. As if she would deny her daughter a place in the house she grew up in! Enough was enough. Stel would take her daughter to one side all right, but instead she would let her know what Ian Robson was doing to her. Knowing Viv, she'd drive straight to the police station and hopefully they'd do what they had to before he plastered those pictures all over the public domain. It was a risk she had to take because she couldn't handle any of it any more.

Stel took her time putting on the covers, glad to be out of his sight and temporarily free from being checked up on. He'd found her diary with all her passcodes in it and used them to access the search history on her PC, her emails and online bank statements. As well as her mileage, she knew he recorded how long she spent in the supermarket and scrutinised what she bought from the till receipts. She wasn't even allowed to lock the bathroom door any more. She felt compressed under the weight of his surveillance; but then he wanted her to feel controlled and demeaned, she knew. She hadn't mentioned her future Sundays with the Old Spice Girls because she didn't want to inflame him, but she could have guessed he considered those were at an end.

Stel plopped Basil back on the bed when she'd finished making it and sat at Viv's desk where she had parked her box of bottles and test tubes and felt herself lifted up by a crest of euphoria that she was going to be out of this mantrap of misery soon. Today.

One of the phials caught her eye: Dancing Sunshine. She'd feel like sunshine was dancing inside her as soon as she and Viv walked out of the front door together. Whatever misery Ian planned to unleash when he realised she'd broken free from him would be better than staying in this hell. Stel's eyes moved across the rack of perfumes. Viv thought of some lovely names for her mixtures: Storm-on-the-Moors, Misty Morning, Wildflower Cottage ... There was a larger bottle with 'Geraldine' on the label. Stel unscrewed the lid of the bottle and inhaled. *Oh that's lovely,* she said to herself. She tipped it upside down to put a dab on her finger but Basil jumped up on her lap and she dropped it, down her shirt and over his back before it fell to the floor and started glugging all over the beige carpet.

Stel bounced to her feet. 'You silly lad, Basil,' she said, picking up the nearly-empty bottle and setting it back on the desk. 'I'd better get a cloth before you start licking your-self.' He was already bending his head back and trying to dry himself off. Stel ran down to the bathroom for a cloth before he made himself sick.

Chapter 95

Viv set off back to Pogley Top but she didn't go straight to her mum's house as it felt more Ian's than Stel's territory now. His stuff had invaded the house like a rampaging weed. She didn't fancy enduring the atmosphere there any longer than she had to and thought she'd pass another hour or so in a place she had always liked to go to. But tomorrow, without fuss or ceremony, she would suggest they went out for Sunday lunch – alone – mum and daughter for a catch-up. She wanted to check that everything was all right, especially after what Al had said.

There was a little-known clearing by the Stripe, so-called because it was a pathetic 'stripe' of river that dribbled through the wood. 'It's hardly worth its bother to flow,' her Nana Blackbird used to say. 'It's even too bloody lazy to dry up.' There was a commemorative bench there with a brass plaque on the back. *Edith Crabtree. She Loved this Place.* Viv and her Nana used to come here with a bag of homemade egg and salad cream sandwiches and a net from the corner shop and Viv would sit on the bank and try and catch one of the sticklebacks that journeyed down it; approximately one every six years. Halley's comet was spotted more than fish in Pogley Stripe.

Viv sat on the bench and opened a bottle of cold pop. And tried not to think about Wildflower Cottage and everyone there, because that's where her thoughts veered whenever they had any freedom to travel.

Chapter 96

Ian was trying to watch the highlights of the match, but the sound of Stel's feet tip-tapping up and down the attic stairs was doing his head in. He gave the ceiling a nasty glare, switched his attention back to the screen, then heard her at it again.

He launched himself from the sofa and took the stairs two at a time.

'What the frigging hell . . .'

He walked into a fug of too familiar scent. *Her scent.* As it swirled around in his head, graves in his memory started to yawn open and the contents sprang alive. *The bitch nearly killed him. She came out early from prison, slipped through his fingers.*

He thundered into the attic to see Stel on her knees dabbing at the carpet.

'Where's that smell coming from?'

'Viv's case,' said Stel, shoulders hunched, arms tucked in, making herself small.

Ian started to plunder through it.

'Don't, that's Viv's stuff,' yelled Stel, making a grab for

his arm. Then she grunted as the backhander sent her flying.

He was pulling stoppers out, sniffing, throwing phials and bottles everywhere.

'Which fucking one is it?' He was snarling like a dog.

'It's the one with "Geraldine" written on it. There,' Stel pointed, hoping to stop him damaging Viv's precious things. 'I've spilled most of it.' She touched her face and there was blood on her fingers but adrenalin was numbing any pain.

Ian picked it up and inhaled. Then his head made a sudden sinister twist to Stel. She lay hunched like a kicked dog on the floor, but her eyes were defiantly wishing him dead.

'Where was she staying?'

'Who?'

'Who do you think, you fucking moron.'

Stel's mind fell blank with panic. 'I can't . . . I can't –'

A punch. She grunted. A kick. His hand clamped onto her throat and she was lifted to her feet that way.

'It was called Ironmist,' gurgled Stel. 'Wildflower Cott . . .' She couldn't breathe and her heart was thumping so hard that she could hear it in her ears. Her last thought before she passed out was that he was going to kill her.

Chapter 97

Viv stared down at the Stripe, following the passage of a leaf as it bumped against the bank and waited for the spit of water to dislodge it so it could resume travelling to wherever it was going, when she heard an alerting cough behind her.

'Didn't think anyone knew about this place.'

Viv twisted round to see a girl, younger than her – about eighteen, she guessed. She was wisp-thin and pale-skinned with grey eyes and long white-blonde hair and carrying a dog lead.

'I've been coming here since I was a child,' said Viv.

'Have you?' said the girl. She plonked herself down on the bench and Viv shuftied up, because she was taking up most of the middle.

'Where's your dog?' asked Viv.

'Haven't got one,' said the girl. 'I just carry this with me in case I bump into any undesirables up here. Not that I ever have, but there's always a first. If I did, the plan would be to whistle "Come on, boy".'

'And pretend you've got a Rottweiler?' suggested Viv.

'Got it in one,' said the girl.

Viv lifted her face to the bars of sun straining through the leaves and for a moment imagined she was sitting outside the kitchen door of Wildflower Cottage and in the distance were the moors and Ironmist Castle.

'Can't handle the sun, me,' the girl said. 'I prefer the shade. It's my colouring.' There was a pause then she asked, 'You smell nice. What's your perfume?'

'I can't remember putting any on,' Viv answered.

'Well it must be you, it's not me.' The girl leaned over and sniffed at Viv as if she were a pig searching for a truffle. 'It's on your clothes. Is it a fabric conditioner? Which one?'

Viv lifted the neckline of her top up to her nose. She still couldn't smell anything – and if she couldn't, she doubted anyone else could.

'Smells a bit like the seaside,' said the girl. 'Have you just come back from your holidays?'

'I've been staying on the moors,' replied Viv.

'Near Haworth? That's the only place I know on the moors.'

'No. It's a place called Ironmist. I doubt you'll have heard of it,' said Viv.

The girl tilted her head one way then the other as if the name were a ball and she were trying to place it in a relevant hole in her head.

'Nope, I haven't heard of it. Was it nice?'

'Yes. Very.' *The loveliest place you could imagine*, Viv added to herself.

The girl rocked to her feet and coiled the lead around her hand.

'I'd better get back,' she said, heading off towards the path. 'Been nice talking to you. See you again, sometime.'

'Bye,' smiled Viv. 'Was nice talking to you too.'

She thought the girl had gone so she didn't expect to hear her voice again.

'If it was that lovely, you should go back. Really you should. Now.'

'Sorry?'

Viv turned round but all that was there was the faintest trail of mist that dissolved as soon as her glance touched it.

Chapter 98

Viv left the clearing, walking quickly down the path to catch up with the girl, but she reached the long straight main road without seeing anyone. There were no other cars on it but her own, nor any walkers or cyclists. That was odd, she thought. As was the feeling that she should get straight back to Stel's. She was gripped by an inexplicable sense of urgency and she knew she'd been right to rush when she opened the door to her mum's house and found it weirdly flooded with Geraldine's perfume.

'Mum?' she called, her scalp prickling with anxiety.

She edged into the lounge, hearing voices, but it was only a football match on the TV turned down low. No one was in the kitchen either.

'Mum?'

Viv ventured upstairs into her mum's bedroom but it too was empty, as was the bathroom and her old room, now completely taken over by Ian's belongings.

Something shifted above her head.

'Mum, are you all right?' she called again.

The aroma of Geraldine's perfume was becoming more

overpowering with every step towards the attic bedroom. As she opened the door, she found Stel on the floor, back propped against the wall, blouse stained with oil, in a sea of smashed test-tubes. Her hands were trembling and covering her throat protectively. Her breathing was laboured as if her windpipe was barely open and her usual smiling grey-blue eyes were a mass of exploded blood vessels.

Viv dropped to the floor and threw her arms around her mother. 'Mum, what's happened? Did Ian do this?'

'Oh Viv,' said Stel, clinging to her darling girl. 'He wanted the name of the place where you'd been living.' Her voice was a terrified, damaged rasp. 'He kept asking me who Geraldine was.'

Then Viv knew.

Chapter 99

Viv closed her eyes and willed herself to concentrate. *Focus, Viv.* She needed to decide what to do first.

Stel was her priority. She flew down the stairs, leaped over the communal fence and rapped on Al's front door urgently, and again. He opened it within the half-minute though it felt like much longer.

'Viv, love, you all right? I've just come out of the shower. What's on fire?'

'It's Mum, Al. Can you come? That Ian has beaten her up.'

Al didn't say a word. He was straight out of the door and into Stel's house. He took the stairs like a Olympian and his face creased up when he saw her.

'Aw Stel,' he sighed. 'Viv, I think we should get her to hospital. I'll take her in the car, it'll be quicker.' He looked at Stel's face and he could only recognise one side of it as being hers. It was as if the other had been pumped up with air. He helped Stel to her feet but her legs were crumbling. 'Sod this for a lark,' he said and lifted her up. He took her down the stairs carefully and it was a testament to what a state Stel was in that she didn't protest.

Behind him Viv was ringing Wildflower Cottage on her mobile. No one answered, but then Geraldine avoided answering the phone like the plague unless she recognised the name on the display. Heath had programmed some in for her, but not Viv's. Then the answer-machine responded and she heard Heath's voice. *This is Wildflower Cottage Animal Sanctuary. Please leave a message after the tone and we will get back to you. Thank you.* But this was no time for sentiment.

'Please pick up if you're there, it's Viv, it's urgent.' She waited a few beats before continuing, but no one picked up. 'Geraldine, if you're listening, please lock all the doors and phone the police immediately or get out of the way. Ian Robson is on his way over to you. He's been seeing my mum. He's in a red car. Heath, if you're there, please keep Geraldine safe. He's dangerous. You must ring the police. Please ring me back to let me know you've got my message. This is urgent. I have to know you're safe.' And she left her number slowly and clearly, unlike the garbled, hurried message which preceded it.

Viv had no idea if Heath knew anything about Geraldine's past and hoped, if he found the message first, that he would take it seriously enough. Then she remembered that the answerphone never flashed an alert. She needed to speak to a person, not a machine; and as Geraldine didn't have a mobile, she would have to call Heath.

She scrolled down in her address book. She had meant to delete his number but thank goodness she hadn't yet. She pressed the phone symbol next to his name. Frustratingly it went to voicemail. *Shit.* As she was leaving a message, the incoming call alert sounded. She accepted it. His voice.

'Viv. Where are you? I've been look—'

'Where are you?' she gabbled.

'I'm in Sheffield trying to find you. Viv, I have to talk to you—'

'Heath, listen,' Viv cut him off again. 'I think Geraldine's in trouble. I might be overreacting, I really hope I've got this totally wrong, but you need to get back to Ironmist because she's not picking up the phone. I think her ex knows where she is. He's dangerous, Heath. I've rung the pol—'

'Viv, I'm . . . the . . . other side . . . take me . . . hour at . . .' The line went dead at his end.

As soon as they were outside, Al set Stel onto her feet whilst he ran back into his house for the keys. Viv held onto her, not wanting to let her go, but she was safe – and it was Geraldine who was in danger now. She had to drive to Ironmist. The words of the strange girl with the dog lead were going round and round in her head: *You should go back, really you should. Now.*

'Mum, I'm going to have to get hold of Geraldine. I think Ian knows her and he's on his way over to her. I'll be back as soon as I can. Promise.'

Stel nodded and squeezed her daughter's hand.

'I wish I could split myself in two.' Viv's eyes pricked with tears but she blinked them away because this was no time to be overtaken by emotion; she needed to be sharp and clear and focused.

'I'll sort your mum,' said Al, appearing behind her. He looked down at the old hockey stick in her hand that she'd taken from the umbrella stand. 'You'd better not be going after him, Viv. You ring the police and let them deal with it.'

'He's dangerous, Al. I have to make sure my friend is safe.' Viv gave her mum a tight hug.

'Ring the police, Viv,' Al insisted. 'Though God knows I wish I'd known sooner because there wouldn't be enough of that bastard left to arrest.'

*

Viv rang the police whilst she was driving. Frustratingly, the emergency call centre operator kept cutting off what she was trying to say and the situation wasn't helped by the intermittent mobile signal on the remote Woodhead Pass which traversed the Pennines. Viv kept having to repeat herself and shout to be heard, and the operator seemed more intent on rebuking her for raising her voice than recording details. Eventually the operator said that a squad car would be on its way as soon as possible and Viv had to hope that was true because the call had drained the battery on her mobile to four per cent and she was presently in the middle of nowhere.

Chapter 100

After Geraldine had finished mopping the kitchen floor, she put the kettle on the Aga to boil. She'd overfilled it, as was her habit, but that was all right, because it would just be whistling by the time she'd finished cleaning out Jason Statham's hutch. Steadily, she got down on her knees and transferred the rabbit to Bub's old wicker cat basket then she set to with the dustpan and brush. She had meant to clean him out yesterday but what with Heath being away trying to locate Viv, she'd had too much to do and something had to give. She wished he would find her and bring her back. Viv meant a lot to him, to them all. Wildflower Cottage was missing something whilst she wasn't there; it felt incomplete. There hadn't even been a wisp of mist for two days.

Pilot suddenly jumped up and gave a woof at the door.

'Shh, Pilot. There's nobody there,' Geraldine threw over her shoulder.

Then she went rigid because behind her, she heard the voice from her nightmares say:

'But there is, Vonny. *I'm* here.'

*

There was a bottle-neck of traffic at Tintwistle and Viv noticed her petrol gauge had nudged into red which meant she had about thirty miles-worth of petrol left, unless she had to use it all idling here, sandwiched between a bus and a Transit van. She considered turning off the engine then had a sudden vision of trying to restart it and hearing only a laboured turning, or worse a solitary click, as happened in horror movies. It took ten minutes for the traffic to start nudging forwards, but it felt like hours.

*

'I see you're down on your knees, Vonny. Just where I like you best,' *he* said.

In her head, Geraldine was screaming, but her mouth wasn't moving. She was trapped again inside her own body. Running around inside it, trying to find the way out.

Ian stroked Pilot's head. The gentle old dog let him. It trusted everyone to be nice to it. It had never learned. Geraldine's eyes were glued on his fingers. *Please don't hurt Pilot.*

'Nice dog. Does he bite?'

Her voice was a frightened mouse-whisper. 'No.'

'I do. Do you remember, Vonny? Or am I supposed to call you Geraldine now?'

Chapter 101

Viv spotted a petrol station coming up on the left-hand side. She daren't risk running out of fuel so pulled in. Luck was on her side as there was a vacant pump. A tenner's-worth of unleaded later, she was back on the road.

*

Ian Robson gave a dry, nasty chuckle. 'Who would have ever thought I'd find you again because of your perfume. Isn't life funny? Aren't some things just meant to be?'

Geraldine's whole body felt heavy, limp, as if she were a puppet being controlled by someone else. Which she was at this moment and had been for many years by the puppet-master standing in front of her. He hadn't changed at all since she last saw him. Not one bit; he was his same vile, smirking self with those small horrible eyes. But she was changing by the second: from content, free Geraldine Hartley back to crushed, frightened Yvonne Taylor.

Pilot moved away of his own accord and out into the yard, and Geraldine released a secret breath of relief.

'Now, I haven't thought this through,' said Ian, rubbing his chin, 'but the sooner we get out of here the better, I think, so up you get, Vonny.'

Geraldine started to lever herself up. Behind her the kettle was boiling now, puffing out steam into the air. Ian was talking but she was only half-listening because her focus had switched to the tiny mirrored tiles that formed a pattern of a cat on the wall. In them, she saw her jigsawed image couched in cloud and momentarily mistook herself for Isme, come to save her. The thought brought with it a surge of hope and gratitude – but mainly adrenalin. As Geraldine groped for purchase on the lip of the sink, her fingers fell on the handle of the copper-bottomed frying pan in the bowl.

'Hello kitty-witty.' Ian bent down to stroke the friendly black cat who was weaving in and out of his legs and Bub, presented with a rare opportunity for carnage, was determined not to waste it. Not only did he wrap his front paws around Ian's arm, but brought the back legs into play as well: a gift of eighteen synchronised claws-worth of damage plus teeth. Ian was so fixated on shaking off the cat intent on puncturing his bone marrow that he wasn't aware of the pan swinging in the direction of his face until his nose was busted by it. His pain receptors had just commenced screaming when the pan came full circle, landing on the back of his skull. He collapsed like a dynamited building.

'If you think I'm going back to you after what I've got used to here, you're very much mistaken, duck,' said the fully reformed Geraldine Hartley.

Chapter 102

Viv sped along the drive to Wildflower Cottage to find Ian Robson's car was parked halfway down. She guessed it was so Geraldine wouldn't hear him coming. There was no presence of a police car, bloody incompetent cow. Viv picked up the hockey stick and was about to get out of the car when she saw her wonderful, dear Geraldine appear in the cottage doorway.

Viv couldn't have run faster to her. Words tumbled out of her mouth: *Are you all right? It's the same man as my mum's been seeing. I was so worried about you.* And where was he?

'Have the police got him?' Viv took back everything she had thought about that operator.

'Not yet,' said Geraldine. 'I've only just rung them. He's on the floor. I've trussed him up with some of the birds' training cord. Not bad considering I did most of it with one hand.'

Geraldine took Viv's hand and pulled her into the kitchen. She stood over the groaning, pinioned man whose nose resembled a burst strawberry tart.

'See that,' said Geraldine, poking his leg with her medical

sandal, 'I wasted over ten years of my life on it. When the police have carted him off, we'll have a cup of tea and a good chat. Sounds like we've a few things to talk about.' She squeezed Viv's fingers affectionately. 'It's so good to see you, duck. Heath's been looking everywhere for you . . .'

They could hear a car in the distance. Geraldine limped over to the window.

'It's the police,' she announced. 'Maybe I should have rung for an ambulance as well.'

As Viv went to the door to meet them, she noticed the infamous mop bucket standing full of dirty water waiting to be emptied into the drainhole outside. There was just time, she reckoned. It might even bring him round. She quickly snatched it up and tipped it above Ian Robson's sorry face.

'And that's from me and my mum,' said Viv, rejoicing in his spluttering. If it was good enough for the Leightons, it was good enough for him.

*

The operator had sent a squad car straight round, as it happens, but it had been diverted to a high-priority incident in Hyde. Crime-wise, it had been a too-rich morning. The present team had had to come over from Fennybridge.

'I thought hitting people with frying pans only ever happened in Laurel and Hardy films,' said the younger of the two policemen. The older one held up his finger to admonish him for that remark.

Robson was in the back of the police car now, head down, concentrating on surviving the pain claiming his whole upper body.

'We'll be in touch,' said the older policeman, stroking the big dog.

'I'll be here if you want me,' said Geraldine. 'I'm not going anywhere. Ever again,' and she grinned because she felt bloody marvellous. She'd had a momentary bout of hysteria and seen a goddess rising from the mists come to save her; and it might have turned out to be a reflection of herself with a kettle boiling behind her, but still it had served to empower her enough to face her biggest demon and beat it.

The police car trundled off down the drive. Geraldine filled up the mop bucket with water and bleach to clean up the mess which Ian Robson had left. She smiled as she mopped and wrung, ridding the tiles of his every trace.

'Whatever anyone says, I know more than ever, after the events of this week, that Isme is here in this place, Viv, looking after us all. Does that make me a mad woman?'

Viv thought of the pale-haired girl with the dog lead. 'I don't think it makes you mad at all, my dear Geraldine.'

'As soon as I've done this, we'll talk,' beamed Geraldine. 'There's so much I have to say to you – and hear from you.'

'I'm just going to ring to see if my mum is okay,' said Viv. 'My mobile is dead. Could I use the the office phone?'

'Of course. You don't need to ask,' said Geraldine. 'Tell her to come and visit. I can help her make sense of what I suspect he's put her through.'

Viv went into the office for some privacy and rang the Admissions department in Barnsley Hospital and they transferred her to the relevant ward. They let Al take the call on the nurse's station and he told her that Stel was a bit bruised and battered and though they were keeping her in for the night, she had nothing to worry about. Not now. And Viv told him briefly what had happened at her end and asked him to give her mum a kiss for her.

*

'That was your Viv on the phone,' said Al, taking hold of Stel's hand in his big rough bear paw. 'She said I'd to give you this.' He leaned over and delivered a soft kiss to her cheek.

'Ah, that was nice of her,' smiled Stel, her voice a ragged croak.

'They've got him, Stel. He went up to that place where your Viv worked and he tried attacking another lass. And she cracked him with a frying pan, bust his nose all over his face. She'd like to see you, and talk to you.'

'I'm an idiot, Al,' said Stel, tightening her grip on his fingers, drawing warmth and comfort from them.

'You are where fellas are concerned, Stel Blackbird,' Al replied. 'Why aren't you as good at picking them as you were at picking a daughter?'

'I never have been. Anyway, I'm done with men,' said Stel. 'I'm going to get myself a wimple and become a nun.'

'You could have had me, you know,' Al said, head down, waiting for Stel to laugh at the thought. But she didn't.

'You never asked me, Al Thackray. And all them fish-finger sandwiches my mam cooked for you an' all. She loved you.'

'You were always out of my league, Stel.'

'Me?' The word came out as a squawk. 'Are you kidding? I was never out of your league. I'm from Holton Road not bloody Beverly Hills. You're the one swanning about on a Jim Davidson bike and moving to a big posh house ... so I think you've got that the wrong way round, love.'

Stel didn't want him to leave the street. It wouldn't be the same without him next door to her.

Al studied Stel's fingers and didn't recognise them. She'd always had lovely nails, pointed and polished not bitten right down as they were now. He wanted to kill that piggy-eyed streak of piss.

'I've still got loads of his stuff in my house,' Stel said, closing her eyes against the thought of going back home and seeing all his belongings everywhere.

'If you tell me what you want shifting, I'll load it into my van and get my mate to store it. You don't want to get done for criminal damage. He's taken enough of your head space up.'

He stroked her hand, as if he were stroking the back of the guinea pig they had in their class at school. He'd been given a certificate by the teacher for being the boy who handled her the gentlest.

'Will you come up and see my new house?' asked Al. 'Help me pick curtains and things like that?'

'Course I will,' replied Stel. 'But you're good at all that stuff yourself.'

'You're better.'

'Thank you,' said Stel and she smiled at him. 'Not just for saying I'm better at choosing soft furnishings, I mean for being my friend.'

Al nodded, too choked up to reply. Stel's face was swollen and dark with bruising but she was still gorgeous to him. He'd always loved Stel Blackbird. When all this was done with and she'd had time to herself, he hoped he could dredge up the way-overdue courage to ask her out. But if she said yes, he'd make sure they had the longest, slowest, courtship in bloody history.

Chapter 103

When Viv went back into the kitchen from the office, she found Heath was there sitting with Geraldine. He looked worn out and drawn but his green eyes sparked with light when they fell on her and though every sinew and muscle in her body screamed at her to run to him, she just couldn't do it.

'I'm going to have a nice bath,' said Geraldine, doing a very unsubtle job of getting out of the way. Even Pilot followed her out of the room.

'Viv, walk with me,' asked Heath. 'Please,' and he got up from the table.

'All right.'

She would let him say goodbye, then she would go.

They walked side by side, down past dear Bertie, Roger and Keith, Ray and Roy and Wonk nodding half-asleep in the sunshine. They stepped over the banks of blue-violet flowers and through the ghost-mist that hovered above the grass, until they came to the bench in the bird arena. Heath sat down. Viv followed his lead, leaving space between them.

He didn't look at her as he spoke, but kept his eyes low,

forward, focused on nothing. 'Geraldine doesn't know what I'm about to tell you, which is why she ...' He stopped, swallowed, took a breath, began again. 'The best of people make mistakes, Viv.'

Why was she even here? Whatever he said couldn't put it right. 'Heath, I'd hardly call what you did a mistake.'

'Please, let me finish. I'm not talking about a mistake that *I* made.'

There was a long pause. Confused by what he had said, Viv nodded that he had her attention and he resumed.

'When I married Sarah, I didn't know her heart had been broken by someone else. I was the rebound boyfriend, part of her healing process. She married me to show someone that she didn't care what he'd done to her, but she did. And she hadn't stopped loving him.'

His lips were dry and cracked. And so was his voice as he spoke.

'He realised he should never have let her go. They started an affair. I didn't see it because I was busy looking after Dad; then he died. Sarah had known she was ill herself but she was terrified of doctors so she kept her symptoms secret, hoping they'd just go away. It was a very aggressive form ... even if the doctors had discovered it earlier, there still wouldn't have been anything they could have done.'

Viv saw his jaw clench as he fought hard against an onslaught of emotion. She hadn't expected to hear any of this.

'When she knew she was dying, she had to tell me about the other man and how much she loved him because she wanted to spend her last days with him, not me. But she felt so guilty because I'd just lost Dad. How could I deny her what she asked me for?'

His long fingers pushed his hair back from his drawn, tired face.

'On the night she left, she begged me to tell her that I didn't love her any more and that she should leave, so she could go to him with her conscience clear. So I said the words she wanted to hear, only so she could die being loved by him. I had no idea that Geraldine was worried by our raised voices; we didn't know she could hear us . . . not that we were shouting exactly . . . it was just that the situation was so intense. She heard Sarah say that what she needed in her last weeks was to be with the person who loved her the most. She heard me say that I wished it could have been me but we both knew it wasn't. She heard me asking Sarah to give me back her wedding ring and go. She didn't know that Sarah's lover was waiting for her up the drive in his car.'

Could all this be true? She wanted to believe him so much.

'But why do her family hate you?'

'Because I was the one who was married to Sarah. I should have stayed with her, they said. I shouldn't have encouraged her to act like a slut. The Bernals are a fine, upstanding family, you see, Viv.' There was a sneer to his lip. 'They didn't want it known that their daughter left me for a lover. So it was far better to twist the story. *Merlo is a man so bad that he abandoned his dying wife.* I could take it. I knew what I'd done was right for her.'

He felt Viv's small warm fingers burrow into his hand.

'But it's so unfair.'

'I think a lot of people now know there's another version of the truth than the one the Bernals parade. It doesn't matter to me anyway. What does matter to me is that Sarah died at peace with the only man she'd ever loved at her side.'

Viv knew he'd told her the truth. She felt it. *This is a good man, Viv Blackbird*, her heart was shouting inside her, and as he turned to her and her eyes locked onto his, every black doubt she'd had about him was blasted away by the honesty shining there.

Heath lifted his arm and wrapped it around her, pulling her close.

'Will you stay?' he asked. 'I will now be able to supply a decent wage, plus a variety of eggs and unending tales of Isme and her bloody mists courtesy of Geraldine.'

'Oooh,' Viv sucked in a spaghetti string of air. 'Tempting. Anything else to add to the mix?'

'I can promise you as much hay and straw as you can shift with a pitchfork and the best compost heap in town.'

Viv pinched her fingers together. 'Nearly there.'

'I will never again laugh at names like Dancing Sunshine when you're mixing your weird oils.'

She grimaced. 'So, so close.'

'I can promise you a whole sweep of sky to fly a white owl in,' said Heath. 'And me.' She turned her lovely face to his and grinned.

'Mr Merlo, I think we have a deal.'

Epilogue

One month later

Linda had pushed the boat out on the buffet that Sunday. It was her mother's eighty-third birthday and all was well in their world. Andy was home on leave, Freddie was still living with them and the Pawson twosome couldn't pull their strings any more. The boot was well and truly on the other foot. It was a victory for grandparents everywhere. And Iris had met a dapper gentleman called Sid at a recent Golden Surfers mingle. He had whisked her off to the Wetherby Whaler in Wakefield and impressed her with his magic tricks at the table.

'What he can't do with a serviette and a two-pound coin isn't worth talking about,' she said, patting her new hairdo with one hand and proffering fish goujons with the other.

'I'm made up for you, Iris,' said Gaynor. 'I really am. I think it's lovely that you've found someone to have a good time with.'

'There's a lid for every pan, even old ones,' smiled Iris.

'Well, I'm staying a milk pan for a long, long time,'

replied Gaynor, refilling her teacup. Life as a widow was a huge improvement on life as a rejected wife. It commanded respect and dignity. She wore her status like an OBE. 'And I've booked a three-week Caribbean cruise at Christmas for Leanne and me.'

'You're talking again then?' Linda asked.

'As much as Leanne and I ever do.' Gaynor blew out her cheeks. 'I was hoping that a few rum punches might help us bond a bit better. I'm not expecting miracles.'

'I don't know about the rum ...' Iris began and Linda butted in. She had a sickening feeling that her mother was going to wade in with something about punching Leanne. Having a boyfriend had done nothing to neutralise her acidic mouth.

'No news from you-know-who, Gaynor?' She meant Danira, of course. Who turned out to be Caro's niece. That was a shocker, hearing that Caro was a Bellfield. It was like finding out that Princess Anne was born a Kray. Not that it made the slightest bit of difference to what they all thought about her.

'Not a word and long may that continue,' said Gaynor. 'We have no connection, other than a historical one where she seduced away my husband and failed to keep him.'

'I'll drink to that,' said Caro, toasting Gaynor with her teacup. Having thought long and hard about the business with Danira, she was convinced that given time, Mick really would have yearned for his old life back with Gaynor. She hadn't lost any sleep about her machinations, anyway.

'Talking of nasties,' said Iris, addressing this to Stel, 'what's happening with buggerlugs?' And she wafted her hand over her shoulder as if that were the direction his prison was in.

'He's safely tucked away in a cell until his trial,' croaked Stel.

Linda put her hand on Stel's arm and gave it an affectionate shimmy. Ian Robson had damaged her throat and cracked her cheekbone which seemed to have taken forever to heal, but now she was well on the mend, mentally as well as physically. And even though they'd all hoped she would have a decent gap between fellas, Al Thackray was an exception. They collectively welcomed him into their friend's life.

'Al okay? Has he got his house sorted?'

Everyone smiled when his name came up in conversation. He would never have believed that he had that effect on people.

'He's good and his house is gorgeous,' Stel replied. 'Bless him, did I tell you that he moved all the furniture round in my bedroom for me so it feels like a totally different space.' She bent forward as if imparting an important secret. 'He can lift wardrobes by himself. He's like Britain's Strongest Man.'

'Well, he'd have to be if he carried you from the attic to his car,' said Caro with a wink.

'Cheeky,' replied Stel with mock affront. That day felt so long ago now.

'Well, he wants someone to look after because he's good at it, you need someone to look after you because you're bloody useless and you've known each other forty-odd years. There are worse starts to a relationship,' quipped Iris, making them all laugh.

Gaynor wiped her forehead. 'Got any more of those fans, Linda?'

'Sodding hundreds,' smiled Linda, reaching into a drawer and throwing one over.

'I went to see Geraldine again at Viv's,' said Stel. 'She's such a lovely woman.'

When they first met, Stel and Geraldine fell on each other like sisters who'd shared a terrible experience and emerged battered but alive from the other end of it. No therapy session could have been more valuable. And they'd both learned things. Geraldine had first got together with Ian when he had found her little missing dog. Until she heard how Ian had found Stel's cat, she didn't realise he must have taken him in the first place. And Stel learned that she must have been drugged, that horrible night of the photos. He'd done the same to Geraldine, and a lot more besides. Stel had been lucky to escape his clutches so early on.

'Did the police manage to hack into his phone in the end?' asked Caro, crossing her fingers in hope as she said it.

'They did. He hadn't sent those photos anywhere. He'd been too concerned with getting to Geraldine,' said Stel. 'She broke his nose with that frying pan, you know. And gave him a right bash on his skull.'

'Good,' huffed Gaynor. 'I hope it cracked like a bloody egg.'

Stel sighed. 'If only I'd not been so stupid . . . '

Linda wasn't having that. 'You're not stupid, Stel. You're kind and open and people like Robson prey on good nature.'

'But I—'

Iris cut her off. 'If ifs and buts were cakes and nuts, we'd have ourselves a party. That's what my mum always used to say.'

'Yes, and if ifs and buts were cocks and nuts, we'd have ourselves an orgy,' giggled Caro.

'How old are you again?' Linda gave her a look of jokey disapproval. She'd only been saying to her mum the other day that once upon a time she imagined all women over fifty wore bedjackets and had false teeth. She never expected to feel eternally seventeen, whatever contrary evidence the mirror displayed.

'Do you think your Viv will stay over there?' asked Iris, reaching for a lobster bite. Linda had gone mad in Tesco. She had visions of Freddie diving head first into what was left of that chocolate birthday cake when they took it through to the kitchen later.

Stel smiled, thinking about her girl in that lovely place. And the handsome vet with the dark beard and big green eyes. Viv looked happy in her setting of countryside and animals like a precious stone in the right piece of jewellery. And Stel never thought she'd see the day when Viv walked towards her with a big white owl perched on her arm. So long as Viv was happy, Stel was too.

Stel always *knew* – no evidence, only mother's intuition on which to base her suspicions – that Viv had gone looking for her real parents when she took the job in Ironmist. They'd shared only the briefest conversation about it, the last time they'd met up, because she had to know if she'd been right.

'Did you find them then?' Stel had dared to ask.

'You're the only parent I've got,' said Viv. 'Or want.'

And that had been the end to it.

Linda walked over to the fridge in the corner.

'I've got some pink Champagne. I thought we'd have a tipple today, to celebrate your birthday, Mum.' She pulled off the foil, twisted the metal and pulled out the cork with a satisfying *thwop*.

Iris's face wrinkled up as she received her glass. 'I hope it doesn't taste of feet,' she said.

'Oh shut up, Mum, just for once.'

'Happy Twenty-first Birthday, Iris,' Caro led the toast.

'Thank you, fellow Old Spice Girls,' said Iris, raising her glass to them.

'Cheers to the bloody lot of us: battle-scarred war horses, fighters, survivors, saucepans, milk pans, frying pans, wives, mothers, daughters and queens of the menopause,' said Stel, taking a sip of the chilled fizz that bubbled up to her brain, bringing with it a hit of contentment. How she wished she could bottle this happy, wonderful feeling inside her and ask Viv to make her a perfume out of it. It would have a top note of fun and laughter, a middle note of acceptance and warmth, and a long-lasting base note of support and love. She'd have called it simply *Friendship*.

In order to be irreplaceable,
one must always be different

COCO CHANEL

Acknowledgements

What deep joy I had writing this book. Especially because it forced me to do lots of research with fascinating beautiful birds of prey. So I thank Colin, Kerry and Nikki Badgery and David Horseman from Thirsk Birds of Prey Centre (www.falconrycentre.co.uk) for allowing me into their wonderful world – and their extended family, because that's what the birds are to them. I've had an absolute hoot mingling with vultures and eagles, owls and hawks – none of whom are 'just birds'. They are fabulous, intelligent, amazing creatures and thank goodness there are centres like this around. Trust me, if you haven't felt the weight of a bald eagle on your glove, watched a snowy owl's angel-like wings in flight at close quarters, you haven't lived.

I also have my wonderful publishing team to thank for their support, kindness and fabulousness: Clare Hey, Sara-Jade Virtue, Suzanne Baboneau, Laura Hough, Sally Wilks, Emma Capron, Ally Grant and Emma Harrow. I love you all and am so glad I'm with you.

A special mention to Sally Partington, an absolute

goddess of a copy editor. If she hasn't got white hair and nervous tics after this book, she never will have.

To everyone at my agency David Higham Associates who are top notch but a special huge hug to the divine Ms Lizzy Kremer. Every writer should have someone of her calibre. I feel blessed to have her.

And, of course, my wonderful TEAM MILLY ladies who are like an army but with fewer Kalashnikovs and less body armour and more lipstick and scones.

I have so much support from Andrew Harrod and Steph Daly at the *Barnsley Chronicle*, and the Radio Sheffield Team. And from fellow Barnsley people in general. Thanks, Tykes!

A huge thank-you to Mike Bowkett at Gardeners and Morrisons and Angela Addington at Morrisons. You can't buy the level of support I get from them.

My family are always amazing and put up with so much. It's not easy living with a writer especially when we're at final edit stage when we turn into coffee-guzzling grizzly bears. So thank you Mum and Dad, Pete, Tez and George for realising that I don't have a normal job because I'm not normal. And for being okay with that.

Special mention to my pal Tracy 'Traz' Harwood. She has to deal with my full spectrum of highs and lows whilst we are dog-walking. The fact that she remains my friend and is still (relatively) sane, must show she is either a really strong person or totally daft. Either works for me.

Thank you to my readers – I wouldn't have a job if it weren't for you lot. You keep me fed and watered with your smashing reviews and letters. You turn up to support me and my charities and I feel honoured that you love what I do.

And lastly, a special mention to some brilliant shining

stars which the world has lost this year, people who had a great influence on me. Alan Rickman, because every hero I've ever written has a little part of his Colonel Brandon in it. David Bowie, whose music was the backdrop to my life. Victoria Wood, a comedic genius who had a massive influence on what I wrote. Frank Finlay, who inspired a few of the real gentlemen in my books, and the fabulous Barry Hines, author extraordinaire and local Barnsley lad whose book *A Kestrel for a Knave* kicked off my love of birds of prey too many years ago to count. This book was always extra special because it is set in my home town and if you haven't ever read it, you should. Barry died after a horrible battle with the very cruel Alzheimer's. I'd like to think his soul was carried up to heaven on the back of the most beautiful hawk.

SIMON &
SCHUSTER

Milly Johnson

The Yorkshire Pudding Club

Three South Yorkshire friends, all on the cusp
of 40, fall pregnant at the same time following
a visit to an ancient fertility symbol.

For Helen, it's a dream come true, although her
husband is not as thrilled about it as she had hoped. Not
only wrestling with painful ghosts of the past, Helen
has to deal with the fact that her outwardly perfect
marriage is crumbling before her eyes.

For Janey, it is an unmitigated disaster as she has
just been offered the career break of a life-time. And
she has no idea either how it could possibly have happened,
seeing as she and her ecstatic husband George were
always so careful over contraception.

For Elizabeth, it is mind-numbing, because she knows
people like her shouldn't have children. Damaged by her
dysfunctional childhood and emotionally lost, she not only
has to contend with carrying a child she doubts she can ever
love, but she also has to deal with the return to her life
of a man whose love she must deny herself.

Paperback ISBN 978-1-84983-410-0
Ebook ISBN 978-1-84739-483-5

**SIMON &
SCHUSTER**

Milly Johnson

The Birds and the Bees

Romance writer and single mum Stevie Honeywell has
only weeks to go to her wedding, when her fiancé Matthew
runs off with her glamorous friend Jo MacLean. But Stevie
knows exactly how to win back her man. By undergoing a
mad course of dieting and exercise, she is sure things will
be as sweet as nectar again before very long.

Likewise, Adam MacLean is determined to win back his
lady. All he needs to do is convince Stevie to join him in
his own cunning plan – a prospect that neither of them find
attractive, seeing as each blames the other for the mess they
now find themselves in.

But when her strategy of self-improvement fails dismally,
Stevie finds that desperate times call for desperate
measures. She has no option but to join forces with the big
Scot in a scheme that soon reaches lengths neither of them
could ever have imagined. So, like a Scottish country jig,
the two couples change partners but continue to weave
closely around each other. And Adam and Stevie find they
have to deal with the heartbreaks of the past before they can
deal with those of the present. When Adam's crazy plan
actually starts to work, the question is: just who will he
and Stevie be dancing with when the music stops?

**Paperback ISBN 978-1-84983-409-4
Ebook ISBN 978-1-84739-482-8**

SIMON &
SCHUSTER

Milly Johnson

A Spring Affair

When Lou Winter picks up a dog-eared magazine in the
dentist's waiting room and spots an article about clearing
clutter, she little realises how it will change her life. What
begins as an earnest spring clean soon spirals out of control.
Before long Lou is hiring skips in which to dump the
copious amounts of junk she never knew she had.

Lou's loved ones grow disgruntled. Why is clearing
out cupboards suddenly more important than making his
breakfast, her husband Phil wonders? The truth is, the more
rubbish Lou lets go of, the more light and air can get to
those painful, closed-up places at the centre of her heart:
the love waiting for a baby she would never have, the
empty space her best friend Deb once occupied, and
the gaping wound left by her husband's affair.

Even lovely Tom Broom, the man who delivers
Lou's skips, starts to grow concerned about his sweetest
customer. But Lou is a woman on a mission, and
not even she knows where it will end ...

Paperback ISBN 978-1-84739-282-4
Ebook ISBN 978-1-84739-866-6

SIMON &
SCHUSTER

Milly Johnson

A Summer Fling

When dynamic Christie blows in like a warm wind
to take over their department, five very different
women find themselves thrown together.

Anna is reeling from the loss of her fiancé. So when a
handsome, mysterious stranger takes an interest in her,
she's not sure whether she can learn to trust again.

Then there's Grace, in her fifties, trapped in a loveless
marriage with a man she married because, unable to have
children of her own, she fell in love with his motherless
brood. Grace worries that Dawn is about to make the same
mistake: orphaned as a child, engaged to love-rat Calum,
is Dawn more interested in the security that comes with his
tight-knit, boisterous family?

At 28, Raychel is the youngest member of their little
gang. And with a loving husband, Ben, and a cosy little nest
for two, she would seem to be the happiest. But what dark
secrets are lurking behind this perfect facade, that make
sweet, pretty Raychel so guarded and unwilling to open up?
Under Christie's warm hand, the girls soon realise
they have some difficult choices to make.

Indeed, none of them quite realised how much they needed
the sense of fun, laughter, and loyalty that abounds when
five women become friends. It's one for all, and all for one!

Paperback ISBN 978-1-84739-283-1
Ebook ISBN 978-1-84983-102-4

SIMON &
SCHUSTER

Milly Johnson

Here Come The Girls

Shirley Valentine, eat your heart out ...

Ven, Roz, Olive and Frankie have been friends
since school. They day-dreamed of glorious futures,
full of riches, romance and fabulous jobs.
The world would be their oyster.

Twenty-five years later, Olive cleans other
people's houses to support her lazy, out-of-work
husband and his ailing mother. Roz cannot show her
kind, caring husband Manus any love because her
philandering ex has left her trust in shreds. And
she and Frankie have fallen out big time.

But Ven is determined to reunite her friends
and realise the dream they had of taking a cruise
before they hit forty. Before they know it, the four
of them are far from home, on the high seas. But can
blue skies, hot sun and sixteen days of luxury
and indulgence distract from the tension and
loneliness that await their return?

Paperback ISBN 978-1-84983-205-2
Ebook ISBN 978-1-84983-206-9

**SIMON &
SCHUSTER**

Milly Johnson

An Autumn Crush

**In the heart of the windy season, four friends
are about to get swept off their feet ...**

Newly single after a bruising divorce, Juliet Miller
moves into a place of her own and advertises for a flatmate,
little believing that, in her mid-thirties, she'll find anyone
suitable. Then, just as she's about to give up hope,
along comes self-employed copywriter Floz, and
the two women hit it off straight away.

When Juliet's gentle giant of a twin brother, Guy,
meets Floz, he falls head over heels. But, as hard as
he tries to charm her, his foot seems to be permanently in
his mouth. Meanwhile, Guy's best friend Steve has
always had a secret crush on Juliet – one which
could not be more unrequited if it tried ...

As Floz and Juliet's friendship deepens, and Floz
becomes a part of the Miller family, can Guy turn her
affection for them into something more – into love for
him? And what will happen to Steve's heart when Juliet
eventually catches the eye of Piers – the man of her dreams?

**Paperback ISBN 978-1-84983-203-8
Ebook ISBN 978-1-84983-204-5**

SIMON &
SCHUSTER

Milly Johnson

A Winter Flame

The final part of the brilliant seasonal quartet...

**'Tis the season to be jolly ... But can Eve f
ind happiness through the frost ...?**

Eve has never liked Christmas, not since her beloved
fiancé was killed in action in Afghanistan on Christmas
Day. So when her adored elderly aunt dies, the last thing
she is expecting is to be left a theme park in her will.
A theme park with a Christmas theme ...

And that's not the only catch. Her aunt's will stipulates
that Eve must run the park with a mysterious partner, the
exotically named Jacques Glace. Who is this Jacques,
and why did Aunt Evelyn name him in her will?

But Eve isn't going to back down from a challenge.
She's determined to make a success of Winterworld, no
matter what. Can she overcome her dislike of Christmas,
and can Jacques melt her frozen heart at last ...?

Paperback ISBN 978-0-85720-898-9
Ebook ISBN 978-0-85720-899-6

SIMON &
SCHUSTER

Milly Johnson

It's Raining Men

**A summer getaway to remember. But is a
holiday romance on the cards ...?**

Best friends from work May, Lara and Clare are
desperate for some time away. They have each had a
rough time of it lately and need some serious R & R. So
they set off to a luxurious spa for ten glorious days, but
when they arrive at their destination, it seems it is not
the place they thought it was. In fact, they appear
to have come to entirely the wrong village ...

Here in Ren Dullem nothing is quite what it seems;
the lovely cobbled streets and picturesque cottages hide a
secret that the villagers have been keeping hidden for years.
Why is everyone so unfriendly and suspicious? Why
does the landlord of their holiday rental seem so rude?
And why are there so few women in the village?

Despite the strange atmosphere, the three friends
are determined to make the best of it and have a holiday
to remember. But will this be the break they all need?
Or will the odd little village with all its secrets
bring them all to breaking point ...?

Paperback ISBN 978-1-4711-1461-8
Ebook ISBN 978-1-4711-1462-5

**SIMON &
SCHUSTER**

Milly Johnson

The Teashop on the Corner

Spring Hill Square is a pretty sanctuary away
from the bustle of everyday life. And at its centre is
Leni Merryman's Teashop on the Corner, specialising
in cake, bookish stationery and compassion. And
for three people, all in need of a little TLC, it is
somewhere to find a friend to lean on.

Carla Pride has just discovered that her late husband Martin
was not who she thought he was. And now she must learn
to put her marriage behind her and move forward.

Molly Jones's ex-husband Harvey has reappeared
in her life after many years, wanting to put right
the wrongs of the past before it is too late.

And Will Linton's business has gone bust and his
wife has left him to pick up the pieces. Now he
needs to gather the strength to start again.

Can all three find the comfort they are looking
for in The Teashop on the Corner? And as their
hearts are slowly mended by Leni, can they return
the favour when she needs it most . . .?

Paperback ISBN 978-1-4711-1464-9
Ebook ISBN 978-1-4711-1465-6

**SIMON &
SCHUSTER**

Milly Johnson

Afternoon Tea at the
Sunflower Café

Love and friendship bloom at the Sunflower Café ...

When Connie discovers that Jimmy Diamond, her husband
of more than twenty years, is planning to leave her for his
office junior, her world is turned upside down.

Determined to salvage her pride, she resolves to get
her own back. Along with Della, Jimmy's right-hand
woman at his cleaning firm, Diamond Shine, and the
cleaners who meet at the Sunflower Café, she'll make
him wish he had never underestimated her.

Then Connie meets the charming Brandon Locke,
a master chocolatier, whose kindness starts to melt her
soul. Could he be her second chance at happiness?

Can the ladies of the Sunflower Cafe help Connie scrub
away the hurt? And can Brandon make her trust again?

Paperback ISBN 978-1-4711-4046-4
Ebook ISBN 978-1-4711-4047-1